Charles Francis Richardson

American Literature - 1607-1885

Vol. II: American Poety and Fiction

Charles Francis Richardson

American Literature - 1607-1885
Vol. II: American Poety and Fiction

ISBN/EAN: 9783337206260

Printed in Europe, USA, Canada, Australia, Japan

Cover: Foto ©Andreas Hilbeck / pixelio.de

More available books at **www.hansebooks.com**

AMERICAN LITERATURE

1607–1885

BY

CHARLES F. RICHARDSON

COMPLETE IN TWO VOLUMES

VOL. II.

AMERICAN POETRY AND FICTION

NEW YORK & LONDON

G. P. PUTNAM'S SONS

The Knickerbocker Press

1889

CONTENTS.

CHAPTER I.

PAGE

EARLY VERSE MAKING IN AMERICA, ... 1

CHAPTER II.

THE DAWN OF IMAGINATION, . . 23

CHAPTER III.

HENRY WADSWORTH LONGFELLOW, . . . 50

CHAPTER IV.

EDGAR ALLAN POE, ... 97

CHAPTER V.

EMERSON AS POET, ... 137

CHAPTER VI.

POETS OF FREEDOM AND CULTURE: WHITTIER, LOWELL
AND HOLMES, ... 172

CHAPTER VII.

TONES AND TENDENCIES OF AMERICAN VERSE, 219

CHAPTER VIII.

THE BELATED BEGINNING OF FICTION, . 282

CHAPTER IX.

JAMES FENIMORE COOPER, ... 297

CHAPTER X.

NATHANIEL HAWTHORNE, ... 330

CHAPTER XI.

THE LESSER NOVELISTS, . . . 390

CHAPTER XII.

LATER MOVEMENTS IN AMERICAN FICTION, . 413

INDEX, ... 451

CHAPTER I.

EARLY VERSE-MAKING IN AMERICA.

POETRY is the rhythmical expression of beauty or imagination, the verbal utterance of the ideal, and therefore the highest and most permanent form of literature.

According to this definition, it is easy to see that very little poetry was produced in America before the close of the eighteenth century. Much of the early verse of the colonies and states was unrhythmical, and most of it was neither beautiful nor imaginative. The human soul was here, and the glory of nature; but genius was smothered or non-existent, and poetic art was almost wholly lacking. Puritan theology in New England could no more produce poetry than it could paint a Sistine Madonna. Its theological force was intense, but it was neither gracious nor serene. Something more than intensity is needed in the production of a true poem. Puritanism could preach, write diaries and descriptions, and make an occasional eloquent speech for liberty; but of the poetic art it had not an idea. It believed that saints were born, not made; but its poets were neither born nor made. The broad, thorough culture of John Milton, who could apprehend Dante and Shakespeare, as well as

I

Moses and Paul, was impossible in early Massachusetts. Even an Andrew Marvell was not to
be expected there. The soul was a part of the
scheme of redemption, not a spontaneous singer
of the beautiful. Nature, whether august on the
sea-coast or fragrant by the brook-side, was of a
lost world; and the Puritan had no idea that any
earthly beauty could be its own excuse for being.

In the middle and southern colonies the state
of things was no better. I suppose I shall hardly
be required to demonstrate the statement that
poetry was not to be expected from the brains or
hands of the Dutchmen of New Amsterdam. The
Pennsylvania Friends were as estimable and honest as they are now; but then, as now, they were
unliterary. The various representatives of non-
English nations, in the middle colonies, neither
transplanted their own literatures nor aided the
English. The Roman Catholics of Maryland
were not a book-making folk; and the cavaliers
of Virginia left behind them the lyrical power of
the aristocratic songsters of England in the seventeenth century. The poetic prospect in the
Atlantic colonies, prior to 1700, was more discouraging than it is in Canada to-day; and it
must be confessed that the promise of better
things had not become brilliant even as late as
1800. It is my opinion that only one true poem
was produced in America before the latter year;
and I am sure that no one could select a dozen
pieces, of all the verse then in existence, deserving the name of poem, under the most liberal
definition.

There is a bibliographical curiosity much prized by collectors of Americana, and well known to antiquarians, called "The Bay Psalm Book." This famous volume, which appeared in 1640, was the first printed book produced within the present limits of the United States. It consists of a (so-called) metrical version of the Psalms, translated directly from Hebrew into English by several ministers of Massachusetts Bay. One hesitates to declare definitely that this is the worst book of verse ever produced in America, for the candidates for the lowest place are many, and I can recall at least one "poem" produced in our own day, the author of which proceeded on the theory that blank verse consists simply of ten prose syllables, beginning with a capital letter. But the "Bay Psalm Book" is so wretched a collection of pious doggerel that, on the whole, the philosophic reader rejoices at its badness. American verse had made a beginning, and was sure to rise, for the adequate reason that it could not sink any lower. In comparison with the "Bay Psalm Book" that dullest of Middle-English poems, the "Ormulum," is a masterpiece of genius and a model of metrical skill. When we consider that these translators of the Psalms might have availed themselves of the noble versions in the Wycliffe, Bishops', and King James Bibles, but preferred to spoil everything for the sake of wretched rhymes or lines quite defying scansion, we are tempted to a severity that is mitigated by the

The Bay Psalm Book, 1640.

reflection that poetry is still confused with sing-song in many excellent minds; and that the worst metrical hymn is sometimes deemed more devout than the best chant of rhythmical prose.

Notwithstanding the wealth of poetry then existent in England, the Puritans had no notion of the difference between good verse and bad. Productions whose poverty of thought and naked-ness of form were nothing less than pitiful, they accepted with gratitude and hailed with extrav-agant enthusiasm. One writer produced a "poem," and another, perhaps in verse, greeted that poem with loud acclaim; but both the praiser and the praised have long since been shrouded in the obscurity from which, indeed, they never emerged save in the provincial esti-mate. Not until the poets of the "Dunciad" are revered as masters need the literary historian analyze the achievements or record the names of New England's clerical bards of the seventeenth century. Let us give them the credit of gal-lantry, however, for they politely found their Tenth Muse in Anne Bradstreet, the first woman in America who entered the ranks of authorship, and the first person who put forth a volume of verse in that part of the country from which the best American poetry was to spring. The merit of Mrs. Brad-street's poems is rather negative than positive; they are not so bad as they might have been, and occasionally proffer a good thought or a decent line. It would be possible, it seems to me, for

Anne (Dudley) Bradstreet, 1612–1672.

some other person than a literary historian, or
a proof-reader, to read her "works," especially
when adorned by the fair type and broad margins
of the excellent modern reprint.* To be sure,
when wandering through her elegiac verse, the
reader will exclaim, with Southey, "my days
among the dead are passed," though he can
hardly add that these dead are "the mighty minds
of old." His courage will flag long before the
end of the ponderous poems devoted respectively
to "The Four Elements" and "The Four Mon-
archies," and at last he will think affectionately of
the colophon of some ancient volumes : "Explicit
Liber : Laus Deo." But Mrs. Bradstreet, though
not a poet, possessed a thoughtful mind, which
she developed to the best of her meagre opportu-
nities ; and some of her miscellaneous reflections
in prose, entitled "Meditations, Divine and
Moral," are of decided merit, easily surpassing the
most ambitious of her labored productions in
verse.

"The Day of Doom," by the Reverend Michael
Wigglesworth, far surpassed in popularity the
much-praised productions of the Tenth Muse. A
good motto for the poem would have
been these two lines from a hymn
once sung in the churches :

Michael
Wigglesworth,
1631–1715.

> "My thoughts on awful subjects roll,
>   Damnation and the dead."

"The Day of Doom" was an attempt to apply

---

* Edited by John Harvard Ellis; Charlestown, Mass., 1867.

the principles of extreme seventeenth-century Calvinism to the final adjustment of the unseen and unknowable, and incidentally to produce a poem. This attempt was not, in my view, entirely successful; but a different opinion was held by the many readers who thumbed its pages for a hundred years. They were sure it was true, and so they bought and prized it, in edition after edition, at a time when the vaporings of "A Midsummer Night's Dream" or the semi-pagan moral virtues of "The Faerie Queene" were unknown in Massachusetts, even by title.* Cotton Mather said that it had often been reprinted in Old England and New, and might perhaps instruct children "till the Day itself arrive." The work is absolutely devoid of merit, save in its evident sincerity. At great length, and with the most deliberate argumentation, it teaches the horrible doctrine of the damnation of non-elect infants because of the sin of Adam as federal head. Jonathan Edwards' famous spider sermon, with all its mixture of brimstone and blood, was at least more tolerable than this, for it treated (presumably) of adults, and made no pretension to be a poem.

"The Day of Doom," like "The Bay Psalm

---

* "Before 1700 there was not in Massachusetts, so far as is known, a copy of Shakespeare's or of Milton's poems; and as late as 1723, whatever may have been in private hands, Harvard College library lacked Addison, Atterbury, Bolingbroke, Dryden, Gay, Locke, Pope, Prior, Steele, Swift, and Young. . . . . Shakespeare was not reprinted in New England until 1802-1804, nor do I find Milton until 1796, though it was found twenty years earlier in Philadelphia."—Mellen Chamberlain, librarian of the Boston Public Library; address at the dedication of the Brooks Library, Brattleborough, Vt., Jan. 25, 1887.

Book" and Mrs. Bradstreet's volume, is not a
piece of literature; the student notes it only as a
curiosity, and as a pitiful indication of the literary
poverty of the days and the land in which it was
popular. Its most famous line, in which Wigglesworth metamorphoses the child-loving and child-
blessing Christ into one who assigns lost infants
to "the easiest room in Hell," occurs in a poem of
which one part is as bad as another, from the
literary stand-point, though perhaps not as repug-
nant to the moral sense as this celebrated example
of the author's modesty and charity. The children say, in the course of their appeal for mercy:

> O great Creator, why was our Nature
>   depraved and forlorn?
> Why so defil'd, and made so vil'd
>   whilst we were yet unborn?
> If it be just, and needs we must
>   transgressors reck'ned be,
> Thy Mercy Lord, to us afford,
>   which sinners hath set free.

But the judge elaborately refutes them, with such
arguments as these:

> Would you have griev'd to have receiv'd
>   through *Adam* so much good,
> As had been your for evermore,
>   if he at first had stood?
> Would you have said, we ne'r obey'd,
>   nor did thy Laws regard;
> It ill befits with benefits
>   us, Lord, so to reward.

> Since then to share in his welfare
>   you could have been content,

> You may with reason share in his treason,
>   and in the punishment.
> Hence you were born in state forlorn,
>   with Natures so depraved :
> Death was your due, because that you
>   had thus yourselves behaved.*

And this was the favorite poem of that New England which was to produce an Emerson, a Longfellow, and a Poe,—a poem written during the lifetime of Milton and Dryden, and locally overshadowing the fame of the best of their productions.

In the pre-revolutionary procession of New England bards, half forgotten and all unread, there are some picturesque figures, standing forth because of personal rather than poetical qualities, and therefore unmentioned here; though Mrs. Bradstreet's clerical companions on the Massachusetts Parnassus were for the most part an indistinguishable group, without salient characteristics or individual merits. It is not strange, perhaps, that Mrs. Bradstreet herself keeps a little larger place in our minds because she was the earliest of our professional poets, and the earliest American woman who won any literary renown. Yet more conspicuous in quaint loneliness was that poor negro girl, Phillis Wheatley, whose clever verses, neatly turned according to the prevalent English

Phillis Wheatley, 1750?–1784.
fashion, pleased the Bostonians during the latter half of the eighteenth century. Born in Africa, Phillis was a precocious household pet, in the last days of African slavery

---

* I quote from an edition published in Boston as late as 1828.

in New England. Her little booklet of "Poems
on Various Subjects, Religious and Moral," was
published in London in 1773, and has several
times been reprinted,—as poetry, as a curiosity,
or as an abolition argument. There seems no
reason to doubt the genuineness of the poems, as
compositions of the girl herself; the early editions contained attestations signed by eighteen
aristocratic Bostonians, to the fact that they
"were written by Phillis, a young negro girl, who
was but a few years since, brought an unculti-
vated Barbarian from Africa, and has ever since
been, and now is, under the disadvantage of serving as a Slave in a family in this town." Some of
the poems are of decided excellence; good lines
of the prevalent "classic" style, are not hard to
find; the general merit of the collection easily
surpasses that of Mrs. Bradstreet's; and when
we make allowance for its artificiality, we may
readily admit that it equals the average first
volume of poems to-day—written, like these, "for
the amusement of the author," who of course
"had no intention ever to have [*sic*] published
them." The book remains the principal literary
achievement of the colored race in America.

Toward the close of the eighteenth century the
storm-centre of American poetry seemed to move
southward, hovering for a time over Yale College
and Connecticut. Timothy Dwight, grandson of
Jonathan Edwards, and president of Yale
from 1795 to 1817, published at Hartford, Timothy
in 1785, "The Conquest of Canäan, a Dwight,
Poem, in Eleven Books." The author, in his 1752-1817.

Johnsonian preface, written in the balanced sentences then in vogue, felicitates himself that " the poem is the first of the kind which has been published in this country"; and not unnaturally, therefore, dedicates it " To his Excellency, George Washington, Esquire, Commander-in-chief of the American Armies, The Saviour of his Country, The Supporter of Freedom, and the Benefactor of Mankind." If the soldier Washington ever read these stories of the wars of " Canäan," he found them decorously written in rhymed iambic pentameters, fashioned strictly in accordance with the prevalent English style, and duly equipped with antitheses, " hovering accents," and all the requisities of artificial-heroic verse :

> Behold these scenes expanding to thy soul !
> From orient realms what blackening armies roll !
> See their proud Monarch, in yon glimmering car,
> Leads his strong host, and points the waste of war.
> Till, rais'd by Heaven, the youth, whose early bloom
> Gives a fair promise of his worth to come,
> That second Irad, Othniel, lifts his hand,
> And sweeps the heathens from his wasted land, etc.

There were 304 pages of verse like this, " including 9,672 lines," wrote a long-dead hand on the last page of the copy before me. Most could raise the flowers in 1785, for all had got the seed. Dr. Dwight's trig little epic, in its strong leather covers, was found in many a meagre bookcase in the early days of the republic. If its qualities are those of industry and occasional stiff merit, rather than genius, and if it is no longer read, can we say anything better of the verse of the great Doctor Johnson himself? This poem, and Dr. Dwight's historico-didactic pastoral called "Greenfield Hill," showed that Americans were feebly gaining a little in metrical skill, though originality seemed as far off as ever. Dr. Dwight, who was as modest as he was learned, fairly measured the success and the failure of himself and his fellows, by the frank motto from Pope, on the title-page of "The Conquest of Canäan :"

> " Fired, at first sight, with what the Muse imparts,
> In fearless youth we tempt the height of arts."

At this time a tendency toward the selection of American themes began to be apparent in poetry. "Greenfield Hill," despite its pretty title, and its pleasant suggestion of Sir John Denham, showed no more than moderate ability ; but its subject and scenes were at least taken from the author's own Connecticut town. A great poet is both national and universal ; we had no great poets, and therefore could not produce poetry of catholic interest or value ; hence it was better for our bards to try to be natural and American than to be artificial and European. The patriotic jingles evoked by the Revolution were of course partially spontaneous, though but imperfectly poetic. Trumbull's "McFingal," a sort of transformed "Hudibras," in which American freedom and new-world progress took the place of Butler's Toryism, was in its John Trumbull, 1750–1831. way a promoter of the spirit of the Revolution,

and was largely bought and read by the colonists,
who were beginning to get reading-matter which
they really liked, besides that which they felt that
they ought to like. Some colonial follies, as well
as Tory bigotries, were wholesomely chastised in
the swiftly-moving, slipshod verse of " McFingal."
Not even the combination of patriotism, duty, and
beautiful typography could give popularity to
Joel Barlow's plumbean epic, " The Columbiad,"
which failed as disastrously as its predecessor, " The Vision of Columbus."

Joel Barlow,
1755–1812.

Barlow ascribed its failure to the fact
that the Federalists controlled literary criticism,
while " The Columbiad " was written by a Demo-
crat ; but Federalists did not hesitate to read and
praise his widely-popular and still-read mock-
heroic, " Hasty-Pudding," despite some mildly disgusting passages which give more offence to the
readers of our fastidious age than they did to our
tough-brained great-grandfathers. On the whole,
these Yale graduates were giving more help to
future American literature by their semi-original
excursions to Parnassus than had all the colonial
manufacturers of British pentameters, though
turned as neatly as some of the lines in such a
poem as the weak but smoothly-written " Philosophic Solitude " (1747), by William Livingston,
another Yale man, afterwards governor of New
Jersey, Continental Congressman, and member of
the Constitutional Convention.

The most conspicuous names in the period
under discussion are those of Trumbull, Barlow,

and Freneau. Trumbull's "McFingal" and Barlow's "Hasty-Pudding" have been reprinted in
our own time, and may be said to have an occasional reader. Of the early American verse these
are the best-known examples. Philip Freneau is
talked about, but is not read. His
name is known, in a vague way, as   Philip Freneau,
that of "the poet of the Revolution";   1752-1832.
and those unfamiliar with his voluminous verse
are ready to believe that he was a patriot, a wit,
and a successful lyrist. He was indeed a patriot,
who had no words too bitter for King George the
Third and his generals and ministers, but most of
all for the American Tories. He liked the New
England Puritans little better. Freneau wrote
swiftly and carelessly on a multitude of subjects,
usually without producing anything very witty,
satirical, or lyrical. In his time his patriotic and
humorous poems were called brilliant; to us they
seem "very valueless verses," to borrow the epithet
applied confidently, by a living critic, to the poetical work of a famous American author of later
years. Freneau must have known the difference
between his good work and his doggerel rhymes,
hurriedly written and instantly printed; but his
public neither knew nor cared for the difference,
in those troublous times of political struggle,
Revolution, and nation-making. Freneau, besides
his political, satirical, and descriptive poems, also
essayed rattling social verse, in which he was
surpassed by some of his contemporaries—for
instance, by James McClurg, of Virginia, whose

" Belles of Williamsburg " celebrated the beauties of the aristocratic little capital between the York and the James.

The average excellence of Freneau's verse is small; but occasionally one finds a line, a stanza, or even a whole poem marked by imagination or by poetic thought.   It is a pleasure, after the dull hymns and weak imitations produced in America during the first century and a half of colonial life, to come upon one little lyric, if no more, like Freneau's " The Wild Honey-Suckle ":

> Fair flower, that dost so comely grow,
>   Hid in this silent, dull retreat,
> Untouch'd thy honey'd blossoms blow,
>   Unseen thy little branches greet :
> No roving foot shall find thee here,
> No busy hand provoke a tear.
>
> By Nature's self in white array'd,
>   She bade thee shun the vulgar eye,
> And planted here the guardian shade,
>   And sent soft waters murmuring by ;
> Thus quietly thy summer goes,
> Thy days declining to repose.
>
> Smit with those charms that must decay,
>   I grieve to see your future doom ;
> They died—nor were those flowers less gay,
>   The flowers that did in Eden bloom ;
> Unpitying frosts, and Autumn's power
> Shall leave no vestige of this flower.
>
> From morning suns and evening dews
>   At first thy little being came :
> If nothing once, you nothing lose,
>   For when you die you are the same ;

The space between is but an hour,
The frail duration of a flower.*

This is imperfect and irregular, but it is genuine. Freneau's masterpiece, which seems to me the best poem written in America before 1800, is "The House of Night, a Vision," in one hundred and thirty-six four-line stanzas, which appeared in his 1786 collection. Its occasional "The House faults of expression and versification are of Night." manifest, but in thought and execution, notwithstanding the influence of Gray, it is surprisingly original and strong, distinctly anticipating some of the methods of Coleridge, Poe, and the English pre-Raphaelite poets, none of whom, probably, ever read a line of it. To those who enjoy a literary "find," and like to read and praise a bit of bizarre genius unknown to the multitude, I confidently commend "The House of Night." In it Death lies dying at midnight in his weird and sombre palace; doctors surround him, and a young man whose love Death has killed, forgivingly ministers to him. Then Death, having composed his own epitaph, most woefully perishes; there follows his grim burial in a grave doubly defended against the Devil, so late his trusty friend. The poem ends by pointing us toward a righteous earthly life and an unending immortality. It is not great, and not always smooth; but its lofty plot is strongly worded in

* "Poems Written between the Years 1768 and 1794, by Philip Freneau, of New Jersey. Monmouth, N. J.: Printed at the Press of the Author, at Mount Pleasant, near Middletown Point; MDCCXCV."

sometimes stately verse. I know not why Freneau, in the 1795 collection of his poems, threw
away all but twenty-one stanzas, which he printed
under the title of "The Vision of the Night, a
Fragment." Surely none of his American predecessors or contemporaries had thought or sung, as
did Freneau in this alliterative and assonant
poem, of

> "The black ship travelling through the noisy gale,"
> " A mournful garden of autumnal hue,"
> "The primrose there, the violet darkly blue,"
> "The poplar tall, the lotos, and the lime,"
> " the scarlet mantled morn,"
> " a grave replete with ghosts and dreams,"

and

> "The ecstasy of woe run mad."

None but a poet could have written lines like
these :

> "Trim the dull tapers, for I see no dawn ; "
> " so loud and sad it played
> " As though all musick were to breathe its last."

The American mind produced a psalm-book at
the beginning of the seventeenth century ; at the
close of the eighteenth, by a change that was
gradual, not violent, it gave some promise of
bringing forth that "native American drama"
which has never risen into the plane of true literature. The chronicles of the stage in the
The early
American United States are by no means uninter-
drama.
esting, but they concern the literary student even less than do the chronicles of the Eng-

lish stage for the corresponding period. The
wild or magnanimous Indian, the patriot of the
Revolution, the society belle, the fashionable villain, the honest back-woods Yankee, and the old-
time volunteer fireman of New York, have hurried through many an original play, but the results have not been for the library lamp. Not
even the success of great actors in leading parts
could metamorphose into literature John Howard
Payne's "Brutus"; John Augustus Stone's "Meta-
mora; or, The Last of the Wampanoags";
Robert Montgomery Bird's "The Gladiator," or
Frank Murdock's "Davy Crockett." There has,
on the other hand, been no lack in America of
plays written, but not produced; yet the closet
drama, from Thomas Godfrey's "Prince of Par-
thia" (written about 1759) to Longfellow's "The
Spanish Student," has, in accordance with its
deserts, won little more fame than the acted play.
When one has named George H. Boker's "Francesca da Rimini," the American list of dramas
possessing fair literary rank is nearly exhausted.

A hundred years ago, however, the prospects
of the American play were relatively bright.
Dwight's "Conquest of Canäan" had appeared in
1785, and had been chronicled with chastened
pride in Dr. Abiel Holmes' "Annals of America"
as "the first grave poem of the epic class, written
by an American poet, printed in America." Two
years later was presented at the John Street
Theatre, New York, with similar gratulation in
the Prologue, the first American play ever publicly

2

presented by professional actors. This was "The Contrast, a Comedy; in five acts: written by a Citizen of the United States," to wit, Royall *Royall Tyler,* Tyler, afterward Chief-Justice of Ver-*1758-1826.* mont. "The Contrast,"* its authors' first venture in literature, was certainly a better production, in its way, than "The Conquest of Canäan." If we can imagine that the same individual, in those days of Puritan hatred of the drama, happened to read the "epic" and also to hear the play, he might well have prophesied that the American manufacture of comedies would be livelier and more praiseworthy than the making of religious or patriotic epics. "The Contrast" is far from being a great comedy; it is crude and imperfect; but it is in parts bright and witty; its "stage Yankee" was the worthy prototype of a long line of similar creations; and it possesses at least one advantage over many a play of famous authorship: that of adaptability for public presentation. Much inferior, in every way, was *William Dunlap,* William Dunlap's "The Father; or *1766-1839.* American Shandyism. A Comedy in five acts: written by a Citizen of New York." This play, produced in 1788, reflects the sentimentalism then rising to its highest power; the successful lover is a sort of feeble American Grandison; and the Father, the foiled villain, and the

---

* Beautifully and accurately reprinted, under the editorship of Mr. Thomas J. McKee, as No. 1 of the publications of the Dunlap Society, New York, 1887. The second issue in this series, edited by the same competent specialist, is Dunlap's "The Father, or American Shandyism," and the fourth is Dunlap's "André."

several women, certainly avoid the danger of
offending human nature by any over-accurate representation of virtues or vices. Dunlap wrote and
adapted more than sixty plays ; and by his books,
paintings, and personal influence decidedly and
wholesomely promoted the American drama and
American art. Not a genius, and neither a good
playwright nor a good painter, he performed a
pioneer work now cordially remembered and properly honored. His failure in " André " was no
worse than that of many successors in trying to
make a drama out of a tempting but difficult
theme.

John Howard Payne equalled Dunlap and far
outstripped Tyler in the number and pretentious-
ness of his dramatic undertakings. The list of
his tragedies, comedies, and operas, as chronicled
by his enthusiastic biographer, includes
more than sixty names, and cannot fail
to strike with surprise all but specially-
John Howard
Payne,
1792–1852.
informed readers. Save " Brutus " and perhaps
" Charles II.," these productions are impartially
forgotten ; and the name of Brutus, even, is associated in the public mind, with certain actors and
not with the author. " Brutus," as materially
revised by the players of its leading part, is a vigorous and dramatically-effective play, marked by
an obvious strength of situation, and by something
praiseworthy in the delineation of character.
Were it included among the volumes of such an
Elizabethan dramatist as Middleton, it would

easily and justly find occasional readers, and
admirers whose enthusiasm would not be unpardonable. A Booth need not be ashamed, as an
American, to repeat with his wonted grace and
strength such lines by an American playwright as
these which I transcribe as the best in the play :

                              here all are slaves
None but the fool is happy.

Tarquinia comes. Go, worship the bright sun,
And let poor Brutus wither in the shade.

                    Hark ! the storm rides on,
The scolding winds drive through the clattering rain,
And loudly screams the haggard witch of night.

When forth you walk, may the red flaming sun
Strike you with livid plagues !
Vipers that die not slowly gnaw your heart !
May earth be to you but one wilderness !

                    Behold that frozen corse !
See where the lost Lucretia sleeps in death !
She was the mark and model of the time,
The mould in which each female face was formed,
The very shrine and sacristy of virtue.

If mad ambition in this guilty frame
Had strung one kingly fibre,—yea, but one,—
By all the gods, this dagger which I hold
Should rip it out, though it entwined my heart.

I am not mad, but as the lion is,
When he breaks down the toils that tyrant craft
Hath spread to catch him.

Son of Marcus Junius,
When will the tedious gods permit thy soul
To walk abroad in her own majesty,
And throw this vigor of thy madness from thee,
To avenge my father's and my brother's murder?

To the moon, folly! Vengeance, I embrace thee!

Poor youth! Thy pilgrimage is at an end!
A few sad steps have brought thee to the brink
Of that tremendous precipice whose depth
No thought of man can fathom.

I could select similar lines that fall from the mouths of other characters in the play, sometimes with an Elizabethan aptness:

Yet sometimes, when the moody fit doth take him,
He will not speak for days; yea, rather starve
Than utter nature's cravings; then, anon
He'll prattle shrewdly, with such witty folly
As almost betters reason.

I have seen
A little worthless village cur all night
Bay with incessant noise the silver moon,
While she, serene, throned in her pearlèd car,
Sailed in full state along.

It is not to be forgotten, however, that Payne, with acknowledged and Elizabethan freedom, "had no hesitation in adopting the conception and language" of his seven predecessors in the same theme, and that bombast and weakness are easily to be found in his own work.

Seldom have the annals of literature proved more conclusively than in Payne's case, that the production of one heart-lyric is almost the easiest way to win a long renown. For Payne the playwright, actor, editor, miscellaneous poet, and obscure diplomat, the public now cares nothing ; but Payne as author of one little song is enshrined in the popular heart ; his body was honorably brought from his foreign death-place to rest in his native land ; and needless monuments preserve the fame of him whose renown depends upon a universal knowledge of his masterpiece. "Home, Sweet Home," severed from its well-known music, and measured by strictly artistic canons, is but a poor little poem ; yet it is genuine and catholic, hence it outweighs the hundreds of acts and scenes which Payne presented to the play-going public of America and England.

The "national drama" may be dismissed with the remark that when Americans produce plays of sound and original construction, of felicitous decoration, of national spirit, and of general interest, they will attain the dramatic success hitherto denied.

CHAPTER II.

In the year 1794, just after the constitutional history of the United States had fairly begun, there appeared in New York a little volume entitled "The Columbian Muse: a Selection of American Poetry, from various Authors of Established Reputation." The muse was more Columbian than poetic; and the authors' reputations do not now appear so firmly "established" as they were thought to be a century ago. The book sampled the work of Livingston, Freneau, Dwight, Trumbull, Barlow, Dunlap, and others even more obscure. In one sense it was a sufficiently discouraging sign, but it showed that poetic industry had appeared, though genius was lacking. Imagination had not characterized our theological treatises, though some of them proved, at least, their right to be called visionary and evanescent; nor had it marked our political speeches and public documents, notwithstanding an occasional eloquent apostrophe, or clear vision of the future results of a noble theory. The dawn of true literature, however, was not long to delay; in prose the work of Irving was about to interest readers in two nations, and in verse we were to have something better than mechanical

23

pentameters or painfully artificial rhymes. The
"rosy fingers" of this long-expected dawn were
first to brighten the skies above the Hudson, not
those which hung above the more melancholy
waters of Massachusetts Bay; and
the legendary land of Rip van Winkle
was to be visited by a poet who found
his theme in fairy-land, not in Columbia nor in
Canäan.

Joseph Rodman
Drake,
1795-1820.

"The Culprit Fay," by Joseph Rodman Drake,
appeared in 1819, when the author was twenty-
four years old; it was the outgrowth of a conversation between Drake, Halleck, and Cooper concerning the unsung poetry of American rivers.
Its little story of a sinning fay's contrition, confession, and satisfaction is told in a way that
charmed my early boyhood and pleases still; for
it shows that American verse, under Drake's
hand, had emerged from pious propriety into the
realm of fancy and the borderland of imagination.
Drake wrote swiftly, and deemed his poems valueless and only worthy of the fire; but one finds
something savable in lines like these:

> The stars are on the moving stream,
>   And fling, as its ripples gently flow,
> A burnished length of wavy beam
>   In an eel-like, spiral line below;
>
> The winds are whist, and the owl is still,
>   The bat in the shelvy rock is hid,
> And naught is heard on the lonely hill
> But the cricket's chirp, and the answer shrill
>   Of the gauze-winged katydid,

And the plaint of the wailing whippoorwill,
   Who mourns unseen, and ceaseless sings
Ever a note of wail and woe,
   Till morning spreads her rosy wings,
And earth and sky in her glances glow.

'Tis the hour of fairy ban and spell :
The wood-tick has kept the minutes well ;
He has counted them all with click and stroke,
Deep in the heart of the mountain oak,
And he has awakened the sentry elve
   Who sleeps with him in the haunted tree,
To bid him ring the hour of twelve,
   And call the fays to their revelry ;
Twelve small strokes on his tinkling bell—
('Twas made of the white snail's pearly shell)—
" Midnight comes, and all is well !
Hither, hither wing your way !
'Tis the dawn of the fairy day."
They come from beds of lichen green,
They creep from the mullein's velvet screen ;
Some on the backs of beetles fly
   From the silver tops of moon-touched trees,
Where they swung in their cobweb hammocks high,
   And rocked about in the evening breeze ;
Some from the hum-bird's downy nest—
   They had driven him out by elfin power,
And pillowed on plumes of his rainbow breast,
   Had slumbered there till the charméd hour ;
Some had lain in the scoop of the rock,
   With glittering ising-stars inlaid ;
And some had opened the four-o'clock,
   And stole within its purple shade.
   And now they throng the moonlight glade,
Above—below—on every side,
   Their little minim forms arrayed
In the tricksy pomp of fairy pride.

Drake's services to nascent American poetry also included the composition of a spirited lyric to "The American Flag," familiar in the anthologies, and long a favorite with the school-boys of the nation. Its tropes are somewhat strained, and its sensational scheme narrowly escapes bombast; but on the whole—like a greater poem, Shelley's "Cloud"—it avoids the bathetic and produces an honest and stirring effect upon the reader. The "azure robe of night," "stars of glory," "gorgeous dyes," "milky baldric," "lightning-lances," "thunder-drum of heaven," "gory sabres," "shoots of flame," and "meteor-glances" of Drake's poem are parts of a symmetrical whole and are accompanied by expressions of true thought. The lyric, in its entirety, easily surpasses such bald, rude rhymes as Robert Treat Paine, Jr.'s, "Adams and Liberty," Joseph Hopkinson's "Hail Columbia," or Francis Scott Key's "Star-Spangled Banner." These last-named songs, like "Yankee Doodle" itself, are so inseparably connected with certain airs, and so closely enshrined in the patriotic heart, that no one stops to think of their literary poverty. The young American nation had found no such singers as those who voiced the stirring hopes of Germany in the days of Napoleon's attempted abduction and murder of a continent.

When young Drake died, his friend Halleck put his deep and unaffected grief into that tender poem of which four lines are universally known:

Fitz-Greene
Halleck,
1790-1867.

Green be the turf above thee,
    Friend of my better days;
None knew thee but to love thee,
    Nor named thee but to praise.

Drake and Halleck worked together as friends and fellow-lovers of poetry. With much that was perishable or valueless, in which division their humorous verse must be included, they produced some things that have attained what may fairly be called a lasting renown, though not the highest. Drake's "American Flag" and Halleck's "Marco Bozzaris" were read, and memorized, and printed in the collections, because people liked them and were stirred by their patriotism or pathos. Limited in range and modest in achievement, American poetry had reached a time when its principal productions could take care of themselves. A "poem" that depends for readers merely upon its piety, or its patriotism, or its local color, is sure to be forgotten soon. Halleck was as patriotic as Barlow, and as fond of local themes as Dwight; but he possessed what both Barlow and Dwight lacked: a spark of poetic fire. There was a genuine force in his lament for Drake and his stirring lyric about Marco Bozzaris the Greek. Halleck, in the foolish days of American criticism, used to be mentioned most respectfully as one of our greater bards. This he certainly was not; but his work marked a step in advance toward that literary self-reliance which was at first so painfully lacking in the United states. Halleck, at least, felt the difference between imagination and raw ambition, and this difference he was able to make apparent to his readers, though they did not stop to indulge in close critical analysis.

Elsewhere, along the Atlantic coast, appeared signs of the new day which was lending distinction to the poets of the Hudson. Washington Allston and Richard Henry Dana, on the banks of that river Charles which was to be made famous by Longfellow, were giving to Massachusetts some welcome tokens of future achievement. Allston, one of the pioneers of American art, was a man of fine thought and poetic feeling, which sometimes found expression in verse or fiction. He had lived and studied in Europe ; the pictures of the masters were his models ; and his list of personal friends included famous names. Early transcendentalism, in the form of spiritual receptivity and insight, was beginning to affect England and America ; and Allston shared with Coleridge the powerful effect of the new movement. Like other young Americans, he brought home with him somewhat of that nameless potency, that attitude toward life, which we call culture ; and culture was the very thing the young nation had most lacked. Allston's poems and little romance are forgotten, but his biblical pictures, because of their form and color, will retain some absolute as well as relative fame. Dana, in his long life, beheld the rise of American poetry from humble imitations to the manly triumphs of a free imagination ; and in its early years he aided its progress, and

Richard Henry Dana, 1787–1879.

the development of culture. While Allston was painting and lecturing on art, Dana was expounding Shakespeare to audiences more interested than critical. Dana was one of the Americans who made unsuccessful attempts to domesticate the discursive periodical-miscellany of the Addisonian type; but his editorship of the most famous Boston quarterly still further aided in the spread of knowledge and gracious letters. When his long and once-known poem, " The Buccaneer," was re-issued in a magazine, a few years ago, some critics thought it a new production, so completely had it passed into the shadows. Its metrical evenness and its smoothly-turned descriptive phrases approached, but quite missed, the success won by Bryant. Dana, like Charles Sprague, is one of the bygone figures in our literature, whose relative importance must constantly diminish ; but those venerable Bostonians, when they passed to rest, could feel that they had in some small degree prepared the way, by their creations and their criticisms, for their stronger successors.

When one has patiently read the eight hundred pages containing the " poetical works" of Percival, the chief of the Connecticut bards of the second generation, it is difficult to pay him even the relative praise that belongs to a pioneer. Percival repeatedly James Gates Percival, 1795–1856. crosses, in the wrong direction, the line that separates the sublime from the ridiculous, the soulful from the sentimental. The age of sickly sweet sentimentality had come upon America, and Per-

cival too often yielded entirely to its influence,
instead of accepting that influence in part, that he
might turn it to higher service. He could find,
like Bryant, a poetic theme in "Consumption,"
and could write upon it eighty-two lines begin
ning :

> There is a sweetness in woman's decay,
> When the light of beauty is fading away, etc.;

and he everywhere hunted up themes for so-called
"reflective" verse. The reflective idea is also
favored by that index of first lines which makes
his works seem somewhat painfully decorous and
monotonously unreadable ; but the variety of
subject is surely sufficiently great. Imitating
half a dozen of the greater English poets of his
time, Percival found themes in sky, earth, and
water, in ancient history and in modern episode.
He ranged from "Retrospection" to "Genius
Waking"; from "Midnight Music" to "Perry's
Victory on Lake Erie"; from the Violet or the
Gentiana Crinita to the Good Man :—

> How happy is the pure, good man, whose life
> Was always good, who in the tender years
> Of childhood, and the trying time of youth,
> Was shielded by a kind, parental hand !

who rises with the lark and secretly prays in blank
verse for five pages.

But the voluminous Percival gives evidence of
the fact that the American mind, in his day, was
beginning to have vague and imperfect, but not

insincere, poetic thoughts and hopes; that its verse-product was received with some favor by a widening audience; and that its themes were sometimes taken from nature or from human nature, and treated with a pen that was facile, if too fluent. If we had never produced more than a Percival, there had never been an American literature; but a new land needs many a little builder before its cathedrals rise in the world's view.

Looking back upon Percival's works, the best thing I find is an occasional apt choice and treatment of a subject taken from external nature, not human nature. Percival sang of Seneca Lake:

> On thy fair bosom, silver lake!
>   The wild swan spreads his snowy sail,
> And round his breast the ripples break,
>   As down he bears before the gale. . . . .
>
> How sweet at set of sun to view
>   Thy golden mirror spreading wide,
> And see the mist of mantling blue
>   Float round the distant mountain's side. . . . .
>
> On thy fair bosom, silver lake!
>   O, I could ever sweep the oar,
> When early birds at morning wake,
>   And evening tells us toil is o'er.

Another crude Connecticut poet, J. G. C. Brainard, was writing hasty lines similarly lacking in greatness but similarly marked by occasional genuineness. Now the sea-bird was his theme:

John Gardiner
Calkins Brainard,
1795–1828.

Who hovers on high o'er the lover,
  And her who has clung to his neck?
Whose wing is the wing that can cover
  With its shadow the foundering wreck?
    'Tis the sea-bird, sea-bird, sea-bird,
      Lone looker on despair;
    The sea-bird, sea-bird, sea-bird,
      The only witness there.

Again, he wrote of some local stream, or of the autumn woods he well knew:

The dead leaves strew the forest walk,
  And withered are the pale, wild flowers;
The frost hangs black'ning on the stalk,
  The dew-drops fall in frozen showers.
    Gone are the Spring's green sprouting bowers,
Gone Summer's rich and mantling vines,
    And Autumn, with her yellow hours,
On hill and plain no longer shines.

Less true and more bombastic was Brainard's once famous extemporization on Niagara, which he never saw. Essentially valueless are such meditations as these, worded in feeble blank verse:

                              It would seem
As if God poured thee from his hollow hand;
Had hung his bow upon thy awful front;
Had spoke in that loud voice which seemed to him
Who dwelt in Patmos for his Saviour's sake,
The sound of many waters: and had bade
Thy flood to chronicle the ages back,
And notch his centuries in the eternal rocks.
  Deep calleth unto deep. And what are we,
That hear the question of that voice sublime?
Oh what are all the notes that ever rang

From war's vain trumpet by thy thundering side?
Yea, what is all the riot man can make,
In his short life, to thy unceasing roar?
And yet, bold babbler! what art thou to Him
Who drowned a world, and heaped the waters far
Above its loftiest mountains?—A light wave
That breaks and whispers of its maker's might!

The lyrical spirit, with its love of nature and of emotion, swiftly expressed, was stealing in upon the South as well as the North. From the South was to come our most distinctly lyrical poet, Poë; and there already was Richard Henry Wilde, Irishman, congressman, and man of culture. We have forgotten his long poem, "Hesperia," but remember these "Stanzas"—everybody wrote "stanzas," in those days, unless, indeed, he wrote a "Conquest of Canäan," a "Columbiad," or a "Hadad":

> Richard Henry
> Wilde,
> 1789-1847.

My life is like the summer rose
  That opens to the morning sky,
But ere the shades of evening close
  Is scattered on the ground—to die!
Yet on the rose's humble bed
The sweetest dews of night are shed,
As if she wept the waste to see—
But none shall weep a tear for me!

My life is like the autumn leaf
  That trembles in the moon's pale ray;
Its hold is frail, its date is brief,
  Restless—and soon to pass away!
Yet ere that leaf shall fall and fade
The parent tree will mourn its shade,
The winds bewail the leafless tree—
But none shall breathe a sigh for me!

My life is like the prints which feet
    Have left on Tampa's desert strand;
Soon as the rising tide shall beat,
    All trace will vanish from the sand;
Yet, as if grieving to efface
All vestige of the human race,
On that lone shore loud moans the sea—
But none, alas! shall mourn for me!

The feeble twitterings of the American song-sters were beginning to be heard beyond the ocean. Byron, whose praise depended on fancy rather than reason, was good enough to commend the lyric just cited, which was fairly representative of the minor poetry beginning to appear in one section of the new world; while the good-natured Southey, fond of poetical bombast, bestowed upon Mrs. Maria Gowen Brooks laudations fit for Sappho or Elizabeth Barrett Browning. Mrs.

Maria (Gowen) Brooks, 1795–1845.

Brooks represented sentimentalism at the full; she was called by the name of "Maria del'Occidente;" and in "Zophiel; or, The Bride of Seven," she success-fully transferred to America many of the weakest elements in the English romanticism of 1825. In her verse, zephyrs play with ringlets, lips resem-ble bud-bursting flowers, eyebrows have flexile arches, cheeks are vermilion and feet silvery; the turf is velvet, the noon fervid, the midnight peaceful; the dove responds to love, and lutes reëcho flutes. But all things go to prepare the way for a nation's literature; "Zophiel" is at least better, as well as later, than the "Magnalia Christi Americana."

By this time, however, the day of small things in American poetry had passed, and the country could boast one poet relatively, though not absolutely, of the first rank, and deserving notice and praise even by absolute standards.   The work of William Cullen Bryant is not to be measured as a curiosity, like that of Anne Bradstreet, or a well-meaning attempt, like that of Joel Barlow, or a promise, like that of Drake.   Neither does his place in literature depend upon a meritorious lyric or two, such as Halleck's " Marco Bozzaris " or Wilde's " My Life is Like a Summer Rose."   It is true that Bryant wrote short poems, not epics, dramas, or idyls ; and that his name is closely connected with three or four productions of special fame and merit.   But we feel, in reading his verse, that its successes are not due to accident.   It comes from the brain of a strong man, in full possession of his powers.   It is the product of a thinker and of an artist ; it represents both imagination and art ; and its themes are taken from nature and the soul.   Bryant, as has been said, cannot justly be ranked with poets of the first class.   Neither in range nor in excellence of achievement is his verse of the highest.   Yet his thoughts are deep, manly, and true ; his observation of skies, woods, and waters, and his power of description of the external world, justly entitle him to his wide renown as a "poet of nature."   He has been amiably called our American Wordsworth, but he was no copyist.   He never gave us poetry as

William Cullen Bryant.
1794–1878.

great or apt as Wordsworth's best; but he did
not sink to Wordworth's flatness, nor wander
away to the fools' region of Wordsworth's silliness. Nay more, he interprets the meaning of
nature, as the mirror and teacher of the soul.
That which reflection must dwell upon, and that
which art may portray, in life and its surroundings, Bryant worthily represents, in forms not a
few. All that is lacking in his writing is the
force and fire of genius. It represents meditation and expression almost at their best; but it
belongs not with the work of the greater choir.

It seems proper, therefore, to close this chapter,
on the dawn of imagination in America, with the
name of Bryant. By the length and importance
of his life-work; by his early triumphs, middle-
life successes, and octogenarian achievements, he
left to us a remarkably complete and valuable
literary legacy, enriched, perforce, by a personal
character of serenity and strength, albeit of a certain coldness. Bryant's poems are by no means
lacking in the quality of imagination; but his imagination does not soar and sing in distant and
ultimate skies. Within his limits he need not
have done better: let not his successors complain
of the comparatively narrow tract on Parnassus
on which he dwelt. As Franklin was the first
man to make the American mind felt as a force in
other lands than ours; as Irving was our pioneer
in carrying forth a distinct literary message and
achievement; so Bryant was the first poet to give
us verse that needed no adventitious excuse or

recommendation. When "Thanatopsis" appeared in *The North American Review*, in "Thanatopsis." 1817, true poetry had come to, and had come from, America. Its author was but twenty-three years of age, but he had been spinning rhymes, or making verse, for more than half of his short lifetime. At ten he was a contributor to the country newspapers, and at fourteen a political satirist in metre. It would seem that the poetic spirit could not longer keep silent in the United States.

"Thanatopsis" is a Saxon and New England poem. Its view of death reflects the race characteristics of ten centuries. It shows "no trace of age, no fear to die." Its morality and its trust are ethnic rather than Christian. It nowhere expresses that belief in personal immortality which the author possessed and elsewhere stated. It is a piece of verse of which any language or age might be proud. Yet, as I have just said, this strong and serene utterance of philosophy and of poetry, expressed in the best blank verse of the period, came from a mere boy, who but a few years before had been writing political poems, dashed with fire and vitriol, on "The Embargo" and "The Spanish Revolution." In its earliest publication "Thanatopsis" was much less than perfect, and was manifestly inferior to the final version. But even then it was, as it is now, a microcosm of the author's mind and powers. It includes the thought of "The Ages," read by young Bryant to the Harvard Phi Beta Kappa

Society in 1821; and its mood is not dissimilar to that of "The Flood of Years," which was the fruit of the author's musings in old age. That essential stability of mind of which this early and most favored poem gave witness, never forsook the poet, though of course his choice and art were fallible. Whether he was traveller, story-teller, essayist, biographical orator, political editor, or free-trade reformer, he carried into the varied work of life the solemn and cheering lessons derived from the contemplation of a universe at once majestic and ever-changing.

The results of Bryant's labors, as a man and an author, might easily have been forecast from the evident character of his mind and poetic product.

The author of "Thanatopsis" could
Bryant's Poetic Product. not be a voluminous versifier. He must write comparatively little, and chiefly on themes suggested by nature or by the reflective temper. The residuum of his work is therefore valuable, since his power to treat such themes could not be questioned, after his first success, and since it remained with him to the end. English poetry, after its freshness in the work of Chaucer and of a few lyrists of later periods, had painfully lacked the spontaneousness and beauty of out-door nature. In the eighteenth century its see-saw artificiality had been deplorable. Cowper had prepared the way for Wordsworth and his fellows ; and the romantic revival in England, and even in Germany, was arousing the American versifiers. So far as this revival

was characterized by a willingness to regard nature as the friend and fellow and mentor of man, Bryant was its principal American representative. He forgot not that the poetry of nature, when transferred to the printed page, must be open and free, and accordingly he was not a mere maker of words and metres in the library. But nature, in Bryant's view, had something to say as well as to show ; and the lesson as well as the vision of nature is presented in " A Forest Hymn," " To a Waterfowl," " Monument Mountain," " The Death of the Flowers." The many songs of sky, forest, brook, meadow, and field-path are reëchoed by Bryant only in part. His pages do not resound with the " thousand voices " wherewith " earth worships God." But when we do catch the solemn tone of the " earth-song," in Bryant's lines, we feel no sense of unworthiness. The grandeur may be limited and imperfect, but it is still grandeur. Wayward beauty or tender suggestiveness is not absent, but each is subordinated to the solemn reflections inspired by the scenes in which we live. Some curious students have averred that the key of nature—the resultant of all the voices of the world—is A. This deep undertone is that which Bryant heard, and to which his verse-music responds in fit accord.

It is not necessarily an arraignment of a man of genius to declare that he did not and could not do this or that thing. That Bryant was unable to produce an epic, a drama, a strong delineation of the heroic character, a brilliant lyric of patriotism or passion, a poem instinct with daring imagination, was not necessarily to the discredit of his powers. *Non omnia possumus omnes.* His place was with Gray, not with Milton, Goethe, Browning, or Burns. Intense power was not his, nor broad creative range, nor soaring vision; his marks were thoughtfulness and serenity. But poets of the second order are not so much to be blamed for their deficiencies as measured by their successes within their proper field. Bryant's were apparent, even absolutely, if we do not press the term too far; relatively, as has been seen, they were for a time even commanding. By and by he must yield to Emerson the poetic seer, to Longfellow the catholic singer of sympathy and of art, to Poe the lyrist pure and simple. Bryant's voice sounded out less strong than Whittier's, in distinctly American song; and even as a descriptive poet Whittier, in his artlessness and haste, seemed truer to our local life than Bryant, in his reserve and quiet strength. What Bryant did and was has been neatly summarized in the phrase "narrow greatness,"—only one prefers to think of the greatness rather than the narrowness. There are no mute inglorious Miltons in the field of letters; everyone gets his due; Bryant has exactly received his deserved meed. His limited greatness is made apparent by his loneliness; there is but one Bryant. After all,

whether a poet be great or not great, his place is
his own if we think of his work as being sufficient
in itself ; such, indeed, is the work of the author
of " Thanatopsis."

The chief of our poets of meditation, based
upon observation, are Bryant and Emerson, if we
set aside Longfellow for the moment; since his
poetry, though often reflective, is more often
marked by feeling and sentiment than meditation.
Between the prevalent attitude of Bryant and
that of Emerson is this difference.   Bryant's is
that of solemn acceptance of the exist-
ent order, Emerson's that of optimistic   Bryant's
                                             Solemnity.
faith in that order.   Bryant as surely
avoids the effect of gloom as Emerson avoids
that of gayety.   When Bryant was more than
eighty years of age, in the very year of his death,
he wrote of Washington :

> Lo, where, beneath an icy shield,
>   Calmly the mighty Hudson flows !
> By snow-clad fell and frozen field,
>   Broadening, the lordly river goes.
>
> The wildest storm that sweeps through space,
>   And rends the oak with sudden force,
> Can raise no ripple on his face,
>   Or slacken his majestic course.
>
> Thus, mid the wreck of thrones, shall live,
>   Unmarred, undimmed, our hero's fame,
> And years succeeding years shall give
>   Increase of honors to his name.

There was something in Bryant's mind that was
akin to Washington's ; this steady flow of thought

and purpose, beneath a calm exterior, untossed
by storm or passion, marks Bryant's poetical work
from the first. When he forgets himself, and
essays the playful or humorous, the result is
melancholy indeed, as in that fearful poem on the
mosquito. In general he is the singer of

> "The victory of endurance born;"
> "The eternal years of God;"
> "Old ocean's gray and melancholy waste;"

hills "rock-ribbed, and ancient as the sun;" and
an "unfaltering trust" learned in the groves,
"God's first temples," or from nature's teachings
under the open sky.

Bryant resembles Emerson in the characteristic
of uniformity. His poetry is little affected by
the progress of the author's life, or the
changes and events of the national history. The stale Minerva-comparison is
applicable to the early products of this author's
mind. If we except the political verse of his boyhood, we find little to suggest either youth or age.
His occasional poems are not felicitous, as a rule.
"The Death of Lincoln" is a wooden thing, and
"The Death of Slavery" is lacking in the fire of
Whittier and the art of Longfellow. One of his
distinctly autobiographic pieces, "A Lifetime," is
poorer still; it carries us back to the dreary days
of colonial doggerel:

Bryant's Uniformity of Work.

> She leads by the hand their first-born,
> A fair-haired little one,
> And their eyes as they meet him sparkle
> Like brooks in the morning sun.

Another change, and I see him
　Where the city's ceaseless coil
Sends up a mighty murmur
　From a thousand modes of toil.

And there, mid the clash of presses,
　He plies the rapid pen
In the battles of opinion,
　That divide the sons of men, etc.

There are one-hundred and forty-eight lines of this general kind, whether better or worse, written in old age by a true poet, who had not lost his powers, but who never seemed able to discriminate with certainty between good and bad. What Bryant could do, he could do in youth as well as in maturity; what he could not do in youth, he never learned.

The use of one of his youthful powers, that of story-telling, was given up in later years. With Robert C. Sands and Gulian C. Verplanck he edited for three years (1828–1830) an annual entitled "The Talisman," which in a modest way marked a period in American literary culture. "The Talisman" for 1829, Bryant's Prose. for instance, was a handsome volume, well printed on what would nowadays be called ragged-edged hand-made paper, nicely bound in half leather, gilt top, and illustrated with ambitious but rather feeble steel-engravings of American origin. In its outward form the book was an exact prototype of some of the finer publications of our own day (for there has been no improvement in the art of printing for two centuries);

and, better still, it had in its contents an unquestionable tone of literary culture and power. For this second volume Bryant wrote, in prose, " Recollections of the South of Spain," and a " Story of the Island of Cuba," and also, with Verplanck, some " Reminiscences of New York." Here, as elsewhere, we see how crudeness and self-assertion were yielding to refinement and conscious strength, which indubitably marked these early though essentially unimportant writings of Bryant. His prose work, throughout life, remained in relative obscurity; but his letters of travel, orations commemorative of friends and contemporaries; critical introductions to collections of poetry, of books, of pictures, or historical narrative; newspaper editorials, etc., possessed the negative merit of freedom from haste or extravagance, and the positive qualities of smoothness, accuracy, and good sense. This well-known and successful poet, like so many other American workers in various fields, never shirked the miscellaneous, though ephemeral and unimportant, duties resting upon authors who are creating and developing a new national literature. His position as the literary and civic Nestor of New York society, during many years, rather increased the number of his transitory tasks, and encroached upon the already impaired time devoted to his high and original work. This, however, is a personal, not a literary, matter; we measure literature by achievement only, not by causes or conditions, however they may affect achievement.

Yet Bryant's city life and manifold duties never injuriously affected the quality of his nature-poetry. Born in the country, he was a country resident for a large part of the year. A poet of observation and reflection, his records of sight and insight were most frequent when he was surrounded by congenial scenes, that is, in rural life. Not a lyrist, not a poet of sentiment, not powerfully affected by reading, he was not often tempted to turn aside from his chosen woodland path. The young Longfellow began in a similar line, but was soon attracted by a thousand themes of love, ambition, sentiment, European romance and culture, and American history and tradition,—as Bryant never was. All these themes Bryant touches, but in his central self he is the contemplative interpreter of nature, and of the procession of man through the ages, environed by the eternal hills and the ever variant sea. It is not strange that a poetic mind so austere, solemn, and essentially unchanged as Bryant's, should have served as a model for a few not successful imitators, who could reproduce neither the man nor his verse. Artificial meditation in verse is like an artificial temple, never devoted to the service of the gods. Bryant himself, on the whole, measured his powers and his limitations justly, gave us the utmost results within his reach as poet, and attained in middle life his full due of praise; for, as has been said, his deserts were clearly perceived and amply rewarded.

The place of Bryant in American poetry, then,

differs materially from his place in American prose. In the former he was a pioneer in fact, but not in the character or quality of his work, which was practically independent of its time. In the latter he was a pioneer in every sense, doing what he could to further culture, learning, good manners, and sound politics in a new land ; and employing powers always respectable, but never commanding, in whatsoever task might present itself with adequate claim. Even in prose, however, it is doubtful whether any reserved possibilities of higher achievement, under more favorable circumstances, lay within him.

To return finally to his poetry, upon which his ultimate renown must wholly rest, we note that the principal qualities of that poetry did not depend upon time-conditions. The dawn of American poetry attained its sunrise-light in Bryant ; but his verse, if now presented for the first time, would probably achieve almost precisely the kind and amount of success it attained six or seven decades ago. Its meritorious quality is essential and not accidental or occasional. It is not of the greatest, for it is not highly imaginative, not broadly constructive, not enthusiastic for liberty, not strikingly original, not beautifully musical, not bathed in the ever-changing light of the ideal toward which the noblest poets yearningly peer ; but it is often grave, reverend, profound, highly helpful. Save Emerson, no American poet so

Bryant independent of time-conditions.

often and so well described the Nature familiar to
the residents of the Eastern States, the Nature
which has been the background of most of our
literature. Bryant might have said, with Addison : "Poetic fields encompass me around"; and,
from them, in many a verse and measure, he drew
the lesson of serene obedience to the Power
behind Nature :

> Be it ours to meditate,
> In these calm shades, thy milder majesty,
> And to the beautiful order of thy works
> Learn to conform the order of our lives.

In the provincial days of our literature, a possible Shakespeare or Milton was thought to be
hidden in some village poetaster, while incipient
Byrons and fully-equipped Thomsons were plenty
enough. Born in those early days, when pretentious mediocrity was "hailed" and honored,
Bryant lived until after the close of the first great
literary period of America, and preserved the
dignity and value of his verse to the end of his
career. No American, as yet, has written better
blank verse, and none, in hymns or other sober
lyrics, has more effectually expressed his thought
in iambic tetrameter four-line stanzas, with alternately rhyming lines, or rhyming couplets. No
American, furthermore, has made a worthier
contribution to the accumulating literature of
Homeric translation. Bryant's stately versions
of the Iliad and Odyssey, in blank verse,
have already endured without detriment the

discussions and rivalries of twenty years. With a
part of Homer's genius—his grandeur—
Bryant's Homer. Bryant was in fit and sympathetic accord, and his plainly straightforward and
steadily dignified verse interprets many parts of
the Iliad and Odyssey in a way not inadequate.
Homer is the great problem of translation ; no
one reproduces all his qualities. One translator
offers fire and swiftness at the expense of stateliness ; another, stateliness that is stiff and pompous, and therefore un-Homeric. A regular and
strong rendition of Homer's stories and thoughts,
with a part of the Homeric manner—these Bryant
gives us. His version seems a good one until we
turn to the magnificent Greek itself, when it van-
ishes with all other Homeric translations. But
a history of national literature must not stop to
discuss renditions from other literatures.

The career of William Cullen Bryant was a
peculiarly fortunate one. To few men does life
give more of fulfilled hope and achieved
Bryant's Career. promise. In his literary work he early
took a just measure of his powers, and
by the exercise of those powers won a success
which, though not the greatest or broadest, was
evident and long-lasting. Not many bards could
so confidently say (if I may reverently use the
quotation) : what I have written, I have written.
Not many have given us, so quietly and so
strongly, the best that lay in their minds, leaving
their rank in literature to be settled by inexorable
Time, without distress or reckless ambition on

their own part. Bryant avoided the mistakes of
over-confidence, and yet did not fall into the
weakness of undue literary conservatism. This
honorable and excellent poet, as he looked forward without envy to the brighter days of American literature, might have given an affirmative
answer to the query concerning a broader immortality, with which he closed his poem on " The
Return of Youth:"

> Hast thou not glimpses, in the twilight here,
>   Of mountains where immortal morn prevails?
> Comes there not, through the silence, to thine ear
>   A gentle rustling of the morning gales;
> A murmur, wafted from that glorious shore,
>   Of streams that water banks forever fair,
> And voices of the loved ones gone before,
>   More musical in that celestial air?

CHAPTER III.

FOR many years the most representative name in American poetry has been that of Henry Wadsworth Longfellow. Others have often rivalled or surpassed him in special successes, or in peculiar fields. The poetry of Emerson displays a clearness of vision, a loftiness of plan, an optimistic philosophy, and a profundity of thought to which Longfellow cannot wholly attain ; but it is the splendid poetry of fragment and of swift utterance. Poe's peculiar domain Longfellow neither would enter nor could enter with success. In some few respects Lowell displays powers—and not alone of wit—more significant than those of his friend and neighbor and collegiate predecessor. Such reflections as these, however, cannot profitably be followed far. All in all, Longfellow has been the nation's poet, and has been recognized as such in the other great Teutonic countries as well as in America. From him came the only important poem embodying the myths and imaginative life of the Indian race,—a poem which, alone among all our productions, shows something of the epic spirit, in that it is a characteristic verse-story of the hero of a race and

Henry Wadsworth Longfellow, 1807–1882.

50

time, whose deeds are affected by the courage of man and by the supernatural work of the powers above. From Longfellow, too, came other tales or dramas of by-gone American life and scenery, in New England or in Nova Scotia. " The Courtship of Miles Standish," " Evangeline," and " The New England Tragedies" were distinctly local products, while at least one of them possessed that universal interest which is a mark of true literary achievement. Longfellow, more than any other American, made known to a provincial people the wealth and the charm of continental culture, and of German romanticism in particular. He experimented so successfully with two measures unfamiliar in English—unrhymed hexameter and unrhymed trochaic tetrameter—that in their use he has virtually had neither rivals nor successors. Furthermore, he has been deemed, by thousands, preëminently the poet of sympathy and sentiment, the laureate of the common human heart ; yet none has been able to class him with the slender sentimentalists, or to deny to him the possession of artistic powers of somewhat unusual range and of unquestionable effectiveness. Longfellow has aroused affection on the one hand and stimulated criticism on the other; the personality has hardly been forgotten in the product, and yet the work has made no claims not intrinsic. Like Whittier, Longfellow is beloved; like Emerson, he is honored for his poetic evangel ; and like Poe, he is studied as an artist in words and metrical effects.

His position as leader of the American choir, however, has not been unquestioned, and is not likely to escape sharp challenge in future. Forty

The questioned Leader of American Song. years ago, Poe, with all the energy he could exert, brought against the greater part of Longfellow's shorter poems the charge of prevalent didacticism, followed by the poet at the expense of beauty. The longer productions upon which his fame must largely rest had not then been written; but the same criticism has since been made more than once, in various forms, and will continue to be made. It is sometimes broadened to the claim that Longfellow's work is good but not great, pleasing but not imaginative, and hence of temporary rather than ultimate value.

The real worth of Longfellow's writings is likely to be made apparent by a frank abandonment of that which is transient or faulty. The

His Transient Work. great service which he did to American culture and poetic thought, has been fully stated in a previous part of this history.* We have seen that he studied widely and sympathetically, and that he taught his countrymen well. In two important colleges he served as instructor for many a year, in that drudgery which is so constantly brightened by the responsive work of the more diligent or appreciative students. Graduates from Bowdoin and Harvard bore his message into Philistia, but Longfellow likewise directly educated the general public in

* Vol. I., pp. 397–402.

many and sometimes humble ways. He wrote or
edited text-books in French, Spanish, and Italian ;
he prepared numerous translations, long or short,
from nearly all the Continental tongues; he
edited a huge anthology of European verses, and
compiled one or two little books of selections
from English bards; he portrayed, in gently-
romantic essays, the life and scenes of the Old
World of castles and cathedrals, sunny France,
decadent Spain, and Italy swarming with ghosts
of past greatness; he opened the oaken door to
the then unknown halls of Anglo-Saxon letters ;
and even in his last years he took the trouble to
edit thirty-one trig volumes of the " Poems of
Places," from his native Maine to the far islands
of Oceanica.   All this ephemeral work—in which
I do not include the translation of the " Divine
Comedy"—was of decided benefit to the country,
and far from valueless to the doer himself ; but it
may be dismissed at once as we turn to the estimate of the character and value of Longfellow's
poetry.   It helped to develop American culture,
but did not greatly benefit American verse.

Not much greater worth or permanence distinguishes Longfellow's essays in fiction.   During
all his life he had a certain fondness for excursions and experiments.   Only two years after the
publication of " Evangeline," his first successful
and widely popular poem of length, appeared
" Kavanagh, a Tale."   The brief story is pleasing
throughout; its rural pictures have a   "Kavanagh,
mild idyllic grace, and its gentle humor   a Tale."
approves itself to the reader, who heartily accepts

its lesson: that purpose should be transmuted into action. All that could possibly be said in its favor was thus worded by Emerson in a letter to its author: "It is good painting, and I think it the best sketch we have seen in the direction of the American novel. One thing struck me as I read,—that you win our gratitude too easily; for after our much experience of the squalor of New Hampshire and the pallor of Unitarianism, we are so charmed with elegance in an American book that we could forgive more vices than are possible to you." The same friendly critic also said that he read the book "with great contentment," and found that "it had, with all its gifts and graces, the property of persuasion, and of inducing the serene mood it required." But it soon joined the great company of sketches toward the American Novel. This amiable story is respectably included in the complete prose-works of its author, of whom it was not unworthy, but whose reputation it never enhanced. Produced when Longfellow was forty-two, in length and merit it fairly equals Hawthorne's "Fanshawe," published when Hawthorne was twenty-four. "Kavanagh" leaves upon the mind an impression of limitation rather than of imperfection, but its minor graces are all it can boast.

"Hyperion, a Romance" is decidedly more important than "Kavanagh," which it antedated by ten years. It is longer, its imagina-
"Hyperion, a Romance." tive element is broader and more conspicuous, its creative power is higher, its style is superior, and it is of significance for the light

which it throws upon the author's mind, and upon
the romantic movement of the time, which Longfellow was turning from Germany to the United
States, then in the sweet enjoyment of a period
of musky sentimentalism. The autobiographical
element in " Hyperion " is unmistakable, though
not to be hunted into its fastnesses. We have
in these pages the record of some of the foreign
travels, experiences, and musings of a thoughtful
mind, touched with the gentle but irresistible
lessons of an old land of romance and tender passion. The view of life here presented is optimistic, yet overhung with a purple melancholy, and
affected by that feeling of sadness, not akin to
pain, of which Longfellow elsewhere sings in a
well-known poem. We have in this world—the
book seems to remind us—the lessons of the past,
the wealth of the present, and the hope of the
future. Life is a rich possession, in which joy
and pathos are fitly blent, and in which pure love
sanctifies manly duty. " Hyperion " bore to the
American public a needed message at the proper
time. The sentimentality of many readers was
then both sickly and silly, but Longfellow gave
them a romance sufficiently meditative and unreal-
istic to be satisfactory at that weak period, and
yet so true and so brave that it spoke of aspiration as well as of reflection and "feeling."
" Hyperion " was intelligible to the feebler minds
of the day, and yet not unwelcome to the
stronger. It was " Wilhelm Meister" wholly
restated and fitted for a Saxon audience in

America. With the freshness of a young heart,
beating more quickly in the presence of the
glories of an Old World still comparatively unfamiliar, the Paul Flemming of "Hyperion" taught
many a sympathetic soul to heed the lesson of the
quaint mortuary inscription which forms the
motto of the book : "Look not mournfully into
the Past. It comes not back again. Wisely im-
prove the Present. It is thine. Go forth to
meet the shadowy Future, without fear, and with
a manly heart." This agreeable love-tale, with its
pleasant English and its poetic pictures of life and
landscape, will be enveloped in increasing shadows, cast not only by the fame of other and
greater romancers than Longfellow, but by the
poetical works of the author himself; yet the future will hardly deny that it has merit intrinsic
as well as temporary and personal. "Hyperion"
seems to belong to a past period in American
literature ; but the books of Richter himself are
now comparatively unread in Germany, which at
the moment prefers to put its sentiment and emotion into the form of historical fiction rather than
contemporary romance. The soul and its longings are eternal, but modes of expression vary
with the changing years.

The poetic career of Longfellow may now, if
we turn back to its beginning, be traced without
interruption. With all its breadth of thought and
variation of art, it was a symmetrical career, fitly
related to the character of the man and to the
times in which he lived.

In 1825 Longfellow left Brunswick, a graduate of Bowdoin College, eighteen years of age. The next year was published in Boston a neat volume of " Miscellaneous Poems selected from the *United States Literary Gazette*." Fourteen bear the name of Longfellow, and are printed in the following order, here and there in the book: "Dirge Over a Nameless Grave"; "Thanksgiving"; "Sunrise On the Hills"; "Hymn of the Moravian Nuns"; "The Indian Hunter"; "The Angler's Song"; "An April Day"; "Autumn"; "Autumnal Nightfall"; "Woods in Winter"; "A Song of Savoy"; "Italian Scenery"; "The Venetian Gondolier"; "The Sea Diver." Most of these were not included by the author in the collected editions of his poems, but some have been well and widely known since their first appearance. None attained, or was to attain, the honorable position awarded to Bryant's "Thanatopsis," but all together, with certain obvious faults of juvenility and imitativeness, displayed not only precocity but a distinct, if rudimentary, character and a manifest and efficiently deliberate method of literary expression. The young Longfellow, it was already apparent, was to be a discreet poetic leader, in his day and way, and also a sharer of the contemporary time-influence in new America. His verse shows nature affecting thought, thought purifying feeling, and feeling rising into aspiration and action. When we call Longfellow " the poet of sympathy," as we rightly may, we should not

Longfellow's Early Poems.

forget this rising gamut in his verse. The old term "sensibility," as used in "Sir Charles Grandison" and other books of an elder day, may not inaptly describe a potent cause of Long- fellow's charm and success. He was always an artist of the beautiful; but the beautiful, in his dictionary, was largely synonymous with the true and good. "The heart is the life," and our national heart-singer is Longfellow. His poetic blood does not surge with passion, nor ebb with horror; but it beats firm and true.

I have spoken already, and more than once, of Longfellow's wise service in broadening our American culture in many ways, and of his agree- able union of sentiment and sense in prose fiction. His verse was more important than his prose, and in it, from the first, appear the same qualities. Had imagination and creative power been lacking in him—as most certainly they were not—mere discretion or wise didacticism would have been humble poetic helpers; but when added to a real, however limited, creative gen- ius, their service was invaluable. The genial circumstances of his life—broken only by inevitable death and by one swift tragedy—were largely the result of his own kindly and beneficent nature, which never ceased to affect his writings and his fame. Thus we explain the instant yet lasting recognition of the merits of the collection called "The Voices of the Night," the poet's first original volume, issued in 1839. Besides some of the earlier *Literary Gazette* pieces, and many

Causes of Longfellow's Popularity.

translations, here were but eight new poems and a
prelude; but every one of these eight poems may
fairly be said to have to-day a national and almost
an international reputation. The "Hymn to the
Night," "A Psalm of Life," "The Reaper and
the Flowers," "The Light of Stars," "Footsteps
of Angels," "Flowers," "The Beleaguered City,"
the "Midnight Mass for the Dying Year"—everybody knows them all. Mere popularity is but a
poor test of value in art, but the popularity of
poems showing good artistic quality is not lightly
to be set aside. Criticism is but the record of
intelligent opinion, and he would be a bold critic
who should aver that the favor bestowed upon
Longfellow is chiefly unintelligent. In fact, his
American favor has from the first been given by
the higher and middle classes, in greatest measure. Those who are interested in the cheap
jingles of the comic opera or the popular sentimental parlor-ballads of war or home, are not
affected by Longfellow as much as by the author
of "Beautiful Snow." The common heart responds to many things in Shakespeare, in Wordsworth, in Emerson, as it responds to the "Psalm
of Life," or "The Reaper and the Flowers," or
"Resignation." Few poets have sung its hopes
and regrets so well as Longfellow; but his renown is based, after all, upon a general acceptance of good work, and not upon any of the
tricks adopted by the poetical demagogue.
Mere recognition by the masses of readers, however numerous, is inevitably a temporary thing;

and we have already long passed the period when
it was possible to suspect that Longfellow was the
laureate of emotional unintelligence or sentimental mediocrity.   His broad fame is a credit and
not a discredit to the nature of his genius and the
form of his verse.   Eliminate from Longfellow's
poems all that he owed to Heine and Germany,
to Dante and Italy, to the French singers of the
sunshine, and to the Scandinavian scalds of the
sea ; eliminate all that is ephemeral on the one
hand or unduly sermonic on the other, and there
still remains enough that is true poetry and mere
poetry.   When we read a volume of Longfellow
we do not feel simply that we have been preached
at, or furnished with a code of blue-laws, or made
to memorize the Ten Commandments, or sign the
total-abstinence pledge.   I grant that the effect
upon our minds is one of tranquillity, reverence,
sympathy, optimism ; but I am not yet ready to
admit that these things are to be banished from
literature, or that they form a blemish on the face
of the literary product.   If blemish they are,
our definition of literature, as Milton and Dante,
Wordsworth and Emerson knew it, must wholly
be revised.   Tranquillity, reverence, world-sym-
pathy, and optimism are precisely the qualities of
Emerson the poet, and though there was in Longfellow a gentle melancholy utterly unknown to
Emerson's joyful trust in the existing order of the
universe, both reached a similar end by different
means.   If Longfellow was but a poet of genial
twaddle and mild morality, and if therefore he is

to fall in the days of materialism and soulless art, then he will not fall alone. Twaddle and insipidity are not hard to find in his voluminous versifyings, but they are very easily eliminated.

In reading the lyrics of Longfellow, produced in the long period between his college days and the year of his death, one is reminded of the difference between the typical short poem of our time and those of earlier days in English literature. Longfellow's lyrics, aside from the question of genius, are radically unlike Shakespeare's songs, fresh with the breath of Nature herself; the dainty love-poems and the conceits of "compliment and courtship" which came from Herrick and Suckling; the stately or classically fanciful odes of Milton; Dryden's successful experiments for St. Cecilia's day; or Gray's verse, which so curiously united the conventional and the original. The nineteenth-century short poem, if it would rise to favor, must either be merely and highly beautiful, or touched with some power of description, suggestion, or feeling which shall approve itself to the critic's head and to the reader's heart. Upon the latter quality most nineteenth-century readers are likely to insist. In the first respect Longfellow seldom triumphs; in the second he often succeeds. Intense clear beauty is not to be found in "The Rainy Day," "A Gleam of Sunshine," "The Reaper and the Flowers," "Resignation," or "A Psalm of Life." The last-named poem, perhaps the best loved of all, is perilously near to insipid

Longfellow as a Lyrist.

failure. Mere prosy flatness often encounters us in Longfellow's poems, and here it is reinforced by rugged sing-song versification. But elsewhere, as in "The Day is Done," Longfellow shows his power to express high thought in exquisite verse. That he did not oftener produce work purely lovely in form as well as in thought was surely his own fault. It hardly seems that "A Psalm of Life" and "The Day is Done" could come from the same hand:

> "The day is done, and the darkness
> Falls from the wings of Night,
> As a feather is wafted downward
> From an eagle in his flight;"

this is melody, the melody of the author of "Hiawatha," and of him who wrote such lines as

> "When she had passed, it seemed like the ceasing of
> exquisite music;"

> "The leaves of memory seemed to make
> A mournful rustling in the dark;"

> "I turn and set my back against the wall,
> And look thee in the face, triumphant Death;"

> "It came from the heaving breast of the deep;
> Silent as dreams are, and sudden as sleep."

We look to the poet for an apt and artistic expression of that which we have vaguely thought but cannot fitly frame nor utter as we would. Shakespeare is the world's genius because he phrases, better than any other poet, the world's thought. He is not

The Poet's Soul and the Poet's Hand.

the poet of aristocracy, or the middle classes, or
the "masses." When a singer undertakes to voice
the soul of a subdivision of humanity he meets
the fate of the Reverend Mr. Dickinson, who
thought it necessary to translate the New Testament into really refined English; or of Walt
Whitman. Burns was not Burns because he was
a peasant, nor was Emerson Emerson because he
was a university lecturer on philosophy and the
head of the Concord school. The universal, and
not the local or the social, gave them their place.
So it is in the case of the poetry of Longfellow,
or any other favored singer. Had he deliberately
undertaken to be an artist in verse, or an artificial
workingman, or the representative of America or
the "middle classes," whose laureate and *rates*
some have called him, critics and readers would
not be taking the trouble to discuss his works.
He believed that he had a song to sing; and
though he sang it with his own tone, and sentiment, and native feeling, and culture, and time-
spirit, it was a song not designed specially for
Portland or Cambridge, but for humanity. Our
New-World academic singer was quite willing to
leave to an Oxford professor the congenial task
of chanting for cultured pessimists the charms of
spiritual vacuity, in poetry so exquisite that it
would have been Greek save for the fact that to
the Greek mind it seemed necessary that manly
thought and serene strength should accompany
the meditative mood.

Longfellow wrote for humanity, and humanity

recognized its own hopes and feelings in the plain
aphoristic patience and cheer of "A Psalm of
Life"; the responsive, recognizing love of "Endymion"; the manly endurance of "The Light of
Stars"; the tender and melancholy musing of
"The Day is Done"; the affectionate commemoration of the departed in "Resignation"; and the
ceaseless aspiration of "Excelsior" and "The
Ladder of St. Augustine." The simple and lovely
Christian code of action, from patience and self-
sacrifice up to an ultimate heaven and
the fulness of joy, is phrased gently
and strongly, but not too didactically,
by this singer who looked into his heart and
wrote, that he might make his life and many a
life sublime, though he must wait as well as labor.
Sublimity so great as to overshadow Death itself,
he told us, lay in the power to suffer and be
strong. The heights of eternity, as well as of life,
are attained by "toiling upward in the night";
for though

Poetry and the Religious Sentiment.

> "The air is full of farewells to the dying,
>   And mournings for the dead,"

it is not less true that

> "There is no Death! What seems so is transition;
>   This life of mortal breath
> Is but a suburb of the life elysian
>   Whose portal we call death."

Bayard Taylor, who certainly was neither a
bigot nor a platitudinarian, once wrote to Long-

fellow : "I know not who else before you has so
wonderfully wedded Poetry and the Religious Sentiment." *   I cannot agree with Taylor in his high
praise of "The Divine Tragedy," nor in his favorable comparison between Longfellow and Milton ;
but his remark, as generally applicable to a large
part of Longfellow's work, is both apt and just.
Once when Lowell had become discouraged over
the task of preparing a new edition of his own
verse, he happened to take up a similar edition of
Longfellow, "to see the type." "Before I knew
it," he wrote to the elder poet, "I had been reading two hours and more. I never wondered at
your popularity, nor thought it wicked in you ; but
if I had wondered, I should no longer, for you
sang me out of all my worries." †   Longfellow
sang poets, as well as seamstresses and shopkeep-
ers, out of all their worries ; and the simple reason
was that his heart was human and his art was
poetic.

As we turn the pages of Longfellows successive
volumes of minor verse—"Ballads   Longfellow's
and other Poems," "Poems on   successive volumes
                                                                    of Minor Poems.
Slavery," "The Belfry of Bruges
and Other Poems," "The Seaside and the Fireside," "Flower-de-Luce," "Three Books of Song,"
"Aftermath," "The Masque of Pandora and
Other Poems," "Kéramos and Other Poems,"
"Ultima Thule," and "In The Harbor" (posthu-

---

* "Final Memorials of Henry Wadsworth Longfellow," edited by Samuel
Longfellow ; 174.
 † "Final Memorials of Henry Wadsworth Longfellow," 246, note.

mously published)—we note a gradual diminution of the number of highly popular and universally accepted lyrics. Most readers cared comparatively, little, I fear, even for the longer books of his later life, to which I shall recur. "The New England Tragedies," "The Divine Tragedy," "Judas Maccabæus," and "Michael Angelo," upon which the author worked laboriously and affectionately, were given a reception which was perhaps respectful, but no more. Only "The Hanging of the Crane" and the noble "Morituri Salutamus" aroused anything like enthusiasm. Enthusiasm is not the safest of critical guides, but in regard to Longfellow's work it was somewhat in accord with the calm verdict of criticism, which bestows no high approval upon most of the writings just mentioned. On the other hand, there is in Longfellow's later product an increased power of description of scenery and action, and a multiplication of not unpleasing dramatic or semi-dramatic pictures. Sonnets are also numerous, and the utterance of personal reflection is prevalent. The author's intellectual and poetical powers had not declined, though his old age was less successful than his middle-life in its fresh experiments in verse and theme. He had written his *credo* and uttered his "seven voices of sympathy"; and there was neither need nor wish to repeat them. Had he endeavored to do so, and had he chosen subjects and methods similar to those of his earlier famous lyrics and meditative

poems, he would have encountered criticism severer
than that which met his later books. Emerson's
suggestion that Longfellow "wrote too much"
concerned the number, and not the character, of
his last poems. They were not echoes of an
earlier day. The bitterest, or at any rate the most
unpleasant, criticism is that which states that an
author has outlived his powers and can but try to
repeat old tunes and tricks. Such criticism could
never be applied to Longfellow. It is true that
in all Longfellow's minor verse after the "Flower-
de-Luce" volume of 1866 I find none that can
fairly be awarded the general honors bestowed
upon the old favorites, save "The Chamber Over
the Gate," "Robert Burns," "The Sifting of
Peter," and the sonnet on President Garfield.
Admitting this very fully and frankly, the facts
remain that Longfellow's previous work was done
and well done ; that he was too wise to try to step
in the old footprints ; that his later writing was
marked by some successes of its own ; and that,
in artistic finish, the numerous sonnets produced
in the last twenty years of his life not only
equalled anything he had previously written but very easily put him at the head of Sonnets.
all American sonneteers. The very soul and the
true body of a sonnet are found in the two that
follow, which, it should be added, are nowise
superior to the noble series accompanying his
translation of the "Divine Comedy" :

MY BOOKS.

Sadly as some old mediæval knight
   Gazed at the arms he could no longer wield,
   The sword two-handed and the shining shield
Suspended in the hall, and full in sight,
While secret longings for the lost delight
   Of tourney or adventure in the field
   Came over him, and tears but half concealed
Trembled and fell upon his beard of white,
So I behold these books upon their shelf,
   My ornaments and arms of other days;
Not wholly useless, though no longer used,
For they remind me of my other self,
   Younger and stronger, and the pleasant ways
In which I walked, now clouded and confused.

VICTOR AND VANQUISHED.

As one who long hath fled with panting breath
   Before his foe, bleeding and near to fall,
   I turn and set my back against the wall,
And look thee in the face, triumphant Death.
I call for aid, and no one answereth;
   I am alone with thee, who conquerest all;
   Yet me thy threatening form doth not appal,
For thou art but a phantom and a wraith.
   Wounded and weak, sword broken at the hilt,
With armor shattered, and without a shield,
   I stand unmoved; do with me what thou wilt;
I can resist no more, but will not yield.
   This is no tournament where cowards tilt;
The vanquished here is victor of the field.

The latter of these was written in Longfellow's seventieth year, and the former in his seventy-fifth. I do not see why, according to the best Italian and English models, the death-sonnet cannot fairly be called perfect. He would be an able critic, or a great sonneteer, who could suggest an improvement in it.

It is time, in this survey of the poet's work, to turn to his longer, more ambitious, and more important books of verse, after examining which we shall be able to view more fully the literary attainment of his lifetime.

Late in life Longfellow jotted in his diary: "Our opinions are biassed by our limitations. Poets who cannot write long poems think that no long poems should be written." He must have been thinking of one of Poe's most foolish sayings, which needs no more respectful refutation than this. Longfellow could successfully write both short poems and long. Excellent, numerous, and widely popular as are his lyrics of the heart, they are scarcely more praiseworthy or more widely current than his two best poems of length, "Hiawatha" and "Evangeline." In middle life Longfellow found a new and notable fame awaiting him because of these well-known productions, the spirit and form of which became as familiar as those of "The Rainy Day" or "Excelsior." They are indissolubly connected with his life-work and fame, and their qualities and individual characteristics are Longfellow's, and are not shared, for the most part, by other books of their time.

The first of Longfellow's longer, and in that sense more ambitious, poems was "The Spanish Student," published in Cambridge in 1843. This three-act play is a pretty little affair, no more.   It "The Spanish may be read without difficulty, and Student." with that pleasure which accompanies the sense that a neat plan has been agreeably carried out.   Its Spanish scenes and story formed a part of the equipment of gentle romance which Longfellow got in Europe and so fully shared with his countrymen.   Few indeed have been the meritorious plays written in English during the present century, measured even by the literary or library criterion.   Still fewer have been the successful acted dramas produced by authors of the first contemporary rank.   Longfellow's dramatic compositions,   notwithstanding   some   manifest merits—cheery grace in " The Spanish Student " and the sublimity of rapt paraphrase in " The Divine Tragedy "—fell below the best of his other work.   No other American poet of prominence ever completed a dramatic essay, so that Longfellow's relative failure is not heightened by any comparison with a fellow-worker's success.

When " Evangeline " appeared, in 1847, Longfellow was already the most widely known of our "Evangeline, poets.   Emerson's first collection of a Tale of poems was printed that year, but it was Acadie." long before he could be said to enjoy any wide renown.   Poe's volumes and single successes were already familiar, but the general consent assigned to him a place much below that of the singer whom he so unjustly attacked.   Had there been any doubt as to Longfellow's primacy, it was removed by the instant fame of this widely discussed and oft-read book. The theme, at once idyllic and tragical, and the much-debated measure (unrhymed hexameter) were alike attractive. Many to whom poetry was unfamiliar became interested in the sad lives and loves of the banished Acadian girl and her lost betrothed, who met at last as tender, helpful nun and dying stranger. While the critics and rhymesters were discussing the metre, thousands of readers were sharing the sentiments of Doctor Holmes, who wrote to the poet: "The story is beautiful in conception as in execution. I read it as I should have listened to some exquisite symphony, and closed the last leaf, leaving a little mark upon it which told a great deal more than all the ink I could waste upon the note you have just finished."

"Tell me a story" has been the request made of singers and makers of prose fiction for many a century. "Evangeline" told a story with simple grace and quiet art, and with that human sympathy which pulses through nearly all that Longfellow ever wrote. A new-world theme, taken from an unfamiliar coast or from the wild interior, gave the poem an originality of plot which fitly accompanied its unfamiliar metre. There was in it enough of freshness to separate it from the well-known productions of its author, whose qualities of mind and soul it however reflected sufficiently clearly. He had been deeply and constantly indebted to Europe for poetic theme and color; but here he essayed a long poem of strictly

American tone. The experiment, discreetly made, was a wise one. The story was one suited to his mind, and his previous metrical experiments and obvious artistic powers, enabled him to give it a proper setting. Bold and high imagination, a soaring genius, were not his; but the imagination which is tender, sweet, and human was never far away from his hand. Therefore in "Evangeline" are shown, at large, the patient endurance and gentle love of which he had so often sung in lyrics. Here, too, Longfellow's habitual diffuseness almost ceased to be a blemish, for diffuseness is so essential a part of the English hexameter—alas, how different from the Greek!—that in Longfellow and Clough we scarcely stop to note it. The body and soul of the poem "Evangeline" offer no discordant impression to the reader's mind.

The English novel, at its best, has told the story of the love and life of typical men and The story and the background. women of the English people, seen against a national background. English narrative and idyllic verse, from "The Canterbury Tales" to "Enoch Arden," has followed the same broad general plan as that of "The Vicar of Wakefield," the masterpiece of English fiction. Thus in "Evangeline," a love-romance in verse, and also a poem of idyllic description, the characters and scenes are of the western world, but the love and the pathos, like those of all great works of the sort, belong to universal humanity. The apt literary artist uses enough local color to give

his work a character of its own, and yet employs
the large manner that appeals to a catholic audience. A woman's heart bereft of its lover's heart,
and resting not till the two are reunited—"all the
world loves a lover," and a goodly part of the
world accordingly loves Evangeline and shares her
sorrows. Her people are quaint colonists, near
us in home and in time, yet seeming faint and far
because of their foreign blood and their dispersion
over the earth. Seldom has a poet chosen a
theme more likely to win affection and enthusiasm
from those to whom it has been presented; for
seldom has a verse-painter found or framed a
story so responsive to all his best aspirations and
powers: to human sympathy, gentle pathos, quiet
trustfulness, romantic sentiment, artistic originality.

 "Evangeline" is least successful on its artistic
side. I have no wish to reënter or to reopen the
controversies attending the appearance of this
famous hexameter poem. What hex- Longfellow's
meter *may* be in English is a question Hexameters.
as yet a speculative one, though the history of
our poetry for five centuries is instructive on this
point. The fact remains that most of our poets
have not used it, and that few indeed have used
it well, either in original or translated verse.
There is in it a fatal facility which, at first
thought, would seem likely to tempt many versifiers. But that facility is so slippery and perilous
that few have essayed it seriously or long. English hexameter is nearly prose, and rather weak

prose at that. "All that flams is not flamboy-
ant"; our hexameter resembles the Greek in
little save that it has six beats. Majestic melody
and a beautiful union of fixity and variety are
lacking in it. The quantity and even the accent
are too often arbitrary rather than essential.
Longfellow used it to better advantage than
Clough or Howells, and gave it a variety and
grace of treatment beyond the range of Chap-
man's vigorous but crude powers. But his
dreams of its utility in Homeric translation were
were visions of what can never be. His own
experimental lines from Homer are feeble in
comparison with Tennyson's specimen from the
" Iliad " in unrhymed pentameter. English versification is a rich and noble thing, as strong as the
Greek, as graceful as the Latin, with a better
accent-system than the French, and more musical
than the German. The nineteenth century, in
the work of Shelley, Coleridge, Keats, Scott, Poe,
Swinburne, and Longfellow himself, has given
new and brilliant proofs of the power and range
of the poetry of the English tongue. But hexameter never has been and never will be one of
its strongest instruments. At their best, Longfellow's hexameters had an idyllic sweetness and
grace; at their worst, the clumsy dactyls sounded
like hoof-beats on a muddy road. The chief
value of " Evangeline " as a metrical experiment
was limited but great: it proved that English
hexameters were best fitted for idyllic, rather than
Homeric, narrative. In "The Courtship of Miles

Standish " the charm was once more invoked, but half in vain; in the latter poem we no longer wander through

"Green Acadian meadows, with sylvan rivers among them,"

but listen too often to the cacophonous

" Praise of the virtuous woman, as she is described in the Proverbs,"

or hear how she

" Said in a tremulous voice, ' Why don't you speak for yourself, John ? ' "

But Longfellow's best hexameters, in "Evangeline," though representing neither the force nor the flexibility of the Greek measure of the same name, had a genuine musical beauty of their own. Our language, lacking the inherent or local quantity of the Greek, and its particles and inflections, with their union of expressiveness of thought and rapidity of movement, cannot reproduce the Homeric metre. Not all the praise of enthusiastic friends, and not all the acknowledged skill of Longfellow, could make us approve such an experimental rendition as he once made of the opening lines of the Iliad :

Sing, O Goddess, the wrath of Peleidean Achilles,
Baleful, that brought disasters uncounted upon the Achaians.
Many a gallant soul of heroes flung into Hades,
And the heroes themselves as a prey to the dogs and to all the
Fowls of the air; for thus the will of Zeus was accomplished;
From the time when first in wrangling parted asunder
Atreus' son, the monarch of men, and godlike Achilles.

This specimen (left in Longfellow's diary, and of course not rigidly to be criticised) is almost pitiful in its inadequacy. The question, moreover, is not one of Homeric translation. Bryant and Tennyson have shown that our greatest English metre—unrhymed pentameter—can in some ways reproduce the power of the chief Greek measure. What we learn from Longfellow is not so much the limitations of hexameter, the imperfect shadow of its namesake, as the beauty which it may sometimes show. Critic and general reader are at one in praising such lines and passages as these:

> Naught but tradition remains of the beautiful village of
>   Grand Pré.

> Darkened by shadows of earth, but reflecting an image of
>   heaven.

> Late, with the rising moon, returned the wains from the
>   marshes,
> Laden with briny hay, that filled the air with its odor.

> Under the open sky, in the odorous air of the orchard.

> Sweetly over the village the bell of the Angelus sounded.

> "Benedicite," murmured the priest, in tones of compassion.

> And, as the voice of the priest repeated the service of
>   sorrow,
> Lo, with a mournful sound, like the voice of a vast congre-
>   gation,
> Solemnly answered the sea, and mingled its roar with the
>   dirges.

> Into the golden stream of the broad and swift Mississippi.

Day after day they glided adown the turbulent river.

Over their heads the towering and tenebrous boughs of the
  cypress
Met in a dusky arch, and trailing mosses in mid-air
Waved like banners hung on the walls of ancient cathedrals.

Then in his place, at the prow of the boat, rose one of the
  oarsmen,
And, as a signal sound, if others like them peradventure
Sailed on these gloomy and midnight streams, blew a blast
  on his bugle.
Wild through the dark colonnades and corridors leafy the
  blast rang,
Breaking the seal of silence, and giving tongues to the
  forest.
Soundless above them the banners of moss just stirred to the
  music.
Multitudinous echoes awoke and died in the distance,
Over the watery floor, and beneath the reverberant branches;
But not a voice replied; no answer came from the darkness;
And, when the echoes had ceased, like a sense of pain was
  the silence.

Then he beheld, in a dream, once more the home of his
  childhood;
Green Acadian meadows, and sylvan rivers among them,
Village, and mountain, and woodlands; and, walking under
  their shadow,
As in the days of her youth, Evangeline rose in his vision.

Still stands the forest primeval; but far away from its
  shadow,
Side by side, in their nameless graves, the lovers are sleep-
  ing.
Under the humble walls of the little Catholic churchyard,
In the heart of the city, they lie, unknown and unnoticed.
Daily the tides of life go ebbing and flowing beside them,
Thousands of throbbing hearts, where theirs are at rest and
  forever,

Thousands of aching brains, where theirs no longer are
busy,
Thousands of toiling hands, where theirs have ceased from
their labors,
Thousands of weary feet, where theirs have completed their
journey !

Blame not Longfellow that he did not make better hexameters; praise him that he wrote so good, and framed them into an idyl of true and original beauty.

"Evangeline" was a poem of idyllic pathos; "The Courtship of Miles Standish" a love story tinged with humor, and set against the background of historic Massachusetts. The dry bones of Puritanism lived once more when Longfellow breathed upon them the spirit of the human love that never grows old, and that could not be crushed by the austerity of dogma or the poverty of colonial beginnings. Longfellow, at his best, was a good story-teller; and though "The Courtship of Miles Standish" is distinctly a smaller and lower production than "Evangeline," its constructive merit is considerable. The swinging measure of the hexameter somehow lent itself well to the sly and archaic humor of the tale; and Longfellow, who always required plenty of room in which to make a jest, here pleasantly mingled the amusing, the descriptive, and the passionate. The picture seems possible rather than actual; the humanity of the poetic Evangeline legend appears truer than that of the well-known Puritan story; and

the later book merely pleases where the former
touched the heart. This, indeed, is precisely
what it aimed to do; and we have in "The
Legend of Miles Standish" another proof of the
breadth of range and achievement in which Longfellow surpassed all other American poets, and in
which he was approached by Lowell only, at a
considerable distance. Our chief representative
of continental culture was also a peculiarly American poet, even aside from his masterpiece, "Hiawatha," the most American poem of all.

On June 22, 1854, when Longfellow was
forty-seven years old, he made this entry in his
diary: "I have at length hit upon a plan for a
poem on the American. Indians, which seems to
me the right one, and the only. It is to weave
together their beautiful traditions into a whole.
I have hit upon a measure, too, which I think the
right and only one for such a theme." Longfellow was a painstaking literary artist, who carefully analyzed the thought and as carefully
planned the form. He was a good judge, furthermore, of the merit and probable success of his
productions. It is true that he sometimes erred;
he worked for more than twenty years over his
trilogy of "Christus"; planned but never completed an addition to its closing part, as finally
printed; and sent forth "The Divine Tragedy,"
the portion first in order and last in composition,
with more misgivings than ever accompanied the
advent of any other of his works. This completed trilogy never fulfilled the hopes of "the

consecration and the poet's dream"; and the
reader is not—as the cautious author was not—at
a loss to discover why. But the author's serene
confidence concerning "Hiawatha"—expressed,
let us remember, in a private memorandum, and
not for the public—was perfectly justified by the
result. The poem remains the greatest achievement of Longfellow, and the one surest to arouse
"Hiawatha." interest as the years go by. Its success can never be repeated; its maker
himself wisely essayed no new triumph in the
same field. In theme and in general and special
treatment "Hiawatha," to repeat a phrase already
used, is our "nearest approach to an American
epic." It is a semi-epic *about* a race, and not *from*
it; yet notwithstanding this fact, it is to be
ranked with such productions as "Beowulf" or
"The Song of Roland."

The character of the North American Indian at
his best, described historically by Francis Parkman and romantically by Fenimore Cooper, is
here set forth poetically. An adequate basis of
truthfulness to aboriginal ideas is retained; but
upon it is built a fabric of imagination and dream-
land. Thus, the poet tells us, thought the wild
man of the west, in his loftier moods and more
poetic legends; and his interpreter in verse adds
to his fidelity to the originals a constructive art
lacking in the Indian mind. Here are the skies
and waters, the woods and hunting-life, the fancies and the loves of the white man's predecessors.
Many tales are gathered into a symmetrical whole,

the hero-legend forming, after a familiar plan, the chain upon which lesser stories and mythological narrations are hung. Everything may be included, if it be characteristic. The career of a typical man through life, in his experiences between the unknown and the unknown—such is any race-epic, and such is "Hiawatha" in a full degree. Beside the central figure are his fellows and his love ; above him are the powers of light and darkness ; beneath is the all-nourishing earth ; and before him the land of the hereafter. The plan is rounded and complete ; the scene is filled with representative figures ; the movement is steady and symmetrical ; and yet behind all the poet stands invisible, such is the excellent art he has shown. The race-poem, too, has a universal bearing. It touches the mystery and destiny of all human life. In Hiawatha the reader sees not only the representative of a westward-moving people, but also an allegorical picture of one's own progress onward.

But the reader of "Hiawatha" does not labor over its pages as a student or philosopher, studying ethnology or the mystery of the universe. He turns to it as he would "pore upon the brook that babbles by." Here in these stories are a garland of flowers, a fair and shadowy vision, an odor of an unknown land. Now that the superficial controversies concerning the trochaics of "Hiawatha" have been forgotten, I suppose few will quarrel with the art of the poem. When a metre is musical in itself, is well fitted to the idea

6

and even the nomenclature of its theme, and is
made the natural means of sweetly singing the
song of the author, there would seem to be little
for the critics to quarrel about. Nothing succeeds like success ; and here the artist and poet
accurately measured his theme, his scheme, and
his powers of execution. Let those who have
rivalled or surpassed him in such a measurement
be the ones who may venture to laugh at the
alleged eccentricity of this *sui generis* poem of
the western world. But it is not the art of
" Hiawatha " which most pleases us. We read it
not because of its form but because of its nature.
These legends of prairie-land belong to the great
story-book of the world, that treasury of lay and
legend which delights the childhood of a man and
a people, and brightens long days of labor and
nights devoid of ease, for those, at least, who
carry the childlike heart into middle-life and age.

> Should you ask me, whence these stories ?
> Whence these legends and traditions,
> With the odors of the forest,
> With the dew and damp of meadows,
> With the curling smoke of wigwams,
> With the rushing of great rivers,
> With their frequent repetitions,
> And their wild reverberations,
> As of thunder in the mountains?
>
> I should answer, I should tell you,
> " From the forests and the prairies,
> From the great lakes of the Northland,
> From the land of the Ojibways,

From the land of the Dacotahs,
From the mountains, moors, and fenlands,
Where the heron, the Shuh-shuh-gah,
Feeds among the reeds and rushes.
I repeat them as I heard them
From the lips of Nawadaha,
The musician, the sweet singer."

Should you ask where Nawadaha
Found these songs, so wild and wayward,
Found these legends and traditions,
I should answer, I should tell you,

" In the birds'-nests of the forest,
In the lodges of the beaver,
In the hoof-prints of the bison,
In the eyry of the eagle !

" All the wild-fowl sang them to him,
In the moorlands and the fenlands,
In the melancholy marshes :
Chetowaik, the plover, sang them,
Mahng, the loon, the wild-goose, Wawa,
The blue heron, the Shuh-shuh-gah,
And the grouse, the Mushkodasa ! . . . . . ."

There he sang of Hiawatha,
Sang the song of Hiawatha,
Sang his wondrous birth and being,
How he prayed and how he fasted,
How he lived, and toiled, and suffered,
That the tribes of men might prosper,
That he might advance his people !

Ye who love the haunts of Nature,
Love the sunshine of the meadow,
Love the shadow of the forest,
Love the wind among the branches,
And the rain-shower and the snow-storm,
And the rushing of great rivers,

Through their palisades of pine-trees,
And the thunder in the mountains,
Whose innumerable echoes
Flap like eagles in the eyries :—
Listen to these wild traditions,
To this song of Hiawatha!

Ye who love a nation's legends,
Love the ballads of a people,
That like voices from afar off
Call to us to pause and listen,
Speak in tones so plain and childlike,
Scarcely can the ear distinguish
Whether they are sung or spoken :—
Listen to this Indian legend,
To this song of Hiawatha!

Ye whose hearts are fresh and simple,
Who have faith in God, and Nature,
Who believe, that in all ages
Every human heart is human,
That in even savage bosoms
There are longings, yearnings, strivings
For the good they comprehend not,
That the feeble hands and helpless,
Groping blindly in the darkness,
Touch God's right hand in that darkness
And are lifted up and strengthened :—
Listen to this simple story,
To this song of Hiawatha!

In "Hiawatha" we wander amid woodland
shadows, with the far, light clouds above us
and the black American rivers at our feet. The
smell of pine-needles is in the air, and the whirr
of the partridge or the liquid song of the thrush
occasionally falls upon the ear. Chaucer put the

fresh breezes of old England into his perennially vital tales; Longfellow sings to us ruder legends than Chaucer gathered, and charms us with the stories of those virgin prairies and uncut forests that knew not even a crude civilization like that of the court of King Richard the Second.

These trochaics are excellently suited to the presentation and fit portrayal of that spontaneous beauty which belongs to Nature and her children, unspoiled by arts and civiliza- **Spontaneous Beauty.** tion. The very regularity of the short-line measure is an advantage; it goes along in an agreeably monotonous undertone that reminds one of the accompaniment to Schubert's *Die schöne Müllerin* songs, whereby the steadily purling brook is represented, while the soaring air tells the story of the maid of the mill. In " Hiawatha" the words are the aboriginal song and the measure is the accompaniment, the two being combined in that natural union which marks the true lyric poem, whether of ten lines or ten thousand. Hiawatha, Minnehaha, Shawondasee, Wenonah, Mahnomonee, Nahma, Nokomis—the very names are little poems; while the more guttural and explosive words of the Indian dialect but increase the charm of the melody by their occasional twang of strength or clash of discord.

I suppose the most obvious criticism evoked by " Hiawatha " is based upon its tau- **Repetitions and Parallelisms.** tology and consequent length. The tautology is partly that of translation and partly that of paraphrase. He must be a learned or a fastidious reader who objects to such self-explanatory lines as these, which so often occur throughout the whole poem:

> Forth upon the Gitche Gumee,
> On the shining Big-Sea-Water,
> With his fishing-line of cedar,
> Of the twisted bark of cedar,
> Forth to catch the sturgeon Nahma,
> Mishe-Nahma, King of Fishes.
> In his birch-canoe exulting
> All alone went Hiawatha.

> Through the clear, transparent water
> He could see the fishes swimming
> Far down in the depths below him;
> See the yellow perch, the Sahwa,
> Like a sunbeam in the water,
> See the Shawgashee, the craw-fish,
> On the white and sandy bottom.

As for the parallelisms in the poem, their fitness, then, may be defended on the double ground that clearness was essential, and that the Indian character, like the Hebrew, lends itself readily to this form of utterance. The poem as a whole is not prolix, and any section illustrates the fact that force and even brevity are often increased by the cumulative method which belongs to the parallelism.

Thirty years after the publication of "Hiawatha" we can look calmly at the excited but now unimportant discussions that attended its appearance. We will readily admit that the measure is easily written; but who save Longfellow has mastered it and turned it to the implicit service of a poetic idea? We grant, too, that in the poem the Indian character is idealized; but it is not distorted. One is not ready to aver that a semi-ideal picture of any part of humanity is to be rejected because it is not strictly realistic as regards the average race-type; otherwise we must throw aside Homer, the "Divine Comedy," "Faust," the "Elder Edda," the "Song of Roland." "Hiawatha" possesses the poetic merits of imagination, descriptive power, native originality, and broad interest; and so, fortunately, it is able to take care of its own place in literature. It is a book that seems to its present readers to miss greatness; but it is quite possible that the time will come when, his other writings forgotten or ignored, the name of Longfellow will be chiefly known as that of the author of "Hiawatha."

Of all Longfellow's works the most ambitious, on the whole, was that trilogy which was published in its complete form in 1872, under the title of "Christus, a Mystery." The first part, "The Divine Tragedy," had appeared   *"Christus, a* in the preceding year; the third, "The   *Mystery."* New England Tragedies," in 1868; and the second, "The Golden Legend," as far back as 1851. When issued together, under the final title, they were equipped with two connecting Interludes and a Finale, then first published. The general design of the work was to present three pictures of Christianity, in widely separated ages: those of its founder, of mediæval Roman-

ism in its better estate, and of New England
Puritanism. The plan was a good one, but the
selection of periods, and the execution, very
imperfect. "The Golden Legend" versified an
old German story of a maiden's self-sacrifice for
her prince, who rewarded her with all his love and
half his throne. The story is pretty but not significant, in the broad and long history of Christianity. "The New England Tragedies," in their
division, represent a cold, hard, and temporary
phase of religious life, strong in the ideas of
theism and the "perseverance of the saints," but
sadly lacking in the all-embracing *caritas* of
Christ, which has been the most important note
of Christianity from the beginning. The paraphrase of the Gospels in "The Divine Tragedy,"
the first part of the trilogy, is noble in language
and spiritual in effect ; few writers in Christian literature, from Cædmon to our own day, have so
well succeeded in this difficult task. But the contrast between this division and the two other
selected episodes is grotesque, almost painful. A
score of more significant themes in Christian history might have been selected. The union of the
three parts of "Christus" is so infelicitous as
almost to seem an afterthought, but the final
biography of the poet shows that such was not
the case. To the third and last division he once
thought of adding a picture of the life of the
Moravians in Bethlehem, Pennsylvania, which fit
and characteristic addition was never made. The
poet himself has more than once recorded his mis-

givings concerning the first and third parts of this book; they afford another proof of the general sanity of his art and the justice of self-esteem. Indeed, the whole was less than the sum of its parts; for "The Divine Tragedy" and "The Golden Legend" were good in their respective ways, though not great. In a large composite poem of this sort a partial success is a virtual failure.

In 1863, when he published the first part of the "Tales of a Wayside Inn," Longfellow had reached a critical point in the career of a sucessful author. He was fifty-six years old; his reputation was firmly established, both upon his subjective lyrics and upon "Evangeline" and "Hiawatha"; and the usual question arose, in the minds of his readers, whether that reputation was to be increased, maintained, or impaired in the latter years of his life. New methods and forces in English verse were beginning to appear or to attract the public: Browning, Arnold, and the young pre-Raphaelite poets in England, and Whitman and the western or ultra "American" singers in the United States. The reputation of Emerson, too, was steadily and surely advancing to a point from which it was not to recede; Poe was gaining in foreign renown with the passing years; Whittier and some lesser lyrists were rivalling the Cambridge bard in their poems of the war; and Lowell, in his later work, was displaying somewhat of the depth of Emerson and the musical flow of the verse of his neighbor and friend.

On the whole, during the two remaining decades of Longfellow's life, there was the maintenance of a reputation already won, and not its substantial increase or evident diminution. Accurately measuring his powers, he continued to write admirable short poems of thought, sentiment, or suggestion, which, though not rivalling the popularity of his earlier poems, aroused no feeling of disappointment and no special complaint of inadequacy. Of the merit of his noble and self-contained sonnets I have already spoken.

In " The Tales of a Wayside Inn," Longfellow grouped together by a device familiar since the days of the " Decameron " and the " Canterbury Tales," graphic pictures of local life and character, and duly representative tales from the old world and the new. The merit of the stories and interludes of the several series of " Tales of a Wayside Inn," appearing at intervals during a decade, was on the whole a declining one; but the whole work is an enjoyable, varied, and characteristic miscellany of tales in verse. The weather-beaten old inn at Sudbury; the thinly-veiled characters from real life; the interesting and well-told episodes of narration and song, combined to produce a work that charmed and will charm. The giving of pleasure—that is a true mark of a picture or poem deserving its name; and surely pleasure is to be found in many of these simple, graceful, and pure tales of to-day or of old. The poet seems to sing his natural thought; the public has but to listen and to applaud with the sense that it is still the poet's mission, as in the days of " Dan Chaucer, the first warbler," to tell us of nature and human nature, of wildwood, shaw, and green, and the hearts of men and women.

> These are the tales those merry guests
>   Told to each other, well or ill;
> Like summer birds that lift their crests
> Above the borders of their nests
>   And twitter, and again are still.
> These are the tales, or new or old,
> In idle moments idly told;
> Flowers of the field with petals thin,
> Lilies that neither toil nor spin,
>   And tufts of wayside weeds and gorse
> Hung in the parlor of the inn
>   Beneath the sign of the Red Horse.

Two of Longfellow's larger works remain to be mentioned. In the closing months of 1867, after many a year of preparation, was printed that literal and isometrical unrhymed transla- Longfellow's tion of the "Divine Comedy" of Dante Dante. which remains closely associated with the fame of Longfellow, to whom culture in America already owed so much. Its strict fidelity to the original; the careful scholarship which had literally scrutinized every word, often with the assistance of competent friends who met regularly to aid the translator; the frequent combination of a life-giving spirit with the exact letter of utterance, gave this version a place which it is not likely to lose, at the head, on the whole, of English translation of Dante. The literalist school of translators

does not often receive aid from a more valuable
or learned helper, at once scholar and poet.
Longfellow's Dante possesses nearly every merit
save that of readability; in peculiarly important
passages it   sacrifices too much to the original;
and its unrhymed lines, with their too frequent
use of the feminine ending of the verse, become
wearisome long before the solemn journey from
hell to paradise is completed.   This feminine ending is one thing in Italian, and another in English.   It must be said, too, that Dante's soaring
fire does not flame in Longfellow.

The drama " Michael Angelo," left by the poet
in manuscript, was his latest essay in dramatic
"Michael composition, and one of his longest.   It
Angelo." has some fine lines and strong passages,
but it leaves upon the mind no characteristic impress, no lasting historical or personal picture.
A play that does not in some way stamp itself
upon the memory is an unsuccessful play, especially when it attempts something more than mere
amusement.   Longfellow was not at his best in
his dramas, but in his lyrics, idyls, and narratives,
and in such panoramic poems as " The Building
of the Ship," " The Rope walk," " Rain in Summer," " Keramos," or " The Hanging of the
Crane."   He could admirably present a series of
pictures or a chain of stories ; but he could not
tell us, in forceful scenes and acts and plays, how

> " Men's lives, like oceans, change
> In shifting tides, and ebb from either shore
> Till the strong planet draws them on once more."

In estimating the life-work of Longfellow as a poet, the personality and the product The Man and cannot be separated. The sweet and the Poet sympathetic and strong and self-reliant soul, so fully portrayed in the three-volume life by the poet's brother, ever animates the verse. Long-fellow looked out upon life and sang his thoughts concerning its joys and its mysteries. His lyrics and idyls and dramatic studies and reflective poems illuminate with catholic sympathy and quiet optimism the procession of human exist-ence: childhood, youth with its loves and hopes, middle-life with its bereavements and struggles, age with its wasting and weariness and patiently continued work, death as the transition to another stage of progress and experience. His poems lack not thought, nor feeling, nor art, but well combine the three. What he misses in intellect-ual greatness he possesses in heartfulness. He was the St. John of our American apostles of song. He allowed the poets of intricate philoso-phy, the sad singers of wan pre-Raphaelitism, the cosmic bards of atlas and city directory, and the "howling dervishes of song," to go their way while he went his. His word was spoken to those who work and win, struggle and lose, love and bury. He ranged from the American hearth-stone to the castle-towers of the Rhine. He adorned the simplest thought with spoils of medi-æval and continental culture. An American, he was too wise to refuse to learn of Europe. A man of culture, he knew as well as Hawthorne

that mere selfish intellectual wisdom turns the
heart to stone. A man of books, he carried his
sympathies with him as he entered his library
door. His reading was bent toward the better-
ment and the utterance of his good impulses, and
not to their crushing. A life-long moralizer, he
shunned cant as the twin-devil of hypocrisy. He
made the most of himself, in life and letters.
Neither Providence nor error cut short his earthly
service to song. We dare not say that his service
shall last

> " As long as the river flows,
> As long as the heart has passions,
> As long as life has woes ; "

but it will be until another shall sing the same
songs better.

Nothing is easier than to point out Longfellow's limitations ; not a few have been already
noted in this chapter. His broad range of
achievement, the very number of the things which
he attempted, make these limitations and imper-
fections all the more manifest. But how many
poets proffer a round and perfect life-work ? It is
idle to deny Longfellow's faults; it is equally idle
to shut one's eyes in the presence of his merits.
Neither is it wise to attempt to assign him an
immovable place in American letters, or to label
him, in numerical order, first or second of our
poets. Emerson's thought, as I have said, is
more profound, and his poetic philosophy delves
deeper and soars beyond. Other poets, mayhap,

surpass Longfellow in special powers or achievements. But all in all, Longfellow's place in our
verse-product has deservedly been very broad and
conspicuous, nor can it shrink to narrow limits for
many a year. Without his work, how much les-
sened would the value of the national literature
be. The thoughts of humanity, the gifts of culture, the graces of art, were fused in a poet's
imagination and sent forth everywhere. The
poet sang, too, of

> " Dreams that the soul of youth engage
> Ere fancy has been quelled ;
> Old legends of the monkish page,
> Traditions of the saint and sage,
> Tales that have the rime of age,
> And chronicles of eld."

In this " Prelude " to Longfellow's first book he
exclaimed : " Look, then, into thine heart, and
write ! " Into the depths of that ocean of joy and
beauty and danger and unrest he peered to the
end of his life, and learned its lessons, and wrote
them for the people. The manly and helpful
cheer of his youth was never stilled. Fifty years
after his graduation day at Bowdoin he stood
once more beneath the Brunswick pines "Morituri
and looked forward into the future with Salutamus."
the unquenched ardor of youth, under that night-
time of earth which is the dawn of eternity.
Never did poet more nobly say *ave atque vale*
than did Longfellow in this " Morituri Salutamus " poem, thus closing :

7

Shall we sit idly down and say
The night hath come ; it is no longer day?
The night hath not yet come : we are not quite
Cut off from labor by the failing light :
Something remains for us to do or dare ;
Even the oldest tree some fruit may bear ;
Not Œdipus Coloneus, or Greek ode
Or tales of pilgrims that one morning rode
Out of the gateway of the Tabard Inn.
But other something, would we but begin ;
For age is opportunity no less
Than youth itself, though in another dress,
And as the evening twilight fades away
The sky is filled with stars, invisible by day.

CHAPTER IV.

No book in my library contains a more interesting and suggestive portrait than that which forms the frontispiece of the most extended biography of Poe. It is a photograph copied from a daguerreotype formerly owned by the poet's friend " Stella," Estelle Anna Lewis. The picture is a truth-teller, one of those accurate presentations of the real man which photography is occasionally able to produce. No etcher or engraver has altered the lines or changed the life of the eye; one feels that he is looking at Poe himself. Around the portrait gather the memories of words spoken or written concerning him, by men who were the daily companions of his genius and of his selfishness; and at length the personality of the poet seems almost present—the pale, high forehead, the dark, clustering hair, the deep sad eyes, the supercilious and irresolute mouth, the slight, proud figure, the traces of dissipation marring the evident genius. One side of the face is longer, manlier, and handsomer than the other; we seem to be looking at Doctor Jekyll and Mr. Hyde at the moment when change impends. In our own minds, as we gaze at this counterfeit present-

Edgar Allan Poe, 1809-1849.

ment, so significant and so sad, pity and disgust struggle with the reverence due to genius. Here is a being weakly yielding to intemperance and to worse ingratitude; yet here is one of the most distinct and unquestioned powers in the history of American intellect. "This is the porcelain clay of humankind"—how fragile and how fine.

At the very outset of any critical discussion of Poe's literary products it is necessary to obtain a clear view of two things : the relation between his personality and his work, and the peculiar character of the field occupied by the best of his poems and tales. The life-story of Poe arouses peculiar interest in young minds, and possesses a never-ending fascination for that class of essayists and biographers which delights in attempting to "reverse history," to paint a nimbus around the sinner's head, or to throw mud at Aristides the just. Poe's first biographer, formerly his friend and latterly his literary executor, undoubtedly presented too distorted and ill-favored a portrait of his subject. Later writers, however, not content with appealing from some of Dr. Griswold's severer judgments, have sought to vindicate Poe throughout, a task manifestly impossible. The facts presented in the largest and most laudatory biography (Ingram's) are in themselves enough to sadden or repel the impartial reader. From the careful study of nearly all of the vast mass of Poe literature, and from diligent inquiry among those of his contemporaries with whom I could speak, I am satisfied that

Poe's personality. [margin note]

Poe, on the one hand, was industrious, usually devoted to his wife and her mother, and chaste in thought and life ; while, on the other, he was tactless, imperious and wayward of temper, too fond of sentimental attitudinizing, occasionally treacherous toward loyal friends, and wretchedly intemperate. With these plain statements, to which should be added a denial that he was addicted to the opium habit, the literary historian may dismiss the personality of Poe. Few authors of note have so completely severed the life and the book. All that Poe could have written we have, and we have it in as finished form as his utmost diligence could give. No American author save Hawthorne ever wrote and rewrote with such sane and constant care. The notion that Poe "dashed off" his poems in his wilder moods is at the farthest remove from the truth. Poe's sentimental friendships and personal or local prejudices colored his critical work, it is true ; and of course his genius was deeply moved and modified in its nature by the awful and constantly remembered progress of death through his little world of intense friendships ; but his poems and his imaginative prose, on which, of course, his ultimate fame must rest, were neither weakened nor stained by the sins and miseries of a woe-begone life. The very problem of immortality, around which fell his deepest shadows and above which hung his serenest star, he treated in the manner of a man to whom the "eternal streams" were nearer than the Hudson or the Schuylkill. Poe's

own field is that of the purely imaginative; and
there his chief writings, creations of mere mind,
have

"Left but the name
Of his fault and his sorrows behind."

The genius of Poe expressed itself, from the
first, in a literary field coextensive with the nature
Poe's literary and powers of that genius. His criti-
field. cal writings, earnest and vigorous as
they were, did not express his largest self. They
performed a useful service in banishing many
poor books and weak writers from the field of
American literature; though too often prejudiced,
they were never timid, and they called attention
to some of the deeper elements of literary creation at a time when superficiality was too common. These criticisms, written before the masters had done their best work, and while the mists
of sentimentalism temporarily shrouded the literary landscape, were necessarily of little permanent value. The papers on chirography, cryptog-
raphy, the "automaton chess-player," and similar
themes, were of course the by-play of an active
mind, possessed of unusual powers of analysis.
Poe's fame rests upon his tales and poems; and
the essential nature of the best of them is the
same. They deal with weird and ethereal beauty;
with the desolate sadness of a half-despairing and
half-hoping soul before the iron gate of death;
with the strange lights and unworldly sounds of
the realm of pure romance; with the parable of
shadow and the fable of silence. Theirs is not

the high philosophy of life, the manly, ethical self-reliance of Saxon independence. Had Poe striven often to enter Hawthorne's domain, the allegory of conscience, his failures would have been speedy ; had he sought to repeat the hated Longfellow's "seven voices of sympathy," the result would have been grotesque. We cannot all do all things. Poe knew what he could do and did it. The knowledge and the choice were so instinctive, and the expression was so complete, that never did the spontaneity which is the soul of art make more manifest exhibition than in his best prose and verse. I am far from saying that Poe never over-estimated his powers : he absurdly exalted his "prose-poem" of "Eureka"; he was apparently blind to his failures in the department of the would-be humorous; and he even prided himself on some seemingly learned review which was really the product of a journalist's "cram." But it is to be remembered that the final edition of Poe's writings includes nearly all of his hack-work—literary criticisms of ephemeral and valueless books, personal sketches of temporary interest, newspaper discussions of mechanical curiosities of the day, and stories and sketches written by a poor man for daily bread. The wonder is that the average excellence is so high. Seldom is the task-work of an editor or "regular contributor" so conscientiously performed and so closely related to the real mind of the writer. Poe is not wholly to be blamed for his poverty, nor for the passage of time, nor for the state of American literature when he wrote ; and the fact is indisputable that he measured his mind and entered his true field with a wisdom as confident as that which dominated the life-work of Emerson or Hawthorne. Their serenity toward the things just beyond he utterly lacked ; but in his own domain he was a conscious monarch. This self-confidence of mind is in itself, when justified by achievement, a mark of genius ; the fated sky gives free scope.

There are two measures of literary success, the one relative and the other absolute. Shakespeare *The measure of* is Shakespeare because he rises above *Poe's Success.* the world's best chorus: Homer, Æschylus, Sophocles, Virgil, Dante, Milton, Goethe. But Coleridge, in "The Ancient Mariner," attains a single intense success coextensive with the ambition of the poem If the estimate of an author's rank is in the large sense relative and comparative, we properly consider his breadth of theme, varied aims and triumphs, relations to the problems of the world and the universe of matter and mind. By such an estimate we view a Shakespeare, a Beethoven, a Raphael ; and there can be no question that the world's masters in every art are those of depth and breadth and height of thought and work. But the place of a flower or a gem is as legitimate and true as that of a mountain or a Parthenon. If the artistic act fitly follows the artistic thought, the resultant success and the attendant pleasure are not the less abso-

lute because relatively less great. Considering
that which Poe sought, in a part of soul-land
where few have dwelt and sung as did he, it must
readily be admitted that his poetic attainment followed his poetic search. "Very valueless verses"
have his poems been called by a realistic critic ;
and so they are, when compared with Emerson's
or Wordsworth's apt answers to the riddle of life.
But the shade of Emerson might now say to the
shade of Poe:

"The self-same Power that brought me there brought you."

The field of thought and genius is broad enough
for all three poets ; there is in it a place not only
for Yarrow and Musketaquid but for "an ultimate dim Thule,"

"A wild weird clime that lieth, sublime,
Out of Space—out of Time."

Over the whole earthly life of Poe hung an
eternal vision of pure beauty. If the vision were
in fleshly form, he addressed it with the
reverence of a worshipper entering some
classic temple, as in the familiar fifteen lines
forming the well-known lyric "To Helen":

A poet of beauty.

Helen, thy beauty is to me
Like those Nicéan barks of yore,
That gently, o'er a perfumed sea,
The weary, wayworn wanderer bore
To his own native shore.

On desperate seas long wont to roam,
  Thy hyacinth hair, thy classic face,
Thy Naiad airs have brought me home
  To the glory that was Greece,
  And the grandeur that was Rome.

Lo! in yon brilliant window niche
  How statue-like I see thee stand,
The agate lamp within thy hand!
  Ah, Psyche, from the regions which
  Are Holy Land!

Notwithstanding some alterations in later life, this chaste and round lyric belongs to the poet's earliest years. Its tone of personal address is apparent at a glance; neither Poe nor the majority of the world's poets sang of intellectual abstractions or mere capital-letter personifications of imaginary beauty. But here, as in so many of Poe's poems, the earthly form is made to assume an unearthly and half-spiritual guise; upon the material and fleshly there falls a light from an immaterial world. Beauty and love are all-in-all, but the beauty is not of the court or the street, nor is the love that of this middle-earth alone. No writer of his time ever fell prostrate upon the grave in morbid desolation so utter; but nevertheless the poet's eye turned with clear vision "To One in Paradise":

Thou wast all that to me, love,
  For which my soul did pine—
A green isle in the sea, love,
  A fountain and a shrine,
All wreathed with fairy fruits and flowers,
  And all the flowers were mine.

Ah, dream too bright to last !
  Ah, starry Hope ! that didst arise
But to be overcast !
  A voice from out the Future cries,
" On, on ! "—but o'er the Past
  (Dim gulf !) my spirit hovering lies
Mute, motionless, aghast !

For alas ! alas ! with me
  The light of Life is o'er !
  No more—no more—no more—
(Such language holds the solemn sea
  To the sands upon the shore)
Shall bloom the thunder-blasted tree,
  Or the stricken eagle soar !

And all my days are trances,
  And all my nightly dreams
Are where thy dark eye glances,
  And where thy footstep gleams—
In what ethereal dances,
  By what eternal streams.

He sings not only of the earthly presence and of
the sight of the far-sundered one in paradise, ever
away from the light of this life, but also of a
union of souls so perfect and eternal that material
earth and spiritual heaven are indistinguishable
and at one. From the reverential tribute " To
Helen " and the rapt and constant vision of the
ethereal dance and the eternal stream, he turns
once more in " Annabel Lee " to a love that is
more than love—more than the poor temporary
physical love of earthly space and time, and belonging instead to the illimitable land of " deathless love's acclaims " :

It was many and many a year ago,
  In a kingdom by the sea,
That a maiden there lived whom you may know
  By the name of Annabel Lee;
And this maiden she lived with no other thought
  Than to love and be loved by me.

I was a child and *she* was a child,
  In this kingdom by the sea:
But we loved with a love that was more than love—
  I and my Annabel Lee;
With a love that the wingéd seraphs of heaven
  Coveted her and me.

And this was the reason that, long ago,
  In this kingdom by the sea,
A wind blew out of a cloud, chilling
  My beautiful Annabel Lee;
So that her highborn kinsmen came
  And bore her away from me,
To shut her up in a sepulchre
  In this kingdom by the sea.

The angels, not half so happy in heaven,
  Went envying her and me—
Yes!—that was the reason (as all men know,
  In this kingdom by the sea)
That the wind came out of the cloud by night,
  Chilling and killing my Annabel Lee.

But our love it was stronger by far than the love
  Of those who were older than we—
  Of many far wiser than we—
And neither the angels in heaven above,
  Nor the demons down under the sea,
Can ever dissever my soul from the soul
  Of the beautiful Annabel Lee:

For the moon never beams, without bringing me dreams
  Of the beautiful Annabel Lee;
And the stars never rise, but I feel the bright eyes
  Of the beautiful Annabel Lee;
And so, all the night-tide, I lie down by the side
Of my darling,—my darling,—my life and my bride,
  In her sepulchre there by the sea,
  In her tomb by the side of the sea.

I have reprinted entire these familiar poems—of which the first is artistically the best and the third the most famous—so that the reader may follow them in their order of composition, and thus behold in symmetrical arrangement the three chief planes from which Poe viewed the mystery of life and death. "To Helen" dates from his earliest years, while "Annabel Lee," undoubtedly written in memory of his wife, was almost his own death-song. To claim that these three severed pieces were written as the poet's cumulative *credo* would be nonsense; but it is plain truth to assert that they form a key to Poe's chief mood of song.

This highest mood, however, was not all-prevalent. It dominates these three poems, unsurpassed in essential merit by anything he ever wrote in verse; and it dominates the tale of "Ligeia," which stands with "The Fall of the House of Usher" at the head of his prose. The will dieth not; God himself is but a great will; man by the strength of will conquers death that conquers all else.

The eternity of the individual soul.

This is the answer to the riddle of Poe, and to the vaster enigma of his world. But Poe's high creed was better than his practice, in life and in verse. His own will was sadly fluctuant, and two-thirds of his well-known woes were born of his personal weakness. So, too, in his poems the note of clear and resistless assertion is often changed to that of wailing and ineffectual lament. The ethereal quality of his genius soared

A poet of
weird woe.

above the heart of common humanity, but was too often caught by rough winds and dashed helpless to the earth. Therefore we have poems of the storm-swept desolate grave, or even of the charnel-house ; poems of melodious but utterly melancholy tears and sighs, —of a despair that veers between the shuddering thought that mayhap death is very death, and the welcome idea that the dreamless sleep of forgetfulness is best after all. And yet Poe turned again and again from the " nevermore " of " The Raven," from " the tragedy ' Man ' and its hero the Conqueror Worm,"

" From Hell unto a high estate far up within the Heaven—
  From grief and groan, to a golden throne, beside the King
    of Heaven."

Less than two hundred small pages include the poetical product of Poe. Upon his forty poems,

The singer and
his hearers.

however, rests a reputation which has slowly and steadily advanced in many lands, without successful challenge from the critics or the public, during the forty years since his death. Their obvious and at times painful limitations have by contrast displayed

their conspicuous merits. The maker and the
product have survived the attacks of hostile critics
and the still more foolish and injurious praises
bestowed by the indiscriminate adulation of those
who have made " the Poe craze " a term of mer-
ited contempt. The lonely separation of his
verse, in the history of American song ; its melancholy imagination and its romantic fancy ; its
metrical originality and beauty and its mastery of
assonance and alliteration, have given it a place
and fame, notwithstanding its lack of the moral
might of the masters. Poe could not give us one
of the long poems he affected to despise ; he was
incapable of success in the use of our noblest
English measure, the iambic unrhymed pentameter or " blank verse" ; and he too often forgot
—though at his best he remembered—the words
of a poet as great as himself and in some respects
very like him :

> " Beauty is truth, truth beauty,—that is all
> Ye know on earth, and all ye need to know."

All this, however, does not deny or diminish the
legitimate pleasure with which we read the vague
fantasies of " Ulalume ; " the Tennysonian allegory
of " The Haunted Palace ; " the pallid and silent
and unhuman apostrophe to " The Sleeper,"
environed by ghosts and shadows of No-man's-
land ; the obvious tone-pictures of " The Bells " ;
or the cadenced story of " The Raven." The
commanding popularity of the last named poem,
among its author's works, is due to its apt combi-

nation of things said and things suggested, of pathos and half-humorous lightness of touch, of story for the people and parable for the elect.

The originality of Poe's product explains his fame in America and in Europe. His genius and

Poe's its expression were separate and indi-
Originality. vidual. The peculiar type of the American mind shows itself more or less all through the national literature ; but not many of our authors, like Poe, Hawthorne, Emerson, Cooper, and Whitman, stand isolated and significant. A Coleridge or Tieck may have influenced Poe or Hawthorne, as Carlyle affected Emerson and Whitman ; every author learns something from his predecessors ; but these five American names stand for peculiar powers in separated fields. New-world men and nature were shown to the novel-reading public in the works of Cooper ; but his national tone, characteristic as it is, may be deemed less significant, in one sense, than the might of genius which makes itself independent of time and place, while freely availing itself of both. I am far from stating that these five men are of equal rank, nor do I claim that significance is the only mark of success ; but it is a conspicuous and suggestive mark. These men have deeply affected their students in many lands ; they have aroused the imitation of literary schools, or, like Hawthorne, have left their would-be followers in despair of learning their secret.

Poe's originality of mind and note appears even in his poetical failures, such as the long and dreary and often obscure "Tamerlane" and "Al Aaraaf," or the trashy verses on "Israfel," which form so absurd a contrast to the lovely text from the Koran which inspired their thought.

His cheapest jingles have a quality which is distinctly his own :

> Tottering above
>   In her highest noon,
>   The enamored moon
> Blushes with love,
>   While to listen, the red levin
>   (With the rapid Pleiads, even,
>   Which were seven),
>   Pauses in heaven.

> And never a flake
> That the vapor can make
> With the moon-tints of purple and pearl,
> Can vie with the modest Eulalie's most unregarded curl,
> Can compare with the bright-eyed Eulalie's most humble and careless curl.

> Some have left the cool glade, and
>   Have slept with the bee—
> Arouse them ; my maiden,
>   On moorland and lea.

> The sickness, the nausea—
>   The pitiless pain—
> Have ceased, with the fever
>   That maddened my brain—
> With the fever called "Living"
>   That burned in my brain.

> And oh ! of all tortures
>   *That* torture the worst
> Has abated—the terrible
>   Torture of thirst,

For the naphthaline river
 Of Passion accurst:—
I have drank of a water
 That quenches all thirst, etc.

This is doggerel, but it is Poe's special doggerel. The ease and persistency with which he has been parodied, and the failure which has met the efforts of his more serious imitators, are sufficient proof that all his verse, in its three clearly-marked divisions of good, bad, and indifferent, is impressed with his special seal. The thought and the voice, the light and the touch, are unmistakable. " Le sue piccole ballate sono gioielli poetici, ma anche in esse domina quel *tedium vitæ*, quella malinconia insanabile, diffusa, come lume lunare, su tutte le sue creazione." *

From the small and homogeneous body of Poe's verse two poems stand clearly forth, marked with a general favor they are unlikely to lose. " The Bells " and " The Raven " are in my opinion of merit inferior to that of the trio of poems previously reprinted in this chapter. But their qualities are such as to insure lasting popularity in a world where the majority of readers prefer a lyric to an epic, and sing a song while they leave a drama unread. Poetic conciseness and unity of thought were prime articles in Poe's creed, and in these original lyrics his practice well followed his principle. The heaviest ear can follow the music of " The Bells," and the dullest "The Bells." mind can perceive the varied but pro-

* Gustavo Strafforello, " Letteratura Americana." Milano, 1884; p. 14.

gressive suggestions of the poem; while the
reader of finer tastes need not complain of any
lack of refinement and beauty in the metrical and
verbal workmanship. As an extended illustration
of onomatopœia "The Bells," as Mr. Stoddard has
said, need not fear comparison with "Alexander's
Feast,"—a wonder in its day but no marvel now.
As for "The Raven," it is obvious that our
"Stygian American" never measured
his powers more exactly than in its   "The Raven."
famous stanzas. Its variorum editor boldly
declares that it "may safely be termed the
most popular lyrical poem in the world." A
dozen rival candidates at once occur, beginning
with Gray's "Elegy;" but there need be
no discussion of the wide-spread favor which
the later lyric enjoys. It is "recited" by the
schoolboy, and its melodious earthly despair
inspired the serene heavenly contrast of the
recluse Rossetti's best poem, "The Blessed Damozel." Mrs. Browning, to whom it was manifestly
indebted in form and word, bore testimony to the
"sensation" made in England by its gruesome-
ness and its melody; and its "power which is
felt," to borrow her own words, has not faded with
time. The genesis of the poem, as elaborately
and doubtless in the main truly described by its
writer, fully accounts for its mechanical excellence; while its spirit is that in which Poe chiefly
lived. Its "midnight dreary" was his own most
characteristic hour; and its irregular and ineffectual struggle with the inevitable was thoroughly

8

representative of one of Poe's frequent reflections, in which he consoled himself for personal failure by the thought of the "unmerciful disaster" of destiny. But the spirit and tone of the poem were controlled rigidly, from first to last, by the intellectual force and ratiocinative grip which Poe displayed so constantly in all his literary life. Whatever the limitations of his mental powers, those powers which he possessed were used with the utmost sanity of deliberately measured strength. The best illustration of this fact is to be found in the apt introduction of humor in certain lines of "The Raven,"—a flicker which admirably deepens the shadows darkening toward the close. It is the fashion to say that humor is utterly lacking in Poe; but the statement cannot be accepted, as regards either his verse or his prose. This quality was not his strongest, but it was occasionally used with good effect in heightening the grotesque. Indeed, a romancer destitute of a sense of humor would almost be an impossibility; he must play with his subject and his readers, as Poe does here, before he permits the red glare to rise or the darkening final shadow to fall. His constructive art, like that of the painter, must ever be watched, if it would produce a result which, like "The Raven," contains within itself an element of perennial life.

Midway between the verse and the prose of Poe stand the "Scenes from 'Politian,' an unpublished drama," which have always been retained among the author's collected

"Politian."

writings. These fragments of a never-completed
play have received little praise, even from the
poet's most constant and all-absorbing coterie of
worshippers. It may be said, however, at the
least, that they do not fall below the average of
the weak and unimportant contributions which
America has made to the department of literature
which they profess to enter. Poe's mind was
essentially incapable of producing a long-sustained
effort in either prose or verse; as a rule he contemptuously abstained from essays toward the
"large manner," and assuredly we need not regret
this fact, in view of his failures in "Al Aaraaf,"
"Tamerlane," "Eureka," and "Arthur Gordon
Pym." What Poe would have made of "Politian," had he completed it, I do not know; the
chances of success were against him. But I rank
these existing fragments as the best of his three
poems of more than lyrical aim. They are sometimes grandiloquent, but they mouth well, and
often show more than superficial attractiveness of
words, as in—

A spectral figure, solemn, and slow, and noiseless—
Like the grim shadow Conscience, solemn and noiseless;

I heard not any voice except thine own,
And the echo of thine own;

                Methinks the air
Is balmier now than it was wont to be—
Rich melodies are floating in the winds—
A rarer loveliness bedecks the earth—
And with a holier lustre the quiet moon
Sitteth in Heaven.*

---

* Poe never learned to punctuate; and here, as elsewhere, it is an annoy-
ance to follow the established text.

The subjective element clearly appears in the following longer extract, the spirit of which is closely accordant with that of several of the author's best lyrics,—indeed, with the dominant thought of his life :

> *Politian.* Speak not to me of glory!
> I hate—I loathe the name ; I do abhor
> The unsatisfactory and ideal thing.
> Art thou not Lalage, and I Politian ?
> Do I not love—art thou not beautiful—
> What need we more ? Ha! glory!—now speak not of it :
> By all I hold most sacred and most solemn—
> By all my wishes now—my fears hereafter—
> By all I scorn on earth and hope in heaven—
> There is no deed I would more glory in,
> Than in thy cause to scoff at this same glory
> And trample it under foot. What matters it—
> What matters it, my fairest, and my best,
> That we go down unhonored and forgotten
> Into the dust—so we descend together,
> Descend together—and then—and then perchance—
>   *Lalage.* Why dost thou pause, Politian ?
>   *Politian.* And then perchance
> *Arise* together, Lalage, and roam
> The starry and quiet dwellings of the blest.
> And still—
>   *Lalage.* Why dost thou pause, Politian ?
>   *Politian.* And still *together*—together.
>   *Lalage.* Now, Earl of Leicester !
> Thou *lovest* me, and in my heart of hearts
> I feel thou lovest me truly.

Of all the prose tales of Poe the one most dear to him was "Ligeia"; and in it the reader passes naturally from one great division of the author's writings to the other. The general

The prose of Poe.

theme is here unchanged; the deliberate prose has somewhat of the melody of verse; and here, as before, the living heart beats rebelliously and at last triumphantly against the bars of the dying body. The tale, according to the author's own statement in manuscript, appended to a copy in the possession of Mr. John H. Ingram,[*] was suggested by a dream, " in which the eyes of the heroine produced the intense effect described in the fourth paragraph of the work." Mr. Ingram aptly adds : " A theme more congenial to the dream-haunted brain of Poe could scarcely be devised ; and in his exposition of the thoughts suggested by its application he has been more than usually successful. The failure of Death to annihilate Will was, indeed, a suggestion that the poet—dreadingly, despairingly, familiar as he was with charnel secrets—could not fail to grasp at with the energy of hope, and adorn with the funereal flowers of his grave-nourished fantasy." In Poe's statements concerning the powers and the place of the post-mortem soul there is at times an over-intensity of assertion that seems almost hysterical, and that is far removed from the serenity of settled faith. But

> " There lives more faith in honest doubt,
> Believe me, than in half the creeds."

There is a stolid fixity of faith that is unreflecting and unprepared for questionings; and

"Ligeia."

---

[*] Ingram's " Edgar Allan Poe : his Life, Letters, and Opinions " ; i., 155. London : 1880.

there is, on the other hand, a storm-tossed incerti-
tude that rises *per aspera ad astra*, and at length
exclaims, with a confident "Eureka": "All is
Life—Life—Life within Life—the less within the
greater and all within the Spirit Divine." *

Poe has left on record, with his usual italicized
positiveness, his views of the difference between
poetry and romance. These views have interest
as we turn to "Ligeia" and "The Fall of the
House of Usher," his strongest stories: "A poem,
in my opinion, is opposed to a work of science by
having, for its *immediate* object, pleasure, not
truth; to romance, by having, for its object, an
indefinite instead of a *definite* pleasure, being a
poem only so far as this object is attained;
romance presenting perceptible images with definite, poetry with indefinite sensations, to which
end music is an *essential*, since the comprehension
of sweet sound is our most indefinite conception.
Music, when combined with a pleasurable idea, is
poetry; music, without the idea, is simply music;
the idea, without the music, is prose, from its very
definitiveness." †

This statement, which Poe at some other times
modified or failed to observe, is obviously open to
criticism in several respects. But its
idea that romance should present perceptible images with definite sensations is one that
Poe scrupulously observed in his best tales, such
as the two just named, "The Gold Bug," "The

Definiteness
of Poe's tales.

---

* "Eureka"; complete works (1884 edition), v., 150.
† Letter to B——," works, vi., 571.

Black Cat," " The Pit and the Pendulum," "The
Facts in the Case of M. Valdemar," "The Mystery of Marie Roget," "The Murders in the Rue
Morgue." Upon their unity of thought and painstaking vividness of impression depends their success. However improbable, unworldly, or supernatural was Poe's theme, the figures were presented with the clear-cut distinctness of a silhou-
ette. No "realist" of the next generation was
ever more zealous and fastidious in the selection
and arrangement of details. As far as verisimilitude is concerned this weird and at times apparently distraught romancer stands in the company
led by the author of " Robinson Crusoe" himself.
The romance lay in his thought, but he well knew
that a deliberate literary method, in great and in
small, was needed before the reader could receive
"definite sensations from perceptible images."

This method was often apparent in many
details, despite Poe's great unevenness in literary
style—from the choice of titles to the arrange-
ment of concluding paragraphs. Such phrases as
" The Fall of the House of Usher," "The Fall of
" The Imp of the Perverse," " The the House of
Usher."
Masque of the Red Death," " Some
Words with a Mummy," " The Murders in the
Rue Morgue," "The Pit and the Pendulum,"
" The Gold Bug," and " The Island of the Fay,"
arouse attention in themselves, irrespective of
what follows ; and remain in the memory as repre-
sentatives of original and definite impressions.
Less poetic, but sufficiently clever to serve the

purpose of apt introductions, are the more obviously readable titles of sensational stories like " MS. Found in a Bottle," or " The Unparalleled Adventures of One Hans Pfaal." Poe did not depend, however, upon titles only; sometimes an artistic tale was ill-labelled; and again so rhythmical a collection of words as " The Cask of Amontillado" formed the prelude to ten pages of sub-freshman silliness. It is pleasanter to think of Poe's full triumphs than of his weak failures. " The Fall of the House of Usher " is, in its way, a triumph of art. An intensely dramatic tale, involving both mind and matter, it employs the full powers of art to draw from dark and mysterious scenes and deeds a very definite and impressive literary picture. Language, as the chief means of intellectual impression, was so used by Poe that it imitated some of the effects of painting, of sculpture, and of wordless music.

The chief divisions of Poe's tales, natural or supernatural, are those of life battling with death; of remorseful, overwhelming tragedy; *Divisions of Poe's Tales.* of retribution; of ratiocination; of pseudo-scientific realism; and of humor. In these divisions, " Ligeia," " The Fall of the House of Usher," " Hop-Frog," " The Gold-Bug," " The Unparalleled Adventures of One Hans Pfaal," and " The System of Doctor Tarr and Professor Fether," may be taken as representatives. The verisimilitude of the unimportant long story, " Arthur Gordon Pym," is occasionally overshadowed by Coleridgean mystical tints; while the "prose-poem" of "Eureka" is a dream of the universe, in the waking sleep of an imaginative genius who has dabbled in science. The slight value of both—and to them may be added Poe's third long piece of prose, "The Journal of Julius Rodman"—is easily outweighed by any one of the more characteristic tales mentioned above. Dismissing also the dismally unsuccessful and ephemeral "humorous" sketches of the "X-ing a Paragrab" variety, we may study, without distraction, the qualities of that part of Poe's writings in prose which will survive the passage of years.

"Arthur Gordon Pym," "Eureka," and minor prose.

Some of those qualities are concisely made apparent by the rather obvious and natural comparison between Hawthorne and Poe, who wrote at the same great formative period in American literature. Both were original and characteristic forces, and their peculiar fields in fiction were occasionally contiguous. Hawthorne's method was deliberate and regular; Poe's, though deliberate at last, was sometimes directed by a peculiar choice. Hawthorne's humor was more gentle and constant; Poe's more extravagant and artificial. Both were realists in touch and idealists in thought, but Hawthorne's realism cared little for the mysteries of the detective, for cryptograms or purloined letters, or for semi-scientific dreams. Hawthorne's strongest stories were calm but mighty allegories of soul-triumph or spiritual suicide, of

Poe and Hawthorne.

development or destruction. Poe's, with the exception of those portraying the eternal vitality of the life-principle, were chiefly of supernatural weirdness and horror, or of unearthly beauty. The pellucid literary style of Hawthorne constantly surpassed that of Poe, save in some climax of sombre or romantic description or delineation. Hawthorne was an observer and recorder of the broadest range, possessed of imaginative genius, spiritual insight, and a sure artistic hand; his creations affect us as those of a serene master in the world of life and thought. Poe was a magician who, by the utmost effort of a powerful will, brought before us, in shadow and in sunlight, wonderful beings that were almost beyond his control :

> " Black spirits and white,
> Blue spirits and gray."

Relatively, therefore, the power and range of these stories are manifestly inferior to those exhibited in the works of Hawthorne. Absolutely, however, they stand individually forth, without conspicuous challenge in contemporary literature. Hawthorne and Poe were in no sense rivals, nor did either regard the other as a rival, or even a fellow-worker in the same field. Poe's vacillating review of Hawthorne does not disprove this statement. Indeed, they are so far apart that Coleridge himself seems to stand between them, with something of Hawthorne's humanitarianism on the one hand, and on the other something of

Poe's supernaturalism and fondness for the mar-
vellous. Few authors gain or lose less, in comparison with others, than these two peculiar
Americans, each of whom knew his powers and
used them well.

It has been averred that Poe had but "a
mechanical ideal, that disabled him from doing
any very noble work of his own." His Was Poe me-
work was evidently not noble in vital chanical?
ethical purpose; but at its best it was excellent
in its adequately artistic presentation of an original and legitimate conception. This excellence
hardly permits one to declare, with Tennyson,
that Poe was "the greatest American genius,"
the literary glory of America; but it well war-
rants the critic in assigning him a place among
the world's artists or makers. The French saying, "nothing succeeds like success," is already
sufficiently applicable to the poems and tales
of this favorite of the French literary public.
Neither his thoughts nor his creations were of
the deepest or highest type; but his feignings
were those of definite genius and not of mere
mechanical cleverness, of which the reading world
soon tires.

Poe's chief stories are "tales of the grotesque
and arabesque." Their hold upon plain human
life—such as that portrayed in the Could Poe create
novels of George Eliot—is neither characters?
strong nor constant. Even in the detective riddles of "The Mystery of Marie Roget," we do
not feel the power of a writer whose chief aim was

to delineate actual character.   Poe created few
men and women whose personality stands clearly
forth in the reader's mind.   No Don Quixote,
Gil Blas, Robinson Crusoe, Colonel Newcome,
Sam Weller, Adam Bede, Phœbe Pyncheon,
Natty Bumppo, was added by him to the "dic-
tionaries of noted names of fiction."   With all his
realism and reasoning power, he was no master
in the art of characterization.   Humanity is that
which shapes and warms a hero or heroine in fiction ; and humanity was the quality which Poe
most conspicuously lacked.   The lack was so
complete that its absence hardly troubles us.
Poe's bloodlessness is the true cause of the failure
of the most of his "tales of humor," which are thin
and artificial.   The world of Le Sage and Goldsmith was for him a *terra incognita.*   But his non-
humanity, his failure in creation of characters of
flesh and blood, enabled him to succeed in his own
field.   Destitute of sympathy, his analyses were
intellectual and not spiritual.   Unworldly and
unheavenly, he was empowered by his very nature
to introduce us to the spaceless and timeless
regions of merely mental enchantment and horror.
Unemotional, he was unfettered by the bonds of
earth, but in tombland and ghostland he was a
master.   He was wise enough to endeavor to connect his work with some thought or experience of
man, but of such connection he made a mere
starting-point.   So long as a thought or feeling
was true or sufficiently obvious, he cared not how
vague or unusual it might be.   In the elaboration

of his ideas he willingly and often left the realm
of the real, but he never dropped the central
thread. This union of directness and mystery is
doubtless the chief cause of his literary success.
The directness is of the world of matter, and the
mystery is of the world of spirit; this man so
combined explicit reason with shadowy imagination that he seemed to enlarge the borders of his
readers' universe.

Poe's characters and plots are spectacular and
occasionally impressive, but they do not illuminate
Poe's mind and instruct. The instability and insin-
and heart. cerity which made the man Poe so often
and so weakly fall, were closely connected with
his lack of human heart and sympathy. "The
mind and the heart," says Longfellow in "Hyperion," "are closely linked together, and the errors
of genius bear with them their own chastisement,
even upon earth." Poe's mind was large, in a
way, but his heart was small; hence his personal
career verged dangerously near the course of
Ethan Brand. There is not much heart in his
tales; their light, whether whitely clear or lurid,
lacks warmth; their characters and doings, notwithstanding constant intellectual guidance, are
too often, therefore, thin, pale, and limited. Poe,
in his excursions through hell, purgatory, and paradise, wanders far from Dante's path. Rossetti
put a flesh-and-blood woman into paradise; Poe
peopled earth itself with phantoms and abstractions. In his stories, as in his poems, we cannot
fail to note some influence of the personality of

the writer. They are free from his positive sins,
but they are strongly marked by his negative
signs. On the side of the human soul not less
than the human mind we are forced to perceive
that Poe's field was limited and his success narrow.
A Raphael could paint the heavenly in the
human; Poe never learned the secret. He gave
us high art and pure spirit; but could not give us
high art and all-embracing soul.

The sensational and merely artificial qualities
which disfigure some of Poe's poems—including
"The Raven"—are in one sense less annoying in
his prose. The stories which he wrote merely
for effect may be divided into two classes: those
of strained humor and mechanical gayety, which
have dropped out of sight for lack of inherent
merit; and those in which the clever ratiocination
won a permanent success by sheer force of intel-
Analytic lectual strength. His unending self-con-
power. sciousness, in the latter case, actually became a merit. Conscience was not needed, nor
deep spiritual sympathy; analytic reason was
demanded, and in this no American author was
ever stronger than Poe. He often wrote of
strength of will, but his own was very weak; and
most of his literary limitations may be connected
with this lack of a strong, dominating individuality. But in the matter of thought and its logical processes he needs no apology or defence,
personal or literary. His mental integrity—if I
may coin a phrase—was high. All charges of literary dishonesty may be dismissed from his case.

He wrote hack work, at times valueless; but its worthlessness was not due to lack of expenditure of such intellectual resources as were at hand. He who wasted weeks in deciphering newspaper correspondents' cryptograms, when time was money, was a conscientious workman in that part of his mind which was uninvaded by his folly or weakness.

Conciseness and neatness of literary workman-ship, from method down to word, were to be ex-pected from a mind constituted as was his. He is always verbally intelligible, however remote or unfamiliar his theme. Clearness in rhetoric is a first pre-requisite of force, *Clearness of speech.* and by its almost invariable use Poe secured its natural result. "The Purloined Letter," or "The Gold Bug," is as straightforward as Web-ster's description of the White murder at Salem. They represent a class of stories in which a whole school of lesser novelists has imitated Poe, but has for the most part failed, through the careless-ness which is born of over-sympathy. Poe "hitched his wagon to a star"—the Black Maria of the detective story to the cold star of in-tellectual insight. Strange to say, he was en-abled to carry this clearness of exposition all the way from such obvious stories as "The Oblong Box," or "The Premature Burial," which any magazinist could have written, up to "Ligeia" and "The Fall of the House of Usher." It failed him only when he undertook to portray the great mysteries of the spiritual universe, for the

reason that mere intellectual insight is insufficient
for the reading of the riddle. Poe was right
when he announced that deduction, or poetic
thought, was the proper starting point in many
great movements; but his failure—as in "Eureka"—was in the quality of the thought required. He could not use a key which he did not
possess.

There is a numerous class of readers delighting
in speculations concerning the unfulfilled possibilities of literature. What if Keats had lived? what
if Byron and Burns had been temper-
ate in life-habits? what if Poe had
not given way to temptations which
formerly limited the earthly career of genius to a
period far shorter than that of the Tennysons
and Longfellows of to-day? The might-have-
been is a subject for guess-work more entertaining than valuable. In Poe's case its value is re-
duced to its lowest terms. His clearness, directness, and force in literature, as I said at the start,
apparently suffered little from his personal irregularities, and even from the hack-work necessities
of his life. Poe, though he earned his living by
his pen at a time when sentimentalism was better
paid than genius, refused to stoop below, nor
could he rise above, the plane he had chosen,
wisely or unwisely. Seldom, in the history of
literature, can we say so confidently that the work
adequately represents the man. Poe needs no
apologies or extenuations, which his proud nature

*Poe's product
the best he
could offer.*

would have been the first to scorn. His field was his own; his triumphs were those won by his genius, and his failures were natural and deliberate, not the result of intemperance, accident, or fate. Many of his poems were revised again and again, and the revision always moved toward the style which is most characteristic of the author.

The obedience with which Poe's pen obeyed his mind is well displayed in " William Wilson," a story, which, though comparatively neg- "William lected by his readers, possesses a signifi- Wilson." cance peculiar to itself. It is partly autobiographical; it vividly describes the buildings and environment of the school at Stoke Newington, England, in which some of Poe's boyhood days were spent; and, in later pages, it unquestionably contains a personal element. Its theme is perennial: the struggle between good and bad in one man; between conscience and the self-destroying principle of sin. Neither of the two William Wilsons—he of the echoing whisper, the haunting presence in sin or danger, and the solemn monitions; and he of the heedless and selfish downward way—is lightly to be declared the real Poe, for the tale is, of course, dramatic. But it is impossible not to read this deeply religious allegory without feeling that nowhere else do we come so near the real man. The author of " William Wilson " must have seen at times the Dantean and Miltonic vision of mighty right and hideous wrong, and must have possessed in his own soul

9

the power of that ultimate rectification which heeds the voice from the Paradiso and not the Inferno.

A few of Poe's productions in prose were written with an idea of the prose-poem in the author's Prose-poems. mind. Not content with the music of verse or with occasional careful presentations of euphonic phrases in his better stories, he essayed occasionally the art of deliberately melodious utterance in prose. By the choice of a single isolated thought or a significantly romantic theme, and by the use of that archaic English which is instinctively connected with the attempt of prose to express the ideal, he sought to secure results which would have attracted more notice had they been more numerous or sustained. As it is, they occasionally produce effects not essentially different from those which follow the reading of parts of the best of the poems and stories; but since their central ideas are less potent in their grasp upon the reader's mind, they are little heeded by the majority of Poe's public. Weird music, interpreting thoughts of the ethereal or the horrible, is so frequently heard from Poe's hand that it ceases to be novel in pieces which would arouse interest if more exceptional in tone. They are similar to the author's other work, and not strong enough to command a place for themselves. The "Silence; a Fable." brief study entitled "Silence, a Fable," however, is at least worth a deliberate reading :

"'Listen to *me*,' said the Demon, as he placed his hand upon my head. 'The region of which I speak is a dreary region in Libya, by the borders of the river Zäire, and there is no quiet there, nor silence.

" ' The waters of the river have a saffron and sickly hue ; and they flow not onward to the sea, but palpitate forever and forever beneath the red eye of the sun with a tumultuous and convulsive motion. For many miles on either side of the river's oozy bed is a pale desert of gigantic water-lilies. They sigh one unto the other, in that solitude, and stretch toward the heavens their long and ghastly necks, and nod to and fro their everlasting heads. And there is an indistinct murmur which cometh out from among them like the rushing of subterrene water. And they sigh one unto the other.

" ' But there is a boundary to their realm—the boundary of the dark, horrible, lofty forest. There, like the waves about the Hebrides, the low underwood is agitated continually. But there is no wind throughout the heaven. And the tall, primeval trees rock eternally hither and thither with a crashing and mighty sound. And from their high summits, one by one, drop everlasting dews. And at the roots strange poisonous flowers lie writhing in perturbed slumber. And overhead, with a rustling and loud noise, the gray clouds rush westwardly forever, until they roll, a cataract, over the fiery wall of the horizon. But there is no wind throughout the heaven. And by the shores of the river Zäire there is neither quiet nor silence.

" ' It was night, and the rain fell ; and, falling, it was rain, but, having fallen, it was blood. And I stood in the morass among the tall lilies, and the rain fell upon my head—and the lilies sighed one unto the other in the solemnity of their desolation.

" ' And, all at once, the moon arose through the thin ghastly mist, and was crimson in color. And mine eyes fell upon a huge gray rock which stood by the shore of the river, and was lighted by the light of the moon. And the rock was gray, and ghastly, and tall,—and the rock was gray. Upon its front were characters engraven in the stone ; and I walked through the morass of water-lilies, until I came close unto the shore, that I might read the characters upon the stone. But I could not decipher them. And I was going back into the morass, when the moon shone with a fuller red, and I turned and looked again upon the rock, and upon the characters ; and the characters were DESOLATION.

"'And I looked upward, and there stood a man upon the summit of the rock; and I hid myself among the water-lilies that I might discover the actions of the man. And the man was tall and stately in form, and was wrapped up from his shoulders to his feet in the toga of old Rome. And the outlines of his figure were indistinct—but his features were the features of a deity; for the mantle of the night, and of the mist, and of the moon, and of the dew, had left uncovered the features of his face. And his brow was lofty with thought, and his eye wild with care; and in the few furrows upon his cheek I read the fables of sorrow, and weariness, and disgust with mankind, and a longing after solitude.

"'And the man sat upon a rock, and leaned his head upon his hand, and looked out upon the desolation. He looked down into the low unquiet shrubbery, and up into the tall primeval trees, and up higher at the rustling heaven, and into the crimson moon. And I lay close within shelter of the lilies, and observed the actions of the man. And the man trembled in the solitude;—but the night waned, and he sat upon the rock.

"'And the man turned his attention from the heaven, and looked out upon the dreary river Zäire, and upon the yellow ghastly waters, and upon the pale legions of the water-lilies. And the man listened to the sighs of the water-lilies, and to the murmur that came up from among them. And I lay close within my covert and observed the actions of the man. And the man trembled in the solitude;—but the night waned, and he sat upon the rock.

"'Then I went down into the recesses of the morass and waded afar in among the wilderness of lilies, and called upon the hippopotami which dwelt among the fens in the recesses of the morass. And the hippopotami heard my call, and came, with the behemoth, unto the foot of the rock, and roared loudly and fearfully beneath the moon. And I lay close within my covert and observed the actions of the man. And the man trembled in the solitude;—but the night waned, and he sat upon the rock.

"'Then I cursed the elements with the curse of tumult; and a frightful tempest gathered in the heaven, where before there had been no wind. And the heaven became livid with the violence of the tempest—and the rain beat upon the head of the man—and the flood of the river came down—and the river was tormented into foam—and the water-lilies shrieked within their beds—and the forest crumbled before the wind—and the thunder rolled—and the lightning fell—and the rock rocked to its foundation. And I lay close within my covert and observed the actions of the man. And the man trembled in the solitude; —but the night waned, and he sat upon the rock.

"Then I grew angry, and cursed with the curse of *silence*, the river, and the lilies, and the wind, and the forest, and the heavens, and the thunder, and the sighs of the water-lilies, And they became accursed and *were still*. And the moon ceased to totter up its pathway to heaven—and the thunder died away—and the lightning did not flash—and the clouds hung motionless—and the waters sunk to their level and remained—and the trees ceased to rock—and the water-lilies sighed no more—and the murmur was heard no longer among them, nor any shadow of sound throughout the vast illimitable desert. And I looked upon the characters of the rock, and they were changed, and the characters were SILENCE.

"'And mine eyes fell upon the countenance of the man, and his countenance was wan with terror. And hurriedly, he raised his head from his hand, and stood forth upon the rock and listened. But there was no voice throughout the vast illimitable desert, and the characters upon the rocks were SILENCE. And the man shuddered, and turned his face away, and fled afar off, in haste, so that I beheld him no more."

*　　　*　　　*　　　*　　　*　　　*　　　*

"Now there are fine tales in the volumes of the Magi—in the iron-bound, melancholy volumes of the Magi. Therein, I say, are glorious histories of the Heaven, and of the Earth, and of the mighty sea—and of the genii that overruled the sea, and the Earth, and the lofty Heaven. There was much lore too in the sayings which were said by the sibyls; and holy, holy things were heard of old by the dim leaves that trembled round Dodona—but, as Allah liveth, that fable which the Demon told me as he sat by my side in the shadow of the tomb, I hold to be the most wonderful of all! And as the Demon made an end of his story, he fell back within the cavity of the tomb and laughed. And I could not laugh with the Demon, and he cursed me because I could not laugh. And the lynx which dwelleth forever in the tomb, came out therefrom, and lay down at the feet of the Demon, and looked at him steadily in the face."

This ambitious sketch is the best example of Poe's deliberate picture-writing, and on the whole it must be called thin and artificial. The quality of artificiality is the bane that poisons much of his work. Where his conceptions were at once original and within the scope of his mental powers, they were presented with an art that will live; where he sought to startle or impress by useless incantations he very naturally and speedily failed. It is easy to imagine how De Quincey or Hawthorne would have written " Silence," and it would not have been in this thin and impoverished style, with its multiplicity of "ands" and its downright carelessness where art should have been flawless. "And the hippopotami heard my call, and came, with the behemoth, unto the foot of the rock, and roared loudly and fearfully beneath the moon." That is, the hippopotami came with the hippopotamus and so managed their snorting and blowing as to produce a loud and fearful roar. This is not the only production of Poe in which he seems like a sublimated sophomore.

Time has done much, within the space of the forty years that have elapsed since the poet's death, to correct misjudgments concerning Poe's

life and work. The mass of writing concerning
him—critical, laudatory, or denuncia-
tory—has not been exceeded in the Time and Poe.
case of any other American writer. At the one
extreme of opinion is the curt and contempt-
uous statement that his writings, if now freshly
offered to the public of readers, would not attract
serious attention. At the other are such words as
M. Jules Lemaitre (in his " Dialogue des Morts,
a propos de la préface du ' Prétre de Nemi '" *)
puts into the poet's mouth :

"*Edgard Poe.*—Vous dites bien. J'ai vecu vingt-trois
siècles après Platon et trois cents ans après Shakespeare, à
quelque douze cents lieues de Londres et à quelque deux milles
lieues d'Athenes, dans un continent que nul ne connaissait au
temps de Platon. J'ai été un malade et un fou; j'ai éprouvé
plus que personne avant moi la terreur de l'inconnu, du noir,
du mystérieux, de l'inexpliqué. J'ai été le poète des halluci-
nations et des vertigues; j'ai été le poète de la Peur. J'ai
développé dans un style précis et froid la logique secrète des
folies, et j'ai exprimé des etats de conscience que l'auteur d'
Hamlet lui-meme n'a pressenti que deux ou trois fois. Peut-
être aurait-on raison de dire que je différe moins de Shakespeare que de Platon: mais il reste vrai que nous presentons
trois exemplaires de l'espece humaine aussi dissemblables que
possible."

Plato, Shakespeare and Poe!—is our bard, luck-
less in life, to go down the ages in such company
as this, gravely weighed and compared with the
very masters of the human mind? Is he absolutely matchless in his delineations of the terror
that lurks in the shade of the soul's mysterious

* *Les Lettres et les Arts,* Janvier, 1886.

night-time? Not so, the French admirers of his genius, misled by the intensity of a taste national rather than catholic, would give to the clever magician honors belonging to the profound philosopher. Poe is absolute master only of the young or the superficially impressionable. He cannot affect our whole lives as does a Hawthorne in prose, nor can his eye sweep from zenith to nadir in the poetic vision of Emerson. His realm of heaven-lit night is narrow, and his rule is that of a noble and not of a king; but realm and rule will endure.

CHAPTER V.

EMERSON AS POET.

The literary history of past centuries, in many lands, shows to us numerous prose-writers who have written verse, and not a few poets whose prose letters, journals, or weightier works have been treasured up. Prose is the natural utterance of the mind; therefore it falls from poets' lips or pens; poetry is the highest form of literature, therefore it is essayed by those who write chiefly in prose. But not until the nineteenth century have authors of eminence written in prose and in verse almost indifferently, and with nicely balanced success. The greater poets of contemporary England, indeed, still write verse alone. The tendency of the time, however, is to make the man of letters seek many modes of expression, and try varied forms of work. In America, with much to say and to do, with the pressure of newness ever making itself felt upon the mind, most poets write prose at wish or at need, and eminent prose-writers are not guiltless of "iambs and pentameters." Longfellow gave us a sentimental romance, an idyllic novelette, and some good criticisms; the young Whittier was biographer, essayist, or historical novelist; Bryant was traveller and commemorative orator, and in his

Poetry and Prose.

youth could spin a fair tale in prose; Poe's high
continental renown is based upon his tales as truly
as upon his poems; Holmes the Autocrat, and Professor, and novelist, shares honor with Holmes
the poet of "The Last Leaf" and "The Deacon's
Masterpiece"; and Lowell, in the time devoted to
criticism of others, has stolen that which would
have enhanced his standing in the muses' court.

The prose of Longfellow, Whittier, and Bryant
will pass out of sight; and prose *or* verse rather
than prose *and* verse, will finally be preferred by
the test of time in other cases. In the writings of
Ralph Waldo Emerson, however, they
need not be and cannot be separated in
final verdict or present estimate. Emerson was a seer and utterer; a great mind looking out upon the universe, and telling the world
what he saw and thought. His words were spoken
in prose or poetry as seemed to him fit; but the
purpose and the general plan were ever the same.
There is no intrinsic reason why his prose and
verse should be considered in separate chapters.
Their treatment in different volumes of this history
forms, I believe, the only notable exception to the
general desirability of the plan of the work,
whereby, in symmetrical progress, the two great
divisions of non-imaginative and imaginative
American writings are viewed without vexatious
interruption. Even in Emerson's case, however,
the changed point of view—as in looking at Canterbury Cathedral—but illustrates the variant
unity of a great intellectual product.

Ralph Waldo
Emerson,
1803-1882.

The poetry of Emerson occupies a peculiar position. It is obedient, as a rule, to the canons of poetic art; much of it is highly lyrical and of exquisite finish; but on the whole it is simply to be considered as a medium for the expression of thought which could not so concisely be uttered in prose. When Emerson wished to speak with peculiar terseness, with unusual exaltation, with special depth of meaning, with the utmost intensity of conviction, he spoke in poetic form. He who misses this fact cannot rightly interpret Emerson the poet.

His themes are of the highest that can engage the singer's or the sayer's attention. The collected body of his verse, in the final edition, is but a single volume of moderate size; but within those three hundred pages how much is packed! Emerson stands on our *Emerson's Poetic Theme.* earth in the middle years of the nineteenth century, and looks about him. He peers into the past of Greece and Rome, of Palestine and Egypt, and of remoter India. He studies minutely the woods, and waters, and birds, and beasts, and men and women of his town and neighborhood. He gazes upward to the stars of heaven and downward to the central fires. He stands by the bed of sickness and the open grave, and peers beyond to the hereafter of the soul. In all he is the optimist rather than the pessimist, the philosopher, not the mere bystander. Idealism appears to him a thing lovely and of eternal truth; materialism hateful, and to die with the perishing matter

from which it sprung. Above and in all, for him,
is the spiritual meaning and mission of nature to
the individual soul. For that soul the whole
universe is the ethical teacher.

For the reasons stated, one would expect to
find the poetry of Emerson irregular, unconven-
His Method and
Limitations. tional, at times careless. Emerson
was too much an artist to neglect the
artistic element, but it is invariably made subor-
dinate. Clear expression of high thought is his
perpetual desire. His very wish to be terse sometimes makes him obscure, and oftener causes him
to seem obscure. In this respect, as in some
others, there is a parallel between Emerson and
Browning. The two poets, with manifold differences of mind and of method, are at one in their
broad view of life's mysteries and duties, and of
the poet's relation to God and to man. Both are
unpopular among the multitude, and beloved by
the few to whom they are masters and benefac-
tors. Emerson could not be, like Browning at
times, a stirring lyrical poet of battle and of the
fire of life, but he could be sweetly melodious,
charming his readers and hearers by the form and
expression of his song. Not a constructive dramatist, Emerson had the dramatic instinct in so far
that he could put himself in the stead of others,
and imagine himself in a "far or forgot" place
and time. As a poet, he sung when he must or
would, not merely when he should or could.
Emerson, in his last years, declared that Longfellow wrote too much; Longfellow might have

retorted that Emerson wrote too little. In Longfellow, true poet though he was, art sometimes
usurped the place of genius ; in Emerson, genius
too often refused the needed aid of art. Emerson
could write a poem "round and perfect as a star,"
or set "jewels five words long" in immortal verse ;
but, like Wordsworth, he sometimes strayed into
the regions of the ridiculous. His devotion to
poetic art increased toward the close of his life ;
his later poems show a gain in form and finish,
and he left behind him unpublished pieces surpassing not a few of those printed in his first
book of verse. On the whole, however, there is
a certain impression left upon the minds of the
readers of Emerson's verse which, for lack of a
better expression, may be described by the word
fragmentary. It should by no means be implied
that his poems are mere broken bits of genius, or
imperfect indications of the irregular powers of an
idle or self-destructive mind. The mere supposi-
tion would be absurd. An English critic has said
of Coleridge, as poet : "all that he did excellently might be bound up in twenty pages, but it
should be bound in pure gold." The poems of
Emerson are golden leaves which do not need to
be bound separately from his prose essays, of
which they are the companion and interpreter.
Whatever fragmentary character they may have
is due not to failure or incompleteness, but to the
fact that Emerson was, in a true sense, a sort of
oracular philosopher and prophet ; and philoso-
phers and prophets do not feel bound to produce

epics in twelve books, or dramas in five acts, or even blank verse poems, fifty pages long. When Emerson had said his say in verse, he stopped. His poems are more artistic, of course, than his essays; more than the essays, they have their fixed beginnings, progress and end; verse, in Emerson's mind, was the finest condensation of thought and utterance. That rigid and austere governance of English verse which Gray got from classic study, Emerson derived, when he wished, from the nature of his own mind. Even in his poems that apparently run rapidly on, each line is packed with thought—packed so closely, sometimes, that the wise reader cannot discover what the poet meant to say.

The poetry of Emerson is by no means that of a mere preacher. In a previous criticism I once said of him: "Both in poetry and in prose his influence is as spontaneous as that of nature; he announces, and lets others plead." I may be permitted to repeat the statement, for convenience' sake, because I cannot better claim for him the character and work of the true poet. Keats himself, in his world-famous line, " A thing of beauty is a joy forever," did not more loyally or more fitly describe nature's and poetry's self-existent loveliness than did Emerson in his poem, "The Rhodora: On being asked, Whence is the Flower?"

His Sponta-
neity.

"The Rho-
dora."

In May, when sea-winds pierced our solitudes,
I found the fresh Rhodora in the woods,
Spreading its leafless bloom in a damp nook,
To please the desert and the sluggish brook.

The purple petals, fallen in the pool,
Made the black water with their beauty gay;
Here might the red bird come his plumes to cool,
And court the flower that cheapens his array.
Rhodora! if the sages ask thee why
This charm is wasted on the earth and sky,
Tell them, dear, that if eyes were made for seeing,
Then Beauty is its own excuse for being:
Why thou wert there, O rival of the rose!
I never thought to ask, I never knew;
But in my simple ignorance, suppose
The self-same power that brought me there brought you.

This is the poet's *credo*, and it could hardly be better stated. It is not heartless "art for art's sake," nor does it try to make poetry "turn the crank of an opinion-mill." The poet sings because he must, for very joyance, and for the sharing of nature's beauty. But nature, in Emerson's verse, is something more than mere prettiness; it is now a mirror of mind, now a spiritual parable, now a revelation of the supernal goodness of the All-maker. Thus viewed, nature becomes an inspiration unknown to the materialist, on the one hand, or the sour moralizer over a "lost world," on the other. Emerson's poetry of nature has the broadest range, from noon-day sky to swampy pool, from snow-capped mountain to skipping squirrel on the tree:

For Nature beats in perfect tune,
And rounds with rhyme her every rune,
Whether she work in land or sea,
Or hide underground her alchemy.
Thou canst not wave thy staff in air,
Or dip thy paddle in the lake,

But it carves the bow of beauty there,
And the ripples in rhymes the oar forsake.
The wood and wave each other know,
Not unrelated, unallied,
But to each thought and thing allied,
Is perfect Nature's every part,
Rooted in the mighty Heart.

Emerson's general reputation as a writer dates from the publication of his essay on "Nature," which slowly worked its way into fame. The circumstance was no accident, for the material world, as the background—or, more properly, the companion and friend—of the intellectual and spiritual, is never long lost to sight in the prose pages of Emerson. In his verse it is equally important; <small>A poet of nature.</small> it would be as just to call Emerson the poet of nature as to apply the familiar phrase to Bryant. Nature-poetry made great progress between the time of Thomson and that of Shelley and Wordsworth. It would be idle and valueless to institute a comparison between poets as unlike as Wordsworth and Emerson; for the originality of the latter is unquestionable. In external form Shelley's "Life of life, thy lips enkindle" lyric in "Prometheus Unbound," which Mr. Palgrave, in his "Golden Treasury," entitles a "Hymn to the Spirit of Nature," is far from the Emersonian type; but Shelley and Emerson were not dissimilar in their rapt devotion to the beauty and all-pervading charm of the external world. Both were called pantheists, at one time or another; and the Englishman and the American reproduced, in various forms, certain Greek conceptions and expressions. The old truths, ancient as the world and fresh as the new dawn, are given a nineteenth-century application in many of Emerson's lines; take, for instance, a few stanzas from " The World Soul " :

> For Destiny never swerves,
>   Nor yields to men the helm;
> He shoots his thought, by hidden nerves,
>   Throughout the solid realm.
> The patient Dæmon sits,
>   With roses and a shroud ;
> He has his way, and deals his gifts,—
>   But ours is not allowed. . . . . .
>
> When the old world is sterile,
>   And the ages are effete,
> He will from wrecks and sediment
>   The fairer world complete.
> He forbids to despair;
>   His cheeks mantle with mirth ;
> And the unimagined good of men
>   Is yeaning at the birth.
>
> Spring still makes spring in the mind
>   When sixty years are told ;
> Love wakes anew this throbbing heart,
>   And we are never old.
> Over the winter glaciers
>   I see the summer glow,
> And through the wild-piled snowdrift
>   The warm rosebuds below.

Parts of these stanzas, and other parts of the same poem, suggest at once the relations between

10

Emerson s poetic thought and poetic expression.
Thought In the latter, we sometimes find art, some-
and times artlessness, sometimes deliberate
expression. crudity. A Tennyson or a Longfellow
would not have permitted some of the lines just
quoted to pass without artistic revision. Not
even Wordsworth pressed so dangerously near
as did Emerson at times, the borderland of what
is bald, or juvenile, or apparently silly. The third
and fourth stanzas of Emerson's poem on
" Tact " (dropped from the final edition) are sorry
doggerel :

> The maiden in danger
>   Was saved by the swain ;
> His stout arm restored her
>   To Broadway again.

> The maid would reward him,—
>   Gay company come,—
> They laugh, she laughs with them ;
>   He is moonstruck and dumb.

This is on the artistic level of Wordsworth's

> " Fretted by sallies of his mother's kisses,"

or that estimable stanza of the same pious poet :

> "'And now, as fitting is and right,
>   We in the church our faith will plight,
>   A husband and a wife ;'
>   Even so they did ; and I may say
>   That to sweet Ruth that happy day
>   Was more than human life."

Wordsworth, in his revolt against eighteenth
century academic poetry, went far toward the

absurdity of over simplicity; just as the pre-Raphaelite English poets and painters, half a century later, carried their rebellion against formalism so far that there could be found no stiffer formalists than themselves. This is an old story, in literary, artistic, political, and religious revivals.

Emerson's rawness and roughness were not due to the fact that he was trying to break down one school, or set up another. They resulted from his ever-present idea of the commanding importance of the thought, and the insignificance and relative unimportance of the means of expression. But Emerson, like Wordsworth before him and Browning beside him, was deliberate in his poetic utterance. If not always artistic in form, it was because he did not choose to be. Flat, and foolish, and egotistic as Wordsworth seems at times, he was the poet who sang to us of "faith become a passionate intuition;" of a violet

> "Fair as a star when only one
> Is shining in the sky;"

of

> "The light that never was on sea or land,
> The consecration, and the poet's dream."

The bard of "Peter Bell" was also the bard of the "Ode on Immortality" and the sonnet on sleeping London. So, too, whatever flaws we find in Emerson's verse, we also find such lordly and lovely lines as

> "Earth proudly wears the Parthenon
> As the best gem upon her zone."

lines that in themselves are a gem of poetry. Wordsworth hardly seemed to know when he was on the mountain-tops of art, and when in the valleys; but Emerson would measure his every mood and mental state.   Said he:

> " But in the mud and scum of things
>   There alway, alway something sings; "

and that song in his catholic ear was as sacred as the song of the spheres.   He was deliberate in his noblest lines and most polished poems; he was no less deliberate in his quaintest, most irregular, and cacophonous verses.   The poetry of Emerson must be taken as it is.   Its writer had the power, when he chose, to give it all needed adornment of art; he also had the will, when he deemed it necessary, to utter his thought in the baldest form.   With him the *must* was more potent than the *may;* he cared more for the *why* than for the *how.*

We thus can see and understand the position of the poetry of Emerson in the literature of his country and his time.   It is more truthful to call him a great man who wrote poems, than to call him a great poet.   It seems to me essential to remember this definition, that we may avoid errors in either direction.   His poetry at its best reaches heights which Longfellow or Bryant could not attain.   Its august purpose renders comparison with the verse of Poe utterly out of the question.   Emerson was a greater man than any one of these three; and once in a while he

wrote lines as artistic as Longfellow's, as stately as
Bryant's, as melodiously beautiful as Poe's. He
was more than an eminent prose writer who produced verse. His poetry would give him a high
reputation were his prose blotted out. And yet
his prose overshadows his verse ; his character as
literary force seems higher than his rank as poet.
His three hundred pages of poems, read them and
praise them and revere them as we will, but
restate concisely the message of his essays. So
long as this result was chosen by Emerson himself, his readers may well accept it without
regrets or attempts at denial. He wrote, as one
of his fragments tells us,

> " For thought, and not praise ;
> Thought is the wages
> For which I sell days,
> Will gladly sell ages,
> And willing grow old,
> Deaf and dumb and blind and cold."

Though Emerson conscientiously wrote " for
thought and not praise," from the beginning of
his career to its close, he could in a The Test of
limited but true sense be called a Popularity.
popular author, even before his death. Not one
word in his lectures or essays was apparently
written with popularity in view, yet he slowly
climbed to the sure height of a deserved renown
based on high achievement. I do not mean, of
course, that he ever found half as many readers as
the contemporary novelists of a day, whose

methods and movements the newspapers think so
important ; but he found a public of thoughtful,
studious, benefited, and sometimes raptly enthusiastic readers, which could both relatively and
absolutely be called a large public.   But these
readers were affected by his prose more than by
his verse, in the mathematical ratio in which the
quantity of his prose exceeds that of his verse.
In Emerson's lifetime appeared two volumes of
poems, and one book of selections from the two.
After his death was published a complete edition,
with previously uncollected fragments.   These
collections had a circulation small beside that of
the books of any other American poet of equal
standing.   This fact could not have been due to
the obscurity of Emerson's poems as a whole, for
some are "sun-clear"; nor to the remoteness of
their themes, for some treat of the simplest and
nearest emotions or natural objects ; nor to their
small bulk, which was greater than that of Gray's
or Poe's poetry.   Its cause, as I have said, is that
Emerson delivered his one message in many
forms, not all of which were designed for all
hearers and readers.

All the great poets of the world have been great
poetical artists.   In Homer, Sophocles, Virgil,
Dante, Milton, Shakespeare, we find not only the
power of thinking grandly and freshly, but also
of constructing nobly and decorating
beautifully.   Not many can endure a
comparison with these great makers of
the world's verse ; but if we pass to the list of

Emerson and
the Greater
Poets.

poets of the lesser order,—to Sappho, Horace,
Petrarch, Heine, Gray, Wordsworth,—we discover
a similar union of the internal with the external,
so that both make a poetic whole. Those who
aver that great nuggets of unpolished poetic
thought are to be accepted as readily as " Hamlet,"
the odes of Sappho and Horace, Gray's " Elegy,"
or Wordsworth's best sonnets, must revise the
entire intellectual and artistic history of the world.
It is perfectly true that

> "Thought is deeper than all speech,
> Feeling deeper than all thought,"

but it is equally true that wisdom must be married
to immortal verse before it can pretend to be immortal poetry. Feeling that cannot express itself in
formulated thought, thought that cannot embody
itself in fit speech, speech that cannot be framed
according to the noblest verbal art, may be true
and valuable, but are not poetry. We do not
propose to revise the artistic canons of all literary
history for the benefit of those who aver that the
poet need only throw before us a mass of jewels
and dirt, leaving to us the cleansing and polishing
of the occasional glittering stones. Emerson
makes for the poet no such claim as this. When
he gives us plain, compact instructions or reflections he pretends to do no more. When he gives
us deep thought in artistic form, then and
then only does he tacitly rank himself among the
poets. Sometimes he does the one, sometimes
the other. There is enough of his verse of the

latter kind to entitle him to the name of poet in the usual limited sense. Art and form, lovely and self-contained, find their place in not a few of his poems. When he courted the muse she smiled upon him; when he turned his back upon her he made no pretence of standing in her favor.

It may at first seem a paradox to say that the quality of evenness marks the poetry of Emerson. No American writer of verse more freely followed his will, in the choice and treatment of subjects. But there is no essential difference between his earliest verse and his latest. The chronological order, so important in studying the writings of some poets, is almost valueless in the case of Emerson. We know that certain of his poems were produced in his youth, and others in his maturity or old age. Some were written for occasions, or were drawn forth by that great civil war which threw its shadows across the seventh decade of the sage's life. But this knowledge is interesting, rather than essential, in the particular instance, and not valuable in the general estimate. In one of the stanzas just quoted Emerson reminds us that

Evenness of Emerson's Work.

> "Spring still makes spring in the mind
> When sixty years are told."

The noble lines are worth repeating. No modern writer more clearly shows the truth that immortal existence is an eternal now, notwithstanding the correlated law of beginnings and developments. Not even the fact that the man Emerson outlived

his mental powers can blind us to the perception
that the mind Emerson was of perennial freshness,
youthful and mature at once. This statement is
no idle compliment, in words that have lost their
meaning ; it goes to explain the poet's apprehension of remote India on the one hand and modern
Massachusetts on the other. He was as old as
the mystic Brahman and as young as a Middlesex
stripling. His heart and thought included the
Hindoo seer and the Concord farmer. Who
but he would write as the first line of a poem
bearing the far-off and ancient title, " Hamatreya,"
such a rugged list of contemporary American sur-
names as

> " Minott, Lee, Willard, Hosmer. Meriam, Flint " ?

But in such apparent eccentricity and roughness
he was not careless but deliberate. Here, and in
a hundred other instances, he was stating hoary
truth in the every-day language of his neighbors.
He frankly said :

> " What all the books of ages paint, I have."

In poetry, as in prose, Emerson prepared his
bits of material when he would, and afterward
elaborated them into symmetrical wholes, at leisure
or on the fit occasion. Some of these bits, never
elaborated, but printed posthumously as mere
" Fragments on the Poet and the Poetic Gift,"
are in themselves better than many poems which
have cost their authors

> " Long days of labor
> And nights devoid of ease."

Indeed, we have no reason to doubt that, in some true sense, Emerson labored long on such fine though fragmentary work as many of these incomplete poems or parts of poems. Let us read some of them at random, without classification, just as they were apparently written, and without trying to give them titles or explanations which they lack but do not need :

That book is good
Which puts me in a working mood.

Unless to thought is added will,
Apollo is an imbecile.

What parts, what gems, what colors shine,—
Ah, but I miss the grand design.

Forebore the ant-hill, shunned to tread,
In mercy, on one little head.

The brook sings on, but sings in vain,
Wanting the echo in my brain.

On bravely through the sunshine and the showers!
Time hath its work to do and we have ours.

Thou shalt not try
To plant thy shrivelled pedantry
On the shoulders of the sky.

Teach me your mood, O patient stars !
Who climb each night the ancient sky,
Leaving on space no shade, no scars,
No trace of age, no fear to die.

If bright the sun, he tarries,
All day his song is heard ;
And when he goes, he carries
No more baggage than a bird.

But Nature whistled with all her winds,
Did as she pleased and went her way.

The passing moment is an edifice
Which the omnipotent cannot rebuild.

Tell men what they knew before;
Paint the prospect from their door.

From such fragments as these, quoted as left in Emerson's manuscript and printed by his literary executor after his death, there is no long step to the finish and completeness of his stately poem entitled "Days:"

Daughters of Time, the hypocritic days,
Muffled and dumb like barefoot dervishes,
And marching single in an endless file,
Bring diadems and fagots in their hands.
To each they offer gifts after his will,
Bread, kingdoms, stars, and sky that holds them all.
I, in my pleachéd garden, watched the pomp,
Forgot my morning wishes, hastily
Took a few herbs and apples, and the Day
Turned and departed silent. I, too late,
Under her solemn fillet saw the scorn.

This posthumously published quatrain is in its way as complete as an epic:

Go, if thou wilt, ambrosial flower,
Go match thee with thy seeming peers;
I will wait Heaven's perfect hour
Through the innumerable years.

The thoughts and wordings of the last pages of Emerson's volume of poems send the reader's mind wandering back through the centuries, from Walter Savage Landor to the Greek anthology.

Emerson, never a deep classicist, was sometimes half Greek in his way of looking at things, and also in his way of wording his thought. The statement seems either an exaggeration or a platitude, but I know not how to express my meaning in other language.

The compactness of Emerson's writing, whether in prose or in verse, is apparent to the most careless reader. The quatrain I have just quoted, "Teach me your mood, O patient stars", really includes the thought and the lesson of the eight stanzas comprising one of Matthew Arnold's best known poems, that beginning:

His conciseness.

> "Weary of myself, and sick of asking
>   What I am, and what I ought to be,
> At this vessel's prow I stand, which bears me
>   Forward, forward, o'er the starlit sea."

Emerson's four lines surpass, I think, the best four lines of Arnold's thirty-two, which are:

> "From the intense, clear, star-sown vault of Heaven,
>   Over the lit sea's unquiet way,
> In the rustling night-air came the answer:
>   'Wouldst thou *be* as these are? *Live* as they.'"

The superiority extends not only to the quatrain as compared with the poem, but to the choice of particular epithets and phrases. One of Mrs. Browning's best sonnets,

> "'O dreary life!' we cry, 'O dreary life,'"

has the same theme and general method; and though it comes nearer Emerson's felicity, with

" * * the unwasted stars that pass
In their old glory,"

it does not surpass that felicity. Mrs. Browning's thought was sometimes fused and compacted by the fires of intense feeling, but Emerson's was made concise by calm and cold selection. Yet his calm is not the calm of Arnold, himself sometimes as diffuse as Mrs. Browning; but that of one who will not speak or sing at all until the urgency of his poetic desire is joined with the sense of fitness of poetic expression. This statement applies even to the queerest and most rapidly moving of Emerson's metres. Aside from the question of the value of his poems, we cannot deny that they were the best he could write. The apt union of words and thought in "The Snow-Storm" is as good a proof of this "The Snow-proposition as can be found: Storm."

Announced by all the trumpets of the sky,
Arrives the snow, and, driving o'er the fields,
Seems nowhere to alight: the whited air
Hides hills and woods, the river, and the heaven,
And veils the farm-house at the garden's end.
The sled and traveller stopped, the courier's feet
Delayed, all friends shut out, the housemates sit
Around the radiant fireplace, enclosed
In a tumultuous privacy of storm.

Come see the north wind's masonry.
Out of an unseen quarry evermore
Furnished with tile, the fierce artificer
Curves his white bastions with projected roof
Round every winded stake, or tree, or door.
Speeding, the myriad-handed, his wild work

So fanciful, so savage, naught cares he
For number or proportion. Mockingly,
On coop or kennel he hangs Parian wreaths ;
A swan-like form invests the hidden thorn ;
Fills up the farmer's lane from wall to wall,
Maugre the farmer's sighs ; and, at the gate,
A tapering turret overtops the work.
And when his hours are numbered, and the world
Is all his own, retiring, as he were not,
Leaves, when the sun appears, astonished Art
To mimic in slow structures, stone by stone,
Built in an age, the mad wind's night-work ;
The frolic architecture of the snow.

This is as simple a nature-poem as Whittier's
"Snow-Bound,"—less subjective, indeed, and
much less subjective than two other of New
England's notable winter-pieces, Longfellow's
"Snowflakes" and Lowell's "The First Snow-
Fall." The seer and the mystic could treat nature in the simplest descriptive fashion when he
had no other purpose in view ; and seldom was he
so inexcusably inaccurate an observer as in the
first line of the poem just quoted. No simpler or
more Saxon language need be asked than that in
which are written such poems as the "The Rhodora," "The Humble-Bee," "Woodnotes," or
"Ode to Beauty," some of which teach deep
spiritual and vital lessons. Johnsonian expressions and Latinized words are also conspicuously
absent from "The Problem" and "Initial, Dæmo-
nic, and Celestial Love," despite the portentous
title of the latter. This poet's method of teaching
is well-illustrated in his "Hamatreya." He begins

by giving a list of some of his neighboring families in Concord; tells how they owned land, raised crops, added field to field, and then were laid under their own sod, "a lump of mould the more." Then comes, in the "Earth-Song," the moral of it · "Hamatreya."

> Mine and yours;
> Mine, not yours.
> Earth endures;
> Stars abide—
> Shine down in the old sea;
> Old are the shores;
> But where are old men?
> I who have seen much,
> Such have I never seen.
>
> The lawyer's deed
> Ran sure,
> In tail,
> To them, and to their heirs
> Who shall succeed,
> Without fail,
> Forevermore.
>
> Here is the land
> Shaggy with wood,
> With its old valley,
> Mound and flood.
> But the heritors?—
> Fled like the flood's foam.
> The lawyer, and the laws,
> And the kingdom,
> Clean swept herefrom.
>
> They called me theirs,
> Who so controlled me;

Yet every one
Wished to stay, and is gone.
How am I theirs
If they cannot hold me,
But I hold them ?—

When I heard the earth-song,
I was no longer brave ;
My avarice cooled
Like lust in the chill of the grave.

In bold simplicity this curious " Earth-Song " reminds one of the earliest poetry of the Saxons, Teutons, or Icelanders. The suggestion of parts of the " Elder Edda " is peculiarly strong, and in grim earnestness the poem also recalls the expressions of the Hebrew psalmist. If Emerson had called " Hamatreya " a sermon, with Psalm xlix: 10, 11 for its text, he would have been strictly accurate ; for what is the poem but an expansion of the idea of the two verses of the Hebrew poet :

" The fool and the brutish together perish,
And leave their wealth to others.
Their inward thought is, that their houses shall con-
tinue forever,
And their dwelling-places to all generations ;
They call their lands after their own names."

On the heights of poetry one is often reminded of Æschylus, Sophocles, Dante, Shakespeare, Milton, but not less truly of David, Job, Isaiah, and Joel. We have become so accustomed to call the Bible " holy," and to make it a fetich, that we half forget to call it literature. Emerson and the

greater minds, however, have not forgotten the
literary character of its best books, which they
paraphrase both consciously and unconsciously.

Emerson's conciseness of expression and his
loftiness of religious thought may further be
illustrated by quoting, entire, one other poem,
that which he entitled " Brahma." This much
discussed and almost famous utterance
appeared in the first number (November, " Brahma."
1857) of *The Atlantic Monthly*, and stirred those
circles in which the name of Emerson was considered honorable. Not even the members of the
Emersonian cult were able to give it unanimous
approval, or to aver that they all understood its
meaning. To the uninitiated it was food for
laughter, or at best an interesting puzzle, about as
intelligible to a modern reader as the Riddles of
Cynewulf—the hardest reading in the English
language. Emerson's biographer * says, with his
habitual neatness of wit, that " to the average
Western mind it is the nearest approach to a Tor-
ricellian vacuum of intelligibility that language
can pump out of itself." I do not read Emerson
on my knees, sure that his every word is crammed
with wisdom ; and I make not the slightest claim
to peculiar literary insight. Certainly, too, one
must feel a little diffidence in questioning so
deliberate a statement as Dr. Holmes makes when
he says that " Brahma " was " one of his [Emer-
son's] spiritual divertisements" ; and that Emerson merely " amused himself with putting in

* Oliver Wendell Holmes, " Ralph Waldo Emerson," p. 397.

11

verse." "the 'Yoga' doctrine of Brahmanism."
"The oriental side of Emerson's nature delighted
itself in these narcotic dreams, born in the land of
the poppy and of hashish. They lend a peculiar
charm to his poems, but it is not worth while to
try to construct a philosophy out of them." Of
course not; Emerson would have been the last
to claim that "Brahma," or fifty poems combined,
offered the reader a complete philosophy. But
I cannot call "Brahma" a "divertisement" until
I am ready to apply the same term to Coleridge's
"Hymn Before Sunrise in the Vale of Cha-
mouni," or Shelley's "Life of Life, thy lips
enkindle." The poem is dramatic; Emerson is
not speaking for himself, save as every dramatic
or subjective poet must; and his theme and
reflection are of a far-away land and soul. But
"Brahma," given its subject, is simple and
austere. Certainly it does not belong with the
class of poems to which Dr. Holmes by implication assigns it when he says a little farther on:
"Emerson's reflections in the 'transcendental'
mood do beyond question sometimes irresistibly
suggest the close neighborhood of the sublime to
the ridiculous. But very near that precipitous
border-land there is a charmed region where, if
the statelier growths of philosophy die out and
disappear, the flowers of poetry next the very
edge of the chasm have a peculiar and mysterious
beauty." Nothing would be easier than to cull
from Emerson lines, stanzas, and whole poems
that seem, and are, across the border-land of the

ridiculous. Emerson himself tacitly acknowledged the fact, in his revisions; and there is no reason why his students should deny it. To prove it by quotations would be superfluous, for the winnowing of time has already thrown to oblivious winds most of the Emersonian chaff, which, after all, is but a very fraction of his poetic crop. Enough that is good remains, and "Brahma," unless I am sadly mistaken, is a part of this selected and choice remainder. Read it again :

> If the red slayer thinks he slays,
>   Or if the slain think he is slain,
> They know not well the subtle ways
>   I keep, and pass, and turn again.
>
> Far or forgot to me is near;
>   Shadow and sunlight are the same;
> The vanished gods to me appear;
>   And one to me are shame and fame.
>
> They reckon ill who leave me out;
>   When me they fly, I am the wings;
> I am the doubter and the doubt,
>   And I the hymn the Brahmin sings.
>
> The strong gods pine for my abode,
>   And pine in vain the sacred Seven;
> But thou, meek lover of the good!
>   Find me, and turn thy back on heaven.

A paraphrase of this brief poem seems almost superfluous and absurd, and cannot, in prose, equal its terseness of expression : If he who kills think that his act is final, if he who is killed think that he falls without present part in the divine plan, or future hope, neither has any idea of that rule of the universe which bides long for the full adjustment after seeming indifference and delay. Divine power is omnipresent and omniscient ; in its plans virtue and vice play their appointed parts ; of it the rude divinities of the past were prototypes ; and its measures of man's success or failure are not the world's measures.   To be without God in the world is to die to all true life, for he is all and in all ; he recognizes his own among those deemed heretical, as well as in the services of the "orthodox" churches or religions of any age.   The greatest and best have longed for him, but he is found most by those who are meek and self-sacrificing, and who do not good works for the mere hope of reward.

Thus does Emerson, from an oriental text, re-state the lesson of man's relation to him whom the Anglo-Saxon poet named in that mighty word, "All-walda," and whom the Hebrews called Jehovah.   Some parts of the poem could be paralleled from the words of the Bible, which instantly occur to the mind in connection with such lines as "Far or forgot to me is near," or "When me they fly, I am the wings."   The paraphrase in the last instance must have been intentional.   That God is in nature, that man aspires to complete communion with God, and that high love is the means toward this communion—if this thought is obscure then the founders of Christianity were themselves riddle-makers.*

The poetry of Emerson is valued, at least in some of its parts, both by those who find enjoyment in smoothly lyrical expression of common and obvious meditation or observa- General tion, and by those who are willing estimate of Emerson's to give to verse a deep study, if but that Poetry. study be rewarded by the discovery of intrinsically valuable or novel thought. Here are pure sunshine and simple bird songs—the mere pleasure of existence and joyous perception; here, too, are intense peerings toward zenith and nadir. Emerson's verse, like his prose, might not inaptly be called "Thoughts on the Universe,"—the title of the *magnum opus* of Master Byles Gridley, in Dr. Holmes' novel "The Guardian Angel." The universe, in Emerson's eyes, was a great and ever-present ideal teacher, whose lessons he studied and tried to interpret for others. Sentient and

---

* Interesting parallelisms between "Brahma" and "Hamatreya" and passages from Eastern and other sources which may have been suggestive to Emerson's mind are given by several correspondents of *The Critic*, Feb. 4, Feb. 18, and March 3, 1888. Dr. C. A. Bartol's communication of the last date is so valuable a comment that it is worth preservation here:

"The store Emerson at one time set by this poem ['Brahma'] appears from his resisting, as Mr. J. T. Fields told me he did, a proposal to omit it from a collection the publishers were making of his works. This he said must go in, whatever else stayed out. Not that he thought much of his verses in general. To Dr. F. H. Hedge he said that he composed lines because he happened to have a nice lead-pencil and some good paper. He told Mr. Sanborn he doubted if he could write poetry, to which the reply was, 'Some of us think you can write nothing else.' But he disparaged his own rhymes and put none of them into 'Parnassus.' Perhaps it was his admiration of the Oriental genius that made him insist on the claim of

non-sentient Nature, with the individual and self-reliant soul at the top, mirrors for that soul the spiritual element, instructs and helps it, and foretells the future which its Maker has in store for the upward-striving creatures made in his own image. This sentence may be said, not unfairly, to be the key-note of Emerson's oft-expressed answers to the riddle of life. The answers are—as I have said—in substance identical, whether expressed in poetry or in prose; the poems, at their best, are more concise than the prose, more intense, and more ideal in thought and expression; at their worst, they are more obscure, fragmentary, and unsatisfactory. The union of blind thought and crude art is a dreary thing, but it is a thing too often present in Emerson's verse. His poetry was his serenest heaven and his most convenient rubbish-heap.

Some of the statements thus far made are sufficient to explain the present and probably the future lack of the highest fame for Emerson's

Brahma. It went, indeed, to the heart of his religion and philosophy, in which the *One* was all. To a friend doubting immortality, he said such a question betrayed lack of intellect. But he did not think Jesus taught it as a doctrine apart from life. In his last days he affirmed for the soul *identity* despite death, whether he meant individual persistence, or the oneness with the Father Jesus affirmed, or both as conjoined in the same truth. What he resented was any implication of that truth with a particular period, here or hereafter, of time. Infinite Presence forbade, with him, consideration of there or then. His idea of spirit as eternal and its own evidence disinclined him to spiritualism or the acceptance of any prodigy as proof, or to transmigration as the process of survival. Yet the charm for him of speculation in all the religious books of the far East indicates a peculiar constitution in an American, and is one of the most interesting facts in our literary history."

verse. Popularity is a relative term; in Its Future. one sense Sophocles, Dante, and Shakespeare are not popular. Without stopping to discuss this broad question, it is evident that Emerson, though deserving, as we have seen, to be called a favored writer, is not popular as poet, in the sense in which we apply the adjective to Shelley or Keats, Bryant or Longfellow, for instance. His own prose has reached many highly intelligent minds to which his verse is still comparatively unwelcome. This fact is not wholly due to the general intelligibility and popularity of prose as compared with poetry; for it is equally true, by converse, that the wings of song can carry a thought farther afield than the slow steps of prose; and that a poem is more likely to be widely loved than is an essay. Emerson's own verse shows that his highest and noblest poems, when most artistically written, are the most widely popular. Orphic sayings, bluntly or rudely put, may fail because of their bluntness; but the same high thought, nobly sung in melodious numbers, will become widely current. Shakespeare is not world-famous because he is superficial, but because he fitly words the deepest thoughts of the race. We may properly conclude, therefore, that the failure of a part of Emerson's poetry, compared with that produced by minds of the same general literary rank, or with the average of his own prose, was his own fault and not that of his readers. In a certain way he failed for the same reason that the classicist Walter Savage Landor failed; but

Emerson's prose, of course, so far surpasses
Landor's that it throws a friendly radiance on his
kindred verse. Landor was a poet of limited but
true power, who also wrote prose; Emerson wrote
both poetry and prose, for an identical purpose;
the likeness between Landor and Emerson rests
in the fact that they did not impress their poetic
gift upon the world-heart as the great poet ought
to do. No amount of special pleading can deny
the fact that ultimate high success is the final seal
of the poet's mission.

But in speaking of Emerson's failure the term
is used relatively, and with reference to no
more than a part of his verse. He wrote poetry
under peculiar circumstances and with peculiar
aims. His purposes were self-recognized, and
they met with all the success he
*Success as far
as Success was
sought.* desired or expected. His limitations
and terminations were known to none
better than to himself:

> Best boon of life is presence of a Muse
> That does not wish to wander, comes by stealth,
> Divulging to the heart she sets on flame
> No popular tale or toy, no cheap renown.

So long as his heart was set on flame he cared
neither for cheap renown nor for high. He
knew what he did not do, or could not do, as well
as what he did and could. A serene nature like
his would be the last to complain; it made the
most of itself, and that was enough, in both senses
of the word. Emerson gave us so much that

there is no reason for lamenting that he did not give more. He was neither one who was cut off in youth, like Keats, nor one who left only exquisite fragments, like Coleridge. No American had a better right than he to say (in his poem entitled " Terminus ") that he obeyed the voice at eve obeyed at prime.

The poetry of Emerson, whatever its special manner or theme, is the poetry of acquiescence, optimism, idealism, spiritualism, individualism. It often has a didactic and magisterial The Poetry of tone, rather than the moralizing tone of an Optimist. Wordsworth or Cowper. " Do this," "shun that," it swiftly says. " Be not a fool, not a money-maker, but a poet and a lover of the beautiful and the good." Nature, rightly understood, is a fit and lovely thing, and so is the soul at its best. Poetry notes and intensely describes some of the qualities of each, or of both. It was no wonder that Emerson anticipated, in half-a-dozen poems, the later conclusions of the evolutionists. He was the singer of the upward march of nature and the onward march of man. His poetic field was too broad to be tilled thoroughly in many parts. He was too proverbial to be a great constructive artist. He gives us saws, sayings, admonitions, flashes, glimpses, few broad constructed pictures. With these we are content, and do not ask him for epics, tragedies, or " Excursions," having poems like those already named ; or " Good-bye, Proud World," " The Sphinx," and the " Concord Hymn " ; or lines like

He builded better than he knew;

Earth proudly wears the Parthenon
As the best gem upon her zone;

The silent organ loudest chants
The master's requiem;

And conscious law is king of kings;

Or music pours on mortals
Its beautiful disdain.

Emerson's poetic art was at times of exquisite quality, a lovely presentation of noble thought. The perfection of verbal melody exists when the reader or hearer cannot conceive of any other way of singing the thought; and not a few of Emerson's lines or poems well bear this test. When this art gives place to grim force we do not feel, as Lowell said of Whittier, that Emerson as poet is

"Both singing and striking in front of the war
And hitting his foes with the mallet of Thor,"

for Emerson's stern strength is not that of a Taillefer but rather that of a Saxon law-maker. He announces, with all his force, but does not wage war in defence of the sayings he has uttered with oracular positiveness. Emerson is one more illustration of the fact, too often forgotten, that a poet can be forcible and lyrical at the same time; rooted in cold, deep thought and giving to the warm winds the loveliest flowers of beauty. Emerson, more than any American poet, severely tests and almost defies the laws of poetics, as they have been deduced from other languages and applied to English scansion ; but yet from his work may be selected many an example proving anew that English is capable of fine and deliberate metrical and melodious effects. He who recognizes Emerson's aims and methods will attempt neither to prove all his failures to be glorious successes, which men are too blind to see ; nor to declare him rugged or unmelodious or obscure,—the poet who, when he would, could sing so sweet and clear a song.

CHAPTER VI.

POETS OF FREEDOM AND CULTURE: WHITTIER, LOWELL AND HOLMES.

IT would seem natural to look to the United States, the world's most successful experiment in democratic government, for a literature peculiarly expressive of the idea of freedom. A certain disappointment is therefore felt when one finds, in two centuries and a half of English his-

The Idea of Freedom in American Literature. tory on American soil, so much second-hand and second-rate theology, such weak and imitative semi-religious philosophy, and not a little that is conventional or negative as far as freedom is concerned, in Irving, Longfellow, and dozens of lesser writers. Is our literature, from the "Bay Psalm Book" upward, a pale reflection of better things abroad, unmarked by the national characteristics which commend the society and government of America to the half-reverent study of the old world, perplexed by the problems of the closing years of the nineteenth century?

Yet let us not forget, in the first place, that the ideas of Greek, Roman, French, German, or English individualism color but a small part of literature; so that no disproportionate claim should be made upon American writers. In the second place, when timid provincialism gave way,—and never did it sooner yield in a colony,—the line of freedom's light became strongly and constantly apparent in Franklin's state and miscellaneous papers; in hundreds of speeches, from Otis' and Henry's to Webster's and Lincoln's; in the spiritual protests or asseverations of Channing and Emerson; and here and there in the histories of Bancroft, Motley, and Parkman. Imaginative or ideal themes chosen by poet or romancer, though less closely connected with the liberty-thought, demand free air for their development; Hawthorne's democracy liked an aristocratic background, but it was democracy still, and in its love for humanity it studied aristocracy and feudalism from the outside. Cooper sometimes carried patriotism into Buncombe County; Bryant made the solemn hills preach discreet political sermons; Emerson's "Concord Hymn" is bone and sinew of the Saxon race in their latest home; and the poetry of our wars, though poor by absolute standards, is relatively not inferior to that of other lands. Fortunate indeed, and sufficiently prominent in the patriotism of its literature, is a country that within fifty years can produce such a singer for liberty and for home as Whittier, and can proffer, as in Lowell's verse, the hot fire of localism and the calm culture of deliberate study.

The prime rhetorical requisite is to have something to say; and so we demand of the would-be poet that he sing to us a true song. Whittier, in his passionate anti-slavery

<small>John Greenleaf Whittier, b. 1807.</small>

ballads, his lyrics and idyls of the plain New England home, and his serene hymns of religious trust, sings from the pure depths of a sincere soul. His verse is diffuse and of irregular merit ; from it there might be drawn an instructive glossary of mispronunciations and excruciating rhymes ; and it contains a large percentage of those "occasional" poems which would be a literary pest were they not so promptly and efficaciously covered by the recurrent tides of time. Yet Whittier, without being able to avail himself of the spoils of classical culture, and with all the disadvantages incident to the calling of the political poet, has succeeded by the strength of his conviction,—a conviction affecting, as well as relying upon, the spontaneous grace of a natural melodist. Sometimes his lame muse of language "goes halting along where he bids her go free"; but at other times thought and form unite in unstudied beauty. Not one of the chief American poets, in the strictest use of the adjective, Whittier has slowly reached, in a green old age, a recognized fame which the cold classicist in verse, or the restless sensationalist, might well envy. In fresh naturalness of utterance, as well as in his rise from the humble life of the sturdy New England Quaker yeomanry, he is in a small way the American Burns ; yet how different his serene and undisturbed career—amid the glare and hate of the anti-slavery conflict—from the woe and excess of the short life of the great Scotch lyrist !

The numerous books by Whittier, the non-sig-

nificant titles of which do not call for recapitula-
tion, have been for the most part small collections
of miscellaneous poems, taking their names from
the first, or longest, or most noteworthy lyrics or
descriptive pieces. He began to send Whittier's
"verses" to a local newspaper, printed Books.
near his Massachusetts birthplace, when he was
but seventeen. The muse of song beckoned him
when a farm-lad or shoemaker's helper, and she
still led him forward at fourscore years. At the
district school or the town academy of Haverhill,
and at the editor's desk in Haverhill, Boston,
Hartford, Philadelphia, or Washington, his
thought and pen were never long sundered, and
he produced an uninterrupted series of songs of
American country life; bugle blasts in the van of
freedom; or organ strains of deep religious faith
and hope. Whittier, on the whole, has lived
nearer the homely heart and life of his northern
countrymen than any other American poet, save
Longfellow. His reformatory lyrics have been
saved from a shrill strident tone by his refreshing
habit of turning aside to the simplest and most
peaceful country scenes and characters; and the
chief idyl of New England, "Snow-Bound,"
resembles "The Cotter's Saturday Night" in its
presentation of the soul as well as the body of the
people's life. With the exception of "Snow-
Bound," the greater part of his poetical product
has been exactly and constantly of the character
which attracts, instructs, and benefits for the time,
but lacks the inherent elements of perennial great-

ness. Whittier was honest and wise when he
said that, though not insensible to literary reputation, he set a higher value on his "name as
appended to the anti-slavery declaration of 1833
than on the title page of any book."

Behind all his work appears the character of
the man, which may be called more attractive
The Character than the work itself. Admiration spon-
of the Man. taneously and often springs toward the
sweet pictures and pure pathos of his village
poems, the burning force of his scornfully indignant lyrics attacking the horrors of human
enslavement, the story of the honored patriotism
of poor old Barbara Frietchie during the Confederate invasion of Maryland, the unfaltering trust
of such a religious utterance as "My Psalm."
But Whittier as idyllist, reformer, patriot, or
preacher is less closely connected with his readers'
hearts than Whittier the man. Criticism is not yet
quite ready to eliminate the personal element from
its estimates ; and nowhere else in American song
does that element come so near. The personal
and subjective poets are usually those who are
most fluent in descriptions of unimportant characteristics of their time and place ; and so
Whittier, like the greater Wordsworth, burdens
his pages with much that is trivial and inartistic.
His subjectivity, too, like Longfellow's, is for the
most part of an obvious and readily intelligible
kind. And yet shall the clearness and common-
ness of love of home and country, memory of the
dead, hatred of cruelty, devotion to duty and

God, remand these sentiments to the lower order
of verse? Not so, thought Shakespeare. Whittier's art, imperfect in expression, is grounded in
the verities and eternities; his sentiment will live
when its utterance has ended a temporary work,
—and there is as yet no sign of death in "Maud
Muller," "Barbara Frietchie," "Skipper Ireson's
Ride," "In School-Days," "Laus Deo," or "Snow-
Bound." *

In Whittier, as in tens of thousands of the
world's brave soldiers, love of the country and
love of country seem almost identical. His country-
The young editor in various eastern heart.
cities never lost his constant and affectionate
memories of the lovely Essex county which gave
him birth; and he carried into his political work
the placid strength of the Merrimack in its
familiar meadows near the sea. Like Bryant,
Whittier has always been a ruralist at heart; but,
more fortunate than Bryant, he has spent the
latter half of his life amid the rustic scenes so
often portrayed in his verse. In the Revolution
and the civil war many a soldier, from North or
South, spent in flame and blood the strength
acquired in fields and woods; and so Whittier
the reformer has ever been all the mightier for
his country heart. His Friends' "inner light," too,
kept him from the uncharitable and unchristian
excesses of so many of the Abolitionists, whose

* Mr. Whittier's pleasant prose has already passed into the shadow,
and calls for no mention here; nor does his kindly and frequent service as
editor or preface-writer.

self-wisdom and self-righteousness would not brook the slightest divergence from the individual say-so. Had Whittier been less loving, he would have been a mere dogmatist and destructive ; had he been less stern, he would not have been found

> " Both singing and striking in front of the war
> And hitting his foes with the mallet of Thor."

It is not the poetry of politics, however impassioned or effective, upon which long renown is based. As the years go by, we chiefly prize Whittier's lyrics of anti-slavery and war Transient and permanent. for what they were rather than what they are. Even "Ichabod," wherein Whittier thought he wrote the doom of Webster's fame, is now read, if at all, because of its connection with an orator who is challenging Burke's renown in English prose. But when, in reform or in battle, the poet finds a theme which he transfigures with the glory of imaginative genius or intellectual might, the poem lives, like Milton's sonnet "On the Late Massacre in Piemont." Our war-verse thus keeps in its choicest division Whittier's noble ballad of "Barbara Frietchie," with its simple grace and its throb of the heart of all humanity. Though we pass by the "lines written for" this or that occasion, we treasure the stanzas of "The Farewell of a Virginia Slave Mother to her Daughters sold into Southern Bondage," for their lyrical swing is as attractive as their monitory woe is strong :

> Gone, gone,—sold and gone,
> To the rice-swamp dank and lone.

Where the slave-whip ceaseless swings,
Where the noisome insect stings,
Where the fever demon strews
Poison with the falling dews,
Where the sickly sunbeams glare
Through the hot and misty air,

> Gone, gone,—sold and gone,
> To the rice-swamp dank and lone,
> From Virginia's hills and waters,
> Woe is me, my stolen daughters!

This lyrical power is often and obviously present in Whittier—the power of sweetly singing a thought of ideal truth. Sometimes it is *Lyrical power.* manifested side by side with some rugged sign of haste in word or rhyme; sometimes its melody beautifies an entire poem. None but a poet could frame such lines as

The dear delight of doing good;

And pale remorse the ghost of sin;

Evermore the month of roses
Shall be sacred time to thee;

For thee thy sons shall nobly live,
And at thy need shall die for thee;
But life shall on and upward go;

Th' eternal step of progress beats
To that great anthem, calm and slow,
Which God repeats.

Whittier's readers readily admit that his mental character and chosen method of composition have scattered rich thoughts here and there, without striving, first of all, to co-ordinate them in artistic unities; but the pleasure and profit found in the somewhat random product amply atone for the apparently wayward defect. The "fatal fluency" to which criticism has made objection seems like self-sacrifice on the poet's part : he gives to humanity the songs he might have given to eternal art. Warm love, in the spiritual world, is better than cold praise ; and when the praise is deserved and given, it is glowing and free. After all, we are what we are, and each man, by being himself, gets his precise deserts in the world of letters as in the world of life. Whittier's lyrics remind us that if we cannot always have the results of hand-work and soul-work, we are at least spared the coldly technical success and its incident sense of spiritual disappointment. The simple song, the narrow range—and Whittier's homestead-love, humanitarianism, and piety are really one—are those we best love in our tenderer moods. Here, as in so many other in-stances, the poet has measured his powers and surveyed his field, and rests content with work and reward. Said Whittier, once : " I never had any methods. When I felt like it, I wrote, and I had neither the health nor patience to work over it afterward. It usually went as it was originally completed." But this spontaneous song-power is able at times to produce such a symmetrical and beautiful result as " The Pipes at Lucknow," which seems to me the lyrical masterpiece of Whittier, and the best of the poems called forth by the event described. It is all lovely, but the best stanzas for illustration are the three which follow :

> O, they listened, looked, and waited,
>   Till their hope became despair;
> And the sobs of low bewailing
>   Filled the pauses of their prayer.
> Then upspake a Scottish maiden,
>   With her ear unto the ground:
> "Dinna ye hear it?—dinna ye hear it?
>   The pipes o' Havelock sound!"

> Hushed the wounded man his groaning;
>   Hushed the wife her little ones;
> Alone they heard the drum-roll
>   And the roar of Sepoy guns.
> But to sounds of home and childhood
>   The Highland ear was true;—
> As her mother's cradle-crooning
>   The mountain pipes she knew.

> Like the march of soundless music
>   Through the vision of the seer,
> More of feeling than of hearing,
>   Of the heart than of the ear,
> She knew the droning pibroch,
>   She knew the Campbell's call,
> "Hark! hear ye no' MacGregor's,—
>   The grandest o' them all!"

The nature and exercise of Whittier's powers have been precisely those best calculated to promote his work as people's poet. A strong-souled man, trained in rural New England, early given the benefit of cosmopolitan work in troublous political times, at length permitted to return to his favorite country scenes,

Nature and exercise of Whittier's powers.

and belonging by inheritance and conviction to a
religious body making much of the "inner light"
of God in the heart, Whittier has by his free and
natural songs made freedom a duty and religion
a joy.   His genius is wholly instinctive and
national.   When peace followed the storms of
political struggle and of civil war, he returned
naturally to the themes and methods of nature
and the soul.   Unvexed by literary envy, and
oblivious to mere fame, he became the laureate of
the ocean beach, the inland lake, the little wood-
flower, and the divine sky.   The strength and the
songs of youth and middle-age were freely given
to humanity, often at the expense of art ;   but his
life has been so spared that he has produced distinctly literary work enough for a more than
transient fame.   The gold in his verse is plenti-
fully mixed with dross, but it may readily be
found.   It is the gold of the man's heart, quickly
wrought by the facile artist's hand.   It is but a
step from the prose thought to the poetic verse :
thus the thought "that the natural circumstances of
death cannot make any real change of character ;
that no one can be compelled to be good or evil ;
that freedom of choice belongs to both worlds,
and that sin is, by its very nature, inseparable
from suffering" sings itself in the spontaneous
music of such stanzas as this :

> I know not where his islands lift
>   Their fronded palms in air ;
> I only know I cannot drift
>   Beyond his love and care.

Whittier's merits are best summarized in his New England winter idyl "Snow-Bound," from which his customary defects are creditably absent. Upon this poem, as the years go by, will chiefly rest its maker's fame. It combines his descriptive and lyrical powers with "Snow-Bound." his accustomed expression of the thoughts and hopes of the human heart. Whittier's early success in poetizing New England legends, Indian and other, had been very moderate, a fact which the poet had recognized by abandoning many of his earliest productions. Aboriginal myths and Indian conflicts were to him, as to many others, tempting themes; but he missed the triumph attained by no more than one of his fellow-singers. "Snow-Bound," however, was an inspiration of his own heart and life. Home is as narrow as the ancestral walls, but as broad as humanity; and here is a work both local and general,—of the kind which tends to make the whole world kin. It is a little sphere seen through the transparent soul and style of the simple poet. Notwithstanding the freshness of spring, the luxuriance of June, and the sober wealth of autumn, winter is the most characteristic season of that land to which the Pilgrims came in December; and therefore "Snow-Bound" is a fitly chosen title for Whittier's characteristic scenes and portraits. The muse, like the man, after the fierce work of abolition, came back at last, and found that "East, west, hame's best." Having strongly helped to shape the political history and social life of the nation,

Whittier turned to sing of one of its typical hearth-stones. Here were needed no fruit of foreign culture, no high search for the ideal, no philosophic didacticism ; the home-bred singer, like so many of his predecessors, framed the simple chant of that which he best knew. The wasteful irregularity and hurried excess which have diminished or destroyed the value of so much of Whittier's writing—and so much of American literature—here give place to the simplicity of artless art, lightly touched and slightly transfigured by gleams of that ideal excellence toward which life and its reflecting literature aspire.

Little by little, during the decades since the publication of " Snow-Bound," it has become almost axiomatic in America to say that the poem deserves mention with "The Deserted Village " and " The Cotter's Saturday Night." Perhaps this verdict, though common, is too hurriedly confident ; but it is certain that the qualities of the poem are the same as those which have given lasting renown to its famous forerunners ; and that it shows " no sign of age, no fear to die." In its native character and indigenous worth its nearest rival is " The Biglow Papers"; and " The Biglow Papers," written in dialect, during twenty years, cannot be considered a unity. Sometimes homely pathos and kindly humor combine with facile art to produce, as here, a rounded literary result. We see and learn to know and love this plain country home, with its honest faces illumined by the great fire of an " old-fashioned

winter," and with its surrounding and imprisoning
glory of the ample northern snow. And from it
all there rises the world-hymn :

What matter how the night behaved?
What matter how the north-wind raved?
Blow high, blow low, not all its snow
Could quench our hearth-fire's ruddy glow.
O Time and Change !—with hair as gray
As was my sire's that winter day,
How strange it seems, with so much gone
Of life and love, to still live on !
Ah, brother ! only I and thou
Are left of all that circle now,—
The dear home faces whereupon
That fitful firelight paled and shone.
Henceforward, listen as we will,
The voices of that hearth are still ;
Look where we may, the wide earth o'er,
Those lighted faces smile no more.
We tread the paths their feet have worn,
 We sit beneath their orchard-trees,
 We hear, like them, the hum of bees
And rustle of the bladed corn;
We turn the pages that they read,
 Their written words we linger o'er,
But in the sun they cast no shade,
No voice is heard, no sign is made,
 No step is on the conscious floor!
Yet love will dream, and faith will trust
(Since he who knows our need is just),
That somehow, somewhere, meet we must.
Alas for him who never sees
The stars shine through his cypress-trees !
Who, hopeless, lays his dead away,
Nor looks to see the breaking day
Across the mournful marbles play !

Who hath not learned, in hours of faith,
  The truth to flesh and sense unknown,
That Life is ever lord of Death,
  And Love can never lose its own !

There is naught of unkindness or injustice in
saying that Whittier as poet is not great but
good, in every sense of the adjective.* Who
would not be satisfied with such a life work in
letters, self-crowned at nigh four-score years by a
book so true as " Saint Gregory's Guest, and
Other Poems?" Of the poet himself might be
spoken the words he therein sang of a dead New
England painter :

Magician, who from commonest elements
  Called up divine ideals, clothed upon
  By mystic lights, soft blending into one
Womanly grace and child-like innocence.
Teacher! thy lesson was not given in vain.
  Beauty is goodness ; ugliness is sin ;
  Art's place is sacred : nothing foul therein
May crawl or tread with bestial feet profane.

There is an interesting contrast between the
lives of the two principal poets of anti-slavery
Whittier   in America. Whittier was born in a
and Lowell. country town, of Quaker parentage ;
obtained a meagre English education by his own
efforts ; served here and there in the humdrum
toils of the editor ; and at length permanently
retired to the Arcadian simplicity of rural quiet.

* " If men will impartially, and not asquint, look toward the offices and
function of a poet, they will easily conclude to themselves the impossibility
of any man's being the good poet, without first being a good man."—Ben
Jonson, dedication of " Volpone ; or, The Fox."

Lowell was born in a Boston suburb; his father
was minister of a prominent city church; his
education was in the oldest American college, the
somewhat slender resources of which—even in its
Augustan literary period—he supplemented in
the cultured circles of eastern Massachusetts; in
mature youth he took his seat in the Harvard
chair of modern languages, as Longfellow's
successor; thenceforward, for many years, he
lived a literary life quite closely corresponding to
that of old-world centres of authorship; and at
length, in Madrid and London, he represented
the United States in ancient and important
courts. But Lowell, the representative of culture
and of what has been called the "Brahmin caste
of Boston," will chiefly be remembered as poet
because of his New England heart and voice—
his idyls of the Junes and Decembers of Massachusetts, and his verse of anti-slavery and patriotism, beginning with the fierce blasts against the
pro-slavery Mexican war of 1848, and ending
with the serene fervor of the Harvard Commemoration Ode of 1865. With more humor and
romantic sentiment, Lowell resembles Whittier in
his two chief lines of poetic work and success.
To the thought of freedom, rural and national,
have been added some of the spoils of time, but
the general theme and temper are unchanged.

There was not much in a large part of Lowell's
early verse to promise that he would be a characteristic American humorist, satirist, idyllist, and
critic. It was simply the lyrical product of a

young man of sentiment, and sometimes of senti-
Lowell's
Early Poems. mentality. To write a " Serenade, " lines
sent " With a Pressed Flower," " songs "
and " stanzas " on this or that, addresses " To the
Past " and " To the Future," " incidents " of one
sort or another, and miscellaneous personalities
" to," or moral reflections " on,"—all these were
marks of an age the spirit of which was felt by
Longfellow, Whittier, and all. Irené, Allegra,
Hebe, and Perdita are the ladies who figure prom-
inently in such *juvenilia* as these, which must distress the calm soul of the mature re-reader. The
moon and the sea, of course, were sometimes able
to express the conditions and longings of the
poet's soul, which, however, was occasionally
forced to utter itself in a grand combination of
the methods of the early Tennysonian lyric and
of the novels of the junior Cobb :

> I waited with a maddened grin
> To hear that voice all icy thin
> Slide forth and tell my deadly sin
> To hell and heaven, Rosaline !
> But no voice came, and then it seemed,
> That if the very corpse had screamed,
> The sound like sunshine glad had streamed
> Through that dark stillness, Rosaline !
>
> And then, amid the silent night,
> I screamed with horrible delight,
> And in my brain an awful light
> Did seem to crackle, Rosaline !
> It is my curse ! sweet memories fall
> From me like snow,—and only all
> Of that one night, like cold worms crawl
> My doomed heart over, Rosaline !

The poet, like the fat boy in "Pickwick," evidently "wants to make your flesh creep."

But it is far easier to criticise the old sentimental revival of American letters, than it was to resist its influence at the time. Irving had paved the way; and an emancipated nationalism, affected by novel religious and social reforms, and stirred by a fresh sense of power, naturally turned our young writers toward extravagance and artificiality. England herself was sharing the same feeling, which, indeed, had already affected France and Germany, where Goethe had many a time crossed the line separating bombast from power. There was in young Lowell, after all, an evident, though by no means regular, thought-strength and word-strength; his best ideas were true; of the imaginative quality of his mind there could be no question; and in his earliest books he promptly struck some notes of originality. Maturity and good judgment are precisely the qualities which marked Lowell's brilliant literary review in verse, "A Fable for Critics," described at some length in a preceding chapter of the present history. A young man who could characterize a literature, scarcely older than himself, with the insight and the prophetic wisdom which Lowell displayed at the age of twenty-nine, was assuredly in no danger of being permanently bound by the iron fetters of custom or the flowery garlands of a fleeting fashion.

As we re-read Lowell's early verse, good and bad, in many strains, we recognize the courage of

the poet in retaining so much of it. The mind of
the imaginative genius cannot be restricted to any
narrow range of thought or song. In later years
Lowell has been a conservative, in his publication
of none but his best; the same principle was
doubtless his guide in youth, but his early best
was irregular. The poetic product has varied
greatly in value, but it has almost always seemed
sincere. When, as in the absurd poem from
which stanzas have been cited, Lowell yielded to
a notion, he at least yielded himself without
reserve. The singer who was willing to sacrifice
so much for the sake of anti-slavery and unpopular religious movements, and to write a whole
series of poems, with his utmost force, against a
popular war, is certainly not amenable to the
charge of weakness. The lack of Addisonian
Manly   care in the preparation of his prose is par-
Sincerity. alleled by a certain lavishness in the production of his verse; but on the whole Lowell
was more likely to be endangered by conservatism than by spontaneity. We pardon the occasional silly jingles and the bathos in his first
books, for the sake of their idyllic promise, their
romantic and poetic feeling, and their strong
creative originality in some fields. The worst
fault in his volumes of verse produced before
middle life is, after all, that of prolixity; the
greatest merit, of course, is the conspicuous presence of the poetic gift.

The human element in Lowell, when it finds
expression in verses of life, is far from Poe's

bloodless passionateness, though it hardly beats
with the warm heart of Longfellow.
Lowell's non-political and non-humorous Humanity.
verse is usually that of tender thoughtfulness.
There is a place in our song for his " A Requiem "
as well as for " Annabel Lee" or " Resignation " :

> Now I can love thee truly,
>   For nothing comes between
> The senses and the spirit,
>   The seen and the unseen;
> Lifts the eternal shadow,
>   The silence bursts apart,
> And the soul's boundless future
>   Is present in my heart.

The grave reflectiveness of the scholar but serves
to heighten the simple grief and the earnest hope
of the man. Later he wrote, in a poem free from
every fault of his earlier work :

> Not all the preaching since Adam
>   Has made Death other than Death.

but yet in this darkest doubt, he exclaimed :

> Immortal? I feel it and know it,
>   Who doubts it of such as she?

The conflicting moods of this mature poem,
" After the Burial," often appear in the earlier
verse. Lowell is a poet of the eternal mystery
of life and death ; and his answers are neither
those of hasty faith nor those of long despair. In
reply to the questions of the open grave his best
lyrics are sung :

As a twig trembles, which a bird
  Lights on to sing, then leaves unbent,
So is my memory thrilled and stirred;—
  I only know she came and went.[*]

I know not how others saw her,
  But to me she was wholly fair,
And the light of the heaven she came from
  Still lingered and gleamed in her hair;
For it was wavy and golden,
  And as many changes took
As the shadows of sun-gilt ripples
  On the yellow bed of a brook.[†]

Even in his poems of the heart, Lowell's poetic
fancy made him too lavish in illustration and
Lavishness.   epithet. A discreeter bard would have
restricted his figurative language, and
won greater fame. His facility and fertility
pleased the few and repelled the many. Lowell's

O'er yon bare knoll the pointed cedar shadows
Drowse on the crisp, gray moss: the ploughman's call
  Creeps faint as smoke from black, fresh-furrowed mead-
    ows;
The single crow a single caw lets fall:
  And all around me every bush and tree
  Says Autumn's here, and Winter soon will be,
Who snows his soft, white sleep and silence over all

is poetical, but it delights no more than one
reader of the ten who take pleasure in Bryant's

The melancholy days are come, the saddest of the year,
Of wailing winds, and naked woods, and meadows brown
    and sere.

---

[*] "She Came and Went."   [†] "The Changeling."

Few indeed are the poets of nature or the heart who can make obvious the ideal and universal. Lowell attempts to give us too much; the forty long stanzas of "An Indian Summer Reverie," full of apt allusions, we gladly exchange for the few well-known June-lines of "The Vision of Sir Launfal." Seldom indeed can a singer succeed by the very opulence of suggestiveness, as in Shelley's "Cloud," which is itself dangerously near such repetition or confusion as one notes in Lowell's "To a Pine-Tree," which just escapes grandeur, but escapes it utterly.

Few readers know what deep and rich philosophy, what fruits of thought and culture, are to be found in some of Lowell's work: Philosophic for instance, in "Columbus," "Beaver Thought. Brook," "On a Portrait of Dante by Giotto," "Stanzas on Freedom," "The Ghost-Seer," "Prometheus," and a dozen others as good. If our literature shall ever fade and die in the coming centuries, and some future reader shall stumble upon Lowell's books, he will easily and excusably wax highly enthusiastic over the unquestionable wealth of thought therein discovered. As he founds a new cult, he may confidently exclaim, in Lowell's own language:

> Great truths are portions of the soul of man;
> Great souls are portions of eternity.

And yet there is a sad possibility that he will at

13

length see the blemish of too many of these
poems, the blemish already mentioned
Verbosity. here, and expressed by that most coldly
satirical of criticisms : " Words, words, words."

There is no use in denying or minimizing this
fact, to which must be added the equally apparent fault of careless expression on Lowell's part.
Not often, in the history of poetry, does one find
a poetical product at once so genuinely valuable
and so annoyingly irregular. It is easy, of
course, to name a dozen poets who have written
too much or too hastily—who is exempt from one
or the other fault ? But in Lowell's verse there is
a peculiar and an aggravating variety of impulsive
ideas and swift expressions. Force and fire are
secured on the one hand, at the expense, perhaps,
of the consistency of art. An artist may fail, like
Tennyson in his dramas ; but at least Tennyson
does his best,—the failure is likely to be inherent
in the singer or his theme. There is in Tennyson, now and then, a misapprehension, perhaps
grotesquely complete, a fall, perhaps pitiful ; but
it is not one of carelessness or hurry. A close
study and minute analysis of Lowell's language,
whether in prose or verse, brings promptly to
view an array of errors which cannot be paralleled
in the works of Emerson, Bryant, Longfellow, or
Hawthorne, his fellow-workers and contemporaries. A scholar of thorough culture in more
than one field, he vexes the refined sense as truly
as Whitman and more often than Whittier.

But James Russell Lowell is a wit and a genius : wit sparkles through whole essays and long poems, and in the best parts of "A Fable for Critics" or "The Biglow Papers" it fairly proves that it *is* genius. Who would exchange such results, so brilliant and so illuminating, for a ten-fold number of machine-essays or Odes to Propriety? The very faults are human and helpful. Lowell is a poet of freedom, of nature, and of human nature. His intellectual freaks and sallies are those of a patriot and reformer, a man whose spontaneity is better than his imitativeness or his deliberateness. The qualities of such great books as "The Vicar of Wakefield" or "Gil Blas"—irregular pictures of an irregular world—are those which now and then reappear in the pages of this Yankee idyllist, foe of slavery and of war, and lover of special American humanity seen against the background of the old-world's centuries. We could not have had the "Commemoration Ode," or "The Courtin'," or even "The Vision of Sir Launfal," from a man without a human heart and brain. And time, in his case, will once more carry forward the slow and unerring process of saving from the mass the select literary "remnant" of the lastingly valuable.

In a previous chapter and volume of this history I have already noted the injurious effect of the varied and elementary demands of American life upon our scientists, to the injury of what ought to have been their large and originally valuable creative work.

I shall have occasion hereafter to study the influence of the same multifarious industry or prodigality upon recent fiction. Its mark is plain, also, upon the work of Whittier and Lowell. But character is a higher thing than art, after all ; and there is character in these two men, and in nearly all of their books. Lowell the editor, abolitionist, religious liberal, critic, diplomat, is also the writer of that noble allegory of good deeds, "The Vision of Sir Launfal," with its lofty lesson and its "The Vision of warm glow of idyllic sunshine. All at Sir Launfal." once, forty years ago, his rich mind could give the world an intellectual and moral store so varied as that of this evenly-presented " Vision "; the stern political warning of " The Present Crisis "; the pungent satire—though sometimes coarsely written for quick effect—of the first series of " The Biglow Papers," in which he taught his readers to love the New England "The Biglow fields, and to hate the pro-slavery Mexi-Papers." can war; and the swift survey of our nascent literature proffered in the unsurpassed " Fable for Critics." Work at once so rapid and so good never came, within so brief a period, from an American pen. With all Whittier's love of New England soil and men, and all his hate of oppression and political truckling, Lowell also displayed wit and humor that sent his shafts straight home, but, unfortunately, made thousands of careless readers believe him a mere jester or at best a vitriolic satirist, as in " What Mr. Robinson Thinks," a poem upon which its unfortunate subject's reputation chiefly rests. "The Biglow Papers" in their two series (1848--1867) are not only satire and idyllic picture, but also a valuable philological contribution, with their careful display of the Yankee dialectic pronunciation and phraseology.

No other American poet has succeeded so constantly, and with such strong indication of high powers of observation and delineation of Yankee character, in portrayal of the New England men as they are. Take the excellent pictures in "Fitz-Adam's Story," the only printed part of a never-fulfilled plan for a group-poem to be entitled "The Nooning," and to be composed of serious or humorous tales in verse. The chief of these pictures is a personification of Yankee stinginess in a hypocritic garb—a type sadly familiar. In other pictures, however, and very often, Lowell fully and aptly and most justly sets before us the rustic folk-mind in its strength, shrewdness, helpful kindness, and simple reliance on God and self. The characteristics which reached their utmost manifestation in the face of Emerson will not be lost to literature so long as Lowell's poetical works continue to be read. In this regard the poet was born in the right place at the right time.

Delineation of Yankee character.

Lowell's heart-words, when uttered against slavery or political war, or in delineation of rural life or natural beauty, have been heard with something like the general welcome accorded to his rollicking productions in the vein of wit or humor.   As a sentimentalist, however, his public has been more limited than Longfellow's or Whittier's. From his verse of sentiment or imagination or more frequent fancy one can select a goodly list of meritorious poems, but most of them are not widely known. They are not indispensable, as the best poetry must always be, and as his "Auf Wiederschen," "Das Ewig-Weibliche," "The Changeling," "The First Snow-Fall," "The Courtin'," "After the Burial," Lowell's "The Miner," and "Ode Recited at the best lyrics. Harvard Commemoration" seem to be. Most of us would be content to have written these eight alone, or even the last, the best American poem of occasion, and the chief literary result of the civil war. Such songs, lovely or noble, outweigh the store of thought in "The Cathedral," or the richly varied nature-panorama in the second series of "The Biglow Papers," quaintly and modestly entitled "Sunthin' in the Pastoral Line."

Notwithstanding his high success in the "Commemoration Ode," Lowell has not always shown the confident powers which the ode-maker must possess. The ambitious ode on Agassiz is valuable for its portraits of the subject and his friends, but the metrical system seems over-cumbrous ; where success is won it is in spite of the system, not because of it. Lowell is usually Man and strongest where he is freest, as in the artist. felicitous personal "Epistle to George William Curtis." In the sonnet, however, he is not fettered by a form that too severely binds some others; but he finds within its "narrow room" ample chance to express political admiration or scorn, or to make such tender tributes as are offered in the "Bankside" series to the memory of Edmund Quincy, one of the true gentlemen in American thought and letters. Despite his extensive readings and studies in English and continental poetry, the personality of Lowell dominates that which he writes; we are almost always conscious of the man and his mind; no artistic result eliminates him and leaves us only the work.

Mr. Lowell's productions, from first to last, both in verse and in prose, have occasionally been subjected to severe or violent critical condemnation. Even the "Commemoration Ode" has been most contemptuously characterized by an able but eccentric English poet and scholar whose vocabulary contains no adjectives midway between "heavenly" and "devilish." We have been told, by various writers, of his mixed metaphors; culinary comparisons; inconsistencies of utterance; willingness to introduce coarse jokes more akin to the wild western "humorist" than the Cambridge scholar; and use of forced rhymes worthy of a country bardling or the intensest modern mediavalist. These faults, which must at times be recognized and plainly described, really spring from the very qualities of alertness and freshness of speech which make Lowell the poet both of

The secret of Lowell's Successes and Failures.

scholars and of a part, at least, of the common people. It is hard to distinguish, sometimes, between a "more than Shakespearean felicity" and a dangerous carelessness, individuality, or obscurity. Lowell approaches all these things; and for this very reason few of his critics agree in their lists of his best and worst productions. He writes, furthermore, for his own time; a more A Poet of selfish or discreet bard—a Bowles or a the time. Rogers—would have left us a trim little book of metrical reflections, without the lyrical grace, and without those faults which poor N. P. Willis very aptly called "hurrygraphs." But I, for one, am willing to give up neither the quick sparkle nor the lasting worth, neither such dialect wit nor such a scholarly introduction as may be found in the second Biglow series. It might be better to separate the 'prentice-work and time-work from the results of art, long and true; Lowell has not separated them, but neither did Wordsworth, nor Shakespeare himself, whose art was sometimes worse than his hack writing for the expectant play-house. Lowell, more than calm Emerson, gentle Longfellow, blatant, bustling Whitman, cold Bryant, or unhuman Poe, writes at once as man and scholar, wit and artist, reformer and poetic maker. Therefore Whittier and Lowell reap the American reward, while they lose some sprays of the Greek laurel. Of either of them might be said, as Lowell wrote of Abraham Lincoln :

His was no lonely mountain-peak of mind,
Thrusting to thin air o'er our cloudy bars,
A sea-mark now, now lost in vapors blind;
Broad prairie rather, genial, level-lined,
Fruitful and friendly for all human kind,
Yet also nigh to heaven and loved of loftiest stars.

The time will come, I presume, when two hundred million English-reading people will occupy the
present territory of the United States. Literature does not necessarily grow with numbers or
wealth—the greatest glory of the greatest of the
world's literatures is still the Elizabethan English.
We shall then, however, have ample *The Amer-*
leisure for a serener art. In the teeming *ican Song.*
years of the future, American authors will hardly
be forced, or tempted by their ready zeal, into
works so multifarious as those of Lowell in these
early and shaping days of American letters. A
booklet designed to aid in a thorough study of his
writings discusses them under the several heads
of nature; the poetic ideal; a "portrait gallery"
of thirty or forty authors delineated in his verse;
legends, history and religion. In the historical
division the claim is made, and justly, that,
"Lowell's patriotic verse lights every part of our
national chronicle; there are poems about the
discoverers, the forefathers, the men of '76, the
nation from 1787 to 1820, the rise of abolitionism,
the annexation of Texas and the Mexican War,
the 'Irrepressible Conflict,' the Commemoration
Ode, the reconstruction." Such a range of subjects would be impossible for some poets, and

dangerous to all; but Lowell bears the test with substantial success,—a success somewhat more lasting than the swift and earnest singer expected in youth. "Unless to thought is added will," says Emerson, "Apollo is an imbecile"; this Cambridge Apollo adds will to thought, and produces a result distinctly American, and often distinctly poetic. His full mind and ready pen turn without hesitation from the practical to the ideal ; now they pack into four lines a somewhat strenuous argument for international copyright :—

> In vain we call old notions fudge,
>   And bend our conscience to our dealing,
> The Ten Commandments will not budge,
>   And stealing *will* continue stealing,—

and now he peers toward the ultimate home of poetry and religion, Shelley's "land where music and moonlight and feeling are one," of which Lowell sings :

> Happier to chase a flying goal
>   Than to sit counting laurelled gains,
> To guess the soul within the soul
>   Than to be lord of what remains.
>
> Hide still, best good, in subtile wise,
>   Beyond my nature's utmost scope;
> Be ever absent from mine eyes
>   To be twice present in my hope!

To refuse to try to separate wheat from chaff in Lowell's rich garner would be to abdicate the critical function. I have faithfully, however imperfectly, endeavored to search for the soul of the

poet behind his varying songs and philosophic
verses. The endeavor is that which Lowell himself has more successfully made in his criticisms
of European singers. As he has told us: "Not
failure, but low aim, is crime." His aim is high
and his failure non-essential as compared with his
success. Two lines in " The Cathedral," "The
a poem worthy of Browning, remind us Cathedral."
that

> God is in all that liberates and lifts,
> In all that humbles, sweetens, and consoles;

and he is therefore in Lowell's verse. And the
didactic is not less welcome, nor more, than the
pure spirit of poesy phrased in the same profoundly meditative poem :

> The bird I hear sings not from yonder elm ;
> But the flown ecstasy my childhood heard
> Is vocal in my mind, renewed by him,
> Haply made sweeter by the accumulate thrill
> That threads my undivided life and steals
> A pathos from the years and graves between.

In divine thought and in human perception, thus
phrased, in the three quotations last made, Lowell
recalls and restates for us the very secret of existence, taught by seer and poet to man in his upward march. Whittier, too, in unmystic and
simple phrase, has many a time unriddled this
mystery :

> Beneath the moonlight and the snow
> Lies dead my latest year;
> The winter winds are wailing low
> Its dirges in my ear.

> I grieve not with the moaning wind
> 　As if a loss befell;
> Before me, even as behind,
> 　God is, and all is well!

> His light shines on me from above,
> 　His low voice speaks within,—
> The patience of immortal love
> 　Outwearying mortal sin.

Whittier and Lowell, our poets of freedom, could not have sung the American song had they not learned and interpreted to a willing folk the same lesson of the higher and poetic optimism which underlay Emerson's every line. Such men must be reformers, but their earthly battles are fought beneath a heavenly star.

The name of Oliver Wendell Holmes is naturally and honorably associated with those of Whittier and Lowell as that of our third poet of freedom and culture. His literary life began with a ringing lyric of patriotism, easily surpassing the best of the revolutionary songs. The English-reading world well knows those indignant verses, flung forth in answer to a proposal to dismantle the frigate Constitution, or "Old Ironsides":

Oliver Wendell Holmes, b. 1809.

> Ay, tear her tattered ensign down!
> 　Long has it waved on high,
> And many an eye has danced to see
> 　That banner in the sky;
> Beneath it rung the battle-shout,
> 　And burst the cannon's roar;—
> The meteor of the ocean air
> 　Shall sweep the clouds no more!

Her deck, once red with heroes' blood,
 Where knelt the vanquished foe,
When winds were hurrying o'er the flood,
 And waves were white below,
No more shall feel the victor's tread,
 Or know the conquered knee;—
The harpies of the shore shall pluck
 The eagle of the sea!

Oh, better that her shattered hulk
 Should sink beneath the wave;
Her thunders shook the mighty deep,
 And there should be her grave;
Nail to the mast her holy flag,
 Set every threadbare sail,
And give her to the god of storms,—
 The lightning and the gale!

Not less intense, though more sober and re-strained, is the noble song which Holmes wrote forty years later for the ceremonies attending the laying of the corner-stone of Harvard's great Memorial Hall, built in honor of her sons slain in the Civil War. Here is the American mind, and here the unmistakable touch of true poetry. In the swing of these stately and musical lines are the fervor of patriotism and the calm restraint of academic contemplation, the latter tempering the former, but never quenching a single heat-ray of forceful devotion. Holmes, within these sixteen lines, was performing the same service done by Lowell in his great Ode; he was laying the laurel of learning upon the reddened sword of national honor:

Not with the anguish of hearts that are breaking
　Come we as mourners to weep for our dead ;
Grief in our breasts has grown weary of aching,
　Green is the turf where our tears we have shed.

While o'er their marbles the mosses are creeping,
　Stealing each name and its legend away,
Give their proud story to Memory's keeping,
　Shrined in the temple we hallow to-day.

Hushed are their battle-fields, ended their marches,
　Deaf are their ears to the drum-beat of morn,—
Rise from the sod, ye fair columns and arches !
　Tell their bright deeds to the ages unborn !

Emblem and legend may fade from the portal,
　Keystone may crumble and pillar may fall ;
They were the builders whose work is immortal,
　Crowned with the dome that is over us all !

There were poets at Harvard a generation ago !
Mr. Stedman well says of Holmes, in his essay
on that poet : "Though the most direct and
obvious of the Cambridge group, the least given
to subtilties, he is our typical university poet ; the
minstrel of the college that bred him, and within
whose liberties he has jested, sung, and toasted,
from boyhood to what in common folk would be
old age. Alma Mater has been more to him than
to Lowell or Longfellow,—has occupied a surprising portion of his range ; if we go back to
Frere and Canning, even to Gray, for his like,
there is no real prototype." But Holmes,
"always a university poet," is a singer of freedom
as well as of culture. "When the Civil War
broke out, this conservative poet, who had taken

little part in the agitation that preceded it, shared in every way the spirit and duties of the time. None of our poets wrote more stirring war lyrics during the conflict, none has been more national so far as loyalty, in the Websterian sense, to our country and her emblems is concerned. He always has displayed the simple instinctive patriotism of the American minute-man." *

" The " scholar in politics," or in national life, does not always show the aggressive radicalism of the young Lowell; and Holmes did not share in all the intense pioneer reforms in state-craft, religion, and social life, which were promoted by some of his friends and literary contemporaries in Massachusetts. But no one can long read in any one of his books, prose or verse, without discovering that 'he is patriot, Unitarian, and republican, though not radical abolitionist, " free-religionist," or phalansterist. The " Autocrat," " Professor," and " Poet " at the Breakfast-Table, those original and valuable books of essay-talk, display the man and his mind in round and attractive completeness; and they show that the books are the author, and the author a nineteenth-century American in thought and outlook. What I mean will be apparent to every reader of the Autocrat series, and it is hardly less apparent in Holmes' novels : " Elsie Venner," " The Guardian Angel," and " A Mortal Antipathy." These books, in their fresh-

Wholesome American conservatism.

---

* " Poets of America," 276-7, 298-9.

ness, alertness, and brilliancy of delineation, are
Holmes' essays and novels. thoroughly of New England; they
could not have been written in another
land; and their descriptions and their solid (and
yet progressive) discreetness of thought are
representative of the soil and the time. Common sense—the Franklinian quality—has no
better representative; and it is this very common-
sense that prevents Holmes from reaching the
highest success in fiction. "The Guardian
Angel" narrowly escapes being a great novel;
but in it, as in the less meritorious "Elsie Venner" and the weaker "Mortal Antipathy," the
author's personality invades the artistic field.
Every page or two he interrupts the narrative to
make a thrust at religious orthodoxy or medical
heterodoxy; to discuss his favorite theme of
atavism; or to utter, like his own Master Byles
Gridley, a few "thoughts on the universe." His
themes are half Hawthornesque, but their treatment is that of the analytical and tersely didactic Harvard professor. The man behind the
machine is an inartistic spectacle, in prose fiction,
even if the man is mindful and masterly. The
personality that is a delightful companion in the
essays, and a "guide, philosopher, and friend" in
the biographies of Motley and Emerson, intrudes
in the pages of what should be a novel or a
romance. The contents of the minor volumes of
essays—"Soundings from the Atlantic," "Cur-
rents and Counter-Currents in Medical Science,"

" Mechanism in Thought and Morals," etc.,—will not keep within their covers, but spread into the would-be artistic product.

The personal element, however, is ever welcome in the poems, and I may add indispensable. Holmes has kinship with Hood, Praed, Thackeray, and even Pope, *mutatis mutandis*, as also with Montaigne, Sterne and Lamb. Such a singer must be intimately and constantly connected with his song. He is preeminently a lyrist of humor, pathos, and occasion ; and poets of this class are poets who put their individual selves into iambus and trochee. They instruct while they amuse, and their personal attractiveness is transmuted into poetic force. They are spectators of the comedies and tragedies that make up life : Balzacs in theme, but treating their themes with somewhat of the heart and humanity that spontaneously sang themselves in the lyrics of Burns. Something akin to affection connects such poets and their readers, when poet and reader are at their best. They cannot be Shelleys, but they win by warmth though they dazzle not by splendor. The wit of Holmes is human as well as intellectual, though it stops far short of the vulgar or the sensational elements which are the bane of the lower American fun, and sometimes of the higher. Whatever Holmes writes is not only manly and characteristic, but characteristic of the man. His themes and methods are sufficiently varied, but they are all

Personality of Holmes' poems.

14

closely connected with the author of " Every Man his own Boswell." Variety and quick wholesome suggestiveness and helpfulness in the poems come from the same qualities in their writer.

Before speaking of his pathos and humor, and of his voluminous and here-unsurpassed occa-
Holmes the sional verse, one notes at the start that
lyrist. of all the company of American singers, after Poe, the two who versify most swiftly and sweetly, our American *improvisatori*, are Holmes and Bayard Taylor. Lyrical grace and aptness are theirs ; and one of them is likely to be our chosen singer when we want not Longfellow's sympathy, Bryant's austerity, Lowell's incisiveness, Emerson's masterful thought. This singing power gives pleasure in Holmes' rollicking descriptions and bits of mere fun ; his after dinner sallies ; his ephemeral contemporary satires ; his best songs of occasion, like the noble Harvard hymn just quoted ; and his downright masterpieces, " The Last Leaf " or " The Chambered Nautilus."

In its humblest estate this lyrical power is the pleasing jingle which properly accompanies and increases the pleasure derived from the telling phrases of the occasional poems. There is a legitimate enjoyment in sing-song, the border-line between which and scansion is not easily traced. One enjoys reading aloud, with somewhat undue stress of accent, the least ambitious of Holmes' clever rhymes, such as

Where, O where are life's lilies and roses,
  Nursed in the golden dawn's smile?
Dead as the bulrushes round little Moses,
  On the old banks of the Nile.

Where are the Marys and Anns and Elizas,
  Loving and lovely of yore?
Look in the columns of old Advertisers,—
  Married and dead by the score.

This easy verbal music is as legitimate in its
way as Swinburne's or Poe's, as Moore's or
Scott's. Holmes intentionally plays with a lyrical
faculty that is ready to do his bidding in more
stately and splendid, more devout and inspiring
verse :—

Say not the Poet dies !
Though in the dust he lies,
He cannot forfeit his melodious breath,
  Unsphered by envious death!
Life drops the voiceless myriads from its role ;
  Their fate he cannot share,
  Who, in the enchanted air
Sweet with the lingering strains that Echo stole,
  Has left his dearer self, the music of his soul !*

Her hands are cold ; her face is white ;
  No more her pulses come and go ;
Her eyes are shut to life and light :—
  Fold the white vesture, snow on snow,
  And lay her where the violets blow.†

Not less serenely musical are those sacred songs
that are like oases in the deserts of the hymn-

---

* Poem at the dedication of the Halleck monument, July 8, 1869.
† "Under the Violets."

books : "O Love Divine, that stooped to share," and "Lord of all being, throned afar." Many a time does the reader of Holmes' verse, in its changing tones, speak to it as did its author to the fountain at Stratford-on-Avon :

> Welcome, thrice welcome is thy silvery gleam,
>   Thou long imprisoned stream !
> Welcome the tinkle of thy crystal beads
> As plashing rain-drops to the flowery meads,
> As summer's breath to Avon's whispering reeds!

The writer of poems of occasion, like the after-dinner orator, must pay a high price for immedi-

Occasional verse.

ate applause. He gets hearty laughter and spontaneous praise, at the expense of being called merely "clever" or "neat." A great event sometimes, though rarely, calls forth a great poem; but occasional verse seldom lives long. The collected edition of Holmes' poems contains no less than thirty-two pieces connected with the reunions or the deaths of his Harvard class of '29, and some seventy-five more called forth by Phi Beta Kappa anniversaries, centennials, medical meetings, birthday feasts, scenes of welcome and farewell, theatre-openings, and similar seasons. His writing is largely "Rhymes of an Hour," as he modestly entitled one of his collections. It cannot live, for the adequate reason that most of it is not re-read. Originality,

"Rhymes of an Hour."

brilliancy, the surprise which is the essence of wit, rhythmical melody, cannot save it. But its sum-total of agreeable memories

has materially and justly been added to our
appreciation of the merit of the author's more
ambitious and enduring verse. These occasional poems, like the lyrics destined for longer
life, are eminently free from imitativeness. The
emancipation of American letters from foreign
fashions—not necessarily from foreign thought
—owes much to Doctor Holmes' sturdy and
successful, because natural, display of independent genius. The " cleverness " of this characteristic writer, not less than his deeper pathos
and humor, has played its part in the intellectual
movement of his time; it has made it easier for
everybody to follow his own bent and say his
own say. Holmes' occasional poems have simply
amused hundreds of delighted hearers, most of
whom have hardly stopped, at the moment, to
think of any higher result ; but sooner or later they
reflect that here is more than an individual neatness,
here are an alertness and daring felicity that have
in them something national. It is even apparent
elsewhere ; for an English writer, whose name I
know not, has justly associated, in this regard,
" Mr. Lowell and Dr. Holmes—men who combine
the culture of the Old World with the indefinable
and incommunicable spirit of the New."

As I turn over the leaves of Holmes' complete
poetical works, I find just half-a-dozen poems
which stand out most in my mind as Holmes mas-
significant : " The Last Leaf," " The   terpieces.
Chambered Nautilus," " The Voiceless," " The
Deacon's Masterpiece," " Æstivation," and

" Homesick in Heaven." "The Last Leaf" is one of those creations which are struck off at a heat and remain unique in literature. That union of pathos and humor which distinguishes every great wit is manifestly here, expressed with the novelty of form which must be added to naturalness of picture, if the word-painter would make a highly significant impression :

I saw him once before,
As he passed by the door,
    And again
The pavement stones resound,
As he totters o'er the ground
    With his cane.

They say that in his prime,
Ere the pruning-knife of Time
    Cut him down,
Not a better man was found
By the Crier on his round
    Through the town.

But now he walks the streets,
And he looks at all he meets
    Sad and wan,
And he shakes his feeble head,
That it seems as if he said,
    "They are gone."

The mossy marbles rest
On the lips that he has prest
    In their bloom,
And the names he loved to hear
Have been carved for many a year
    On the tomb.

My Grandmamma has said—
Poor old lady, she is dead
　　Long ago—
That he had a Roman nose,
And his cheek was like a rose
　　In the snow.

But now his nose is thin,
And it rests upon his chin
　　Like a staff,
And a crook is in his back,
And a melancholy crack
　　In his laugh.

I know it is a sin
For me to sit and grin
　　At him here ;
But the old three-cornered hat,
And the breeches, and all that,
　　Are so queer!

And if I should live to be
The last leaf upon the tree
　　In the spring,
Let them smile, as I do now,
At the old forsaken bough
　　Where I cling.

I must remember that these pages attempt to present a history, not an anthology ; but the quaintly successful poem repeats itself in my ear. This " Last Leaf" is printed on the first leaf of the collected edition of Holmes' poems; but it will indeed be the last to fall, for such an artless piece of art, such a rare union of unadorned humor and tender pathos cannot die. Poe (in *The Pioneer* for March, 1843) made it the subject of an elaborated metrical analysis, in which his well-known skill in scansion failed to present a proper scheme, notwithstanding his patient discussion and elaborate nomenclature.* The music of the pathetic song, in its author's mind, was

> "More of feeling than of hearing,
> Of the heart than of the ear,"—

it sung itself, like the best of Wordsworth's "Lyrical Ballads." Scansion, the botanizing of poetry, is a fit and needful study, but sometimes it is well to let the poem and the flower alone in their beauty. "The Last Leaf" is a lily which neither Poe nor I can paint.

"The Chambered Nautilus," originally printed in the "Autocrat," is one of the illustrations of Holmes' occasional fondness for the measures of the ode, which he might have used, had he wished, more often, and with an evident success. To write an ode is as hard as to write blank verse, but more than once does Holmes show the promise and potency of a triumph never fully essayed. Meanwhile he here achieves a success hardly less: that of writing a poem of self-evident beauty, inculcating a moral lesson. "The Voiceless" is a laurel-wreath of recognition and reward, laid upon the grave of mute, anonymous human

* This analysis had a curious history. It was not retained in the collected edition of Poe's works; a part of the manuscript was given after many years to Dr. Holmes by Robert Carter, one of the editors of *The Pioneer*, who had evidently forgotten how it came into his possession; and this part was reprinted as unpublished matter in the introduction to an illustrated edition of "The Last Leaf," 1885.

suffering. "Homesick in Heaven," in its idea, suggests a parallel with Rossetti's "Blessed Damozel," but is manifestly an outgrowth of the author's own thought, which more than once had touched upon some kindred theme. Here, as seldom occurs when such a thought rises in Holmes' mind, the execution falls manifestly below the idea.

Of all the many humorous poems produced by Holmes in half-a-century, my favorites are "The Deacon's Masterpiece" and "Æstivation." The first, with its swift movement, its Yankee spirit, its country pictures, its *sui generis* catastrophe, and its delicious ultimate line—"Logic is logic. That's all I say"—is faultless fun. The second poem one longs to send back the ages, or beyond the "iron gate" of which Holmes afterward sang, to that true prose-poet and heartful old English doctor, Sir Thomas Browne, whose chief writings James T. Fields once aptly dedicated to John Brown and Oliver Wendell Holmes.

As the literary career of Doctor Holmes is viewed from the close of the century it so nearly covers, one perceives that he has been a poet as well as a humorist, a teacher as well as a "man-pleaser," if I may use the word in an innocent sense. This specially representative Bostonian poet has been a natural and catholic singer, and he has constantly upheld right canons of living. Bigotry, of many names, is saddened by the reflection that his books are not wholly mortal. Manliness finds in him a friend, Holmes' career.

and culture a companion.   Though as a poet he is almost great but assuredly not great, while as a prose essayist he must ever stand below the greater American whose biography he wrote, his place on the shelf is characteristic and likely to remain undusty.   A later Franklin in riper days, he has added to the valuable part of creative literature, while he has shown how an intense and perpetual localism, under the touch of a true though narrow genius, and aided by culture, may earn a place in the world's republic of letters.

CHAPTER VII.

TONES AND TENDENCIES OF AMERICAN VERSE.

AFTER poetry in America could make some boasts in the matter of quantity, and even in that of quality in a lesser degree, it was struck by that wave of sentimentality which, following the legitimate revival of romanticism, had ^{Sentimentality.} submerged so much of the English literary field. I need not stop to say that when poetry ceases to express sentiment it will die; and that Heine and Longfellow need not retreat before criticism or classicism or any other rival spirit in modern song. The prevalent lack of sentiment is a fault in Emerson's verse, notwithstanding its obvious power; while the presence of deep, true feeling in poets like Shelley or Keats increases the royal splendor of the one and the Hellenic grace of the other. But sentiment that consists in part of bombast, Parnassian attitudinizing or extravagant apostrophe is not usually a thing which the centuries value. Nor, when these things are absent, is it a mark of the greatest genius to express the cheaply obvious in thinly tinkling rhymes. "Feeling," to be sure, is better than indifferentism, and if either heart or brain must depart from letters we will dismiss the latter first; but we prefer imagination to that quality which

219

the old novelists called "sensibility." In American sentimental verse, forty or fifty years ago, it is not difficult to discover the objectionable qualities just named ; and the general absence of the element of imagination has already banished it to the forgotten land once occupied by Mrs. Hemans, " L. E. L." and Eliza Cook.

It should fairly be admitted, at the start, that in the poems of Willis and Mrs. Sigourney, as well as of Mrs. Frances S. Osgood and the lesser lights, there is

Nathaniel Parker Willis, 1807–1867.

something of high thought, sincere feeling, occasional effective utterance, and poetic touch. The time-spirit of a sentimental age was not so foolish as to be utterly misled in its enthusiasms. From Willis and Mrs. Sigourney can readily be selected a few poems that have survived the critical contempt, or indifference worse than contempt, which followed upon a temporary fame once equalling Longfellow's and far surpassing Emerson's. Willis, and not Bryant, was the typical New York poet, forty years since; while in distant country towns his metrical paraphrases of the Bible, his verses of observation, and his lyrics of affection and reflection, had a hearty welcome among men and women whose devout or secular aspirations and emotions had not elsewhere found so apt expression. But that is all ; his " Poems Sacred, Passionate, and Humorous" are mostly forgotten, in their three divisions ; and his many books of once-enjoyable stories and sketches of life and travel have gone the way of the dead

magazines and newspapers in which some of them
were printed. He chose, though possessed of
brilliancy, to be affected and hurried, and paid the
penalty. Not even the discreet endeavors of his
biographer, Professor Beers, could popularize the
best of these prose productions in a recently-
selected volume; the ordinary reader knows little
more of Willis than the not unmeritorious script-
ural pieces upon Absalom and Hagar in the Wilderness, and the lyric beginning "The shadows
lay along Broadway," which Poe (whom Willis
nobly befriended) so heartily admired, and in
which he found a true imagination and an impressive grace, dignity, and pathos. Willis was a
sort of lesser Southey, in his money-making literary industry and facility in prose and verse, his
occasional strength or music of utterance, and his
beautiful and unjealous self-sacrifice in promoting
the work and fame of other writers. He was a
power not to be ignored in the development of
letters in New York.

Among Willis' contemporaries, beloved by
many readers who sincerely believed that they
were "fond of poetry," were some men and more
women who were capable of manufacturing verses
that were occasionally pleasing, and of turning
out rhymes in which the sense was not always
sacrificed to the sound. Copious illustrations of
their products may be found in that indispensable
piece of pioneer industry, the Duyckincks' "Cy-
clopædia of American Literature," or in the still
more voluminous anthologies of Rev. Rufus Wil-

mot Griswold. Upon many of them Poe bestowed a critical smile or frown. Their "poems" were declaimed by school-boys and pasted into the scrap-books of young lovers; and to this day some of them are warmly remembered by readers who cannot deem just the neglect which has enveloped them. Their one great merit was their tender heart; but not even this could cover their multitude of literary sins. In brief, they had most of the demerits of Mrs. Browning without her unquestionable genius. Their work was on the whole humbly beneficent, for it helped the general public in a transition time,—at least negatively, while it could not harm the abler minds, nor, in its nature, could it be lastingly mischievous. When I think of the genuine love of man and nature, the sincere moral helpfulness, and the half-a-hundred blameless volumes of Mrs.
Lydia Howard Sigourney, I regret that literary justice (Huntley) permits the critic to do no more than Sigourney, chronicle the death of her fame. But 1791-1865. facts are inexorable; such verse cannot long outlive the contemporary fugitive prose; and obvious sentiment expressed with hurried facility is a mark of the humbler and more perishable forms of poetry. The epitaph of nearly all such productions, once deemed "contributions to American literature," is to be found, alas, in the first of Holmes' stanzas quoted on page 211.

Literature, however great, does not take the place held by sentiment and religion in the hearts of the majority of mankind. Tastes and capacities, furthermore, are not always Shakesperean or Emersonian. Some of the successes of Longfellow and Whittier are merely the result of their attainment, by similar but more successful methods, of that which Willis and Mrs. Sigourney could but seek. Our best patriotic ballads and popular lyrics are of course based upon sentiment, aptly expressed by the poet and instinctively felt by the reader. Hence, just is the fame and true is the love bestowed upon the choicest songs of our "single-poem poets": upon Samuel Woodworth's "Old Oaken Bucket," Albert G. Greene's "Old Grimes is Dead," Thomas Dunn English's "Ben Bolt," George P. Morris' "Wood- man, Spare that Tree," Coates Kinney's "The Rain upon the Roof," Mrs. Allen's "Rock me to Sleep, Mother," Julia Ward Howe's majestic "Battle Hymn of the Republic," Thomas Buchanan Read's "Sheridan's Ride," or Francis M. Finch's "The Blue and the Gray." Kinney, neither dazzled nor misled by the glow of spontaneous favor bestowed upon his best-known poem, continued through life to study and to polish, until, in his seventh decade, he collected, in a volume of no great size, poems so wise in optimistic thought and so definite in their varied artistic form that they would readily have given him fame in our early verse-days, fifty years agone. The American singers, with all their rush of enthusiasm, have not been utterly lacking in reserve, though too few have followed Kinney's sanely deliberate method.

Popular lyrics.

Coates Kinney, b. 1826.

To this select list of lyrics I must not allow
personal preference to add the poems of the late
Elbridge Jefferson Cutler, nor an anonymous
tribute to "The Confederate Flag,"—the gem of
the Southern poetry of the civil war.

A certain "seal of approval," though not a
large one, has been set by popular verdict, and by
the iterated opinion of competent critics or poetic
associates, upon the "War Lyrics" of Henry
Howard Brownell, almost the only Northern poet
Henry Howard
Brownell,
1820-1872.
whose reputation, though a dwindling
one, rests solely upon his vigorous lyrics and graphic descriptions of the
great internecine struggle.   His "Bay Fight" is a
swiftly effective verse-story of Farragut's battle at
Mobile, and might well be read beneath St. Gau-
dens' spirited statue of that great naval com-
mander, whose deeds it enthusiastically commem-
orates in lines that can hardly stop to obey the
stricter laws of scansion, but hurry along like
those of a newspaper report of the engagement.
Similar, but marked still more by the *currente
calamo* manner, is Forceythe Willson's "Rhyme
of the Master's Mate," describing the fresh-water
conflict at Fort Henry.   Appearing almost simul-
Byron For-
ceythe Willson,
1837-1867.
taneously with Brownell's lyrics, it was
not unnaturally assigned, by some
readers, to the same hand.   Willson's
"Old Sergeant" is better known, being, indeed,
one of the most familiar of the civil war poems ;
but aside from its subject it is essentially less
worthy of praise than Willson's "Autumn Song,"

"No More," or "The Voice"—the last is a poem
which any writer might deem one of his successes,
as measured by its fit union of thought and form.

Among all American songs of sentiment, none
are more characteristic of the soil, none more
genuine and spontaneous than the folk-songs
of which both words and music were written
by Stephen C. Foster. "The Old
Folks at Home," "My Old Kentucky Stephen
Home," and others scarcely less popu- ¹⁸²⁶⁻¹⁸⁶⁴.
lar, voiced very sweetly and aptly the hopes and
fears, the happy home-life and the bloody inexorable tragedy of the Southern slaves before the war.
Both light and shade of African life are here—the
sunny noontide joy and the midnight woe. The
words, with their simple pictures of nature and
their unsophisticated pathos, and the music, melodiously expressing the whole thought of the
words, are of the land, the climate, and the time.
The crude strength of the interesting and indigenous slave-songs of semi-Israelitish oppression and
prophetic triumph seemed to serve as Foster's
basis, upon which his art built symmetrical songs,
all his own and yet such as the slaves, under more
favorable conditions, might have framed for themselves. That Foster was a poet is proved—one is
tempted to say—by a single line like

By'n by hard times comes a-knocking at the door

in "My Old Kentucky Home," which seems to
me worth quoting entire, as a true poem :
15

The sun shines bright in the old Kentucky home,
   'Tis summer, the darkies are gay;
The corn-top's ripe, and the meadow's in the bloom,
   While the birds make music all the day.
The young folks roll on the little cabin floor,
   All merry, all happy and bright;—
By'n by hard times comes a-knocking at the door,
   Then my old Kentucky home, good-night!

Weep no more, my lady,
   Oh! weep no more to-day!
We will sing one song for the old Kentucky home,
   For the old Kentucky home, far away.

They hunt no more for the possum and the coon,
   On the meadow, the hill, and the shore;
They sing no more by the glimmer of the moon,
   On the bench by the old cabin door.
The day goes by like a shadow o'er the heart,
   With sorrow, where all was delight:
The time has come when the darkies have to part,
   Then my old Kentucky home, good-night!

The head must bow, and the back will have to bend,
   Wherever the darkey may go:
A few more days, and the trouble all will end,
   In the field where the sugar-canes grow.
A few more days for to tote the weary load,
   No matter, 'twill never be light,
A few more days till we totter on the road,
   Then my old Kentucky home, good-night!

Weep no more, my lady,
   Oh! weep no more to-day!
We will sing one song for the old Kentucky home,
   For the old Kentucky home, far away.

" The Old Folks at Home " is not less veritably
a poem; and in its melody Foster created the

best musical composition as yet produced in a country that pours its gold into the pockets of European singers and players, but is even poorer than England in its original musical product. But music, as a rule, lags behind the other arts of civilization.

None but superficial critics or jaded readers insist that the only characteristic and original element in American literature is that which distinctly and constantly "smacks of the soil." We have traced the local and national idea through the development of American thought, and have noted its constant appearance in the writings of the greater American poets. One should not claim that this idea, definitely expressed, is the sole test of value and interest in verse; he should rather find in it a theme of occasional but genuine power, appearing as often as usual in other literatures, and displaying itself according to the varying influences of place, time, and man. Fidelity to scene and character explained the wide popularity which was won by Dr. Holland's narrative poem "Bitter-Sweet," and the more sentimental and less meritorious "Kathrina." In these, and in his readable and "native-American" novels,—"Miss Gilbert's Career," "The Story of Sevenoaks," etc.,—the author made wholesome national honesty and pluck, against that background of cheap rascality that is so easily to be found, a theme for descriptive verse and permissibly didactic fiction. None of our writers has

Poetry of the soil.

Josiah Gilbert Holland, 1819-1881.

better understood the average national heart.
The real country-life of eastern America also appears in the novels of J. T. Trowbridge,
whose "Neighbor Jackwood" surpasses any story by Holland as a prose-
drama, faithful to the New England character and
its environment. A wholesome and sympathetic
portrayal of human nature underlies his best piece
of fiction, "Coupon Bonds," and his most successful poem, "The Vagabonds," both of which take
their place in the complex library of national delineation. Trowbridge sang of the homeless wanderer and his dog all the more effectively because
he had elsewhere described so well the comfortable home-life of the American farmer's family.
Tender knowledge is the groundwork for all success in folk-song. This "criticism of life" has
been called the poet's theme; and it appears here and there even in the midst of
the rollicking fun and inveterately mul-
tiplied puns of the burly, manly, friendly Ver-
monter Saxe, the facile humorist of a bygone
day, who wrote at least one lyric worthy of Praed :
"Wouldn't You Like to Know."

John Townsend Trowbridge, b. 1827.

John Godfrey Saxe, 1816–1887.

The essential unity of American life, increasing
rather than diminishing as the great tide of population sweeps westward, is shown in such a book
as Piatt's "Idyls and Lyrics of the Ohio
Valley," in which man and landscape and
tone are characteristically at one. The prairies of
the westernland, and the sunshine and pathos of
the full rural life of the broad interior states,

John James Piatt, b. 1835.

while they have a flavor of their own, in such
idyls as these, are closely kin to the heart of
Bayard Taylor's Pennsylvania ballads and Whittier's songs of New England. I like to turn to
the admirably-drawn frontispiece to Mr. Piatt's
"Idyls," and look long and half-reverently at the
rough and homely yet characteristically manly and
self-reliant face of Piatt's "Mower in Ohio," an
incarnation, whether in picture or verse, of average American manhood.

The old man is making hay all alone,—

> "And only the bees are abroad at work with me in the clover
> here,"—

for he has sent his boys to triumph or to die with
the Northern army. Meanwhile to Hayne and
Timrod, far in the south, their deathless heroism
seems paralleled by the devotion of the Confederate youth. With equal sincerity the
laureates of blue and of gray were exclaiming, with Hayne, in those tumultuous years :

Paul
Hamilton
Hayne,
1831–1886.

> Look round us now ; how wondrous, how sublime
> The heroic lives we witness ; far and wide
> Stern vows by sterner deeds are justified ;
>   Self-abnegation, calmness, courage, power,
>   Sway, with a rule august, our stormy hour,
> Wherein the loftiest hearts have wrought and died—
>   Wrought grandly and died smiling.

But South and North seemed too benumbed
with wound, or scared by fire, to sing many songs
of fit honor and acclaim for the heroic living and

the martyred dead. Hayne's poems of peaceful
life and lovely nature are better than his war-
songs; and, indeed, his historical, Revolutionary
"Battle of King's Mountain" is a nobler lyric
than those he sang in the later strife.

The South has thus far produced but one poet
of the first rank—Poe, though haply born in Boston and living in Philadelphia and New York, is
to be ranked as a Southerner in his origins of
ancestry and education. Of its singers of the
second grade Hayne is chief; his verse displays
the wealth and warmth of the landscape of South
Carolina and Georgia, the loneliness of the "pine
barrens" where nature seems unmolested, or the
swish of the wild Southern sea. As a sonnetteer,
too, his place is not far below Longfellow's;
American achievements in this important division
of verse have not been inconsiderable. When
Hayne, for a short period in his life, fell under
the influence of Morris-mediævalism, the merit of
his verse dwindled to that of occasional lines or
passages; but when he sang his own song in his
own land it was that of a true poet, who heard

> "Low words of alien music, softly sung.
> And rhythmic sighs in some sweet unknown tongue."

Far from the distributing centres of literature,
and unaided by the stimulus or the criticism
that come alone from association with brother
authors, Hayne wrote too much, nor polished
with sufficiently painstaking art. Hard, too, is
the lot of the bard whose whole life is devoted to

letters in a lonely land. I do not think, however, that deductions and limitations of excess or of failure can deny the poet's crown to him who wrote " Lethe," " Under Sentence," " Above the Storm," " Pre-existence," " Underground," " The Dryad of the Pine," " The Pine's Mystery," " Love's Autumn," " The Vision at Twilight," " The Inevitable Calm," " The Dead Look," " Over the Waters," " Forecastings," " The Visionary Face," the sonnets " At Last " and " Earth Odors after Rain," and the dramatic sketch " Antonio Melidori."

Another characteristic poet in Georgia was Henry Timrod, whose poems Hayne edited. His little book of verse is so good in its Henry Timrod, martial and general work, that it 1829-1867. makes us speculate on the possibilities which might have come in a longer life of one whose inspiration was so vivid that he half expected the incarnate spirit of springtide to appear in rosy flesh before him, in his woodland walks, exclaiming,

" Behold me ! I am May ! "

The poetry of a third Confederate, Sidney Lanier, is dear to an audience fit and now more than few, which often cherishes the memory of the early dead singer in biographical sketch, memorial tablet, or commendatory verse. None can fail to recognize in his poems the time-spirit, the land-song, and the true poetic touch, especially in " The Marshes of Glynn," " Sunrise," " The Song of the Chattahoochee," "The Mocking-Bird," or the more ambitious "Corn." His were a larger mind and a stronger hand than Timrod's or even Hayne's, yet his was a fatal fault : he lacked that spontaneity which is the chief pleasure in the verse of Hayne and Timrod. In the midst of the products of a genius that certainly at times seemed large, and that was bold to the extent of eccentricity, are the too-conspicuous signs of mere intellectual experiment and metrical or Sidney Lanier, verbal extravaganza. Lanier theorizes 1842–1881. in verse ; the practice-hand seeks to strike chords than can only come from the impassioned and self-forgetful singer of nature and the soul. His analytical and exhaustive musical studies—applied to literature in "The Science of English Verse"—greatly harmed his creative work.

The wild western scenes of the numerous poems of "Joaquin" Miller owe their success chiefly to the interest aroused (especially in England) by their descriptions of men and Cincinnatus Hiner Miller, women and skies utterly unfamiliar to b. 1841. readers in the older environments. Miller is the Sierra minstrel, who, on the basis of a natural aptitude fortified by an enthusiastic study of Byron and Swinburne, easily sings of the romantic experiences of a rich *terra incognita*, where the dash and fire of personal life stand forth against the background of snowy mountain, —"lonely as God and white as a winter moon,"— darksome gulch, or tropical river. His poems,

however, are but essays in song, perishable utterances of a freedom that must more slowly take
to itself the lessons of lasting art.

Another phase of nineteenth-century verse in
America, as marked and as characteristic as sentimentalism, the natural lyrical outburst, or the
local idyl or romance, has been the poetry of
thought and culture produced by men
and women of a fame and power below
Emerson's, who still have shared the
influence of the various upward movements of the
time. Thoreau, Jones Very, the younger Ellery
Channing, John S. Dwight, Cranch, and Mrs.
Hooper show how the broad Transcendental
revival of 1840 affected minor verse of many
tones,—now in the direction of religious or philosophic meditation, now in that of concise appeals
for courageous activity in life, and yet again in
mere reflection or observation of nature. The
volumes of *The Dial*, with much that is simply
quaint or hopelessly eccentric, contain verse of no
small merit, and the books of some of the writers
—they were not "singers"—just named are full
of what seems, after all, essays toward poetry
rather than poetry itself. Jones Very, a sort of
Unitarian monk and mystic, packed into many a
sonnet or meditative hymn rich and
weighty words of reverence and consecration, which he deemed inspired by ghostly
power from above, and which he wrote in implicit
obedience to the spiritual voice within. Some of
these poems are harmed by a semi-Buddhistic

Poetry of Thought and Culture.

Jones Very, 1813-1880.

Christian Quietism, as though Molinos had been
incarnated anew in the Salem streets; others display the serene sure beauty of church-yard lilies.
But the many preferred, and justly, a more
obvious and rememberable phrasing of vital
truth, such as Dwight made in his effective
poem entitled " Rest:"

John
Sullivan
Dwight,
b. 1813.

> Sweet is the pleasure
>   Itself cannot spoil!
> Is not true leisure
>   One with true toil?
>
> Thou that wouldst taste it,
>   Still do thy best;
> Use it, not waste it—
>   Else 'tis no rest.
>
> Wouldst behold beauty
>   Near thee? all round?
> Only hath duty
>   Such a sight found.
>
> Rest is not quitting
>   The busy career;
> Rest is the fitting
>   Of self to its sphere.
>
> 'Tis the brook's motion,
>   Clear without strife,
> Fleeing to ocean
>   After its life.
>
> Deeper devotion
>   Nowhere hath knelt;
> Fuller emotion
>   Heart never felt.

> 'Tis loving and serving
> The highest and best!
> 'Tis onwards! unswerving—
> And that is true rest.

The gospel of life and eternity shines through these seven stanzas! Mrs. Ellen Sturgis Hooper, like Dwight, displayed to the Massachu- setts circle of readers, in her brief life, the fact that culture was not incompatible with directness, earnestness, and reverence,—that, indeed, will must fertilize thought before thought can do its proper work in the world. The anthologies do not allow us to forget these half-dozen lines of hers, which I quote because they exactly show how Transcendental idealism set young Americans at work:

Ellen (Sturgis) Hooper, 1816-1841.

> I slept, and dreamed that life was Beauty,
> I woke, and found that life was Duty.
> Was thy dream then a shadowy lie?
> Toil on, sad heart, courageously;
> And thou shalt find thy dream to be
> A noonday light and truth to thee.

There is in Unitarianism a deeply devout spirit, as every reader of Bryant, Holmes, Longfellow, and such hymn-writers as Sir John Bowring, E. H. Sears and Mrs. Sarah Flower Adams well knows. The individualism and insight of the Transcendental movement was developing this spirit into a vital connection with literature, a connection to which other American books than those of Emerson and Thoreau are directly or indirectly indebted. Cranch went straight to the

Christopher
Pearse
Cranch,
b. 1813.

heart of the whole matter,—to the heart of spiritual perception,—in his oft-quoted lines:

> "Thought is deeper than all speech,
> Feeling deeper than all thought;"

and when he immediately added:

> "Souls to souls can never teach
> What unto themselves was taught,"

he truly phrased the essential loneliness of innermost experience. But the success of Transcendentalism, notwithstanding all its follies, lay in the fact that in Emerson's words, and in those of some of his associates, the "inner light" of one was made the illumination of others.

One from whom much was expected, in the days of *The Dial*, was the younger Channing,

William Ellery
Channing, Jr.,
b. 1818.

nephew of the eminent divine. Emerson sent some of young Channing's verses to Carlyle, who found them "worthy indeed of reading"; the poem on "Death," in particular, being "the utterance of a valiant, noble heart," of which, in rhyme or prose, Carlyle thought to hear more in the future. The same crisp critic, in the letter to Emerson in which he spoke thus kindly, added this reflection: "Let a man try to the very uttermost to speak what he means, before singing is had recourse to. Singing, in our curt English speech, contrived expressly and almost exclusively for 'dispatch of business', is terribly difficult." The history of

English verse, from Chaucer to Tennyson, instantly refutes this statement; the advice, however, was salutary at a period when even the Transcendentalists were falling into the time-fault of diffuseness. Channing's Miltonic line

"If my bark sinks, 'tis to another sea,"

like the best poetic product of Emerson, Thoreau, and their associates, was meritorious because it packed more thought in verse than prose could express. But no poet of his time is more addicted than Channing to the habit of maundering along through page after page of dull pseudo-poetry, like "The Wanderer" or "Eliot," never read by most and instantly forgotten by the patient few. Channing's thoughts are sometimes strong and new, and they are never contracted or tame; but when obscurity and ruggedness are added to prolixity we refuse to pardon the result, save in the case of one great poet of our time.

A later singer, of limited but valuable achievement retained much of the Transcendental lordly view of thought and life, and made verse express in terse and remember- *Edward Row- land Sill, 1841-1887.* able words the proper application of ideals to daily duty. Read once more E. R. Sill's six lines on "Life":

"Forenoon, and afternoon, and night,—Forenoon,
And afternoon, and night,—Forenoon, and—what?
The empty song repeats itself. No more?
Yea, that is Life: make this forenoon sublime,
This afternoon a psalm, this night a prayer,
And Time is conquered, and thy crown is won."

The American poetry of pure intellect deals not in abstractions alone, nor yet does it assoil pure thought or degrade the ideal, when it "hitches its wagon to a star." Sill was able, within his sphere, to show the relations between idea and act, while offering an ennobling conception of both, in clear language and few words—an ability which has not been tiresomely common in New England.

Many of the contributors to *The Dial* were women; and one of its editors was Margaret Fuller. Among the Brook Farm group, however, and among such later singers as Alice and Phœbe Cary, Celia Thaxter, Margaret J. Preston, and Lucy Larcom—whatever the merit of their pleasing verse—none was the peer of Helen Jackson ("H. H."), whose name outranked, at the time of her death, that of any other American woman who ever claimed the name of poet. Mrs. Jackson had the characteristics of the *Dial* group at its best: deep and sincere thought, uttered for its own sake in verse not untinged by the poetic inspiration and touch. In her poems the influence of the mind is felt before that of the heart; they are reflective and suggestive, sometimes concisely argumentative. Certain phases and senses of spirit, brain, and nature lay long in the poet's thought, and at length found deliberate and apt expression in word and metre. The character of H. H.'s product is explained by the frequency with which she chose single words —often abstract nouns—as titles. It is medita-

Helen Maria (Fiske) Jackson, 1831–1885.

tive, not lyrical; it lacks spontaneity and outburst; the utter joyance of the poetry of nature
and humanity, that will sing itself, is seldom
present, even when nature and man are the
themes. Large creative impulse is also absent.
It is therefore poetry that never rises above the
second class, but its place in that class is high.
Emerson, whose aptly-titled and curious anthology
"Parnassus" is chiefly valuable as a commentary
on his own mind and writings, recognized some of
the work of H. H. with a definite praise which he
seldom bestowed upon a contemporary American.
The poems he selected and lauded were constructed on lines partly parallel with his own,
though far enough below. In them it would be
unjust to say that feeling is absent, for H. H.'s
feeling was true, if delicately and reservedly
expressed. In such a poem as "Resurgam," one
of the longest she ever wrote, philosophic trust
becomes religious faith. Indeed, from the very
earliest of her poems, the rugged blank verse
which she wrote in 1865, after the death of her
husband and two children, her writings are usually
subjective and personal. It would be absurd to
call merely cold and intellectual the author of the
strong novel "Ramona"; which, with its precedent
prose-work "A Century of Dishonor," fairly burns
with a woman's just indignation at the wrongs
suffered by the Indians. But the ardor of her
poems is a quiet glow, it is not flame. One may
read them with recognition, it may be with satisfaction or even admiration, but without enthusiasm.

There can be no question that the work of
Woman in woman in American literature, and chiefly
Literature. in fiction and poetry, is hereafter to
command a study as deep as that bestowed upon
the work of men; but the fruitage of many
seeds is not yet, though the flowers are begin-
Sarah Morgan ning to appear.   The time will come
(Bryan) Piatt, when such insight, philosophic obser-
b. 1836   vation, and pithiness as Mrs. Piatt's;
such vital intensity as Miss Lazarus'; and such
Emma Lazarus, bright, gracious nature-chronicles as
1849–1887.   Miss   Edith   Thomas',—who   has
Edith   strayed from the Elizabethan days into
Matilda
Thomas, ours.—will be but preludes to a chorus
b. 1854. triumphant, many-voiced and long.

The effect, upon some few of the more eminent
American poets, of residence and study in France,
Germany, or Italy is sufficiently manifest, and has
elsewhere been discussed in the pages of this history.   The national verse-product, however, has
been little effected by Continental influences, so
The European far as the most of our greater singers
impact.   are concerned.   The European impact
upon the poems of Bryant (notwithstanding his
translations), Holmes, Whittier, Emerson, Poe,
and Whitman was not strong, and Longfellow
alone returned from the Old World with his mind
and genius saturated with the wine of mediæval
romance and modern Continental literature.   The
prose-works of our many literary diplomats have
shown a more potent effect of foreign study than
is visible in the writings of the poets who have

trodden the ancient fields. In some few cases,
however, the arts of the painter and the poet
have been joined in the same person, as in Allston, Cranch, and Read; as those of the sculptor
and poet have been displayed by Story. For
such men an Italian residence has been almost a
necessity, and thus, in the nineteenth century,
American literature has been in some slight way
affected by that land which so mightily taught
England after the Norman conquest had opened
the doors of the Continent to the singers and
scholars of our mother-tongue. Story, a Harvard graduate, son and biographer of the eminent
commentator on the Constitution, William Wetmore
began his career as a lawyer, but Story, b. 1819.
soon turned to sculpture and song, and became
a permanent resident of Italy. His dramatic
studies, of which "A Roman Lawyer in Jeru-
salem," "A Jewish Rabbi in Rome," and the
repulsively strong "Cleopatra" are the chief,
display a philosophic strength or a passionate fire
rare indeed in a division of literature to which
other Americans have made but feeble additions.
Method and result occasionally suggest Browning, but only because the scenes and the historic
thought of Italy seem naturally to have affected
two minds in somewhat similar ways. A few
of Story's delicate and muse-born lyrics, such as
"In the Moonlight," "In the Rain," "Love and
Death," and "In the Garden," are of the poet's
own land—not merely Italy's, but Ariel's and
Endymion's. Yet, notwithstanding the manlier
16

tone of " Io Victis" (the thought of which
Holmes better sang in " The Voiceless "), and
" After Many Days," Story's sweetly verbose
melancholy becomes monotonous, as in all other
followers of Heine save Longfellow. " Sunrise "
and " Moonrise " are longer poems that seem
based upon Shelley, but result in a sort of combination of Whitman and Sidney Lanier. His
books of verse, as a whole, present no more
than suggestive or pleasing material, not wrought
into a true and lasting result.

A somewhat fuller and more symmetrical
though equally limited poetic success is that of
Dr. Parsons, who was born in the same year with
Thomas William Story and Lowell, and who, in his
Parsons, b. 1819. life-task of Dante-translation, has
turned again and again toward the sunny land in
which his brother-poet lives. Parsons' place
among American poets has always been peculiar ;
he has been ignored by the many but prized by a
little public composed for the most part of those
who are themselves poets. The plain brown-cov-
ered book of his " Poems" (1854), worn and
shabby now, is often found in hands that have
themselves written verse as praiseworthy as that
of its author. In its best page, that containing
the lines " On a Bust of Dante," he exclaims :

> "O Time ! whose verdicts mock our own,
>   The only righteous judge art thou."

This judge, in a generation, has not established
Dr. Parsons' reputation on any other basis than

that on which may stand a minor poet of thought
and grace; nor will Parsons sing for a larger
future. To-day his books hold forth some few
finely-wrought verses, enriched by culture,
adorned by the touch of beauty, and occasionally
illumined by the light of the land of Dante's
vision, described by Dr. Parsons in his "Para-
disi Gloria":

> "There is a city builded by no hand,
>   And unapproachable by sea or shore,
>   And unassailable by any band
>   Of storming soldiery forevermore."

The latest Italian influence upon American
verse is to be found in the work of Gilder, collected in three volumes: "The New Day," "The
Celestial Passion," and "Lyrics." The title of
the first at once suggests that of Richard Watson
Dante's "New Life,"—noblest and Gilder, b. 1844.
most beautiful of all the contributions ever made
by Love to literature. In form and spirit, as well
as in name, Gilder shows how reverently and
sympathetically he has studied the prose and
verse of that artistic and picturesque old band of
singers whom Rossetti grouped as "Dante and
his Circle." Sincerity, conscientious and unworldly art, a devotion half-religious toward the
soul of an earthly love, and an attitude of rapt
and almost pietistic devoutness toward the maker
of that physical world whose riddle is transfigured
and so made plain by unworldly affection—these
were the qualities of the mighty, sad, and yet

serenely happy Florentine; and these are the
things that his followers in every age would show.
The self-respecting and unswerving loyalty of this
young singer toward his verbal art, and toward
the spirit that shapes his song, is praiseworthy.
He is in some ways a poet of his city and his
time; but more than either, to him, are the long
verities of his craft. His sincerity not unseldom
shapes itself in a worthy utterance; some of his
sonnets have a fit body for an inspiring thought;
and an occasional blank-verse fragment such as
the poem entitled " Recognition," or a terse lyric
worthy of being read by Landor, approves the
maker's art. Aim and plan, however, as yet out-
run achievement in Gilder's books, which are not
free from excrescences, fettered imitations, failures to reach the sought result, or grotesque
juvenilities like two much-laughed-at sonnets in
" The New Day." " Follow, follow," is still the
word of his muse; and there is no unwillingness
in the mind thus bidden.

The later and living poets of America, as the
nineteenth century draws to a close, hardly find
themselves in the position occupied by
their predecessors, forty years ago.
" The stories have all been told," says a
realistic critic of fiction; we cannot aver that " the
songs have all been sung," but it is certain that
the first national outburst has not been followed
by a second as great. It could not be, for the
flowering came after two centuries of dull and in-
conspicuous preparation and germination. Again,

American
poetry
to-day.

in England itself the romantic revival of 1800 has
long since spent its force, and the later Tennyson
and Browning loom up lone in a chorus of trio-
let-makers, with few save Arnold, Swinburne, and
Morris between their stature and that of the
little crowd. The tides of literature, and especially of poetry, rise and fall though time goes on ;
progress and readjustment will sooner or later fill
the places of Emerson, Longfellow, and Poe.
Meanwhile many a noble note is struck half un-
heard, in the maturer history of American verse,
which would have sounded clear and fine in the
early poverty-stricken days when everybody who
could manufacture a couplet,—pious, patriotic,
or sentimental,—was forthwith deemed a poet.
There was no more than one American writer,
before Bryant, who could have conceived or expressed in a dozen pages, such thoughts, for
instance, as Henry Abbey puts into two lines
like these :

> " Read the round sky's star-lettered page, or grope
> In the abysses of the microscope ; " *

nor could the combined talent of the whole company of our imaginative writers before Drake
(always excepting Freneau) have produced a
poem so good as the same author's " Irak "; yet
Abbey is a comparatively obscure poet. One of
ten thousand massed flowers is less distinguisha-

* " Science and the Soul."

ble than a single weed blossom here and there. But broad prodigality will sometime produce a Milton or at least a Keats :

> " Come hither, Muse, rest on our Western shore ;
> The sea is narrow, and the time is come.
> Heart, home and freedom, and thine English tongue
> Have builded here. Thou shalt have room and love,
> What shady nook, what sunlit stream is yon,
> But we here sunnier, shadier ? Younger lands,
> And greener woods and songs of peace are here." †

I have been considering some names of living singers, but as connected with tendencies the force of which is for the most part spent. Now that I turn to the immediately present names of the second poetic period, I cannot refrain from putting at the head of the list the name of Bayard Taylor, though he went hence now a decade ago. The dissipating and almost destroying tendencies of modern intellectual life, especially in new and multifarious America, seemed almost cruel in the case of that adventurous traveller, attractive Pennsylvania novelist, entertaining lecturer, well-equipped critic, wholesome wit, industrious journalist, and manly man, who ever loved poetry most of all, and who, save Holmes, was at once the most natural and the most accomplished American master of the purely lyrical art since Poe. The melodies of the

Bayard Taylor, 1825–1878.

An Invocation," by William Hayes Ward, D.D.

infinite song rang in his ear, and he almost caught
and reproduced in verse some high strains of the
universe of matter and of man. But

> " Now I hear it not :—I loiter
> Gayly as before ;
> Yet I sometimes think,—and thinking
> Makes my heart so sore,—
> Just a few steps more,
> And there might have shone for me,
> Blue and infinite, the sea."

From his quiet and opulent Chester County in
Pennsylvania to Europe in the east, to California
in the west, to frozen Iceland in the far north,
and to torrid ancient Egypt in the sun-drenched
continent of the south, Taylor travelled with the
poet's wander-staff ; and from nearly every field
he brought back some ballad or other lyric, some
dramatic sketch or Parnassian thought. A few of
these he modestly called " Rhymes of Travel "—
it was at least well to show that America had at
length become rich enough to call true poems
" rhymes," having begun by declaring rhymes to
be poems. The classical influence and spirit,
also, were not wanting in a singer, who, like
Keats, had lacked the mellowing influences of
collegiate life. And what other English-speaking
poet has so reproduced the very atmosphere of
the Orient as did this writer of the lovely " Bed-
ouin Song," this " Western Asiatic," as his friend
and loyal critic Stedman aptly calls him ? The
Yankee Unitarian Emerson, from Massachusetts,
and the Quaker Taylor from Pennsylvania,

stretched forth their hands to the realms of "The Lord's Lay" and "The Arabian Nights." But Taylor was not the less American; he wrote "Poems of Home and Travel," and "The Quaker Widow" is purely of his own soil and time. Nearer still to his own heart and experiences are parts of "The Poet's Journal"—which, in its externals, proffers hexameters almost as good as Longfellow's.

I would call Taylor's last years a period of poetic decline, were it not for its two brilliant successes. When I think of "The Picture of St. John," "Lars; a Pastoral of Norway," "The Prophet; a Tragedy," "Home Pastorals, Ballads, and Lyrics," the resonant but imperfectly successful Ode for the national centennial in 1876, and "Prince Deukalion; a Lyrical Drama," there comes to mind the memory of scattered successes and an irregular conglomerate failure. Seldom does achievement lag so far behind desire as in the case of the "Deukalion." Taylor sought to make it a poem fitly chronicling the entire upward and onward march of man, but overwork and failing powers are sadly manifest.

Yet, after all, neither vain excuse nor word of deep disappointment need embitter our memories of one who produced (albeit in three years) a metrical version of Faust that for practical purposes is faultless, and who wrote (in four days) "The Masque of the Gods," our best addition to the loftiest or religious division of the drama, the highest form of literature.

To George H. Boker, Taylor's friend, editor, and fellow-Pennsylvanian, also belongs George Henry Boker, b. 1823. one of the infrequent American suc- cesses in the department of the drama. As Taylor attained, in " The Masque of the Gods," a serene height of religious expression which Longfellow usually missed in his similar efforts, so Boker, with much of Longfellow's bookishness, added to some of his dramas a playwright's skill. When I read Boker's " Francesca da Rimini " and "Calaynos," in my college days, their *atmosphere* impressed me quite as strongly as their words and deeds ; the student of Italian life, yet most influenced by the mighty plays of the period of Shakespeare and his fellows, brought to his page the far unworldly charm which belongs to letters and the library lamp. But in later years an eminent American actor found in the first named of these plays the acting-quality as well as the closet-beauty. In the desert of the American drama the work of Boker, then, is doubly welcome. It is not " indigenous " or new or indispensable ; it merely offers somewhat of the strength of word, the flame of color, the intensity of act, of the earlier or later English makers of plays, to whom the bloody pages of mediæval history have been so rich an inspiration. That verbal grace which must be added to sincere sentiment, if a good lyric is to be made, is a mark of some of Boker's songs, such as the " Dragoon's Song," the " Lancer's Song," or the " Dirge for a Sailor," beginning :

Slow, slow! toll it low,
  As the sea-waves break and flow,
With the same dull, slumberous motion
As his ancient mother, Ocean,
    Rocked him on through storm and calm,
    From the iceberg to the palm :
    So his drowsy ears may deem
    That the sound which wakes his dream
    Is the ever-moaning tide,
    Washing on his vessel's side.

Others of his lyrics are hurried and imperfect, with weak words and forced rhymes. But as we look back upon the past half-century of American verse his dramatic work, though not of the greatest, stands out the more clearly. We have produced dozens of song-makers, but seldom a dramatic author, and only two writers of acting plays which are also pieces of literature : Payne (" Brutus ") and Boker.

The third singer in the trio of poets which included Taylor and Boker was R. H. Stoddard ; the three were united in bonds of personal friendship and literary enthusiasm as firm as those which for a lifetime joined Lowell the poet, William Page the painter, and Charles F. Briggs the *littérateur*. Boker's literary life has always been connected with Philadelphia—once our greatest city and literary as well as political capital, but more distinguished of late for culture than creation. Stoddard, Massachusetts-born, has long been a leading member of that " New York group " which once, notwithstanding the renown of Irving, Bryant, and Poe,

Richard Henry Stoddard, b. 1825.

was less conspicuous than the Boston and Cambridge and Concord coteries, but which, in these
latter days, is drawing to itself a large part of the
genius of the land. New York is old enough, and
widely-rich enough, to proffer many of the advan-
tages and distractions of a book and periodical
centre like London or Paris; and Stoddard,
therein, has been a man of letters from the first.
His extensive acquaintance with English verse,
equalled only by Stedman's, and his artistic taste
and fearlessness of speech, have been long
devoted to that anonymous literary criticism
which he has contributed to the omnivorous and
short-memoried periodical press, and to his
acknowledged editorial work upon anthologies,
collections of prose essays or *ana*, and editions
of standard authors. But his heart of hearts and
song of songs are the poet's; to his Arcady,
Arabia, and Ind no breath of custom-house, city
library, or newspaper office has ever come. I do
not mean to say that he has not been tempted at
times, by the calls that so frequently beset the
metropolitan man-of-letters, to swift improvisations, extravaganzas, or medleys in verse, designed to fit a temporary wish or demand. The
gap between his best and worst is sadly wide.
But his five hundred pages of collected poems are
full-freighted with the *opima spolia* of observation,
reflection, fancy, imagination. Let him who fears
that American materialism can silence the chant of
the soul and the carol of nature turn to Stoddard
and find sufficient answer in him alone. Though

> "We have two lives about us,
>   Two worlds in which we dwell,
> Within us, and without us,
>   Alternate Heaven and Hell,
> Without the sombre Real,
> Within our heart of hearts the beautiful Ideal,"

yet the poet's

> " Castle stands alone,
>   In some delicious clime,
>   Away from Earth and Time,
>   In Fancy's tropic zone,
>   Beneath its summer skies,
>   Where all the life-long year the Summer
>   never dies."

I remember, as of yesterday, the fresh open-air delight, the seeming presence of bird, breeze, and flower, with which in boyhood I read Stoddard's "Songs of Summer"; and as I return to them I find indeed that their season "never dies," for it is the eternal summer of song. In the proem to the collected edition the poet tells us that

> " These songs of mine, the best that I have sung,
>   Are not my best, for caged within the lines
>   Are thousands better (if they would but sing!)."

So it is in all literature, for so it is in a life the whole secret of which is long development from the imperfect and the confined. There is a place for poets below—far below—Sophocles, Horace, Dante, Shakespeare; for we know not when the sphere-song or the nature-word will come from such lyrics as these. Whether they live in litera-

ture is unimportant, for every message of the
ideal is welcome to some one, in whose true life
it can never be lost. Stoddard is to be recognized
in the muses' court not only because he is one of
the few Americans who can write blank verse (it
is natural that he hails Bryant as our chief bard);
not because the mysteries of the sonnet and the
ode are open to him, but chiefly for the spontaneous and imaginative music which is *ubique gen-
tium* the best credential of the poet, whether he
write epics or the shortest Elizabethan madrigal
or Scotch love-song. I cannot follow Stoddard in
his evident preference for his songs on Asian
themes; nor can I praise the too numerous pessimistic and aging strains betokening overmuch a
sense of life's weariness and uncertain skies. Let
his best and brightest self sing down in a lyric, or
weigh down with some strong line from sonnet or
ode, such anacreontic memories, such cis-Atlantic
echoes or sympathetic answers of Heine,—whose
influence in the world I am almost ready to
declare mischievous. The *credo* of this poet and
of all poets is found in the best work Stoddard
has yet produced, his " Hymn to the Beautiful."
It is conspicuously influenced by Wordsworth's
great ode; it reminds us now of Shelley, now of
Keats; its two first divisions are weak; nor, of
course, is it novel in its deep fundamental devout
idea, underlying many poems and
uttered in many words all adown the
line of the centuries. The idea is the
very soul of art: the thing of beauty that is a joy

The Soul of Poetry: "Hymn to the Beautiful."

forever; the truth that is beauty and the beauty that is truth; the beauty that is its own excuse for being. Never can singer attempt to phrase a deeper thought than this :*

> My heart is full of tenderness and tears,
>   And tears are in my eyes, I know not why,
> With all my grief content to live for years,
>   1   Or even this hour to die.
> My youth is gone, but that I heed not now,
>   My love is dead, or worse than dead can be,
> My friends drop off, like blossoms from a bough,
>   But nothing troubles me,—
> Only the golden flush of sunset lies
> Within my heart like fire, like dew within my eyes.

> Spirit of Beauty! whatsoe'er thou art,
>   I see thy skirt afar, and feel thy power;
>   It is thy presence fills this charmèd hour,
>   And fills my charmèd heart:
> Nor mine alone, but myriads feel thee now,
> That know not what they feel, nor why they bow.
>   Thou canst not be forgot,
> For all men worship thee, and know it not;
> Nor men alone, but babes with wondrous eyes,
>   New-comers from the skies.
> We hold the keys of Heaven within our hands,
>   The heirloom of a higher, happier state,
>   And lie in infancy at Heaven's gate,
> Transfigured in the light that streams along the lands.
> Around our pillows golden ladders rise,
>   And up and down the skies,
>   With wingèd sandals shod,

---

* With the exception of one obvious misprint, I have followed, as in duty bound, the author's revised text of 1880, though not deeming it in all respects an improvement upon that given in the 1852 volume of "Poems."

The angels come and go, the Messengers of God!
Nor, though they fade from us, do they depart—
    It is the childly heart:
    We walk as heretofore,
  Adown their shining ranks, but see them nevermore.
Heaven is not gone, but we are blind with tears,
Groping our way along the downward slope of years!

From earliest infancy my heart was thine,
  With childish feet I trod thy temple aisles,
  Not knowing tears, I worshipped thee with smiles,
Or if I wept it was with joy divine.
By day, and night, on land, and sea, and air,
    I saw thee everywhere.
A voice of greeting from the wind was sent,
  The mists enfolded me with soft white arms,
The birds did sing to lap me in content,
    The rivers wove their charms,
And every little daisy in the grass
Did look up in my face, and smile to see me pass.
Not long can Nature satisfy the mind,
  Nor outward fancies feed its inner flame;
  We feel a growing want we cannot name,
And long for something sweet, but undefined.
The wants of Beauty other wants create,
Which overflow on others, soon or late;
For all that worship thee must ease the heart,
    By Love, or Song, or Art.
Divinest Melancholy walks with thee,
And Music with her sister Poesy;
But on thy breast Love lies, immortal child,
Begot of thine own longings, deep and wild;
The more we worship him the more we grow
Into thy perfect image here below;
For here below, as in the spheres above,
All Love is Beauty, and all Beauty—Love!
Not from the things around us do we draw
  The love within, within the love is born,
  Remembered light of some forgotten morn,

Recovered canons of eternal law.
The painter's picture, the rapt poet's song,
　　The sculptor's statue, never saw the Day—
　　Were never in colors, sounds, or shapes of clay,
Whose crowning work still does its spirit wrong.
Hue after hue divinest pictures grow,
　　Line after line immortal songs arise,
And limb by limb, out-starting stern and slow,
　　The statue wakes with wonder in its eyes :
　　　　And in the Master's mind
　　Sound after sound is born, and dies like wind,
　　That echoes through a range of ocean caves,
And straight is gone to weave its spell upon the waves.
　　　　The mystery is thine,
For thine the more mysterious human heart,
The Temple of all wisdom, Beauty's shrine,
　　　　The Oracle of Art!

Earth is thine outer court, and Life a breath.
　　Why should we fear to die, and leave the Earth?
　　Not thine alone the lesser key of Birth,
　　　　But all the keys of Death.
And all the worlds, with all that they contain
　　Of Life, and Death, and Time, are thine alone;
The Universe is girdled with a chain,
　　　　And hung below the Throne
Where Thou dost sit, the Universe to bless,
Thou sovereign Smile of God, Eternal Loveliness!

On this ever-recurrent theme none is more
worthy to speak than a poet who has surveyed the
entire field of contemporary English and American verse, noting wherein it has followed or
Edmund Clarence spurned the eternal canons. Sted-
Stedman, b. 1833. man's related volumes, "Victorian
Poets" and "Poets of America," are from the pen
of a man who has elsewhere told us that "crit-

icism is the art and practice of declaring in what
degree any word, character, or action conforms to
the Right;" and that "the consensus of the fine
arts . . . . is such that, while each has inexorable
limits, they all move in harmony, and subject
to the same enduring principles." The value of
these critical surveys depends even more upon
their author's perception and delicately-clear but
never impertinent statement of this broad principle than upon his extended and indefatigable
studies and his felicity of expression.* He understands the harmony of the arts—all of them,
whether spoken or written language, dramatic
action, painting, sculpture, architecture, music,
mere means of intellectual and spiritual presentation from mind to mind—and in himself refutes
all idea of the essential severance of the critical
function from the creative, because he makes criticism creation. Naturally we find his poetry to
be that of one who sings because he must, yet
with devotion to the austere principles of an art
that held Shakespeare and Dante in bonds that
none were less desirous than they to spurn. Art
without soul is worthless; soul without form is

* The student of American poetry must turn with constant obligation to
the critical aid furnished by Mr. Stedman's volume thereon—the first adequate study of an important division of verse. In that volume one recognizes Mr. Stedman's breadth and depth of catholic learning, as well as the
illuminating power of discriminating utterance possessed by a poet who
constantly shows how nearly related are the criticism of art and the creation
of art. To him all friends of American letters must constantly remain in
debt;—nor would I attempt to lead my readers through the same paths
were it not made necessary by the general plan of my history, undertaken
years before the publication of "Poets of America," and based, of course,
upon ideas often different from those of my predecessor.

17

voiceless; Stedman's poetry—described unconsciously in his own words concerning another—is
that of

> the brave soul
> Which, touched with fire, dwells not on whatsoever
>   Its outer senses hold in their intent,
> But, sleepless even in sleep, must gather toll
> Of dreams which pass like barks upon the river
>   And make each vision Beauty's instrument;
> That from its own love Love's delight can tell,
>   And from its own grief guess the shrouded Sorrow;
> From its own joyousness of Joy can sing;
>   That can predict so well
> From its own dawn the lustre of to-morrow,
>   The whole flight from the flutter of the wing.*

This is the soul not only of the life-romancer
but of every true lyrist and idyllist. The choice
(and now very rare) London collection of Stedman's best poems written prior to 1879
is fitly entitled "Lyrics and Idyls, with
other Poems." Their author is pre-eminently a
lyrist (as he early indicated in his " Poems, Lyric
and Idyllic "), not many notes of whose Pan-song
have been lost in his banker-life in the metropo-
lis, for the great pavemented city, with its overshadowing masses of brick and stone, has never
been able to banish the idyllic from his thought
and verse. The ready pen of the journalist suggested, in his young manhood, that brilliant but
forgotten social satire " The Diamond Wedding,"
and perhaps the more enduring ante-war ballad.
" How Old Brown took Harper's Ferry." But

A lyrist and idyllist.

---

* Stedman's " Hawthorne and other Poems," pp. 15, 16.

"Alice of Monmouth," published in the dark year 1864, was rightly called in its sub-title, "An *Idyl* of the Great War." Its battle pictures have a vividness that Whitman's verse or prose is powerless to rival :

Friends and foes,—who could discover which,
As they marked the zigzag, outer ditch,
Or lay so cold and still in the bush,
Fallen and trampled down in the last wild rush?
Then the shattered forest-trees; the clearing there
Where a battery stood; dead horses, pawing the air
With horrible upright hoofs; a mangled mass
Of wounded and stifled men in the low morass,
And the long trench dug in haste for a burial-pit
Whose yawning length and breadth all comers fit.

And over the dreadful precinct, like the lights
That flit through graveyard walks in dismal nights,
Men with lanterns were groping among the dead,
Holding the flame to every hueless face,
And bearing those whose life had not wholly fled
On stretchers, that looked like biers, from the ghastly
place.

But in other pages it tells us how

Softly the rivulet's ripples flow;
Dark is the grove that lover's know;
Here, where the whitest blossoms blow
The reddest and ripest berries grow;

or bids us look upward to a diffused sky-glory that is a celestial omen of ultimate brotherhood :

Immeasurable, white, a spotless fire, . . .
Gleams of the heavenly city walled with gold!

The poet's view of life is all-inclusive; city and country, war and peace, present and future, time Life and eternity, are equal for the seer who the Poet. sings of flower or star, life or death, brook or battle-field, and would interpret the secret of the whole. There is no violent or unintentional contrast between the parts of this remarkable and rememberable poem, the metrical wealth of which is alone enough to attract attention to its story and its pictures. And the daintiness of the little lyric called "Toujours Amour"; the rustic spirit of "The Doorstep"; the grim strength of "The Lord's Day Gale" (both of which Whittier might have written); the hearthstone affection of the lines to "Laura, my Darling," are inconsistent neither with the sweet mediæval allegorism of "The Blameless Prince" nor with the distinctive Americanism and vitality of the swiftly-moving John Brown narrative. The singer properly refuses to abstract himself, like Poe, from half of life; nor can we wish it in days when even a Tennyson must perforce turn from Surrey or the Isle of Wight toward the Crimea, or venture the solution of the innermost problems of British society.

The philosophy of Mr. Stedman's poetic product, if the term may be applied without hiding the preëminent singing quality of that product, The Old and if I understand his aim, seems to Thought in lie in his broad view of the relations of New Times. nature and man in time, and of the necessarily catholic function of the poet. He who

has noted the inner purposes and the superficial
fashions of the Victorian bards, and has shown
how the great religious, political, and social
movements from 1840 to 1865 affected the American choir, would be unlikely to write verse unin-
fluenced by the same conditions, and by their
serious observation on his own part. The student
and translator of Theocritus, the lover of the
Elizabethan madrigals, and the editor of that
modern Greek, Landor, he perceives that the poet
may enrich his thought with the spoils of thirty
centuries, and be the more, rather than the less,
fitted to write a Yankee love-lyric or a battle-song
of to-day. There can be no question that our
contemporary poets are readers as well as singers ;
Wordsworth's private library, with its three hundred volumes, would have starved Lowell or Stedman. "Ofte thenkyng," says the Wycliffe version
of Ecclesiastes, "is turment of fleisch" ; and certainly it is a torment to the spontaneity which
should be a mark of the minstrel. But he who
reads in order to sing aright and betimes, may,
like Stedman, find his theme in the daily paper,
nor sacrifice one whit of constant devotion to the
serenely spiritual :

> Above the clouds I lift my wing
> To hear the bells of Heaven ring :
> Some of their music, though my flights be wild,
> To earth I bring;
> Then let me soar and sing ! *

* "The Singer," in "Early Poems."

How often do the poets, in the freshness of
their youth, utter this word of life-long allegiance!
Nor can it be renounced in middle-life or age by
the company of those who, in perennial youth, are
ever "children of the morrow"—and of the moun-
tain-top. The poet's mind is to him a higher
kingdom than that of the "middle-earth" of the
Anglo-Saxons; for though he lives among men he
leads them because of his loftier outlook. To
him, in allegory as well as in fact, as to Stedman
in that one of his "Poems of Nature" entitled
"The Mountain"

> The proud city seems a mole
> To this horizon-bounded whole;
> And, from my station on the mount,
> The whole is little worth account
> Beneath the overhanging sky,
> That seems so far and yet so nigh.
> Here breathe I inspiration rare,
> Unburdened by the grosser air
> That hugs the lower land, and feel
> Through all my finer senses steal
> The life of what that life may be,
> Freed from this dull earth's density,
> When we with many a soul-felt thrill,
> Shall thrid the ether at our will,
> Through widening corridors of morn
> And starry archways swiftly borne.

This central thought of poetry may easily be
pushed to affectation or absurdity; and in its too
eager search we may profess to discover "inner
meanings" which the song was never intended to
bear; but its comprehension is the key of lyric or

idyl, sonnet or epic. This to know is also the utter removal of that foolish provincialism or *quidnunc* superficial curiosity which declares that *American* poetry, if it would exist at all, must be limited to pictures of the wharf, the prairie, and the gulch; to city directories and geographical indexes; to axe-swinging pioneers and moral murderers.

The literary career of Mr. Stedman, then, is in all its course a sufficiently instructive illustration of the dominance of the "gay science" over wordly weal, and yet of the constant friendliness and companionship of the two. The service of art, like that of religion, is perfect freedom, whatever the imprisoning environment. I suppose no more strenuous or forbidding circumstances can be imagined for a poet than the duties of a war-correspondent in the field, or the stress of a banker's daily life. When I add that Mr. Stedman turned aside, in mature years, to make a long prose survey of the multiform poetic product of his time, the dissipation or distraction that has beset him would seem to be complete. Not so; the field of battle, as we have seen, subserved the artistic good of "Alice of Monmouth"; in Wall Street he found the wandering Pan; and from criticism he returned to song with new strength and seriousness of devotion. The poet's life is dual, but however long the soul and the body strive in earth or air, the soul must win. Stedman has kept clear of the increasing sense of sadness that has fallen, mistlike, over so much of

the later verse of his fellow-worker, Stoddard.
As one re-reads his books in course, a steady
progress is marked. After the war-fire of "Alice
of Monmouth" came the serene idyllic romance of
"The Blameless Prince," as from the land of
Morris and Rossetti, but of wholesomer tone;
while such metrical experiments as "Surf" or the
Greek translations, and such stray dramatic
studies as "Anonyma," prepared the way for the
strength and inspiring suggestiveness of the
"Dartmouth Ode," or the fit commemoration of
Hawthorne read at Harvard in 1877. Stedman
has been tempted overmuch, like most American
singers, by current themes of humor or pathos,
dedication or commemoration; but even his occasional verse has risen to the merit of the two
productions just mentioned; the lyric on "Liberty
Enlightening the World"; the terse lines "On
the Death of an Invincible Soldier" (Grant); or
the scholarly ode "Corda Concordia," read at the
opening, in 1881, of the Concord Summer School
of Philosophy. None but a mature strength
could have written the poem on "The Hand of
Lincoln," "A Vigil," "The World Well Lost,"
or the quaintly archaic "Star Bearer." But
whether one read the simpler lyrics of his youth,
the two long poems, the exquisite song beginning

> I know not if moonlight or starlight
> Be soft on the land and the sea,—
> I catch but the near light, the far light,
> Of eyes that are burning for me,

or the statelier and serener productions of later
years, he quickly recognizes the poet; and notes,
as he turns the pages of the successive volumes,
the onward and upward steps of a true minstrel-
journey. If he feels the lack of a large, consoli-
dated product, or at least of an adequately representative product, he thinks of the troubled times
and manifold duties of the poet's first-half of life,
and remembers that the richer years are still
before him.

The poetry of Thomas Bailey Aldrich may be
described, with substantial fairness, in the terse
words wherein Emerson characterizes Herrick:
he "is the lyric poet, ostentatiously Thomas Bailey
choosing petty subjects, petty names Aldrich, b. 1836.
for each piece, and disposing of his theme in
a few lines, or in a couplet; is never dull, and
is the master of miniature painting." Aldrich's
limitations and failures have been recognized
first of all by himself; he has anticipated his
critics in that rigid judgment of his own works
which is so indignantly repelled by the majority
of singers. His literary pathway is strewn with
abandoned books and poems: the pretty juvenile
story, " Daisy's Necklace, and What Came of It";
the romance, " Out of his Head"; many a lyric;
and an occasional blank-verse narrative like " Gar-
naut Hall," which seems to me well worth saving.
Through his early verse stole pleasant echoes of
Keats or Tennyson; in later days he has sometimes essayed, as in " Miantowona," to treat an
Indian legend in an unfamiliar metre, whereby an

injurious comparison with Longfellow has immediately occurred to the reader's mind; and his
dramatic pictures have been studies rather than
creations. "Friar Jerome's Beautiful Book"
proves his success in narrative verse, attested
once more in "Judith," to whom an Anglo-Saxon
singer thus returned a thousand years after the
first of our poems on that attractive but difficult
theme. Large creative force, however, is not the
quality upon which Aldrich relies; whatsoever
belongs to the sweet or dainty or epigrammatic
lyric of art or impression is his. From his experi-
An American ments in subject and treatment he
Herrick. returns to his chosen field of early
youth with renewed confidence and more assured
success. The singer and his readers would laugh,
perhaps, if I were seriously to place him on a
level with Herrick; and yet the aspiration of the
closing lines of his address to that master has
sometimes been fulfilled in Aldrich's work:

> If thy soul, Herrick, dwelt with me,
> This is what my songs would be:
> Hints of our sea-breezes, blent
> With odors from the Orient;
> Indian vessels deep with spice,
> Star-showers from the Norland ice;
> Wine-red jewels that seem to hold
> Fire, but only burn with cold;
> Antique goblets, strangely wrought,
> Filled with the wine of happy thought;
>
> Bridal measures, vain regrets,
> Laburnum buds and violets;

Hopeful as the break of day;
Clear as crystal; new as May;
Musical as brooks that run
O'er yellow shadows in the sun;
Soft as the satin fringe that shades
The eyelids of thy fragrant maids;
Brief as thy lyrics, Herrick, are,
And polished as the bosom of a star.

Passing by those Eastern themes and scenes which have never lost their charm for him— "Dressing the Bride," "When the Sultan goes to Ispahan," "The Sultana," etc.—one finds many a song of delicate quality, assuring to Aldrich, in the history of American poetry, a place of his own,— not that of a masterly bard, not that of a successor of the dead leaders of American song, but that of a maker of lines—or "Intaglios," as he calls them in one division—which we may call "painted trifles and fantastic toys," without any intimation that they are not worthy of due praise. One hardly need turn to the book for songs that sing themselves in the brain: "Before the Rain," "After the Rain," "Tiger-Lilies," "May," "Nameless Pain," "The Lunch," "At Two and Twenty," "Amontillado," "The One White Rose," "The Voice of the Sea," which, whether grave or gay, have something of the charm Aldrich himself describes, as of

Rememberable Poems.

"Four-line epics one might hide
In the hearts of roses."

In my boyhood I used to go about repeating to myself the more ghostly or ghastly verses, such as " Glamourie," " December," " Haunted," " The Tragedy," and " Seadrift ;" nor am I quite willing, even now, to give up poems which had the singing tone, though not the finished art, of " Palabras Cariñosas " or " A Snowflake."

Aldrich has not scorned the obvious and universal in sentiment, as is shown by his widely known " Baby Bell," the Beranger-like "The Flight of the Goddess," " The Bluebells of New England," or the well-turned sonnets " Fredericksburg " or " Pursuit and Possession." The maturer years, however, have enabled him to strike from a reflective mind, with his fullest art, those brief poems of thoughtful conceit which have brought him his best fame and his highest claim to original creation : " An Untimely Thought," " Destiny," " Rencontre," and " Identity," alike admirable in execution and well deserving the attention they have drawn from many readers and an occasional masterful artist. I cannot however, assign to a place beside " An Untimely Thought " or " Destiny " the famous eight lines entitled " Identity " —best known of all Aldrich's poems. Its cleverness of phrase conceals the essential falsity of its underlying thought. If shuddering shapes that have forth-fared have no identity, then, indeed, they are dead when they are dead.

American literature hardly affords a more striking contrast than that between Aldrich and the Walt Whit- last poet to be chronicled in this chapter. man, b. 1819. Walt Whitman has strength without artistic power or desire, and therefore would

remand metre, rhyme, and form in general to the
bygone days of a hollow and artificial literature
and a superficial and conventional life.

In absolute ability he is about equal to Taylor,
Stoddard, Stedman, or Aldrich; but by minimizing the spiritual and the artistic, and magnifying
the physical and the crudely spontaneous, he has
attracted an attention among critics in America,
England, and the Continental nations greater, for
the moment, than that bestowed upon any contemporary singer of his nation, and fairly rivalling
the international adulation of his exact opposite,
Poe. To him the ideal is little and the immediately actual is much; love is merely a taurine or
passerine passion; and to-day is a thing more important than all the past. His courage is unquestionable; his vigor is abounding; and therefore,
by the very paradox of his extravagant demands,
he has impressed some and interested more, and
has induced a limited but affectionate and exceed-
ingly vociferous coterie to attempt, for his
sake, to revise the entire canon of the world's art.
Many famous authors have bestowed upon him
high praise—sometimes revoked or ignored in
the calmer years of advancing life; and though
unread by the masses whose spokesman and
prophet he claims to be, and without special influence or increasing potency, he has been for a
generation one of the most conspicuous of his
country's authors.

Whitman's prose need not detain us long. In
youth he wrote for *The Democratic Review* and

other periodicals brief stories (courageously re-
Whitman's prose. printed in his complete prose-volume,
"Specimen Days and Collect "), which, in
theme and treatment, are about equal to the
forgotten minor fiction of the sentimental time
in which they appeared. Their chief characteristics are obvious morality of the Sunday-school-
book order, and a sensationalism which lacked an
effective literary form. The domestic virtues, the
evils of intemperance, the far-reaching consequences of "One Wicked Impulse," etc., were
portrayed in language which assuredly harmed
none and doubtless benefited some. "The Child
and the Profligate," " Wild Frank's Return,"
" Lingrave's Temptation," " Little Jane," " Dumb
Kate," etc., occupy that pleasant borderland of
literature which is secure from the intrusion of
either praise or blame. The remainder of the
volume is filled with random jottings concerning
the author's life in army hospitals during the war ;
his experiences and sensations in city or country ;
his reflections on literature and life ; his reminiscences of Lincoln and other celebrities ; his impressions of American travel ; his broadly optimistic views of democracy (chiefly expressed in a
long essay entitled " Democratic Vistas ") ; and
various prefaces to successive editions of his
poems. The prose, whatever its theme, is that of
an honest, hearty, healthful man, fond of the
ruddier and commoner elements in humanity,
impressed by natural scenery and out-door life,
ardently attached to his country and his time, and

sincerely believing in that country's future. The pleasant quality of these miscellaneous pages is their outspoken freshness; but their prose style is a model of inelegance and unattractiveness, from the pen of one who never learned to write well, and who fell, in an untutored state, into a lifelong enslavement to the more obvious mannerisms of Carlyle. "Specimen Days and Collect," in brief, has no value save as a commentary upon its author's poetry, and even here its importance is small, for poetry that is not self-interpretative is the possession not of literature but of the estimable company of "conjectural readers" and discoverers of "inner meanings." Whitman would be the last to claim that "Leaves of Grass," his lifework, does not explain its reason for being.

The plan of "Leaves of Grass," patiently, courageously and consistently elaborated piece by piece during the author's whole lifetime (and set forth not only in the poems themselves but in needlessly numerous and verbose prefaces and prose articles by the author, as well as in his spoken words), is to present a complete picture of typical humanity in the author's time and land, especially in its pioneer constructiveness, material achievements, and hearty comradeship, "Leaves of omitting no animal element of the whole Grass." personality which we call man or woman, but celebrating and glorifying all. In this picture, physical passion plays a large part, but in the claim of the author and his friends, not a disproportionate one; other equally important physiological functions, such as digestion and the circulation of the blood, are ignored. The sexuality of Whitman's poems forms their most obvious characteristic, attracting the notice of the evil-minded, disgusting the majority of readers, and ardently defended by the members of the Whitman cult, including men and women of whose moral integrity and intellectual capacity there can be no question. As regards this matter, it is perfectly true that passages as objectionable as those in " Leaves of Grass " may be culled from the best Hebrew, Arabian, Greek, Latin, Italian, French and English literature ; that "to the pure all things are pure ;" and that the nineteenth century is the first, in the history of the world's society, to insist upon the omission of mention of the coarser elements in physical passion. Furthermore, Whitman is not the worst author in the world, even in an increasingly fastidious era. There are some poets, who, without specially indecent illusion, throw around and from their books a mephitic atmosphere more deadening than Whitman's frank and unblushing animalism. The fact remains, however, that the generative faculty, like the sudorific glands elsewhere gloated over by the same author, is not *per se* a poetic theme, and that Whitman's treatment of it is destitute of the artistic form which alone makes literature of the corresponding parts of the " Arabian Nights " or the " Decameron."

There remains another and all-inclusive criticism, affecting the entire plan and ultimate suc-

cess of " Leaves of Grass," and removing all
chance of its association with those great books of
the world with which Whitman's admirers have
unhesitatingly classed it. This criticism is found
in the candid admission from Whitman himself,
that he had planned to sing of man both spiritual
and human, but was able to carry out no more
than the lesser half of the grand thought. This
passage, by far the most important in all Whitman's prose, has been strangely overlooked by
critics ; while his extravagant eulogists naturally
dislike to give it publicity. With a frankness
which some of his disciples might well imitate,
Whitman here states very explicitly his conception of a complete man and a complete poem of
man :

I am not sure but the last inclosing sublimation of race or
poem is, what it thinks of death after the rest has been compre-
hended and said, even the grandest—after those contributions
to mightiest nationality, or to sweetest song, or to the best
personalism, male or female, have been gleaned from the rich
and varied themes of tangible life, and have been fully
accepted and sung, and the pervading fact of visible existence,
with the duty it devolves, is rounded and apparently completed.
It still remains to be really completed by suffusing through the
whole and several, that other pervading invisible fact, so large
a part (is it not the largest part ?) of life here, combining the
rest, and furnishing, for person or State, the only permanent
and unitary meaning to all, even the meanest life, consistently
with the dignity of the universe, in Time. As from the eligi-
bility to this thought, and the cheerful conquest of this fact,
flash forth the first distinctive proofs of the soul, so to me
(extending it only a little further,) the ultimate Democratic
purports, the ethereal and spiritual ones, are to concentrate

18

here, and as fixed stars, radiate hence. For, in my opinion, it is no less than this idea of immortality, above all other ideas, that is to enter into, and vivify, and give crowning religious stamp, to democracy in the New World.

It was originally my intention, after chanting in "Leaves of Grass" the songs of the body and existence, to then compose a further, equally needed volume, based on those convictions of perpetuity and conservation which, enveloping all precedents, make the unseen soul govern absolutely at last. I meant, while in a sort continuing the theme of my first chants, to shift the slides, and exhibit the problem and paradox of the same ardent and fully appointed personality entering the sphere of the resistless gravitation of spiritual law, and with cheerful face estimating death, not at all as the cessation, but as somehow what I feel it must be, the entrance upon by far the greatest part of existence, and something that life is at least as much for, as it is for itself. But the full construction of such a work is beyond my powers, and must remain for some bard in the future. The physical and the sensuous, in themselves or in their immediate continuations, retain holds upon me which I think are never entirely releas'd; and those holds I have not only denied, but hardly wish'd to weaken.

Meanwhile, not entirely to give the go-by to my original plan, and far more to avoid a mark'd hiatus in it, than to entirely fulfil it, I end my books with thoughts, or radiations from thoughts, on death, immortality, and a free entrance into the spiritual world. In those thoughts, in a sort, I make the first steps or studies toward the mighty theme, from the point of view necessitated by my foregoing poems, and by modern science. In them I also seek to set the key-stone to my democracy's enduring arch. I recollate them now, for the press, in order to partially occupy and offset days of strange sickness, and the heaviest affliction and bereavement of my life; and I fondly please myself with the notion of leaving that cluster to you, O unknown reader of the future, as "something to remember me by," more especially than all else.[*]

[*] Preface, 1876, to the two volume Centennial Edition of "Leaves of Grass" and "Two Rivulets,"—reprinted in "Specimen Days and Collect," 281, note.

Nothing could be more definite (in spite of the prose style, involved as usual) than this utterance concerning the written poem and the unwritten one ; it is a credit to the author's mind and soul. But as far as " Leaves of Grass" is concerned, we are limited to that which it is, and must judge its success by the criterion set up by Whitman himself. The feet and legs of clay cannot be made, by mere blindness or vociferation, to take the place of an entire marble statue.

As a poem of the individual, therefore, " Leaves of Grass" is essentially imperfect. There are three parts in creative success : the aim, the means, and the result ; here the aim itself, so far *Its limita-* as the printed poem is concerned, is *tions.* admittedly inadequate. That which we call man or woman includes more than body ; more than external achievement ; more, even, than loyal comradeship and affectionate association. The vicissitudes of life, death, suffering, struggle, aspiration, occasional triumph, all point us toward an eternal development of spirit. If our continued life be a fact, most that Whitman " celebrates " is temporary and unimportant ; while that which he confesses himself unable to treat—the ideal, the ultimately beautiful, the on-faring and forth-faring soul—is the very life of our life. Not so Job, Isaiah, Joel, Homer, Virgil, Dante, Shakespeare. Enough of these comparisons, so dear to Whitman's admirers ! not so Longfellow, Whittier, Emerson, Poe. It has been claimed that there is a great triple underlying thought in " Leaves of

Grass" from beginning to end: the thought of unity, beauty, and progression. If this were so it would be a great poem, at least in aim. But the unity is that of indifferent conglomeration, the beauty is imperfect or unethereal, and the progression is unduly physical and material.

Turning to the second element in Whitman's verse, its form, we find the unrhymed and unmetrical, but not unstudied or unmusical, chant familiar in the authorized English translation of the poetical passages of the Bible, in the so-called *Its verse-* poems of Ossian, in Tupper, and in some *form.* few other writers. Whitman's choice of this potentially noble form was wise; it is, though no novelty, comparatively unfamiliar; it naturally fits his bold and outspoken reflections or descriptions, avoids nearly all the vexatious fetters of verse, and gives a free mind a free medium of utterance. Printed as prose (save in its tedious and oft-recurring catalogues) it would show obvious merits, easily surpassing the avowed prose of its own author. In its present *quasi* verse-form it is often pleasing and sometimes resonant and stately, though seldom becoming the art-product essential in whatsoever is poetry. We do not demand rhyme in poetry, nor always metre; but rhythmical beauty is essential. In its feebler divisions it may be parodied and equalled; in its best estate it may fairly challenge comparison with the higher work of any American poet of the second grade. Chiefly when Whitman's eye turns in the direction of theism, individual immortality, affectionate commemoration of the dead, heartfelt sympathy, loving appreciation of the supernal beauty of nature, does he excel; a fact which shows once more that the misapplication of his powers has stunted and half-hidden his better poetic self. The noblest parts of " Leaves of Grass" are devoted to these themes, and not to blatant egotism or sprawling "Americanism." The poet, after some experimenting in early life, deliberately put his worst foot forward, but he followed the law of negatives so dexterously that he found not the slightest difficulty in arousing and retaining interest, because of his strenuous and oft-repeated assertion of that which was least worth asserting at all. His half-perception of this fact undoubtedly dictates his frequent statement of the experimental and limited character of his pioneer-book, which is occasionally noble, shows many a beautiful thought or line, but is crammed with an undigested miscellany.

In the course of a certain famous American trial, the accused, who was a man of unusual cleverness of speech, said that one of his greatest difficulties was to keep his friends from breaking out into a ruinous defence of him. Whitman (and Emerson) might say the same thing. Both Whitman and Emerson have been wiser than their disciples; the "poet of democracy," whom his adulators compare with Homer, Æschylus, and Shakespeare, not wholly to the advantage of the latter, modestly avers, notwithstanding his dramatic egotism in his poems, that he makes no such claims, and that his work must wait a hundred years for a just estimate. At the end of a century, I think, it will be apparent that " Leaves of Grass " is not " the revealer and herald " of " a religious era not yet reached ;" " the bible of Democracy, containing the highest exemplar of life yet furnished," including " a new spiritual life for myriads of men and women," and " unspeakably important." * Nor is its mission to restore the lost and forgotten spirit of the Golden Rule " to heroic and active influence among men." † Whitman fails strongly to enforce the power of true individuality, not lost in the mass of the population, or in indiscriminate comradeship. His love of neighbor is too ardent, fleshly, immediate, material. He does not peer, like Emerson, far below the bottom of the grave, and high above the cross on the spire-top. The vast relations between God, soul, love, and eternity are but partly visible to this poet of practical progress. The sublimities of the ideal, the everlasting development of the soul, and not merely of man among men, are confused or lost in panoramic pictures of America between 1855 and 1885. His highest thought is not fitly voiced in his verse, which falls short of Whitman, as Whitman falls short of him who sang :

> To read the sense the woods impart
> You must bring the throbbing heart.

What it is not.

---

* Richard Maurice Bucke, " Walt Whitman," pp. 183, 185, 190.

† Ernest Rhys, introduction to " The Poems of Walt Whitman (selected)," page x ; London : 1886.

> Love is aye the counterforce,—
> Terror and Hope and wild Remorse,
> Newest knowledge, fiery thought,
> Or Duty to grand purpose wrought.*

Partial and poor is Whitman's world, thus measured. All that may rightly be claimed for him is found in Emerson, plus an insight into nature, a broader sense of love as ever passing between man's God and God's man, a wider and higher and more spiritual sympathy, a thought more profound, a knowledge intuitively American and studiously classic, an interpenetrative sense of the glory of duty and the serenity of beauty. He who has failed to satisfy his own time that he has portrayed its full life as it knows life, can never be the "poet of the future." Notwithstanding his pioneer spirit and eager outlook, in many respects his face is turned backward toward a far cruder, baser, narrower, past. To limit or to omit the ideal is not to become the leader of times and men yet to be. The ideal is the poet's vision, the soul and body of his song :

> "Thy light alone—like mist o'er mountains driven,
> Or music by the night-wind sent,
> Thro' strings of some still instrument,
> Or moonlight on a midnight stream,
> Gives grace and truth to life's unquiet dream." †

But though Whitman's poetic and spiritual sense may be so defective as to unfit him to be a

---

* Emerson, " The Miracle."
* Shelley, " Hymn to Intellectual Beauty."

seer or an artist, much of his work is admirable

and enjoyable. I have no sympathy with his worshippers, but no greater fondness for the bigots and prudes who condemn him unread. His theory of his life-poem is defective, but so far as it goes is perfectly legitimate. It has been carried out with strength, and forms one of the best examples of poetic development afforded in modern literature. Its assertions of comradeship (hardly of friendship in the large true sense), pioneer manliness, the essential wholesomeness and nobility of average American character, the self-reliant and self-preserving nature of democracy, the worthlessness of feudalism, the dangers of the merely conventional, the possibilities of the future of "these states," are excellent. Whitman's poems, too, readily proffer lines lovely or lordly, pictures freshly creative and spontaneously welcome. The title of poet is not to be denied to him who wrote "Crossing Brooklyn Ferry," " Song of the Broad-Axe," " Pioneers, O Pioneers," " To the Man-of-War Bird," "Come up from the Fields, Father," " The City Dead-House," " Proud Music of the Storm," " Whispers of Heavenly Death," or, best of all, the remarkable commemorative poems " When Lilacs Last in the Dooryard Bloom'd," and "O Captain, my Captain." Whitman is the fittest of all laureates of Lincoln, whose greatness the years are making plainer; and in his non-personal and non-martial verse he is never to be accounted less than an original and significantly interesting bard.

Not to him alone, not to any one man, will fall
the task of moulding the future song of
America, which will be at once catholic
and local, of all time and of its own time.
Each of our spring-tide singers is but a herald of
summer, and to each may we say:

*The future
American
song.*

> I sat beneath a fragrant tasselled tree,
> Whose trunk encoiling vines had made to be
> A glossy fount of leafage. Sweet the air,
> Far-off the smoke-veiled city and its care,
> Precious and near the book within my hand—,
> The deathless song of that immortal land
> Wherefrom Keats took his young Endymion
> And laurelled bards enow their wreaths have won;—
> When from some topmost spray began to chant
> And flute, and trill, a warbling visitant,
> A cat-bird, riotous the world above,
> Hasting to spend his heritance ere love
> Should music change to madness in his throat,
> Leaving him naught but one discordant note.
> And as my home-bred chorister outvied
> The nightingale, old England's lark beside,
> I thought—What need to borrow? Lustier clime
> Than ours Earth has not,—nor her scroll a time
> Ampler of human glory and desire
> To touch the plume, the brush, the lips, with fire;
> No sunrise chant on ancient shore and sea,
> Since sang the morning stars, more worth shall be
> Than ours, once uttered from the very heart
> Of the glad race that here shall act its part:
> Blithe prodigal, the rhythm free and strong
> Of thy brave voice forecasts our poet's song!*

* Stedman, "Music at Home."

CHAPTER VIII.

THE BELATED BEGINNING OF FICTION.

FICTION, at its best, forms the highest division of prose literature. The delineation of life, in its complete sense, is its theme; and this delineation, in fiction as in poetry, must include the body, mind, and soul of man, in his journey from the infinite to the infinite. The "light that never was on sea or land," the ideal that glorifies and interprets the real, the unseen that explains to us the fuller meaning of the seen, belong to Cervantes, Le Sage, Goldsmith, Scott, Hawthorne, as truly as to Dante and Shakespeare, Wordsworth and Emerson. The ideal is far more than the visionary and fanciful, more, indeed, than mere imagination in its lower fields. It is truth in its largest sense, a truth so full and round that but part of its revealed glory is visible at once. Toward it the mind springs ever forward with instinctive recognition and undying delight.

Fiction the highest prose.

Between prose-fiction and imaginative poetry the drama (as in any play of Shakespeare) stands as a middle-ground. Shakespeare's view of life includes, at one extreme, heavenly and earthly things undreamt of in narrow philosophy, and at the other Launce and his dog, or Juliet's nurse.

282

So the prose story, in its scheme, may be the ideal romance, bursting the bonds of space and time, or the simplest unadorned tale of actual sayings and doings. Its possibilities are necessarily inferior to those of poetry, not in thought but in form, for verse can display a higher art than prose.

No long argument, therefore, is needed to show the essential wisdom of studying together the poetry and the fiction of a country or a time. Whatever can be separated in a criti- Unity of poetry cism or literary history, these two and fiction. things are indissoluble. The tales and poems of Poe are one ; and scarcely more severable, in our study of the American intellectual product, are Hawthorne and Lowell, Irving and Drake, Mrs. Stowe and Whittier. Comparisons and associations cannot be pushed too far, but it is evident that the creator of " The Last of the Mohicans " and the creator of " Hiawatha " are products of the same soil, with an art more unified than severed, however unlike their capacities and methods.

In this view of the province of fiction, the earliest achievements of American novelists seem laughable or contemptible. We talk of the ideal and the ineffable, and are obliged to begin with Susanna Rowson and Tabitha Tenney. But English fiction dates back little farther than their day ; and it was long indeed before any Anglo-Saxon prose-writers learned to tread in the steps of Boccaccio, Cervantes, and Le Sage. The downfall of the English drama necessarily preceded the devolopment of the novel, its successor

Art-starvation in America. as a means of intellectual amusement. But America, prior to 1750, had no drama, no joy of art, and no creative impulse outside of politics. Even its theology was a slave in chains. New England, in particular, was virtu- ally blind to the infinite vision which makes life worth living, and inspires religion, philosophy, literature, the arts, and science to struggle toward a more perfect expression. Religion, on its exter- nal side, was a narrow but intense rectitude, as the essential preparation, in a rigid scheme, for a theologically constructed heaven. Philosophy was an assistant to Calvinistic theology, literature was explicitly didactic, the arts were non-existent, and science was timid "natural philosophy." All this, as I have elsewhere pointed out, was valuable in nation-building, but not immediately beneficial to literature. Outside of New England, similar conditions prevailed, especially in New Jersey; in Pennsylvania thrift, incipient practical philanthropy, and botanical and physical science were not influential in art; and in the southern colonies, indifferent toward doctrinal quiddities, politics was the chief form of creative activity, as theology had long been in Massachusetts and Connecticut.

One poor little means of expression, neverthe- less, was at length vouchsafed in fiction. How-

Old novels of "feeling." ever limited, timid, bigoted, inartistic, or ignorant a people may be, it is sure to have "feelings." The growing sentimentalism

which was to affect even the higher poetry and
fiction of Germany and England made its trifling
mark upon nascent American literature. In the
last decade of the eighteenth century appeared
" Charlotte Temple, a Tale of Truth," by Mrs.
Rowson—actress, playwright, poet, school-teacher,
text-book compiler, and voluminous Susanna (Has-
sentimental novelist. Its pages were well) Rowson,
long bedewed with many tears of many 1761–1824.
readers ; and, alone among our few eighteenth
century tales, it survives to-day, if a cheap pam-
phlet issue, addressed to a somewhat illiterate
public of readers, can be called survival. Its long-
drawn melancholy is unrelieved by a touch of art ;
it is not even amusing in its absurdity. After
Mrs. Rowson's burst of tears came Mrs. Tenney's
sarcastic laugh ; she castigated in her Tabitha (Gil-
" Female Quixotism, exemplified in the man) Tenney,
1762–1837.
Romantic Opinions and Extravagant
Adventures of Dorcasina Sheldon," the lachrymose and gushing willingness of young women
to believe in everything superficially romantic.
Dorcasina was an American Lydia Languish, and
was at least an improvement upon Mrs. Rowson's
melancholy heroine—whose misfortunes, unfortunately, were substantially those of a poor girl in
real life. The actual, however, did not exert any
unwholesomely chastening effect upon Mrs. Rowson's imaginary land of trusting maidens, fiendish
deceivers, cypress and rue. These poor old
books were issued by the dozen, proudly printed
by the presses of a provincial little nation, and

marked on their margins with many a pencilled
adjective of admiration or horror. The literary
chronicle, however, cannot pause to note, even as
curiosities, their mottos from " Night Thoughts,"
their sincere morality, and their occasionally
respectable prose or interlarded verse. But there
is something pathetic about the faded melodramatic piety of such a typical book as Caroline
Matilda Warren's " The Gamesters ; or, The
Ruins of Innocence" (Boston, 1805), now as dead
and forgotten as the little glittering moth that
met its own death between two of its heavy
leaves.

American fiction, however, had already made a
distinctly significant and important beginning in

Charles Brock-
den Brown,
1771-1810.
the works of Charles Brockden Brown,
which stand toward our later tales and
romances in a relation similar to that
held by Freneau's " House of Night" toward later
American verse. These old novels : *—" Arthur
Mervyn, or, Memories of the Year 1793 "; " Wie-
land, or, The Transformation " ; " Edgar Huntly,
or, Memories of a Sleep Walker"; " Jane Tal-
bot"; " Ormond, or, The Secret Witness "; " Clara
Howard, or, The Enthusiasm of Love "—were our
first considerable essays in what was to become a
great and growing division of creative literature ;
and Brown was the earliest man of letters, in the
professional sense, in the United States. Their
old-fashioned tone is of course apparent at once ;

* Fitly republished in 1887 in the standard library edition ot Mr. David
McKay, of Philadelphia.

repetitions and confusions are not hard to find;
in "Edgar Huntly" the author falls into the inartistic error of introducing two somnambulists, and
elsewhere he sometimes forgets the personages
introduced or the minor details of the plot as previously developed. "Sensibility" and melodramatic horror violently intrude upon the reader's
notice instead of being allowed to rise in constructive order; the *deus ex machina* is altogether
too visible. In the yellow-fever portrayals to
which Brown reverts more than once, and in certain accumulations of murders in other chapters,
mere numerical increase is made to take the place
of deliberate and orderly art. But whatever the
crudeness and irregularity of these books, whatever their prevalent melancholy hue, they have an
inherent merit by no means small. Brown had
the sense to see, in our period of colonial subser-
viency, that American scenes and characters (including the North American Indian whom Cooper
followed him in portraying) afforded fit
themes for the novelist; and in some Portent of Brown's work.
of his literary effects he anticipated Poe, and
even, in a small way, suggested Hawthorne. The
call-note of our greatest fiction sounded clear,
though faint and far, in Brockden Brown. As
one takes from the shelf any of Brown's books—
even the preposterous "Clara Howard, or, The
Enthusiasm of Love"—he is sure to find, amid a
sufficiency of failures, some touch of what we call
genius; some passport to a corner, if no more, in
the land of imagination.

"Not all the wonder that encircles us,
Not all the mysteries that in us lie"

did Brockden Brown's sad eye miss. Edward
Dowden, in his life of Shelley, tells us that
Brown's novels, with Schiller's "Robbers" and
Goethe's "Faust," "were—of all the works with
which he was familiar—those which took the
deepest root in Shelley's mind, and had the
strongest influence in the formation of his character." That high poet looked beyond the
timidly conventional and the obviously apparent,
and found a thought-kinsman, though of stature
less than his, working all alone in the poverty
beyond the sea.

The similarity between Brown's general romantic manner and the prevalent fashion then regnant
The prevalent in English minor fiction is too obvious
fashion. to need mention. He was a sort of
early American Cyril Tourneur, in whom original
strength and crude expression were alternately
visible in the treatment of weird and deathly
themes. The women of his romances are sometimes over-sweetly, and therefore weakly, portrayed, but they are at least stronger and more
characteristic than most of the pink-and-white
blushing-and-weeping nonentities of the time. In
his day and way, and in his short sick life. Brown
made a beginning of which American fiction need in
no wise be ashamed. If he was unduly influenced
by darksome or lurid romance, by emotions more
vague than properly mysterious, and by a storm
of sentiment that seems far enough away from

the intensely real sentiment of "The Scarlet Letter" and "The Marble Faun," let us remember that all Germany and half England were swept by the flood whose farthest waves moved him in his path. At the worst he never wrote aught so wretched as "The Sorrows of Werther"; while at the best his work foreshowed the triumphs to be won by the three greatest of his successors among American novelists.

From Irving, however, not Brown, came the widely apparent commencement of our native fiction. He wrote no novel, or romance, nor had he the constructive art which would have made such a venture success-

Washington Irving, 1783–1859.

ful. But the Hudson stories in "The Sketch-Book" combine nearly every merit that can be found or wished in a tale of humor. They are local in scene and character, strong in delineation of the personages introduced, and thoroughly artistic in literary form and elaboration. Description of natural scenery, rollicking fun, and suggested pathos are combined in a graceful and delightful whole. Irving, as a tale-maker, applied a confident and manifest linguistic skill to the production and perpetuation of an indigenous literary creation. New York and old England found in him a writer whose charm was instantly recognizable, and was pervasive, not strenuously novel or self-assertive. Pleasure preceded analysis on the reader's part, and the product seemed too spontaneous to suggest the *labor limae* behind. When to novelty in theme and form was

added the easy serenity of an assured and confi-
The true beginner of American fiction. dent literary touch, American fiction had clearly passed beyond the stage of apology and curiosity. A success need not be in the "grand manner" in order to be conspicuous and enduring; if it remain, as the years go on, secure from rivalry or even imitation, and if author and tale seem indissolubly related to each other, readers and critics have but to enjoy and record the triumph. That which is self-centred and manifest in its success is gratefully to be accepted; critical study may follow if it will, or be dispensed with altogether.

Throughout the essays of Irving, as in "The Spectator" and its followers, there runs a thread The novelist in Irving. which suggests the novelist. The pictures of persons in the humorous or pathetic papers of "The Sketch-Book," the delineations of English country life in "Bracebridge Hall," the romantic portrayals of castle or battle in the Spanish histories and biographies, the wider constructiveness of "Knickerbocker's History of New York," at once take us back to the creator of Sir Roger de Coverley. Addison, in "The Spectator," was social satirist, genial essayist, literary critic, religious philosopher, precursor of journalist and magazinist, and forerunner of all eighteenth century English fiction as well. Irving led no procession in which a new De Foe, Richardson, Fielding or Goldsmith appeared, but he taught Americans to "paint the prospect from their door," if they would win any

success worth having. Brown's aim was too high
for his powers or strength ; Irving measured his
capacities of creation, elaboration, and adornment
with entire accuracy, save in the fields of history
and travel. All that lay within him, as far as the
writing of fiction was concerned, he gave us ; and
that his success was no accident, but the nice
adjustment of mind to theme, is shown by the
fact that, in their way, the English sketches are
as good as the American, and that in the many-
toned " Tales of a Traveller" or such a foreign
fun-sketch as "The Spectre Bridegroom" the
charm of the two greater and more characteristic
triumphs is not lost to sight. He who had early
begun to portray with dainty skill, not untouched
by the kindly exaggeration then in vogue, the
several characters introduced in " Salmagundi,"
was able in his many succeeding works to transfer
the same power to other lands and times and
themes.

Irving possessed the sympathy and the observant faculty which should belong to the novelist ;
and his wisdom in the choice of really indigenous themes, combined elsewhere with a catholic
temper and the enrichment of thought which
foreign travel bestows, admirably fitted
him for his task. A single step from his
proper fields, of course, would have made
him ridiculous. However one large novelist
differs from another, we can at least conceive
for him other triumphs than those he wins.
Irving was not a large novelist, and our thought

*His fields
and tri-
umph.*

cannot imagine in his case any triumph different from that which he attained. But in the history of the fiction of his native land his place cannot change. Thus far only Irving, Cooper, Poe and Hawthorne emerge in significance from the multiplying procession, and Irving leads the list in point of time. Without Cooper's broad constructiveness, he at least avoided Cooper's prolixity, flatness, irregularity, and preposterous excursions in the service of patriotic or denominational propagandism. Even his vine-around-the-oak women are not such poor, boneless creatures as those in the pages of his eminent contemporary. Comparisons, however, are not specially illuminating in Irving's case. To claim for him more than we have here done would be folly ; to assert less would be ignorance.

Irving's friend and fellow-worker, Paulding, once mentioned almost on terms of equality with the author of " The Sketch-Book," is now but a figure of the past in the story of American letters. Born a little before Irving, he survived him, dying just previous to the civil war ; so that in his long lifetime as a writer he witnessed the entire development of the national mind in the creative fields of literature. William Irving was Paulding's brother-in-law, and naturally Paulding, whose tastes were those of the humorous essayist and sketch-maker, became a useful co-worker on " Salmagundi," of a second series of which he was the sole writer. Such literature of the town, of

James Kirke Paulding, 1779–1860.

course, could not endure ; of all the rich periodical store of England in the eighteenth century not
a dozen essays, outside of " The Spectator," are
read to-day ; and the "whim-whams" of these
early censors of New York society do not interest
a city that has already forgotten even the " Poti-
phar Papers " of Curtis, written a long generation
later. A certain added dignity, for the time, was
given to Paulding's skits and sketches, patriotic
brochures, life of Washington, poems and novels,
by his important place in politics, for he was long
navy-agent in New York, and was secretary of
the navy in the administration of President Van
Buren (1838–1841). But the name of his best
novel, "The Dutchman's Fireside," survived the
fleeting fame of all his lesser writings, and now-a-
days even " The Dutchman's Fireside " lingers in
the mind as a title rather than a thing. Twenty
years ago several of Paulding's more significant
writings were neatly reissued, under the affectionate yet discreet editorship of his son ; but
they had lost their power to charm or interest any
considerable number of readers. The characters
in his novels were sometimes drawn with conspicuous freshness and strength, and there was swiftly
flashing fire or crackling fun in some of his
satires of the ways of "John Bull," or praises of
the words and doings of honest " Brother Jonathan." As far as local theme and picture were
concerned,—watched with a quick eye and delineated with a patriotic pen,—Paulding was a
useful fellow-worker with those who were begin-

ning to give America a literature of her own ; but
something more is needed in a book that is to
live. Paulding wrote just as he thought, without
the artistic touch and without painstaking development; his first public was not a critical one;
but his later readers properly demanded literary
art, rather than mere spontaneity and vigor. The
spirit of time and place must indeed be caught,
but it must be imprisoned in a definite artistic
form if it would go down the years. One-half of
the novels of Cooper himself are deservedly
neglected for the same reason that leaves "The
Dutchman's Fireside" and "Westward Ho" in
the shadow of the procession of years,—which
is, in brief, that they proffer an original creation
ignobly wrought. Paulding sacrificed too much
to the wish to be bright and readable. This wish
he attained, for certainly "The Dutchman's Fireside," with all its queer union of sentimentality
and playfulness, and its occasional absurdities of
sensationalism, is more readable than the worse
half of Cooper's novels, which sometimes move
with an elephantine tread. Let us not blame too
severely those writers who sought to give vivacity
to American stories and sketches between 1800
and 1850; for assuredly that quality had been
none too apparent in the dull theologico-philo-
sophical days that had filled up so large a part of
the seventeenth and eighteenth centuries in the
colonies. Paulding failed honorably in a pioneer's
path, wherein he lacked for the most part both

critics and models ; his pursuits were not wholly
those of the man-of-letters ; and even in his failures he did some temporary service.

When the Indian peered into the windows that
opened on "The Dutchman's Fireside," he was
typical of the advent of native-Americanism in a
literature which, save in its spontaneous political
outburst, had been too conservatively colonial.
He frightened the little girls who pored over
Paulding's novel-pages and he frightened some of
the timid respectables who thought nothing good
that had an indigenous character, and nothing
bad that was in accord with the approved foreign
models. American literature, between 1775 and
1825, veered swiftly to and fro between humble
subservience to European—that is English—
leadership, and a self-conscious indignant
"Brother-Jonathanism" that really was a different
manifestation of the same feeling, the feeling of
verdancy. But another sign, less conspicuous at
first than the nationalism of Paulding or Cooper,
was slowly beginning to appear. This was the
ability to write smoothly and self-respectingly
without haste or local assertiveness, on whatsoever
theme might be selected. Such ability was really
the cause of Irving's international success, and
the general lack of it, as has also just been said,
made Paulding an ephemeral writer, and remanded some of Cooper's novels to a low plane
of merit. This seemingly artless grace, this
power to write well, was illustrated now and then
in the lesser and anonymous fiction of the begin-

ning of the second half-century of the nation. In
" The Talisman " annual for 1829 (edited by Bryant, Sands, and Verplanck) is an excellent illustration of a quiet power upon which American
fiction was to rely for its greatest triumphs. This
example is in very truth, as its title tells us, " A
"A Simple   Simple Tale "—so simple that it almost
Tale."   seems a capital parody on the very latest
and most resultless "realism" of our day. The
eventless story of a man and a woman, in a plain
village, is told with fine finish, and that is all ; but
what more can be asked of thirty small pages?
At the close of the daintily-turned little story, in
my copy, there is written in the minute angular
woman's-chirography of the period : " Very much
like W. Irving"; and so it is ; but it is also suggestive of Gerard de Nerval, or any other exquisite turner of rural episodes into clear-cut minor
fiction. To take a subject near at hand ; to treat
it well, with deliberateness of art and restrained
delicacy of humor ; and to print the sketch so
made, leaving its fate to take care of itself—all
this was precisely what was significant of the true
beginning of American fiction, whether it was to
be great or little. That beginning had at length
been made ; and though its quiet progress was to
be profoundly affected, and turned forward or
aside, by the individual strength of a force like
Cooper, it was also to be absorbed and magnified
in the more perfect grace of a Hawthorne.

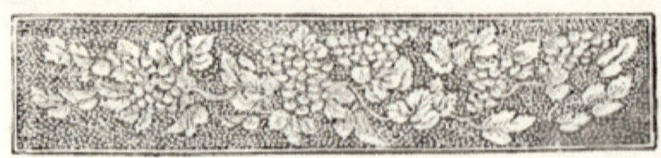

CHAPTER IX.

JAMES FENIMORE COOPER.

In the quartette of greatest American writers of fiction Cooper occupies a sufficiently secure place. To juvenile or hasty readers the charm of his narratives is so quickly apparent that it is uncritically and almost thoughtlessly accepted; while to maturer or more phil- osophic minds his demerits are so constantly visible that some deliberate reflection is demanded before his essential excellence is allowed. A novel by Cooper appears almost a childish performance when placed beside a novel by George Eliot or a romance by Hawthorne. The prevalent taste calls for a nicer analysis and a more delicate touch than the author of "The Deerslayer" could bestow. The graces of art appear but irregularly in Cooper's fiction, and never adorn a complete novel. His success has always depended upon force of creation and vigor of description; and herein lies his proper claim to the renown so long granted. Creation and description, in a novel, are best when adorned with the utmost skill of art; but no one can question their value, even when crudely set forth.

James Fenimore Cooper, 1789-1851.

Personally, Cooper's temper was nothing less

than ferocious; and this temper he sometimes allowed to lead him in choice of themes and treatment of plots. Hence the long list of his books is splashed with frequent blots. An intense patriot, he contrived, both as person and as author, to offend readers at home and abroad. A man whose application of Christian principle should first have been made upon his own irascible character, he undertook to promulgate the faith in the form of polemic fiction. He whose greatest powers, when fully displayed, were those of a strong and brilliant novelist of the trackless woods and seas, essayed to write a "fashionable" novel of society. That old-time string of melodramatic adjectives, "odious, insidious, hideous, and perfidious," was assuredly inapplicable to this great honest straightforward force, whose career of libel-suits and quarrels would best be described by the term litigious. When free, he could be as destructive as Victor Hugo's loose cannon on shipboard; when self-contained in his own proper field, no American could dispute, as none could equal, his solid success. By his triumphs in one place he made us forgive and forget his failures in another. Cooper developed, and by right of eminent domain may almost be said to have discovered, the wilder American field for fiction, and he is the sea-novelist of the English language.

It is axiomatic to say that Cooper was a follower of Scott. But this means no more than that he was a romantic story-teller. The scenes and characters chosen by the two writers could hardly be more unlike than they are. Cooper read Scott, as did everybody ; but his pages are little influenced by the Wizard of the North. The similarities between the two writers are simply those due to the fact that each made a romantic portrayal of humanity, noble and base, cultured and savage, in chivalrous adventure, in exciting plot and counterplot, and in manly and womanly affection and ambition. As well call Victor Hugo the Scott of France as apply to this most characteristic American of his time any term implying servile indebtedness.

The prodigality of Cooper's pen, after it had fairly set to work, was a mark of the English fiction of the century. Half-a-dozen novelists might be named, in Great Britain and the United States, who have among themselves written more stories than a single reader can profitably absorb in a lifetime. That fertility which in Scott was due to pride and consequent financial need, and which in such writers as Trollope and Mrs. Oliphant is mere inveterateness of literary habit, sprang in Cooper from the lusty wealth of his vigorous intellectual nature, to which labor was scarcely more than recreation. A midshipman in youth, he was a hearty literary adventurer in middle life, merely transferring to pen and ink that chivalric combativeness and fondness for novelty that would have made him a discoverer, a crusader, or a pirate, a few centuries before.

This element in his personal character readily

accounts for his literary over-productiveness, and for the irregular value of his long list of books. Let no one go to Cooper, as to Hawthorne, for instruction in the arts of style. Pages, chapters,

Cooper's irregularity of work.

and whole volumes will be found without difficulty, which may quickly be separated from the valuable part of the author's product. Words are sometimes fairly thrown away; a single idea is expanded at tiresome length; and the narrative sadly drags, when that narrative should be all in all. Prolixity and tediousness are serious faults in one whose literary business is to tell a tale. Cooper's tediousness differs from Dickens' in that the latter actively turns and returns in the same corner of a field, while the former seems to try to move, but with sluggish steps. Cooper has been termed a " panoramic " novelist. Everyone who has sat in childhood before one of those innocuous and mildly instructive entertainments which preceded the days of the stereopticon, well remember how the simple machinery would at times halt and finally get hopelessly caught, so that the beholder became wearied of an immovable picture, while the poor manipulator was vainly endeavoring to remedy the evil. So it sometimes seems in the case of Cooper's panoramas. At such times the energetic author, like the panorama-showman, is as vexed as his audience, but hardly knows how to proceed. There are long delays, of course, in any career of adventure; one complains only when they are introduced into the printed page not from artistic intention but from defect of creation.

The mature student of Cooper's works, therefore, finds at the start a sufficiently serious array of demerits. Cooper was fluent but not artistic; he wrote hurriedly, carelessly, and therefore too voluminously; he wasted his strength and his manuscripts in "patriotic," political, and personal squabbles; he failed almost completely as a social painter and as a creator of "novels with a purpose," theological, satirical, or other. He could not undertake with the slightest confidence of success the delineation of women or children. The ordinary class of cultured men he portrayed better, but even here his touch was insecure. Instead of recognizing his defects, and trying either to correct them or to modify his choice of themes and his methods of treatment, he fell into an inveterate habit of replying to, or sueing at law, those who had criticised him. The "grim" humor of some of the characters in his books seemed unfortunately lacking in his own character; its presence would have saved him from many mistakes.

As a preliminary to an examination and hearty recognition of Cooper's great and enduring merits, it will therefore be well, at the start, to eliminate the unimportant titles from his long list of published writings. His contributions to *His minor* periodical literature, with the exception of *writings.* his naval sketches, were few and non-significant, for he early entered upon a career of popularity

which spared him the necessity or temptation to
write miscellaneous minor sketches.   He had no
capacity for the production of short stories, which
he very wisely left unattempted, with one unfortunate exception ; and in his day the monthly magazines of America were unable to pay high prices
for serial fiction.   When he wished to address his
public briefly on any theme of earnest exhortation
or bitter reply, his words were more direct and
forcible than ornate ; as a letter-writer and pam-
phleteer he thought of effect rather than means,
nor did he fully realize how important is style to
Cooper as con-   a Junius, not less than to an Addison
troversialist.   or an Irving.   He was certainly sufficiently violent, and sufficiently comprehensive in
his choice of subjects for attack ; he never learned
to avoid the rhetorical error of attempting too
much.   Once aroused, he hurried along, too fast
and too far, confounding in his onslaught the just
and the unjust, the part and the whole.   With
him, "Hints on the Social and Civic Relations of
the United States of America " easily became positive statements of the demoniac tendencies of the
entire newspaper press of his country, which was
poisoning the national moral sense, and was
existing but as an instrument of wickedness.
James Gates Percival once launched " Salmoneus-
thunderbolts . . . . at the comfortable little city
of Hartford, because the poet fancied that the
inhabitants thereof did not like him or his verses
so much as he himself did ; " * and politely penned
the following request :

* James Russell Lowell, " My Study Windows," 182.

" Wrapped in sheets of gory lightning,
  While cursed night hags ring thy knell,
May the arm of vengeance bright'ning,
  O'er thee wave the sword of hell!

" May a sudden inundation
  Rise in many a roaring wave,
And with hurried devastation
  Whelm thy thousands in the grave.

" When the flood, in fury swelling,
  Heaves their corpses on the shore,
May fell hyæns, madly yelling,
  Tear their limbs and drink their gore."

Cooper, as a controversialist, was scarcely less explicit in the utterance of his wishes, which also found expression in his books of travel, now wholly unread and justly forgotten, and in his satirical "international" novels. Let him who wishes to explore the depths into which a great American writer fell when he sought to satirize the faults of his actual country, and to portray his ideal men and women, endeavor to read that remarkable production, "Home as Found." Cooper, in the very fatuity of foolhardiness, even endeavored to follow Swift in a more general satire, and "The Monikins" was the result. It must be remembered, however, that the sentimentalism of the day, when it turned sour, was very acetic indeed ; and that too large a part of the English press, as well as of the American, showed toward Cooper a virulent injustice that was nothing less than indecent, and would not now-a-days be tolerated for a moment. This injustice was repeatedly displayed by some of the gravest and weightiest periodicals of the language, sample utterances of which may be found in Lounsbury's excellent life of Cooper. But if Cooper's critics lost their manners in their attacks, Cooper himself lost his senses in his replies. However, if there is one thing in the world which Time buries more quickly and more deeply than a book-review, it is an author's reply to that review. The furious controversies, whether *pro* or *con*, which were for so many years connected with Cooper's personal character, records of American and European sight-seeing (calculated, as by the very perversity of unintention, to exasperate Americans and Europeans alike), and comments on American naval history, are impartially consigned to the secure oblivion of some dusty file of defunct newspapers.

A more unkind neglect has also fallen upon Cooper's " History of the Navy of the United States of America " (1839 ; condensed in 1841), and " Lives of Distinguished American Naval Officers " (1846). For the preparation of these works Cooper possessed somewhat unusual qualifications. Naval history and biography. Early familiar with the sea and with the American navy, he never lost his interest in either. Marine adventure, furthermore, was a theme which no one could treat more vigorously and effectively than he ; and many pages of these two works display the characteristics of descriptive style which have made Cooper, and not Marryat, the great sea-novelist.

The volumes, furthermore, were by no means a superficial gloss upon carelessly gathered facts; Cooper sought his materials at first hand, and in their use fell into no fiercer controversies than have beset the literary and personal path of the chief historian of the United States, though, in Cooper's case, these controversies, as usual, got into the courts of law. He sought the truth, published it without fear or favor, and defended it when questioned, earnestly but with unusual gravity and self-possession. The exact reason for the public inattention toward this history is not readily to be stated ; perhaps the decline of the American commerce and navy, only to be revived by broader legislation or some great war, may have something to do with the national neglect of that which once was a matter of intensest patriotic pride. A nearer and more obvious reason lies in the fact that, after all, only the great histories live —those in which a noble theme is deliberately handled with patient research, with philosophic spirit, and with artistic finish. Cooper displayed the first quality in due measure and the second in a degree surprising in view of his usual temptations and failures ; but in the third his haste denied him such successes as were not won by his natural powers in spontaneous action. At a time when Irving's histories and biographies, for reasons elsewhere discussed, are fading rather than brightening, it is not strange that Cooper, as historian, fares yet worse.

Turning finally to Cooper's novels, issued in

20

several competing editions, read by eager thousands, and forming, practically, the sole basis upon which rests his present fame, and upon which all future claims for prominence must depend, we find that some of these also may quite readily be dismissed from the list of those entitled to the most respectful critical mention; or may be abandoned with the flotsam and jetsam of the literary tides. Such, it seems to me, are " The Wept of Wish-ton-Wish," " Afloat and Ashore," " Miles Wallingford," " Satanstoe," " The Chainbearer," " The Redskins," " Wyandotte," " Wing and Wing," " The Two Admirals," " Homeward Bound," " The Crater," " Jack Tier," " The Sea Lions," " The Oak Openings," " The Heidenmauer," " The Headsman," and " Mercedes of Castile." These seventeen novels, though in themselves sufficient to justify the fame of some lesser novelists, are in plan or execution inferior to the masterpieces which chiefly lend honor to Cooper's name. As in the Waverley Novels themselves, we find that inveterate inventiveness and rapidity of composition naturally result in great irregularity of product. " The Wept of Wish-ton-Wish " is worth saving if but for its lovely title—as musical and as characteristically American as Kennedy's " Swallow Barn." This title, however, proved as unwelcome to the foreign reprinters as did that of Hawthorne's " Marble Faun," and was similarly thrown aside. The theme of the book—and the secret of its failure—is to be found in its title as

The lesser novels.

changed in France : "The Puritans of America."
Cooper was always feeble in satire ; and his New
England stories, even "Lionel Lincoln," are
untrue to the local character or ineffective in
its delineation. Into Puritanism, which he not
unnaturally hated, Cooper had no real insight ;
and even a hater must understand if he would
effectively denounce. "The Redskins," too,
proffers at the start an atttactive name, but follows it with hundreds of pages in which, as in its
immediate predecessors "Satanstoe " and "The
Chainbearer," bombast, haste and unmerited
contempt for New Englanders disfigure and
almost destroy the would-be delineations of New
York colonial life and adventure in the eighteenth
century. In addition to his frequent attempts to
ridicule Congregationalism and magnify Episco-
pacy, Cooper was here endeavoring to make
patroon landlords agreeable and "anti-renters"
odious. Now, however attractive may be Epis-
copacy or paternalism in comparison with Puritanism or anarchistic agrarianism, it cannot be said
that Cooper's controversial defences were other
than injurious to the side he espoused. It is
true that "Satanstoe " was not lacking in force,
and that the denunciations, in these stories, of
the selfish ferocity of ignorant communism, and
thieving no-rent land-tenure in general, are instructive to-day; but one regrets that Cooper
did not restrain and command his powers until
they should strike terribly against a terrible evil,

and not waste their force in the moment of the stroke.

"Satanstoe" had been preceded by the four volumes of "Afloat and Ashore"; or "The adventures of Miles Wallingford,"—the third Series of novels. and fourth of which are now reissued under the name of their hero. It was followed by "The Chainbearer," in which the evil deeds of a Puritan product are further elaborated. Judging by this loosely connected series one would say that the prevalent fashion of dovetailing different works of fiction by the introduction of the same characters, scenes or ideas was no element of strength in Cooper; but we shall see that in the "Leather-Stocking" series it was connected with his noblest and more characteristic success. Only when Cooper misjudged his proper field and powers, or slighted his task, did he produce those works which long damaged his reputation and are most advantageous in obscurity.

In those of Cooper's novels which have to do with the sea, such as "The Two Admirals," or "Wing and Wing," the reader is interested in the adventures described but not in the characters portrayed. It seems strange, but it is true, that the creator of the individual and almost immortal character of Natty Bumppo was content to people his pages with preposterous fools; inconsequential heroes; and timid, blushing fainting "female" Turveydrops. As far as the characters are concerned, the reader of "Homeward Bound" is almost sorry that they sur-

vived to visit " Home as Found." But the
events and episodes, the chases and battles and
storms and disciplines of " Homeward Bound,"
"The Two Admirals," or "Wing and Wing,"
and the action in the land novels attract those
who are willing to endure Cooper's tiresome prefaces and long-winded arguments or dogmatic
ipse dixit proofs that a Roman Cath- Cooper as
olic should not marry an infidel ; that an dogmatist.
Episcopal damsel cannot safely bestow her hand
upon a High Arian ; that the Congregational
churches of New England include hypocritical
rascals in their lists of members; or even that, as
in the preposterous finale to " The Crater," a
returning Episcopalian may find his former home,
a Pacific reef, engulfed with all its evil sectarian
population, whether Friend, Baptist, Methodist or
Presbyterian,—so that this excellent liturgist may
triumphantly exclaim in Swinburne's words over
his " Forsaken Garden," that he has lived

"Till the slow sea rise and the sheer cliff crumble,
  Till terrace and meadow the deep gulfs drink,
Till the strength of the waves of the high tides humble
  The fields that lessen, the rocks that shrink;
Here now in his triumph where all things falter,
  Stretched out on the spoils that his own hands spread,
As a god self-slain on his own strange altar,
      Death lies dead."

Meanwhile the greater part of Cooper's public
prefers his accounts of the French privateer to his
defences of the Athanasian creed, and solaces
itself with the author's vigor and vitality, at the

expense of his long prefaces, diatribes against
New England, laudations of placid patroonism, or
violent commendations of the American system
at its best, versus the effete despotisms of Europe.
The various novels just mentioned were one and
all read—and are still read, if at all—as stories
simply. That they could survive their personages
and their preachments indicates that, beneath all
their rubbish, some vital spark must have been
steadily smouldering. But the lesser novels of
Cooper, in fact, are now little read by mature and
critical minds; their public is, as I have said, for
the most part juvenile and unthoughtful, composed of those who "like" the better stories, and
wish to continue the pleasure they have found.
When a discreet reader, familiar, at least in part,
with Hawthorne, Dickens, Thackeray, George
Eliot, Scott and Cooper at his best, takes up one
of them, some impression of inanity, verbosity,
prejudice, or propagandism can hardly be avoided.
As he reads their pages he will be half ready to
declare Cooper an overpraised figure of the past,
whose books have none but a relative interest or
importance.

But now we turn to the golden side and the
nobler books, and find their merits heightened by
His great   the frank contrast we have made. For-
merits.   gotten are the fury of controversy, the lit-
igation of libel suits, the crude satires at the
expense of social errors, the well-meant defences of the ever-attractive Protestant Episcopal
Church, the ill-meant vituperation of the Puritan

New Englanders. There comes into full view the characteristic story-teller of American woods and waters, he who caught and delineated in romantic novels the adventurous spirit of unfettered men and unmeasured Nature. Cooper is, over all, his country's novelist of action, and action ever charms when analysis wearies or invention flags. Antedating Hawthorne in fame, surpassing Irving at least in vigor of stroke and extent of field, and standing utterly aside from Poe, Cooper first wore the novelist's crown in lands west of the Atlantic. His mind was remarkably fertile in planning plots of adventure, and sometimes in elaborating those plots so that incident succeeded incident without wearisomeness or lack of novelty or probability. It has been said that Cooper had no style ; but if his fiery and thrilling episodes of adventure on sea or land are not successful because he was a master of the story-teller's style, his readers have been remarkably influenced by some literary power as yet unnamed. Had he paused longer in search of words, his action, swift in its best passages, would have dragged ; but in such passages he does pause long enough to choose words that fit the purpose in hand. The storms and calms of the ocean and the "inland seas" of the great American lakes ; the fortunes of merchant-ship, privateer or man-of-war ; the peculiar humor of certain vividly-drawn characters previously unfamiliar ; the sombre North American Indian in all his majesty and treachery ; the Pathfinder of the woods, trackless to all but him ;

the infinite wealth of the rude life of the rifle and
the wigwam—of these James Fenimore Cooper
was a master.   Others may yet challenge and surpass his success as a sea-novelist, though, in these
days of swift steamships, iron-clads, and long-range
cannon, none has yet done so.   But as the Indian
character becomes more civilized and the Indian
home moves farther westward, none will repeat
the triumphs of the creator of Chingachgook and
Uncas, and of their Caucasian counterpart the
Pathfinder.   The last-named, and his environment, are not to be criticised ; they are to be
admired.

The five "Leather-Stocking Tales"—"The
Pioneers, or, The Sources of the Susquehanna";
"The Last of the Mohicans, a Narrative of 1757";
"The Prairie, a Tale"; "The Path-
finder, or, The Inland Sea"; "The
Deerslayer, or, The First War-Path"—
were written between 1823 and 1841, "in a very
desultory and inartificial manner," said Cooper in
his final preface to the series.   Having terminated
the career of Leather-Stocking in "The Prairie,"
and laid him in his grave, the author was induced
by "a latent regard for this character to resusci-
tate him in 'The Pathfinder.'"   The logical order
of the five, centreing around this hero, is "The
Deerslayer," "The Last of the Mohicans," "The
Pathfinder," "The Pioneers," and "The Prairie."
Cooper himself perceived that "if anything from
the pen of the writer of these romances is to outlive himself, it is, unquestionably, the series of

The "Leather-Stocking Tales." (marginal note)

'The Leather-Stocking Tales.'" He recognized
their faults of haste and lack of harmony, and was
well aware of the thoughtless way in which his
books were devoured at the time, without reference to lasting value. Nor did he prophesy for
himself with any certainty, even here, a survival
in literature when novelty should have become
worn away. But his "man of the forest," though
"purely a creation," proved to be a creation indigenous, forceful, broadly human, and therefore
perennial. In his creation, too, Cooper exerted
all his own strength, and also relied upon an
essentially fine and often deliberate art—displayed
even in this preface, by far the best he ever wrote.
The hard facts of life and the wiry nature of the
hero were held up in the poetic view of the imagination. Human nature, in unfettered nobility
and a fresh environment, and yet with human sins
and foibles, was nobly painted. So it was with
Cooper's pictures of the Indians who were Natty
Bumppo's fellows and unconscious teachers. "It
is the privilege of all writers of fiction," he justly
said and constantly felt, "more particularly when
their works aspire to the elevation of romances, to
present the *beau-ideal* of their characters to the
reader." Cooper was a large creator and a conscious artist, who perceived a "beau-ideal" even
in—especially in—Bumppo and the redskins.
The American note, *isolated inheritance working
freshly*, was clearly struck in this definite and
lastingly valuable quintette of romantic novels.
Cooper's large and human heart beat responsive

to truth.   He felt what he saw ; and he had the
national faculty of "thinking straight and seeing
clear." Therefore he was both picturesque and
pathetic—how often do those adjectives combine !
—in his delineations of a fading troop and a passing time.   Instead of the artificial Gothicism of
"The Castle of Otranto," the sentimentality of
"The Man of Feeling," the portentous romanticism of "The Mysteries of Udolpho," or, in general, "Man as he Is Not," Cooper gave us a veritable "Simple Story," combining "Nature and
Art," in a "Romance of the Forest," as truly
though not as perfectly as did Goldsmith in the
inimitable "Vicar." *

Cooper's huntsman—brave, cool, slightly sus-
picious and slow of word and act, but honest,
manly and human—was more indigenous and
more widely interesting to his countrymen than
Irving's Rip Van Winkle, Ichabod Crane, or
Knickerbocker Dutchmen.   His Indians, too,
were surely of the soil, though not of the race that
was producing a native literature.   Fortunately
Cooper's greatest strength lay in the creations
which were most needed, most interesting, and
therefore most valuable.   The scenes of domestic
fiction, or its miscellaneous characters, could be
Cooper's better painted by other hands; therein
domain. Cooper failed outright or achieved success
but at random.   His proper domain was the
borderland between barbarism and civilization.

---

* The very titles of these and others in Mrs. Barbauld's "British Novelists" series are historically significant.

In "The Spy" and "Lionel Lincoln," dealing with the Revolution, Cooper also exploited the field of local history, and so far as adventure and action were concerned he was not unsuccessful. Like a trained hound, his powers and beauty were visible in motion rather than at rest; in conflict, not in home-life. "The Red Rover" and "The Pilot," of the sea-tales, excel in their encounters and escapes; they halt in their Sea-tales. love-episodes and conversational discussions. The "problems of life," in the English or the Russian sense, seldom troubled Cooper; and when they did, they troubled his readers vastly more. We go to him with the demand: "Tell us a story," not with the plea: "Help us in solving the riddle of existence." Cooper, therefore, remains the American story-teller, the national novelist of the days before analysis became fashionable. After all, most novelists' fame is built up by large constructiveness and Our novelist of action, on not by decorative details. The major-land or sea. ity of readers is not composed of analysts and critics, constantly bothered with the *why* and the *how*. Cooper created stories which conquered their readers, and he succeeded on the old-fashioned lines. After all, a novel must entertain, and a cloud of witnesses attest Cooper's entertainingness. His most prominent quality, as a novelist, was wholesome independence of thought and speech, a quality that lies at the bottom of the success of the masters, Cervantes and Le Sage, De Foe and Goldsmith. Those story-tellers, too,

were honestly national, as was Cooper. Independence and nationality are not enough to make
a novel, but when the bases of constructive power
they are sure to promote literary triumph. And
careless largeness is more attractive, in the long
run, than careful pettiness. If we must have but
one, let it be the first. Therein is the indispensable element in the " Leather-Stocking Tales,"
which makes us refuse to give them up, or to
challenge their right to their individual place in
literature and in our favor. Natty Bumppo and
Long Tom Coffin are better known to us, more
real personalities, than half our cousins. The
last sea-fight ; the whale-capture, or the killing of
the panther ; the wild justice of the wronged
Indian's vengeance ; the fierce plot and counterplot of the contestants in the Revolution, or of
the pioneers of France and England in the new
world ; and all the parti-colored panorama of the
American man in action, cannot cease to charm
those who have blood in their veins and muscles
in their arms.

Even in our recognition of Cooper's peculiar
and unquestioned triumphs there steals anew
the question: How can these triumphs be consistent with the failures that accompanied them ?
The creator of the " Leather-Stocking Tales "
began his career of authorship with the novel
" Precaution," and closed it with " The Ways of
the Hour." In both, as in so many intermediate
books, symmetry, verisimilitude, and progressive
interest are precisely the lacking qualities. Like

a hundred eminent authors, Cooper could not measure his weakness, though he could, and did, rightly estimate his strength. "The Spy," "The Pioneers," "The Pilot," "Lionel Lincoln," "The Last of the Mohicans," "The Prairie," and "The Red Rover," followed immediately upon the publication of "Precaution," in consecutive order, and in the eight years including 1821 and 1828. I know not where to find, outside of Scott's work, a greater example of affluence in the production of fiction. In haste and uncertainty, with no friendly coterie of discreet advisers, with a public indifferent at home and hostile abroad, Cooper wrote and published that vigorous and enduring book which brought before us the manly, individual American character of Harvey Birch. Single-handed, he gave us a novel and a hero, because the power within him lay. The "The Spy." instant success he won was a proper stimulant toward the production of "The Pioneers." That novel "drags" seriously in the hands of those of us who read it to-day; but it calls for no strong effort of imagination to see how enthusiastically, in 1823, we would have hailed its germs of the "Leather-Stocking" development, in full and final form. The literary possibilities of the hero, of the Indians, and of the opening of the new American land evidently lay in the author's mind, who turned from the Revolution to the forest-clearing with the spontaneity of natural strength. The first month of the very next year added "The Pilot" to the previous successes: a third book, unlike either of its predecessors, and without a prominent prototype in English fiction. "The Pilot," in character and event, perhaps

"The Pilot." seems just to miss the possibilities of the theme ; but the wonder lies in what Cooper could give, not in what he missed. The breath of the book is the salt air of the veritable Atlantic ; its action is that of life. Nowhere else did Cooper come so near an adequate delineation of women's character, or a rememberable portrayal of the natural elements of scenes on water and on land. Its hero is drawn in effective tints, and his figure is both impressive in its distinctness and ideal in its shadows. The marine knowledge is practically infallible, at least for readers on land ; while the Revolutionary times are originally treated by the transfer of the action to a foreign shore. Next came "Lionel

"Lionel Lincoln." Lincoln ; or, The Leaguers of Boston," with its vivid accounts of the great battles of '75 on Massachusetts soil, and with a power not usually shown by its author in depicting his minor characters. "The Last of the Mohicans" may not inaccurately be said to have charmed two continents, in the dash of its doings, the peculiar majesty of its leading Caucasian and Aboriginal characters, and the fresh upland woodsy air that exhaled from its vivifying pages. In "The Prairie" the pathos of inevitable death was mitigated by those visions and reflections which console in every race and literature ; while in "The

Red Rover" we are once more spirited far out upon the scenes of that multiform unity, the ocean.

At the time of the publication of this vigorously-successful tale of adventure on the deep, Cooper had reached a deserved and really commanding popularity. The abounding personality of the man seemed to have freer scope on sea than on land, and in "The Red Rover" we surrender ourselves to a competent literary captain, whose eccentricities and disputatiousness rather add to his attractiveness. When, as in "The Bravo," published three years later, Cooper redoubled his attention to didactic and intense propagandism of democratic ideas, the power of "The Red Rover" or "The Last of the Mohicans," or "The Spy," was really diminished by a non-literary force, pulling partly in a contrary direction. In this, and so many of the later books, unwisdom or extravagance tended to minimize the success already won. But that success was won, and was to endure. For convenience' sake, the worse Cooper has here been studied before the better, that the just impression, in the logical order, might be left upon the reader's mind. But in the chronological order we must not forget that Cooper attained, before he was forty, an established rank which his follies and irregularities might impair but could never destroy. Of his eight first books all but one ("Precaution") was distinctly and lastingly suc-

"The Red Rover."

"The Bravo."

cessful;[*] and several later books were worthy additions to this select list.

James Fenimore Cooper created, developed, and completed, in Leather-Stocking, one of the most natural and significant and attractive characters in the fiction of all lands.[†] He delineated in Chingachgook and Uncas, with that poetic justice which is a proper union of true poetry and strict equity, the character of the Indian at his best. Elsewhere in that remarkable though heterogeneous list of novels whose very titles are

Cooper's special achievements. like characteristic outbursts of natural music, he displayed the literary powers of a leader on the land and a veritable master on the sea.

Considering in its entirety the literary career of Cooper, and viewing it from a point nearly forty years after his death, we can see how it was affected by the conditions of the time in which he

Conditions of Cooper's time. lived and wrote. Timid colonialism had not yet emerged from its state of long-continued deference toward England; and when it occasionally sought to throw off the trammels, it rushed, for the moment, to an opposite extreme of strident self-assertion. Hence, on Cooper's own part, the timidity of "Precaution"

---

[*] I by no means agree with the customary detraction of "Lionel Lincoln."

[†] "The series was a perfect one as it was left. The life of Leather-Stocking was now a complete drama in five acts, beginning with the first war-path in "The Deerslayer," followed by his career of activity and of love in "The Last of the Mohicans" and "The Pathfinder," and his old age and death in "The Pioneers" and "The Prairie."—Thomas R. Lounsbury, "James Fenimore Cooper," 239.

and the contemptuousness of " Home as Found ;"
or on the other hand, " The Pathfinder ;" the
novels attacking the aristocratic feudalism of
Europe, and the honest patriotism of the naval
history and biographies. Meanwhile, Cooper's
public veered long between a fear to praise him
too quickly, and an overweening pride in his
world-wide fame ; between delight at his attacks
upon the effeteness of the old world, and indignation at his outspoken criticisms of the new.
Again, the waste of the American intellectual life
was very apparent in Cooper's work. The Puritans had devoted their mental strength to propagandism of a peculiar religious creed and system ;
so, in his way, and in considerable measure, did
Cooper. The creative vigor of the eighteenth
century, in the colonies, had principally been
applied to the solution of problems of independent statecraft ; and thus Cooper, a few decades
later, felt bound to enlighten two continents
concerning his views of the political fabric and
human society in an actual or ideal state. Freed
from the necessities which have obliged so many
American writers to devote three-fourths of their
time to some wage-earning drudgery, Cooper, in
the very wantonness of that diffuseness and haste
which marked the westward spread of civilization
after 1800, took up most energetically many an
unnecessary task for which he was not fitted ; and
seemed, as a natural state, to be " spoiling for a
fight" of almost any sort. His ideas concerning
" sweetness and light" in human life were about

21

as delicately attractive as his presentation of the "sweet reasonableness" of religion itself. Foremost, in his day, in denouncing American Philistinism, he was himself a Philistine of abounding vitality, to whom rest eternal would have been synonymous with everlasting woe. Claiming to be a proper American aristocrat, in him the ducal qualities of serene self-respect, and a gracious attitude toward less fortunate beings, never appeared in any conspicuous light. Only when he unconsciously lost himself in his work, and heartily threw his great body, his warm heart, and his honest Saxon soul into the written page, did he display the powers of his individuality in their noblest estate. The time in which he lived was not responsible for all his qualities, and certainly it disliked some of them with a cordiality which Cooper, on his part, reciprocated by bewailing or hating his time. But his character was unfavorably affected by the environment, which exaggerated his worse qualities at the very period, and for the very reason, that it gave full scope to his better.

Cooper died September 14, 1851, the day before his sixty-second birthday. A little more than five months later a commemorative meeting was held in New York, the city around which Cooper's literary life had chiefly moved, and which properly deemed itself most honored by those services which belonged to the country at large. Death had silenced those bitter and ephemeral outcries

Cooper, Irving, Bryant, and Webster.

which, chiefly through his own fault, had attended
the novelist's career,—but which, indeed, were
already forgotten by most of those not immediately friendly or personally hostile to Cooper.
Daniel Webster, the representative statesman and
orator of the time, was the presiding officer.
Eight months later he, too, was to pass away, disappointed in his presidential aspirations, fore-
seeing the ruin of the Whig party, and shunned
by the more excitable and mischievous extremists
of both "sections" of the country. To Webster,
however, more than to any other individual, or
any group of individuals, was due the development and consolidation of that discreet and toler-
ant, but intense, Union sentiment which made the
disruption of the republic impossible in the following decade. That masterly man had devoted
his whole life—consistent even in its inconsistencies—to the idea of country, one and indivisible.
Naturally, therefore, the essentially native and
national quality of Cooper's novels was that most
prominent in Webster's mind. "While the love
of country continues to prevail," said he, "his
memory will exist in the hearts of the people. So
truly patriotic and American throughout, they
should find a place in every American's library."
The oration of the day, with equal propriety, fell
from the lips of William Cullen Bryant. After
the death of Irving (who had presided at the
meeting preliminary to this commemoration) Bryant remained for twenty years the most distinguished citizen of New York. Irving had first

showed to America and Europe an indigenous literature, valuable in itself and not merely a curiosity. Cooper had first produced an American series of novels, and had carried the fame of his country's books to the Continent itself. Bryant had turned to solid poetic achievement the promise of those who had begun to sing at the period of the dawn of imagination in the United States. Of the four men, each in his way, had done a great and significant service, and the survivors gladly honored him who was the first to depart.

"It is worthy of note," said Mr. Bryant, "that just about the time that 'The Spy' made its appearance, the dawn of what we now call our literature was just breaking. The concluding number of Dana's 'Idle Man,' a work neglected at first, but now numbered among the best things of the kind in our language, was issued in the same month. The 'Sketch Book' was just then completed; the world was admiring it, and its author was meditating 'Bracebridge Hall.' Miss Sedgwick, about the same time, made her first essay in that charming series of novels of domestic life in New England, which have gained her so high a reputation. Percival, now unhappily silent, had just put to press a volume of poems. I have a copy of an edition of Halleck's 'Fanny,' published in the same year; the poem of 'Yamoyden,' by Eastburn and Sands, appeared almost simultaneously with it. Livingston was putting the finishing hand to his 'Report on the Penal Code of Louis-

[margin note:] Cooper in the early days of American literature.

iana,' a work written with such grave, persuasive
eloquence, that it belongs as much to our literature as to our jurisprudence. Other contempora-
neous American works there were, now less read.
Paul Allen's poem of 'Noah' was just laid on the
counters of the booksellers. Arden published at
the same time, in this city, a translation of Ovid's
'Tristia,' in heroic verse, in which the complaints
of the effeminate Roman poet were rendered with
great fidelity to the original, and sometimes not
without beauty. If I may speak of myself, it was
in that year that I timidly entrusted to the winds
and waves of public opinion a small cargo of my
own—a poem entitled 'The Ages,' and half a
dozen shorter ones, in a thin duodecimo volume."

In the course of this address, one of the earlier
in the irregular series which the veteran Bryant
delivered from time to time at the request of fel-
low-authors and fellow-citizens, he touched very
kindly but perhaps sufficiently plainly upon most
of the demerits, as well as the merits of the novels
of land and sea considered in this chapter. His
estimate of the character of Leather-Stocking, and
of the five books in which his life is painted, is of
historic value, as representing the more intelligent
contemporary opinion at the time of their appearance. "The Prairie," on its publication in 1827,
Bryant read "with a certain awe, an undefined
sense of sublimity, such as one experiences on
entering for the first time upon these immense
grassy deserts from which the work takes its
name." Its Indians were "copies of the Amer-

ican savage somewhat idealized, but not the less a
part of the wild nature in which they have their
haunts." Its pioneers lived "in a sort of primi-
tive and patriarchal barbarism, sluggish on ordinary occasions but terrible when roused, like the
hurricane that sweeps the grand but monotonous
wilderness" in which they dwelt—a "natural
growth of those ancient fields of the west."
Leather-Stocking was "no less in harmony with
the silent desert" in which he wandered. He was
and is "a philosopher of the woods, ignorant of
books, but instructed in all that nature, without
the aid of science, could reveal to the man of
quick senses and inquiring intellect, whose life has
been passed under the open sky, and in companionship with a race whose animal perceptions are
the acutest and most cultivated of which there is
any example. But Leather-Stocking has higher
qualities ; in him there is a genial blending of the
gentlest virtues of the civilized man with the
better nature of the aboriginal tribes ; all that in
them is noble, generous, and ideal, is adopted into
his own kindly character, and all that is evil is
rejected. But why should I attempt to analyze
a character so familiar? Leather-Stocking is
acknowledged, on all hands, to be one of the
noblest, as well as most striking and original creations of fiction. In some of his subsequent
novels, Cooper—for he had not yet attained to
the full maturity of his powers—heightened and
ennobled his first conception of the character, but

in 'The Pioneers' it dazzled the world with the splendor of novelty."

In his peroration, which, as usual in eulogistic oratory, was too glowingly enthusiastic in its tributes and prophecies, Bryant found in the many translations of Cooper some portent that his works might thereby survive the language in which they were written. This speculative compliment need not detain our attention, for the succeeding quarter of a century has shown that English is to be—nay, is —the dominant language of the world, and that its distributing centre, at least as regards numbers of speakers and readers, is to pass to the nation of which Cooper chiefly wrote. Said Bryant: " In that way of writing in which he excelled, it seems to me that he united, in a pre-eminent degree, those qualities which enabled him to interest the largest number of readers. He wrote not for the fastidious, the over-refined, the morbidly delicate ; for these find in his genius something too robust for their liking—something by which their sensibilities are too rudely shaken ; but he wrote for mankind at large—for men and women in the ordinary healthful state of feeling— and in their admiration he found his reward. . . . Hence it is that he has earned a fame wider, I think, than any author of modern times—wider, certainly, than any author of any age ever enjoyed in his lifetime. All his excellencies are translatable—they pass readily into languages the least allied in their genius to that in which he

A national novelist of international fame.

wrote, and in them he touches the heart and kindles the imagination with the same power as in the original English. . . . . Such are the works so widely read, and so universally admired in all the zones of the globe, and by men of every kindred and every tongue; works which have made of those who dwell in remote latitudes, wanderers in our forests and observers of our manners, and have inspired them with an interest in our history. . . . . Over all the countries into whose speech this great man's works have been rendered by the labors of their scholars, the sorrow of that loss which we deplore is now diffusing itself. Here we lament the ornament of our country, there they mourn the death of him who delighted the human race. . . . . The creations of his genius, fixed in living words, survive the frail material organs by which the words were first traced. They partake of a middle nature, between the deathless mind and the decaying body of which they are the common offspring, and are therefore destined to a duration, if not eternal, yet indefinite. The examples he has given in his glorious fictions, of heroism, honor, and truth; of large sympathies between man and man, of all that is good, great, and excellent, embodied in personages marked with so strong an individuality that we place them among our friends and favorites; his frank and generous men, his gentle and noble women, shall live through centuries to come, and only perish with our language."

The cool-blooded Bryant was here too impetuous; but this, at least, we can say in agreement: Cooper, with a hundred faults, possessed the surpassing merit due to a large literary creator in a field which he found and made his own.

CHAPTER X.

NATHANIEL HAWTHORNE.

THERE are some writers—not many, in the literature of any land—whom it is a sponta- Literary artists of the beautiful. neous pleasure to read. In their pages one is not troubled by notable unworthiness of theme, crudeness of plan, imperfection of development, irregularity of thought, infelicity of expression. All parts combine to give a high and true literary pleasure. The critic does not, to be sure, abdicate his function, or declare that the books of such writers are above praise. He prefers this to that, notes and discusses various characteristics of genius and product, and may even declare poem, tale, or large book a mistake or a failure. But the failure, in such a case, has to do with the grand design, not with its details; or perhaps the declaration of failure, means only that creator and critic hold radically different opinions on the subject in question. Of the substantial unity, completeness, natural beauty, and adequacy of the product, or perhaps of the author's whole genius, in its parts and in its entirety, there need arise no troublesome question. Thus, in considering the writings of Dante, one may prefer the " Divine Comedy," another the " New Life ;" or, in reading the

330

longer work alone, one may best like the " Inferno," another the " Purgatorio," and still a third
the " Paradiso." To the stern Protestant lover
of Bunyan's " Pilgrim's Progress," Dante's mediæval Romanism may appear an ineradicable
blemish ; while to the ultramontane Romanist, on
the other hand, his frank treatment of certain
popes and saints may seem sad liberalism. The
canto or the line may be declared indefensibly
poor or unspeakably glorious ; in a word, the
Dante critic may ply his trade with the affectionate zeal of a Longfellow, or with the mathematical letter-counting minuteness of a Dryasdust.
But whatever be the standpoint or method, there
is still in Dante something that makes him a poet
of joy and delight, or of sadness and sorrow that
in themselves have an element of poetic pleasure.
His work, when we study it, takes us out of the
humdrum world, or bathes that world in the new
light and fragrance of genius, so that its earth-
liness, its men and women, its thought and life,
its very atmosphere, seem real and yet ideal, familiar but all above the commonplace. In very
truth there is in the literature of genius a breath
of the New Life which Dante entered under the
guidance of love.

Between Dante and Hawthorne there is no
need to draw a long comparison. The sad-faced
dweller in the land of shades forth-fared _{Dante and}
six centuries ago, while our Yankee _{Hawthorne.}
romancer is remembered by many not yet past
middle life. One wrote verse, the other prose ;

one peered into the unseen for his august theme ;
the other found his subjects in the Massachusetts
soil at his feet. The sadness of Dante was not
so often irradiated with cheer as was the serious
purpose of Hawthorne—a purpose sometimes
mistaken for morbidness or gloom of personal
character. Nor, finally, would any wise critic
aver that Hawthorne, though clearly enough the
greatest author yet produced in America, is to go
down the centuries secure of any fame akin to
Dante's. And yet there are some characteristics,
absolute and relative, which both men had ; and it
will be enough for my present purpose it it be
admitted that Hawthorne's literary creations are
things of genius, and that in reading them we
turn to a region in which study becomes a pleasure rather than a duty. It would be a sorry day
for criticism if it never found a book or poem—
or in a broad sense a whole body of writings—
to which it could say, as to a flower or a
shell :

> " Being everything which now thou art
> Be nothing which thou art not."

Thus gladly we turn toward the singularly
beautiful and characteristic list of writings which
began with " Fanshawe" in 1828 and closed with
the unfinished " Dolliver Romance " in 1864.
Throughout nearly all of them we shall find that
artlessness which characterizes the true genius,
and that art which shows genius to be accompanied by high powers of construction and elab-

oration. An English painter and poet of Hawthorne's own time wrote, in youth, a story which
has for its central thought the idea that "Hand and
"an artist need not seek for intellectual-   Soul."
ized moral intentions in his work, but will fulfil
God's highest purpose by simple truth in mani-
festing, in a spirit of devout faith, the gift that
God has given him."* This idea is one which, in
some shape, often occurs to Hawthorne's readers,
and must more often have been in the romancer's
own mind, though he seldom formulated it.

The delight which we take in Hawthorne is,
then, the joy of perception of the work of an
artist. The several methods of intellectual communication between mind and mind are widely
variant in method and result. We derive one
impression or pleasure from painting, Literature
and another—now stronger, now weaker,   as art.
from sculpture, architecture, action, music; or
from the apprehension of inanimate nature by the
sense. It is the privilege and power of literature,
in the hands of its masters to convey to readers
a sort of combination or intense suggestion of
almost all other methods of thought-transfer or
soul-expression. If printing is the "art preserva-
tive of all arts," literature is the art suggestive
or inclusive of all arts. The author is an artist,
and in direct proportion as he fulfils the highest
artistic function in choice and elaboration of his
creations, does he deserve his craft-name in its
highest sense. The authors who are, by right,

* Edward Dowden, in *The Academy*, Feb. 5, 1887.

nearest of kin to Michael Angelo, Raphael, Beethoven, are those that select some theme from the manifold life of the universe in which we exist, and develop it into a literary form best worthy of comparison, for ideal merit and poetic impression, with the statue of Moses, the Sistine Madonna, or the Eighth Symphony. Usually, the poet and prose romancer most attain success in the development of such literary form; and hence the highest literature of a world or a land, of all times or of any one time, is that of poetry and fiction. The spiritual and physical worlds, the ego and the non-ego, lie peculiarly open to the singer and the story-teller. Our libraries are crammed with the trash of verse and the rubbish of invented story; but now and then their shelves are brightened with a book, in either division, that gives the joy we get from a noble strain or a radiant picture.

The precise success which Hawthorne has attained, in his artist-work, is a matter of debate, which it is hopeless to try to settle definitely as yet. The neglect which once surrounded his Hawthorne name has changed to a too silly and as artist. reverential laudation. Already this modest writer has fallen into the hands of the zealots who study plays or poems of Shakespeare or Shelley or Browning for "inner meanings" or esoteric doctrine. There can no longer be question, however, that Hawthorne is an artist, to be measured by the canons applicable to the broader and more ambitious creations, and to stand or fall in letters according as his writings endure the large tests which they are brought to face.

Often enough did Hawthorne express his knowledge of the tremendous lesson which life teaches to a great artist like a Dante or a Milton, but cannot teach to a Schopenhauer or an Omar Khayyám. Bunyan never insisted more strongly upon the notion of God, duty, and immortality; upon the "sinfulness of sin," as the old preachers used to phrase it, and as the liberal romancer in reality accepted it. The human heart was Hawthorne's highest and most constant theme, and though he never wasted time in orotund sermonizing, and threw away as chaff fit for "Earth's Holocaust" much that creed-makers, from Nice to Plymouth, deem sacred, he was ever, without being less an artist, a force in the world of life and letters. He watched with keen, deep eyes, but sometimes he wrote with a pen of flame. "The heart, the heart,—there was the little yet boundless sphere wherein existed the original wrong of which the crime and misery of this outward world were merely types. Purify that inward sphere, and the many shapes of evil that haunt the outward, and which now seem almost our only realities, will turn to shadowy phantoms and vanish of their own accord; but if we go no deeper than the intellect, and strive, with merely that feeble instrument, to discern and rectify what is wrong, our whole accomplishment will be a dream." *

The romancer of the human heart.

* "Earth's Holocaust," in "Mosses from an Old Manse."

This "inward sphere," the human heart, was Hawthorne's field of study and portrayal. He saw and described its innocence, its purity, its loveliness, its noble hopes, its truest triumphs, its temptations, its sinful tendency, its desperate struggles, its downward motions, its malignity, its "total depravity," at least in appearance, its final petrifaction and self-destruction—the only destruction of which, in the divine plan, it is capable. Life, in Hawthorne's view, was no Human Comedy, as to Balzac, or tragedy of lost souls, as to the early New England theologians, but the struggle of individual men, women, and children with the powers within and without them, and chiefly the powers within. Surely a romancer could have no higher theme, and highly did Hawthorne treat it.

But did he thereby become the less an artist or the more?

The literature of the two great Anglo-Saxon peoples has always had a tolerably clear idea that there is a necessary connection between art and ethics. It has contained many mischievous or frivolous books ; it has wavered between the austerity of Bunyan and the license of the dramatists of the Restoration ; it has been successively influenced by Norman-French, Italian, Latin, and Greek culture ; but it has never lost sight of certain principles peculiarily its own. One of these principles is that a book should have a definite purpose, a real reason for being, if it expects a long life. This principle has not been

Art and ethics.

lost even in the imaginative literature of England and America.

Before the novel, the poem afforded our intellectual ancestors their means of amusement; and in early English poetry the moral element was seldom lacking. The Anglo-Saxons found in the verse ascribed to Cædmon, in the paraphrase of Judith, and even in the non-Christian story of "Beowulf," stern expressions of the inevitableness of retribution and penalty. Like Miles Standish, they liked Old Testament wars better than New Testament peace, but their scanty literature was prized largely for its moral lessons. Later, in Robert of Gloucester's "Chronicle," in the grim and telling force of the satire in "Piers Plowman," and in the "Canterbury Tales," English readers amused themselves while they were getting advice, warning, and entreaty. "Piers Plowman," with its sharp distinctions between righteousness and hypocrisy, and the "Canterbury Tales," with their lifelike pictures of all classes of Englishmen, were in a true sense precursors of the English Reformation. They were novels in verse, but they were something more. Even the "Faerie Queene," with its cumbrous supernatural machinery, never let imagination hide the "XII. Morall Vertues." It was an Italian graft on the tough old English tree.

When fiction took the place of poetry, as an intellectual amusement, the same principle held good. To this day, the best-known work of imagination in English prose is a terribly earnest

22

sermon. It so happened that the growth of the English novel began when English society and religion were once more in a degraded state, but in the indecency and coarseness of the novel of the eighteenth century there still appears something that is not French, not Italian, not Spanish. Rob-

Moral law in
English fiction.
inson Crusoe is a moral Englishman abroad, who has changed his sky, not his disposition. Moralizing, if not morality, is not absent from the loose sayings of Sterne. Swift, in his malignant, half-insane way, at least had reforms in view. Fielding, like Chaucer and the author of "Piers Plowman," felt that accurate delineation was the precursor of a change for the better. Goldsmith's pictures of virtuous rural life are still beloved because, in Taine's phrase, the chief of them "unites and harmonizes in one character the best features of the manners and morals of the time and country, and creates an admiration and love for pious and orderly, domestic and disciplined, laborious and rural life; Protestant and English virtue has not a more approved and amiable exemplar." Samuel Richardson, the precursor of the long-regnant school of sentimental novelists, spent his literary lifetime in trying to show that integrity and uprightness, even of the Grandisonian order, are more attractive than the vice of the "town" in the era of the Georges.

Something more than mere amusement, something behind the story, is still more evident in Scott, the Scheherezade of modern literature; in Dickens, promoting humanity and good fellow-

ship, and attacking abuses in prisons, schools, law
courts, and home-life ; in Thackeray, tilting loyally
against social shams; in saddened but brave
Charlotte and Emily Brontë, amid the Yorkshire
moors ; in George Eliot, describing the Jew as she
believed him to be in reality, doing justice to the
stern righteousness of a Dinah Morris, or telling
how Savonarola was a Protestant in spite of himself. Turning to America, we note, as in England, the almost total disappearance of the outward immorality which defiled British fiction a
hundred years ago, and which still disgraces a
part of French fiction : and more than this, we find
positive qualities, and a belief that story-telling is
something more than story-telling. Irving feels
with the heart of humanity; Cooper, like Scott,
magnifies the chivalric virtues, under new skies ;
and Hawthorne goes to the depth of the soul in
his search for the basal principles of human
action.

What does all this mean ? Is a book great
because its moral purpose is sound, or is all literature bad as art and literature if it lacks the righteous purpose ? Not at all ; neither has Anglo-
Saxon literature monopoly of righteousness and
purpose. It means that this literature has insisted
more strongly than others upon the necessary
connection between art *and* ethics ; that it has
never prized a profitless, soulless _{An inevitable}
beauty; and that, so long as the world _{race-principle.}
can be made better by literature, book-makers can
and ought to help. Between two books of equal

literary merit, but of unequal purpose, it gives greater and more lasting favor to the more useful book. It believes, with the American poet who is usually considered our chief apostle of the merely beautiful, that "taste holds intimate relations with the intellect and the moral sense." Whether it is right or wrong in this general idea, it is certain that any change in it, whether wrought by believers in "art for art's sake," by pseudo Greek poets, by "cosmic" bards who sometimes confuse right and wrong, or by strictly "realistic" novelists, will change a principle in accord with which the race has acted for ten centuries.

In accord with that principle Nathaniel Hawthorne worked from the beginning to the end of his literary life; but he was too great an artist to confuse for a moment the demands of ethics with those of pure art. With this explicit statement at the outset I shall not need to recur again, by the use of the word *ethical*, to this fundamental element in the greatness of Hawthorne's work, save as it may incidentally appear.

Hawthorne's foundation.

Because of his general theme—the heart of man—and the necessary and artistic elaboration of a theme stained with evil, many careless readers and a few superficial critics have been wont to declare Hawthorne morbid, gloomy, fond of repulsive spiritual analysis of depraved or debased characters, or at best a dweller on the "night-side of

Was Hawthorne "morbid"?

nature." Even Emerson made a misleading half-
statement when he said that Hawthorne "rode
well his steed of the night,"—as though he had
been a Poe or a Hoffman. Hawthorne was not a
graveyard ghoul, a specialist in morbid psychology, a black-sheeted monk of the order that
officiates only at funerals. A careful reading of
one of his books—or of the biography of
"Nathaniel Hawthorne and his Wife," by their
son Julian—is enough to dispel the error, which
strangely lingers here and there. Hawthorne
dealt with the profoundest themes of human life
and thought; he saw the mind within the body,
and the soul within the mind. The deep and
lasting consequences of sin, and that most awful
of punishments, the self-slaughter of a soul, he
studied and portrayed in more than one of his
stories. If "morbid psychology" mean the examination and description of temptation, evil, and
the result, then morbid psychology is an element
in Hawthorne's books. But he never describes
evil for the mere pleasure of description; still less
with any pessimistic motive. He delves

"Down, mid the tangled roots of things,
  That coil about the central fire,"

in order to see how they

"Climb to a soul in grass and flowers."

Sin is never disconnected from penalty, and
penalty is applied for the purification of some
imaginary character, or virtually of that very real

character, the individual reader of the story. Hawthorne is never morbid in the sense in which the term is sometimes applicable to Tourguéneff or certain French novelists of general renown, or to Edgar Poe. He does not approach a gloomy theme for the purpose of making a sensation, or producing a gruesome effect, or evoking a brilliant artistic result. Life, in his view, was the most august of themes; and he saw it in its entirety, in its gradations from Roger Chillingworth to little Pearl. When he chose he could create things as evanescent and merely beautiful as a butterfly or a sunlit bubble; but when he passed into the shadow it was for serious portrayals. So far was Hawthorne from being an unwholesome soul that not even his classmate and friend Longfellow was more truly a gentle optimist and lover of existence. His home-life and personal character have been made known to all the world, and rarely has been displayed such a picture of fresh beauty, and serene sunlight, and self-respecting "acceptance of the universe," spiritual and natural. Indeed, his own words to his sister-in-law Elizabeth Peabody are enough: "When I write anything that I know or suspect is morbid, I feel as though I had told a lie."

Hawthorne had the soul and the outlook of a poet. In his story "The Great Stone Face" he says: "The world assumed another and a better aspect from the hour that the poet blessed it with his happy eyes. The Creator had bestowed him, as

the last best touch to his own handiwork. Creation was not finished till the poet came to interpret, and so complete it." According to this
definition, which the writer, of course, had no
thought of applying to himself, Hawthorne did
bless the world with happy eyes, interpret and
complete creation. To him the universe was a
lovely thing of perennial beauty, to be enjoyed
and valued for its own sake, and for the pleasure
of mere existence. This was no lost world, for
religious and irreligious pessimists and agnostics
to practise their wits on, but a veritable earthly
paradise. "There is no decay. Each human
soul is the first-created inhabitant of its own
Eden. We dwell in an old moss-covered man-
sion, and tread in the worn footprints of the past,
and have a gray clergyman's ghost for our daily
and nightly inmate; yet all these outward circumstances are made less than visionary by the
renewing power of the spirit. Should the spirit
ever lose this power,—should the withered leaves,
and the rotten branches, and the moss-covered
house, and the ghost of the gray past ever become
its realities, and the verdure and the freshness
merely its faint dream,—then let it pray to be
released from earth."* Hawthorne's "New Adam
and Eve" light-heartedly "tread along the wind-
ing paths among marble pillars, mimic temples,
urns, obelisks, and sarcophagi, sometimes pausing
to contemplate these fantasies of human growth,
and sometimes to admire the flowers wherewith

* "Buds and Bird-Voices," "Mosses from an Old Manse," Vol. I.

nature converts decay to loveliness." Mere beauty, joy, happiness, to be followed instinctively, are at one side, and that the greater side, of Hawthorne's universe. Toward these all things ultimately ought to tend. At the other extreme from this heaven is the hell he so often described, and which he portrayed in thirty words when he told us, in one of his note books, that "at the last day—when we see ourselves as we are—man's only inexorable judge will be himself, and the punishment of his sins will be the perception of them." To and fro men pass, now hither, now thither, into the shadow or into the sun, and Hawthorne follows them with the serene eyes of a regretful or joyous observer and chronicler, but not with the feelings of the embittered or morbid spectator in the search of mere literary material for woeful romance.

Hawthorne never shared, and indeed must have despised, the silly and sickly sentimentalism of the period in which his literary life began. It was the time—at least in verse and in fiction—of bowers, and casements, and tresses, and wafting breezes, and tears, and sighs; when Vice had horns and a tail and a sulphurous breath, and when sugary Virtue, on the other hand, was equally impossible and almost equally repulsive. Hawthorne was as far from prudery as he was from baseness. His soul was a wholesome one, and it was a soul not content with superficiality, whether of the good or of the bad things in life. As an author, his sunshine

Attitude in the sentimental era.

was brighter and his shadows darker than those of most novelists, for they were the sunshine and shadows of real life, and not of a pallid or utopian picture. When the heroines of other story-tellers were bursting into tears every page or two, Hawthorne's Hester Prynne was walking in the loneliness and silence of majestic sorrow and voiceless remorse. When the guitars of the pseudo-Spanish heroines of the day were tinkling from the lattices portrayed in the steel-engravings then so popular, his Phœbe Pyncheon was showing American readers the fresh and lovely grace of a true little Massachusetts maiden of the Puritan stock. Other novelists of his native land went hunting all afield for types, and plots, and backgrounds ; Hawthorne took those amid which he had grown up, and which he had studied as deeply and quietly as Thoreau studied the depths of Walden Pond, or the depths of the sky above. His world was the world of his place and time, but its light and air were those which surround all humanity. From one he learned all ; in his way he unconsciously heeded that advice of Emerson's, which was found among the philosopher's man- uscripts : he told men what they knew before, he painted the prospect from their door. Men had known more than they could express, Hawthorne's and more than they had read in other outlook. books ; so Hawthorne reaped the reward of the imaginative genius who states or portrays what others have but felt. As a large literary creator, accordingly, no other American occupies a place so high, and no other is so worthy of mention in the study of the world's best literature.

The writings of Hawthorne are, as a whole, of such uniform merit that it is not easy to select illustrative specimens of characteristic significance, as far as thought or literary style is concerned. Though he exercised an unusual freedom in the use of new or unfamiliar phrases, and in coining words, the charm of expression is seldom absent from his later writings, and often appears even in his earliest. It is more important to note that the broad general method of all his books is likewise a method showing few variations between 1828, with its crude little romance of Bowdoin, and 1864, with its unfinished "Aladdin's tower" of the author's fiction. Hawthorne's just judgment of his own genius and powers of expression—a judgment illustrated in his long self-imposed novitiate, and strengthened thereby—enabled him to think and write with unusual freedom from the ill effects of fashion, greed, or prejudice. In this respect he resembled Emerson, from whom he differed widely in most of his mental characteristics. But I believe that it is possible to select from his works one short tale which is a microcosm of his mind and art. From the patient study of such a story as that of "Ethan Brand," in the volume entitled "The Snow-Image, and Other Twice-Told Tales" (1851), may be derived a deeper and more comprehensive knowledge of his true literary life than from any voluminous record of dates, doings, and titles. It contains a picture of the soul and body of the author's work, and may well be taken in hand as the alpha of Hawthorne's alphabet, by those—if such there be—as yet unfamiliar with his method and expression as an author, or by those who have read him merely in a superficial way, without noting the deeper elements in the several stories and romances. Hawthorne's whole philosophy of life, and his point of view, may here be noted and studied within the compass of no more than twenty-two pages. This "chapter from an abortive romance," as the author modestly terms it in the sub-title, is in reality so rounded and complete that it needs no apology, but rather a duly thoughtful attention. Of it Mrs. Hawthorne wrote to her mother in December, 1848: "It is a tremendous truth, written, as he often writes truth, with characters of fire, upon an infinite gloom,—softened so as not wholly to terrify, by divine touches of beauty, —revealing pictures of nature, and also the tender spirit of a child." *

Hawthorne was a pioneer and master of that literary method which, under the name of realism, has so strongly affected the fiction of the latter part of the nineteenth century. He studied minutely, and portrayed with delicate faithfulness, the smallest flower beneath his foot, the faintest bird in the distant sky, the trivial mark or the seemingly unimportant act of the person described. The microscopic

Philosophy of life.

Hawthorne a realist and an idealist.

* "Nathaniel Hawthorne and his Wife," by Julian Hawthorne; 1, 330–331.

artist was not more faithful in noting little characteristics or swiftly-fleeting marks. Such sketches as " A Rill from the Town Pump," " Main Street," " Sights from a Steeple," or " Little Annie's Ramble" are realism in its complete estate. Tourguéneff himself, the prototype of so many followers in Russia, France, and America, is not more watchful with the eye or more painstaking with the pen. But between Hawthorne and Tourguéneff there is an unlikeness as marked as their external similarity of method. Hawthorne, a realist in portrayal, is a thorough idealist in thought and purpose. The weariness and melancholy of Russian life and literature are nowhere present in his writings. Tourguéneff's exquisite " Poems in Prose" virtually end with the query of that weakly pessimistic song the burden of which is : " What is it all when all is done ?" " In Hawthorne's books, to be sure, are the profoundest sin, the deepest veil of misery and mystery, the infinite gloom of which Mrs. Hawthorne wrote ; but always above them the tremendous truth written with characters of fire, and yet with "divine touches of beauty," with many a picture of artlessly lovely nature and life, and with the tender spirit of a child pervading the whole. At the close of Tourguéneff's portrayals silently falls the black impenetrable curtain through which we may not peer, behind which there is nothing. But in Hawthorne's pages, beyond the blackness and woe of sin and of slow spiritual suicide, are the glow and the glory of the triumph that fol-

lows the struggle; of the proved virtue that is
better than untried innocence, and of the eternity
that tells the meaning of time.

The method of elaboration of the idea of
"Ethan Brand" is definite. The plot of the
story seems simplicity itself. It is Hawthorne's
usual plan to take a single thought and develop
it by the aid of an uncomplicated machinery.
Here, as in so many other cases, he
introduces few characters, and describes
no more than one or two scenes, at the
same time contriving to suggest leagues
of wandering and years of passing time. In one
of his earlier walks in Berkshire County, Massachusetts, Hawthorne had come upon a lime-kiln,
luridly and picturesquely burning against the sky
of night; and in his note-book for 1838 is recorded, at some length, its appearance in the
mind of the watchful young romancer. From the
memory of this lime-kiln gradually grew the story
of Ethan Brand, the man with the heart of stone.
Around its central character are grouped the lime-
burner Bartram, rough but not unkindly; his little son, with the innocent curiosity of childhood,
pure amid grime and dirt; the motley group of
village worthies: the bibulous and broken-down
lawyer, the coarse doctor of the period when bru-
tality was deemed requisite in the practice of med-
icine, the withered village wit, and the poor old
white-haired man, whose daughter and whose
mind had been stolen away by the evil Ethan.
As though these were not enough to heighten the

A Hawthorne microcosm: the story of "Ethan Brand."

tragedy of the story, by their more superficial and yet equally miserable badness, we have also, against the solemn background of the hills, a German Jew with his little diorama of the wonders of all the distant world, and his solemn-foolish old dog. Behind them all, in the aloofness of blacker and more deliberate sin, is Ethan Brand, who returns from a world-search for selfish intellectual triumph, to find the Unpardonable Sin in his own breast. Tenderness, sympathy, and love he had deliberately crushed down; the mind he had made everything, the heart nothing, and thus he had become a fiend. The ablest theologians who have speculated upon the nature of that "sin against the Holy Ghost," which shall be forgiven neither in this world nor in the world to come, have concluded that it consists of a persistent barring-out of good influences and good desires. As long as the soul is free, such a barring-out of good must be effectual, and cannot be mitigated until the soul rights itself of its own motion. It may, indeed, notwithstanding the love of the Divine for the creature, go so far that here or hereafter the very heart becomes stony and bloodless. This is the lesson of "Ethan Brand," stated more powerfully than ever a theologian stated it. Hawthorne's creed is as universal as the needs of man; he has no theological axe to grind, wherewith to behead dissentient heretics; he is a literary artist, not a professional sermonizer; and certainly he is above the accusation of the Pharisaic egotism of those who think the

Deity under obligation to manage the world according to the scheme of their sect. But the eternal and apparently inexorable truths of the moral universe he knew and believed as <small>The universe</small> truly as he knew and believed the super- <small>of morals.</small> nal beauty of creation and the yearning love of a Creator who stands ready to forgive whenever a soul turns to him.

On a single page at the close of this story is the contrast between the two phases of truth. Ethan Brand has cast himself into the kiln, and on the calcined dust lies his snow-white skeleton, within the ribs of which is the marble shape of a human heart. But little Joe skips hap- <small>The stony</small> pily about, and cries: "Dear father, that <small>heart.</small> strange man is gone, and the sky and the mountains all seem glad of it!" And meanwhile the serenity and loveliness of the world are portrayed with that dainty touch which suggests, not argues, in the picture of the surrounding landscape :

The early sunshine was already pouring its gold upon the mountain-tops; and though the valleys were still in shadow they smiled cheerfully in the promise of the bright day that was hastening onward. The village, completely shut in by hills, which swelled away gently about it, looked as if it had rested peacefully in the hollow of the great hand of Providence. Every dwelling was distinctly visible ; the little spires of the two churches pointed upwards, and caught a fore-glimmering of brightness from the sun-gilt skies upon their gilded weather-cocks. . . . . . Old Graylock was glorified with a golden cloud upon his head. Scattered likewise over the breasts of the surrounding mountains, there were heaps of hoary mist, in fantastic shapes, some of them far down into the valley, others high up towards the summits, and still others, of the same family of mist or cloud, hovering in the gold radiance of the upper atmosphere. Stepping from one to another of the clouds that rested on the hills, and thence to the loftier brotherhood that sailed in air, it seemed almost as if a mortal man might thus ascend into the heavenly regions. Earth was so mingled with sky that it was a day-dream to look at it.

This idea of the homeward-coming of a world-wanderer was used by Hawthorne in another of his significant stories, "The Threefold Destiny," in "Twice-told Tales." This "Threefold Destiny" is really the counterpart of "Ethan Brand," though we have no indication that the author designed the two to bear a complementary relation. The art of "The Threefold Destiny," though not of the highest, has been so obvious that the story has won considerable favor in France, where literary form is so generally demanded; yet spirit dominates style, as in "Ethan Brand." But notwithstanding its apt title and its relative success as compared with some similar ambitious undertakings by other hands, "The Threefold Destiny," as a piece of literature, is decidedly inferior to "Ethan Brand," and cannot be considered one of Hawthorne's greater products. It illustrates his great general method, but not his highest achievement. The plot is suggestive. Cranfield, the central figure of the tale, wanders far from his village home, in search of world-wide fame and commanding station, a mysterious treasure, and an ideal love; he returns to teach the little school near at hand, to till the poor patch of ground on

which he was born, and to wed a childhood play-
mate. The application follows : "Would all, who
cherish such wild wishes, but look around them,
they would oftenest find their sphere of duty, of
prosperity, and happiness within those precincts,
and in that station where Providence has cast
their lot. Happy they who read the riddle, without a weary world-search, or a lifetime spent in
vain."

In this story we perceive the ill effects which
often attend an attempted union between the
didactic and the artistic. It must definitely be
recognized and stated that in "The Threefold
Destiny" the decoration and construction suffer
at the hands of the ethical purpose. The moral
is somewhat rudely thrown in the reader's face at
the close. We asked for a story, and we got a
"Sunday-school book" instead. Hawthorne, for
once, seems like a professional or salaried moralizer ; and we feel a little inclined, in this instance,
to read what he has to say, and then go and
follow our own will, though it take us to the end
of the earth instead of to our mother's kitchen-
garden or the village school. What is natural in
Miss Edgeworth seems foreign in Hawthorne,
whose usual delicacy of touch and suggestiveness
of style apparently desert him at the climax.
This semi-clerical manner is here not coincident
with any proper success in ideal fiction. The
reader is half ready at the close, to rise for the
benediction, when the "application" and the
"aspiration" have been duly uttered. But the

23

central idea of the story remains significant. It is closely united to Hawthorne's usual method, in which he seldom made failures. It is no easy task to be uniformly spiritual and uniformly artistic, but Hawthorne very nearly achieved this task. We can more readily forgive him for a comparatively poor story, now and then, than for any repeated infidelity to a method at once spontaneous and high, in which he won a success not achieved by any other English-speaking novelist of the century. His deliberate choice of his place in literature was made in full recognition of his powers and preference, as well as of the universal relation between external artistic creation and its guiding purpose within. The literary centuries are strewn with failures in attempts like his; "The Threefold Destiny"—by no means an outright failure—merely reminds us that its author was fallible, and heightens his general success by the passing shade of an occasional unworthiness.

In the previous volume of this history I incidentally mentioned three of Hawthorne's short stories, including the two just considered, as those in which the student could at length perceive the firm purpose underlying the enduring art. The third member of this trilogy—of my choice, not of the author's arrangement—is "Lady *"Lady Eleanore's Mantle."* Eleanore's Mantle," one of the "Legends of the Province House," in the second volume of "Twice-Told Tales." Turning thereto, the reader finds a plan essentially similar, in broad conception, to those of the other allegories, but expressed in an art so admirable as almost to tempt one to use the adjective perfect. In such a story as this Hawthorne appears at his best. The sombre background of early Puritan Massachusetts; the Boston of the days when grim democratic Calvinism struggled with the considerable grandeur of wealth and a provincial court; a few strangely-romantic characters standing plainly against the horizon of the familiar sky, yet seen through the dimmed light of the intervening years that so completely separate the old from the new—all these things Hawthorne could use far more powerfully than any other American.

Some critics have lamented that Hawthorne, so equipped with the strength and weapons of a genius, lacked the historic background Hawthorne's which a great romancer should enjoy. background. They have actually apologized for the poverty of the materials which he was forced to use. On the contrary, it seems to me that he found at hand scenes possessing remarkable capabilities for literary treatment; strong and forceful characters never before portrayed; and (because of the vast changes caused by the Revolution) a sufficient remoteness of time. Castles, drawbridges, black forests, tournaments, battles, and knights and dames had been used so often that none but a Scott could longer make them interesting. But houses of seven gables; witch-haunted Puritan villages, fringed by native woods from which the Indians had scarcely fled; soul-conflicts of stern dogmatists; heart-sorrows of men and

women whose lives were forced back into their
own selves; lovely little maidens from whom the
poetry of nature could not be taken away;
children as pure as the field-springs or half-hidden
violets amid which they played, were unfamiliar
in English fiction before Hawthorne. Irving in
his Hudson stories, or Cooper in his Indian tales,
was not more fortunate in theme nor more original in treatment; while Poe, the only other
American novelist worth mentioning in a chapter
devoted to Hawthorne, did not find Ghostland
itself a better artistic background than Salem or
Concord.

If it be an advantage for a novelist to follow
other great workers in the same field, then Hawthorne lacked such advantage. But the great
Creator, not creator, whether he be novelist or poet,
follower. does not need prototypes and forerunners. He avails himself freely of the lessons
and the work of his predecessors, but he is under
no more than minor obligations to them. The
man of genius is injured by following others,
quite as truly as he is helped. A similar remark
may be made concerning the picturesque or
imposing historic background of literature. Such
a background, in an ancient country, is pretty sure
to be an unduly familiar one. A genius, in point
of fact, takes his background where he finds it; if
at home, and still comparatively unknown, he
follows his national bent and local inspiration; if
not, he forages all afield, without complaining of
the disadvantages of his surroundings. When

Hawthorne chose, he made solemn and august Rome his background; for the most part, however, he was glad to employ the singularly rich unused realm close at hand. It is the weaker novelist that is most concerned to find a fit setting for his plot; a mind like Hawthorne's possesses the element of large natural spontaneity which characterizes the world-author as distinct from the provincialist. A Dante is Italian, a Goethe is German, and even a Shakespeare is intensely English; but in their writings the local typifies the general. To the statement, then, that Hawthorne was imprisoned or disadvantaged by his environment, a double reply can be made: first, that he found at hand a rich and virgin field, well suited to the nature of his working genius; and second, that his powers of invention and assimilation were too great to be crushed down by adverse conditions, had such surrounded him. Indeed, Hawthorne was related to his background as closely as flower to root, so naturally did he grow from it and so truly did he represent it to the beholder's eye.

To return to "Lady Eleanore's Mantle": the story is vivid in its historic pictures, romantic in its plot, and adequate in its perception and portrayal of the emotions, which are the real theme of the highest fiction written during the present century. Its thought is the curse brought by a lovely but heartless woman, who wrapped herself in pride as in a mantle, and whose mantle literally became the source of pestilence to herself and to the whole community. The episode, in other hands, might have been treated feebly or repulsively; its success might have been moral or perhaps sanitary rather than properly artistic; but in Hawthorne's pages the stately and the horrible, the external and the internal, are presented in a literary union of which the reader notes the admirable whole rather than the patiently wrought details. The work of the brain is concealed by the artist who is content to display the finished product; *ars est celare artem.* Hawthorne has indeed shown us, in his note-books, much of his mental habit and method of observation and elaboration; but in his completed work, here and elsewhere, the means seldom cloud the literary result. One might go still farther, and add that the style itself is so transparent that we instantly note the thought and afterward—if at all—the expression.

The powers of Hawthorne, thus displayed in short stories, were made more broadly and largely, though not more truly, manifest in his romances. It often happens that a good writer of short stories is unable to produce a praiseworthy novel

Hawthorne's romances. or romance, while the creator of a meritorious novel cannot, or does not, represent his powers within a narrow space. The history of literature readily affords illustrations of this truth. We do not need to search beyond the brief period of American literature to prove it, for we were given no valuable novel or romance by the hand of Irving or Poe, and no good short story by that of Cooper. Hawthorne, however, having won a true and high (though not widely apparent) place as a story-writer, produced his first romance in middle life, and thereafter achieved his broadest fame as the author of " The Scarlet Letter," " The House of the Seven Gables," " The Blithedale Romance," and " The Marble Faun," rather than " Twice-Told Tales " or " Mosses from an Old Manse." Notwithstanding the obvious merits of " The House of the Seven Gables " and " The Blithedale Romance," it is evident that " The Scarlet Letter " and " The Marble Faun " are conceived in a nobler manner. The first of the two, in important particulars, is the greatest book Hawthorne ever wrote, though comparison between it and some of his other writings—even with the best of the short stories— is neither easy nor valuable in its results. To label books or pictures or musical compositions in order of merit is not an undertaking to be fol- lowed uniformly, nor does it invariably illuminate the study of the productions in question. What- ever be the estimate of the relative rank of those rounded romances, it is evident that the merit of the work of the author of " Ethan Brand " increased in proportion to his breadth of scope— in availing himself of which, of course, he avoided unwisdom in the relations of plot to length, and of his subject to his known powers. At first, I admit, a contemporary critic would hardly have prophesied success for Hawthorne's later books, which now seem the greater in both senses of the adjective. That their success was won was due to the fact of Hawthorne's comprehensive *humanity*,—to his outreaching human tenderness as truly as to his dramatic observation and art.

In "Our Old Home" Hawthorne tells us of a visit paid by several persons of his party to an English workhouse. A wretched child, the offspring of utter degradation and the representative of generations of depravity, insisted upon attaching itself to a gentleman of the party. Its miserable little body was but a living mass of repulsiveness, but its dim eyes, bleared even in infancy, recognized in the kindly man an affection of which it demanded an outward expression. The man was singularly repelled by the physically horrible, but he mastered his prejudice and gave the child the love it craved, taking it up and caressing it as tenderly as if he had been its father. As we read the closing sentence of the description we do not find it hard to think of the general purpose of the series of books beginning with "Fanshawe" and ending with "The Dolliver Romance": "No doubt the child's mission in reference to our friend was to remind him that he was responsible, in his degree, for all the sufferings and misdemeanors of the world in which he lived, and was not entitled to look upon a particle of its dark calamity as if it were none of his concern : the offspring of a brother's iniquity being his own blood-relation, and the guilt, likewise, a burden on him, unless he

(Hawthorne's humanity.)

expiated it by better deeds." Years after this
friend's body was laid in the grave, we were told
that his earthly name was Nathaniel Hawthorne.

I connect this story with a strictly literary
criticism because Hawthorne's humanity was the
basis of his success as the romancer of the human
heart. As tenderly sympathetic as Irving, he
possessed a strength of stroke that Irving lacked.
As original a creator as Cooper, he measured his
own powers with a justice in significant contrast
with Cooper's grotesque misapprehension of himself. As true an artist as Poe, his heart and head
so combined as to lead him to life itself, and not
to the shadowed land between life and death.
Therefore Hawthorne, and not Irving, Cooper, or
Poe, is the chief writer of fiction yet produced in
America.

Thus far have I proceeded without more than
incidental reference to the chronology of Hawthorne's career because it seems to me that the
art-product, in this instance, demands attention
before the man ; not only because it is his permanent literary legacy, self-contained and self-
explanatory, but because it illuminates the whole
story of his personal life. On the foundation
thus laid, our study of his career may now turn
somewhat more definitely to his sixty years, with
their literary gifts to the world of readers.

Hawthorne was born in a plain old house, not
over-large, in what is now a by-street of Salem,
Massachusetts. The city of Salem, near enough

to Boston to share some part of its life, is yet
so far removed as to be able to follow
Nathaniel Hawthorne, 1804-1864. an independent existence of its own, pre-
serving, with a tenacity which a mere
suburb must lose, those peculiar characteristics
which it has retained without essential alteration
for two centuries and a half. English intelligence, here transplanted in sea-coast soil, has long
dominated a society perhaps peculiarly courtly,
and certainly rich in that gentle blood and
thoughtful brain and which constitute the proper
American aristocracy. The old seaport, in 1804,
could boast of money, of spoils of extensive
commerce, and families prominent because of
downright ability. Hawthorne's personal career
in Salem, by an experience not unusual, was
hardly so agreeable to himself or to his fellow-
citizens as it would have been had he followed
the pursuits of a merchant, an attorney, or even a
Hawthorne's Salem. village politician. The man of genius,
if he be a story-teller or poet, naturally
puts the characteristics of his fellows into his
books; and his fellows as naturally fail to be
flattered by portraits not wholly painted in rose-
tints. Local and family prejudices are the passions of human nature first to be roused and last
to be quelled—whether Puritan in Massachusetts
or Creole in Louisiana; and so Hawthorne had
very definitely found when he pleasurably deserted
his ancestral streets to tread less sensitive soil.
Now, however, these difficulties are already
ancient; Salem is proud of the birth of the

greatest of our romancers; and in its graciously conservative shades are shown many of his homes and haunts, around which not a few myths have already gathered. The beautiful old city has the very atmosphere, to-day, which was the vital breath of Hawthorne's books; and though it shows that unsymmetrical combination of raw green-and-white and weather-beaten age which are so sharply contrasted in the highly American but characteristically provincial regions of eastern Massachusetts, the prevalent impression is that of colonial venerableness. Wooden buildings in a salty air grow old quickly, hence Salem, like Nantucket or lower Newport, already seems as restful as some European towns of a fourfold age. As one stands before the birthplace of Hawthorne he seems to see the characteristic New England boy, whose father followed the sea from out the harbor of a rich commercial town; whose mother's ancestral line was Massachusetts-Saxon; and whose own strong frame and brain were nourished by the skies and woods, fruits and streams, traditions and books of that strip of coast-land between the Penobscot and the Hudson, where, for two centuries and a half, average comfort and average intelligence have been greater than in any other spot on the globe.

Upon this seaside strip all Hawthorne's American life was spent, save a little period of rather homesick residence at Lenox, among the At Bowdoin Berkshire hills of western Massachusetts. College. In his college days at Bowdoin, the Brunswick

air was fragrant with the pine-needles and the
neighboring sea-coves of "hundred harbored
Maine." That famous institution of learning, in
its early days, was but poorly equipped with
books, halls, and museums, but it had teachers
who taught and students who studied—the things
most needed in hedge-school or university. The
gracious culture of some homes in the older towns
of the new state, and of its mother Massachusetts,
was at least represented in the class-lists; and
Hawthorne, while "wasting time" in the fashion
so common among under-graduates of bookish or
scribbling tastes, was acquiring—absorbing—a literary style and its informing spirit—which very
likely would have come to him anywhere, but certainly distinguished his college days.

In his old age that beloved instructor at Bowdoin, Professor Alpheus S. Packard, whose career
was almost synchronous with that of the institution to whose loyal service his lifetime was
devoted, wrote at my request his recollections of
the eminent men who had sat before him in the
class-rooms. The clearly written manuscript lies
before me; and from it I transfer his vivid though
brief reminiscences of the greatest of that remarkable group of celebrities whose undergraduate
days were spent at Brunswick in the decade
between 1820 and 1830:

"The College Triennial not unfrequently fails
to denote, in its classical fashion, real celebrities
of a class, because their names have not had
appended what some may regard as the cabala

of academic bodies, the 'semilunar fardels' as the eminent Dr. Cox wittily styled them, or other mystic initials indicating honors, the reward of eminence, or compliments, sometimes forsooth bought at a price. Our own class of 1825 has in its roll the name of 'Nathaniel Hawthorne, Mr.,' all the catalogue shows of a name that does its full share to make that class memorable in college annals.

"The visitor at Salem, Mass., is shown with pride the dwelling in the lower part of the town where Hawthorne first saw the light. His family came from England and settled in Salem early in the last century. The men followed the sea; and his father, a ship-master, died of yellow fever in Cuba when the son was but a child. His mother was said to be of great beauty and extreme sensibility. At the age of ten the boy, on account of his health, was sent to live on a farm on the borders of Lake Sebago, Maine, and at the proper age was sent back to Salem to complete his fitting for college. The writer's memory pictures him distinctly as he sat in the Latin and Greek recitation room, a dark-browed youth, with black, drooping, full, inquisitive eyes; a full head of dark hair; a gentle, grave, low, yet musical voice;—shy as a maiden; always rendering his passages tastefully; writing his Latin exercise with facility, and idiomatically. His English themes were complimented by the professor in charge, Prof. Newman, whose compliments were worth having. He was more a reader than a scholar on the merit roll. I cannot do better than to quote the picture of him by the pen of a classmate, J. S. C. Abbott, recognized, it is likely, by his contemporaries : 'Though singularly retiring in his habits, dwelling in unrevealed recesses which his most intimate friends were never permitted to penetrate, his winning countenance and gentle manners won esteem and even popularity. Though fond of being present at festal scenes, he never told a story or sang a song. His voice was never heard in any shout of merriment; but the silent, beaming smile would testify to his keen appreciation of the scene and to his enjoyment of the wit. He would sit for a whole evening with head gently inclined to one side, hearing every word, seeing every gesture, and yet scarcely a word would pass his lips. But there was an indescribable something in the silent presence of Hawthorne which rendered him one of the most desired guests on such occasions. Jonathan Cilley was probably his most intimate friend in the class. And yet his discrimination would lead him to say : " I love Hawthorne, I admire him ; but I do not know him. He lives in a mysterious world of thought and imagination which he never permits me to enter."' It was of Hawthorne's college days I was to write. His manner of life, and the sources and elements of his fame, are the common possession of the world of letters."

After graduation came that period of seclusion —rather of reclusion, if I may coin a word—in the maternal house at Salem. Seldom, in the

haste and waste of vigorous American life, has a
great author entered the monastery of _{Hawthorne}
home, there to spend the years of strong _{as recluse.}
young manhood in a novitiate preparatory to the
sacred profession of letters. Notwithstanding the
myth and legend that have grown up around
this preparation-time—tales half true, half imaginary, of midnight walks and daily avoidance of
the sunlight, of an invisible eccentric, whose face
was hardly known to his sisters or his melancholy
mother—the common-sense of Hawthorne, in the
matter, was as actual as was his romance of life.
He always shunned much that the world called
existence, but never with utterly unwholesome
idea or lastingly hurtful result. In this determination to read, think, and write for himself, in his
own way, was a large and true sanity, fortunate
for the world of letters. In vigorous health, of a
strong and manly frame, he was pursuing, half-
unconsciously, that graduate-study which some
undertake in the professional school, others in the
university. Years later, in " The Marble Faun,"
he wrote : " If I had an insupportable burden,—if,
for any cause, I were bent upon sacrificing every
earthly hope as a peace-offering toward heaven,—
I would make the wide world my cell, and good
deeds to mankind my prayer." Of the weak and
bilious selfishness which, under the pretence of
spiritual strength and special sanctity, or of high
intellectuality and contempt for the *ignobile vulgus*,
flies from the humanity so needful of help, Hawthorne was as ignorant in his hermit-cave at

Salem as he was later in his capacity of editor, custom-house officer, or consul. His subsequent work, and its deserved and unwavering fame, were based upon a self-control, a willingness to wait, by no means easily secured or maintained in a country where everything was to be done, and in a young literature to which the temptations of sensationalism and sentimentalism, though not of financial reward, were visible on every hand. Hawthorne, in the words of a sage critic, had " the conscientious fidelity of Puritanism in his veins, a thing equally important for literature and for life." * The conscientiousness was the cause of his smaller, more delicate, or realistic successes ; the fidelity of his broader triumphs. Whittier once told the same critic that " when he himself had obtained, with some difficulty, in 1847, the insertion of one of Hawthorne's sketches in *The National Era*, the latter said quietly, ' There is not much market for my wares.' " † Thus patiently, in unruffled temper and quiet determination to do his best, Hawthorne worked on— writing, pruning, destroying. What the world lost by his burning of manuscripts we shall never know ; they must have been better than most writers' best, but our American master of composition may surely be left, if any one may, with a reputation for wisdom in the case of his own genius and the development of its printed expression. His " protecting laziness," as Julian

* T. W. Higginson, " Short Studies of American Authors," 6.
† " Short Studies," 10.

Hawthorne calls it, saved him from crudity or imperfection in literary result ; but in itself it must have been also a discretion that looked toward a high achievement or none.* We must take results as they are ; some books are worth waiting for ; better a decade of toil on a single good book than ten weak volumes in a year. Hawthorne's end crowned the work, and amply atoned for whatever actual indolence or selfishness he may have felt or shown.

At the head of Hawthorne's list of books, in point of time, stands " Fanshawe" (1828), long obscure because unreprinted, and still, in its first edition, a will-o'-the-wisp dancing before " collectors." When reissued in 1876, " Fan- "Fanshawe," shawe " was discovered to be a quiet 1828. pleasant, old-fashioned little romance of an idealized Bowdoin, well enough in its way, but deserving neither praise nor blame. It is easy and agreeable reading, marked by a grace of style not usual among young men, and marred by a vagueness of characterization which Hawthorne afterward outgrew for the most part, though not entirely. His ideal touch here depicted men and women who seemed to live just above our world, or beyond it, not on it. Later, without loss of

---

* " Was there ever such a weary delay in obtaining the slightest recognition from the public as in my case ? I sat down by the wayside of life, like a man under enchantment, and a shrubbery sprung up around me and the bushes grew to be saplings, and the saplings became trees, until no exit appeared possible through the entangling depths of my obscurity."— Prefatory note (to his friend Horatio Bridge) to "The Snow Image, and other Twice-Told Tales."

24

grace and with gain of art, the romantic and the real became one in his stories.

Nine years intervened between "Fanshawe" and the first volume of "Twice-Told Tales," the book that marks the true advent of its author in American letters. It displays in an entirety the idea, the method, and the form of utterance which were to be inseparably connected, in literary history, with the name of the writer, and which have been stated at length in the introductory pages of this chapter. The idea was to portray life in its actuality, as viewed by the romancer, that is to say, the prose-poet. The method was to select characteristic stories, half true and half imaginative, from the past times of colonial New England, a field unknown in fiction, but offering deeper themes than those Irving had found in New Amsterdam or Tarrytown, by the slow-sweeping Hudson. The form of utterance was a pellucid English displaying the poetic sense, and the slily humorous as well, but unmarked by the roundabout facetiousness of the writers who had gone just before. Hawthorne was intelligible to every one who could read at all, and he was found enjoyable by those who like to dwell upon the details of a brook, a landscape, a picture, a poem, or a beautiful woman. Hawthorne was always fully aware of the artistic importance of a title, and here, in the names of the tales and the collection as a whole, he began to show that felicity of nomenclature which did not desert him in his subsequent undertakings.

"Twice-Told Tales," 1837–1842.

He had at length made an auspicious beginning of an unruffled career.

The "childly heart" of Hawthorne, the beatings of which were never stilled until the end of his earthly life, turned him in his earlier years to the writing of children's books,—now of New England history, as in "Grandfather's Chair"; now of such representatives of manhood or womanhood as Cromwell, Dr. Johnson, Sir Isaac Newton, Franklin, West the painter, or Queen Christina of Sweden, whose sketch portraits made up a little book of "True Stories from History and Biography." "A Wonder-Book and "Tanglewood Tales," one work under two names, retell a round dozen of stories from classical mythology. These four volumes, as the collected and final presentation of Hawthorne's juvenile-writing for fifteen or twenty years, are now properly included in all collected editions of his works. Children's story-books at their best are literature of the ideal in a true sense ; the child is an instinctive poet, and often spurns all but the best that imagination can offer. That so few books for children are literary classics is the fault of writers, not of theme or audience. Said Hawthorne, in his prefatory note to the " True Stories from History and Biography" : "This small volume and others of a similar character, from the same hand, have not been composed without a deep sense of responsibility.

> Juvenile Stories: "The Whole History of Grandfather's Chair," 1841; "A Wonder-Book for Girls and Boys," 1851; "True Stories from History and Biography," 1852; "Tanglewood Tales, for Girls and Boys, being a Second Wonder-Book," 1853.

The author regards children as sacred, and would
not, for the world, cast anything into the fountain
of a young heart that might embitter and pollute
its waters. And, even in point of the reputation
to be aimed at, juvenile literature is as well worth
cultivating as any other. The writer, if he succeed in pleasing his little readers, may hope to be
remembered by them till their own old age,—a
far longer period of literary existence than is generally attained by those who seek immortality
from the judgments of full-grown men." The
conscientious workmanship which Hawthorne thus
gave to the myth-stories, and to the retelling of
the tales of the Lady Arbella Johnson, Endicott
and the Red Cross (to that sturdy governor he
recurred again and again), Eliot and his Indian
Bible, Phips' treasure, the Pine-Tree Shillings,
the Liberty Tree, the exiles from Acadia, the
Hutchinson mob, and the Boston Massacre,
resulted in a patient and sympathetic art unsurpassed in his other writings, with which they are
in general agreement as to plan, detail, and verbal style. For a parallel to this fact, which is
demonstrable in an hour's reading, one must go
to the works of Walter Scott.

In these lesser writings there is a charm that
also appears in the minor tales and sketches in
Quiet general, produced at various periods of
charm. Hawthorne's career, such as " Fragments
from the Journal of a Solitary Man"; "Graves
and Goblins" (one of his most characteristic
sketches, and a masterpiece of English); the

brief biographies of Mrs. Hutchinson, Phips, Pep-
perell, Thomas Green Fessenden the satirical
poet, and Hawthorne's college friend Jonathan
Cilley; or even such an unspontaneous bit of
kindly hackwork as the introduction to poor
Delia Bacon's portentous "Philosophy of Shakespeare's Plays Unfolded." Hawthorne's style
sometimes mystified the stupid, as in "The Marble Faun," or the delightful sketch of his dying
years, "Chiefly about War Matters" (1862); but
the style and tone were unmistakable, in their
quiet and agreeable gentleness, which would have
been a mannerism or thin affectation, had it just
missed success, but which, in Hawthorne's strong
hand, was a constant refreshment, as of a cool
and leisurely brook in the shade.

To this quiet strength is due the constant and
characteristic effect produced by the style of such
stories as "The Gray Champion," "The Minister's Black Veil," "Dr. Heidegger's Experiment,"
the four "Legends of the Province House,"
"Peter Goldthwaite's Treasure," "Endicott and
the Red Cross," or "Edward Fane's Rosebud," in
"Twice-Told Tales." There is no radical difference between the two volumes of this work and its
third or supplementary series; while the tales composing the two volumes of "Mosses from an Old Manse" are in all essen- "The Snow-Image, and Other Twice-Told Tales," 1852; "Mosses from an Old Manse," 1846.
tials similar. Nor is there any significance or
importance in the title by which "The Great
Stone Face," "The Canterbury Pilgrims," "The

Man of Adamant," " The Devil in Manuscript,"
and " The Wives of the Dead" are bound
together ; nor, in the latest collection, is there any
but a general relation between " The Birthmark,"
" The Hall of Fantasy," " The Celestial Rail-
road," " The Procession of Life," " The New
Adam and Eve," " Egotism ; or the Bosom
Serpent," " Roger Malvin's Burial ;" or " Earth's
Holocaust." These strong stories were written
deliberately during many years ; printed, in part,
in divers periodicals ; and at last conveniently
collected. There is some difference, of course,
between their average character and that of " The
Gentle Boy" (in which Hawthorne dangerously
approached sentimentalism), or that of his
sketches of peculiar humor and observation, such
as " A Rill from the Town Pump," " Sights from
a Steeple," " Main Street," " Buds and Bird
Voices," or " The Intelligence Office." But the
difference is neither striking nor constant. Hawthorne, with rare lapses, was the patient and
masterful observer and chronicler, unflushed by
contagious excitement, but deeply sympathetic.
The intensely human personages of fiction seized
him as they did Dickens and George Eliot ; but
with slow might they were turned by his arm
before the public eye and fixed there in the
perpetuity of literary presentation. His self-
control was almost absolute, but his perception
and human feeling were not less deep and broad.
The manner sometimes almost mastered him ; but
not often, in an age of mannerisms, did he fail to

create a prose-product of his own, in idea and word. He saw, and made, in the fullest sense; hence his place is with the writers of the highest rank. As an ideal realist he stands at the head of his class, with no other name as a rival in the same field,—neither French nor English in his form and manner. Like Goethe he connected nineteenth-century habits of accurate observation with the ideality of all centuries; but like Emerson he perceived the spiritual meaning of life. Moralist of moralists, his approach was artistically indirect; in cordial sympathy with romance, he was far removed from the excitable and hortatory romanticism of Hugo; a novelist of the heart, he found Wertherism nearly incomprehensible. His pictures of the moral sentiment were of the greatest because none had more completely been able to say, " I am a man."

Hawthorne's large view, combined as it always was with an essentially just measurement of his powers, enabled him to pass without uncertain touch from the twenty-page stories of his early life to the romances of his last fifteen years. This change, however, would have had in it somewhat of an experimental character if either " The House of the Seven Gables " or " The Blithedale Romance " had preceded " The Scarlet Letter." That book was the first of Hawthorne's "The Scarlet romances in point of time, and on the Letter." 1850. whole it remains his best in absolute merit. It delineates the blight of a great sin upon a weak man, a strong woman, a fiend, whose cold blood oozed from a heart of ice, a pure little child, and the community in which they lived. That community was old-Puritan ; the weakling was a minister of the Gospel, and his paramour was the wedded wife of the avenger of a home into which affection came only as the destroyer. The soul-struggles of four human beings, against the background of stern righteousness and witch-superstition, are painted in hues of purple and black, with rays of nature's sunshine and childish innocence stealing across. In " The House of the Seven Gables " there are also but few characters ; the general scene and atmosphere are the same ; and the problematic nature of. the psychological studies is as evident as before. But for Hester Prynne, in her nobility of helpful self-atonement for sinning, Arthur Dimmesdale, ethereal little Pearl, and inexorable Chillingworth, we have here less sombre personages, and a thread of narrative not so pitilessly black. He who had purely written a tale of adultery now turned his nice sense of observation and power of artistic delineation to a cheerier theme. This is the most agreeable of his longer books, and the gentlest and sunniest in its local color. The creator of soulful Hester Prynne, pure, maidenly Hilda, mysterious Miriam, and problematic Zenobia, here added to his gallery of pictures of true women Hepzibah Pyncheon, whose essential excellence consecrates her ancient eccentricity ; and Phœbe, a wood-flower of New England girl-

" The House of the Seven Gables," 1851.

hood. "The Scarlet Letter" is a romance of sin; "The House of the Seven Gables" of heredity;" "The Blithedale Romance" of the forceful might of a woman's character, in struggle with strong environment and stronger self. Somewhat after the fashion of Shake- speare's "Troilus and Cressida," it burns with passion, the while the author stands aloof in a reserve only not cynical. "The Blithedale Romance," 1852.

In "The Marble Faun" the development of character, before and after crime, under varying conditions and in the face of steadily increasing temptations, forms the central theme. The title "Transformation," by which the Eng- lish public know the work, explains this root-idea of the book; though it was hardly worth while to change a poetic title into a commonplace one, for the sake of supposed clearness. The romance is longer and more varied than "The Scarlet Letter." But in both books the char- acters, their environment, and the time in which they live are well presented in an artistic whole, so that the progress of the story and the study is in neither interrupted by irrelevant or injurious details. "The Marble Faun," 1860.

As one notes the large purpose of "The Marble Faun," he is reminded of a few lines of Emerson, who had the art, when he wished, of stating things so neatly that he would have pleased the most critical Gallic lover of *mots*. A lasting truth is here applied to literary criticism :

> "'A new commandment,' said the smiling muse,
> 'I give my darling son : Thou shalt not preach.'
> Luther, Fox, Behmen, Swedenborg, grew pale,
> And, on the instant, rosier clouds upbore
> Hafiz and Shakespeare with their shining choirs."

The preacher has his function and the artist has his ; woe be to the latter if he sermonize when he ought to sing or paint. Seldom did Hawthorne forget the law which Emerson thus phrased. He chose august themes, as the great artists so often do ; but those themes he elaborated from the artist's point of view. When "The Marble Faun" was published, several critics went so far as to declare that its author simply called the reader's attention to some abstrusely interesting problems of love, sin, and woe, and then dropped them at the close of two volumes, without reason or explanation. According to this view, the romancer was surely no volunteer moralizer, but was keeping too closely within the artist's province. Even from the artistic standpoint some disappointed denunciations were thrown at the work, on the strictly artistic ground that it was left incomplete as a mere creation. As time passed, there was bestowed upon the romance an approval denied at first ; and the underlying purpose in the author's mind was seen to be fulfilled as regards both the soul and the form of this "Romance of Monte-Beni." The rosy cloud of which Emerson wrote has tinted the blacker skies which once hung over this latest of Hawthorne's completed fictions ; and with its glow still

above us we shall at least be removed from the
danger of treating "The Marble Faun" as anything else than a work of genius, written with the
purpose which underlies the chief products of the
imagination. "It is one of those works of art
which are also works of nature, and will present
to each thoughtful reader a new set of meanings,
according to his individuality, insight, or experience.*

"The Marble Faun," alone among Hawthorne's
longer works, has its scene in Italy, and is a
direct outgrowth of the author's foreign residence,
which began with his Liverpool consulate in 1853,
under President Pierce.* Its local color is so
true, and its local allusions are so many, that it
has been used by some as a sort of Italian traveller's note-book, or guide-book to Rome. Its
theme is the slow development of utter sin in the
breast of a man at first so pure and true as to
seem a mere conscienceless and spontaneous child
of nature. The story shows how innocence, if
merely negative and lacking the positive qualities
of developed virtue, readily becomes the ally of
sin and the doer of evil. Then follow the rise
of the consciousness of guilt, the growth of
remorse, and the perception that self-mastery, in
some natures, affords a nobler happiness than can

---

* G. P. Lathrop, "A Study of Hawthorne," 255.

* In 1852 Hawthorne had written, for "campaign" circulation, an excellent, and calmly discriminating biography of his college mate and life-long
friend, in whose company at last he died. On accession to office, Pierce
bestowed upon Hawthorne a financially valuable office, and Hawthorne,
naturally, was charged with political time-serving in his small friendly task,

ever be found in thoughtless existence and enjoyment. A witty writer once ably satirized extreme
Augustinianism in an essay entitled "Hell as
the Foundation of the Kingdom of Heaven." In
this apparently repulsive and absurd idea there is
an underlying truth : that while man possesses
free-will, his struggle for mastery may lead him to
a nobler height of joy than that of impeccable and
untempted innocence. But the converse truth,
that complete innocence may in itself raise the
soul to a loveliness that has but to be continued
in the heaven of the hereafter, is portrayed no
less forcibly in the character of Hilda. The few
personages of the romance typify almost a world.
In Brother Antonio we have the shadow, now
deepening, now lifting, of a depravity so deep as
almost to seem total ; in Miriam the blight of a
sin neither accepted utterly nor as yet atoned for ;
in Donatello the spiritual ascent from animal
existence toward a distant but ultimate moral
triumph ; in Hilda a lovely purity sullied only by
the accidental knowledge of guilt ; in Kenyon a
man of something more than average goodness,
yet, compared with Hilda,

"As moonlight unto sunlight, or as water unto wine."

The elaboration of the romance is marked by
that finish which comes of the union of deliberate

---

while Pierce was blamed for favoritism. But it has always been the wise
policy of the American government to send competent literary men into its
diplomatic service ; while Hawthorne sufficiently proved his disinterested-
ness by flatly refusing, in 1863, to withdraw an affectionate dedication to
Pierce (then unpopular in the North), though warned by a discreet pub-
lisher that the book might be ruined.

art in conception with ample leisure for execution. Florence and Rome are portrayed in a series of pictures that are both incidental and essential, and therefore seem pleasurably indispensable. Hawthorne, as we have seen, was too great an author to quarrel with his environment. He most naturally, like all great writers, worked at home; but as his theme was the human heart, not the American heart, he studied it to advantage under Saint Peter's dome, and afterward wrote nearly all the romance on the soil of England. He changed his skies, not his soul, when he crossed the sea. Having patiently thought out his plan, he elaborated it, in this as in his other longer stories, without haste and without rest. He was so sure of the poetry of the idea that he did not weary of the details by which genius was made to take the form of permanent art.

Genius, art, and environment.

That the art of the story (in its original form, and without the final chapter added by Hawthorne after the publication of the work) is permanent, and not a mere study or puzzle, is now perceived by nearly all readers, as it was at first perceived by the wiser critics, such as John Lothrop Motley. To marry or to hang his heroes and heroines was no part of the romancer's plan, notwithstanding the numerous hostile criticisms at first evoked by the book —criticisms of its alleged inconclusiveness and hasty ending. In the familiarity of a friendly conversation Hawthorne once exclaimed: "As

Is " The Marble Faun " incomplete ?

regards the last chapter of 'Transformation' in
the second edition, don't read it; it's good for
nothing. The story isn't meant to be explained;
it's cloudland." * Having detailed, both broadly
and minutely, the dawn, progress, and effect of
sin upon several souls, differently constituted and
differently related to the central crime, Hawthorne leaves to the reader the minute following-
out of future penalty and expiation. The three
parts of repentance, in the Roman Catholic
scheme, are contrition, confession, and satisfaction. Applying this nomenclature to the case in
hand, Hawthorne deems that his effect is made
nobler by the absence of any detailed arrangement of the "satisfaction" division. Mrs. Hawthorne once wrote to a sapient critic of the
smaller order, who doubtless thought he could
have arranged the story much better himself:
" Mr. Hawthorne is driven by his muse, but does
not drive her; and I have known him to be in an
inextricable doubt, in the midst of a book or
sketch, as to its probable issue, waiting upon the
muse for the rounding in of the sphere which
every true work of art is." † In this particular
work of art the author felt that the curtain might
drop upon the play before the playwright attempted to settle everything; and there was
evident wisdom in this course. Great problems
have been studied, and the reader may follow
them on and on, if he can and will. If he cannot,

---

* "Nathaniel Hawthorne and his Wife," II. 236.
† "Nathaniel Hawthorne and his Wife," II. 247.

it is useless to discuss the case with him. Some
novelists and some readers apparently think that
this is a world of completions rather than of
beginnings ; and that the idea of continuance or
aspiration is fatal to any work of art. But art
itself, on the contrary, would be false to life if it
never expressed that constant notion of development and present incompleteness which lies at the
very foundation of things ; which is accepted as
cordially by true science as by true religion ; and
without which the universe would seem to be a
vast mistake.

I have devoted, perhaps, a disproportionate part
of this chapter to the study of "The Marble Faun,"
not because it is Hawthorne's greatest book, but
because it was his last, and suggests in a peculiar way certain elements in his final art. The
literary historian has no right, it seems to me, to
discuss "The Dolliver Romance" and its four
antecedent studies,* though "The Dolliver Romance,"
"Septimius Felton" and "Doc- *Atlantic Monthly,* July,
tor Grimshawe's Secret" seem 1864, Jan. 1865; also, with
another fragment, River-
virtually complete in them- side Hawthorne, XI. 7–67.
selves. Ideas of a bloody footprint, of a life
elixir, and of inherited tendency were slowly shaping themselves in the author's mind. He was

---

* "A Look into Hawthorne's Workshop, being notes for a posthumous
romance by Nathaniel Hawthorne; *The Century,* January, 1883. "The
Ancestral Footstep"; outlines of an English romance (edited by G. P. Lath-
rop); Riverside edition of Hawthorne, XI. 431–521. "Doctor Grimshawe's
Secret, a Romance," edited, with preface and notes, by Julian Hawthorne;
Boston, 1883. "Septimus Felton, or, The Elixir of Life" (edited by Una
Hawthorne); Boston, 1872.

elaborating them into artistic form with unusual care, due both to his wish to write a masterpiece and to his sense of failing physical strength. "The Dolliver Romance" must stand a fragment, like Thackeray's "Denis Duval," or Dickens' "Edwin Drood," and criticism of a fragment is superfluous.

> "The wizard hand lies cold,
>   Which at its topmost speed let fall the pen,
>   And left the tale half told.
>
> Ah! who shall lift that wand of magic power,
>   And the lost clew regain?
> The unfinished window in Aladdin's tower
>   Unfinished must remain!"

From these studies, however, we learn with what reticent care, in an age of hurried bookmaking, especially in fiction, did Hawthorne work. The same lesson is taught by his voluminous note-books of his art and life in America, England, France, and Italy, from which copious extracts were properly published after his death. The English diaries were the precursor and the treasury of the keen sketches afterward printed in finished form as "Our Old Home,"—as kindly and as searching as Emerson's "English Traits," though externally less pretentious. The American note-books, however, are most valuable of all, with their hints for a hundred stories that Hawthorne never wrote and that no other could write.

" Passages from the American Note-Books," 2 vols., 1868; from the English, 2 vols., 1870; from the French and Italian, 2 vols., 1872.

"Our Old Home," 1863.

They are, in their entirety, one of the deepest, truest, and purest personal records which literature can show,—high in thought and remarkably finished in style. It should also be said that they do not reveal to us an aimless night-prowler, a specialist in morbid anatomy, a literary alienist. They are the daily and unstudied memoranda of a mind great in power and true in purpose.

I have thus considered at length, and with such conscientiousness as I could command, Hawthorne's the literary work of a writer who seems faults. to me both relatively and absolutely great. In this consideration the element of commendation has been paramount. Among his faults I have not been able to include morbidness or inartistic incompleteness. That he had faults, however, is unquestionable, and they should be stated definitely and frankly. Pure and fine in mental nature, he was sometimes unexpectedly coarse (I mean coarse, not indecent) in utterance. Descriptions, or at times entire stories, are aggravatingly impassive ; he stands without as a spectator, and what should be the broadly dramatic view falls into an apparent indifferentism which we cannot reconcile with his general purpose and attitude in literature. The unconscious strength summoned from a rich personal experience is missed at critical points. At times, as in reading the works of the Laodicean realists themselves, we are ready to cry out against the frigid philosophy of curious external observation.

Again, while he was a great delineator of representative elements in the characters of men, women, and children, his colors were sometimes too pale and monotonous,—not the colors of flesh and blood. We seldom recognize a " Hawthorne character " on the streets of our daily walk. We are not always in the presence of vitality, but too often in that of personified ideas. His style is unvaried ; half-a-dozen short stories, or three romances, read in succession, may for some readers emphasize this fact to the extent of weariness. The master seems a mannerist ; self-control appears the dead level of a great mountain table-land, as dull as the valley-plains below.

But, after all, these faults are incidental, not inherent. Hawthorne was a great imaginative artist, with a highly ideal purpose and a strong and sure hand ; therefore his fame, small at first, has steadily increased in the quarter of a century since his death, and shows no sign of waning as the years go on. He once wrote: " No man who needs a monument ever ought to have one." Hawthorne's monument is not beside the modest grave above which whisper the pines of Concord's Sleepy Hollow ; nor is it in the commendations or analyses of his many critics. His monument is in his books, which so combine genius and art, imagination and human nature. Those whose eyes may see the fulness of human existence—its bright gayety and its gloomy grief and sin—perceive in Hawthorne's books the breadth of that mysterious thing in

Hawthorne's place in literature.

which we are, and which we call life. In "The
Marble Faun" we are told that "a picture, however admirable the painter's art and wonderful
his power, requires of the spectator a surrender
of himself, in due proportion with the miracle
which has been wrought. Like all revelations of
the better life, the adequate perception of a great
work of art demands a gifted simplicity of vision."
Hawthorne's students, indeed, need not claim that
they must possess high gifts of mind in order to
perceive the art of his books; for he but requires
in his readers somewhat of his own simplicity and
naturalness. They must follow him as a master,
for the time being, and learn in his school. He
whose knowledge of human nature goes beyond
shallow optimism on the one hand, and worldly
cynicism on the other, need find no riddles in
Hawthorne's pages. Perverse or dull was that
French critic who once described Hawthorne as
"un romancier pessimiste." It would be difficult
to frame a statement less accurate, or one more
likely to amuse the romancer himself, if this title
has come to his knowledge in the land of shades.

I have said that Hawthorne's readers may follow
him as a master, and learn in his school. The
same advice is hardly to be given to those who
not only read but write, and who would catch the
secret of his literary success and apply it to their
own novels or romances. Writers as well as
readers, to be sure, may follow Hawthorne in his
habit of minutely-faithful and ever-delicate observation of things great and small; they may dis-

cover that a realism which stoops to note the
color of a single petal may be combined with a
spiritualism which deems a heart-throb more
important than a world of matter. They may
study his pellucid English, simple and yet artistic;
and may learn not to overcrowd their pages with
too numerous figures or irrelevant episodes. He
once made answer to a query as to his style:
" It is the result of a great deal of practice. It is
a desire to tell the simple truth as honestly and
vividly as one can." This seems easy enough;
but there is no likelihood that there will be,
in America or elsewhere, another Hawthorne.
From his name has been derived an adjective, but
we always apply the word " Hawthornesque" to a
single effect or undeveloped idea, and even then
some restriction is usually added to the expression.
His field, method, and style were in a large sense
his own. I repeat that more than a quarter of a
century must have elapsed before we can rank
him with the greatest authors of the world; but I
add with equal positiveness that he made for himself a place unoccupied before or since. There is
an isolation of the greatest geniuses, even when
they have followers; but when no followers
appear, or succeed in their attempts, a genius is
approved by his very loneliness. The Germans,
with affection and reverence not unmixed with a
puzzled awe, apply to their Richter the phrase
" the only." To Hawthorne the same expression
belongs in a higher sense, not only among American authors, but as compared with writers in the

broader field. At first unread, then underrated, then called morbid or at best cold and aloof, Hawthorne now stands before us as in some sense "the greatest imaginative writer since Shakespeare," of whose greatness we are "beginning to arrive at some faint sense,"—a greatness "immeasurably vaster than that of any other American who ever wrote."

In this greatness the spiritual element was of constant importance. Hawthorne, all in all, was no cold observer and impassive chronicler. As author, he looked into the heart of the world, and wrote. As man, this deathless soul could say in truth: "I have no love of secrecy and darkness. I am glad to think that God sees through my heart, and, if any angel has power to penetrate into it, he is welcome to know everything that is there. Yes, and so may any mortal who is capable of full sympathy.

CHAPTER XI.

THE LESSER NOVELISTS.

COINCIDENT with the steadily and symmetrically developing works of Hawthorne appeared numerous novels by numerous hands, some of which attained a circulation remarkable in the annals of fiction, but nearly all of which are now not unkindly forgotten. Fifty years is a long period in the fame of lesser literature, and it seldom leaves the renown of a novel in any glittering or conspicuous state. With the arrival of quiet times in the nation's history—at least as far as foreign wars were concerned—the book-makers had the leisure and the wish to furnish an abundance of stories to the readers so rapidly multiplying. With the spread of circulating libraries there came, of course, a corresponding increase of would-be responses to the all-prevalent human demand: "Tell me a story."

Minor fiction before the war of 1861.

Then, as now, the United States had no international copyright system, and then, as now, the book market was flooded with English fiction in paper covers. But every reading folk demands home-made entertainment, and the history of letters shows that there need be no fear that workers will fail in that division of literary composition which is at once the most remunerative and the quickest to attract individual notice and social notoriety. That novels may be first forgotten is equally true, but oblivion is the common fate of most books in other fields; Edwards' sermons and Willard's "Body of Divinity" are as undisturbed to-day as Mrs. Tenney's story, and even more quiescent than those of Mrs. Rowson.

The lesser novelists of America, in the second literary period, found their themes in American characters, scenes, and historic episodes; in imaginary adventures of foreign travel; in ancient history, and in sentiment or politics. One Northerner endeavored to crystallize the spirit of New England thought and life in a romance at once idyllic and religious; and one Southerner painted for the nineteenth century certain phases of the picturesque life of the old régime in eighteenth-century Virginia. From out this period of activity in lesser fiction there also stands forth, in vivid isolation that may diminish but cannot wholly disappear, the potent name of that individual and characteristic story which was one of the causes of Northern triumph in the war that freed the slave. On the whole, however, the period was characterized by the decline of the Indian romantic novel; the rise and collapse of the sweeter or more superficial sentimentalism in prose; and the comparative failure of the attempt to delineate American home life in various sections; for it cannot be claimed that the writers before the war produced much that equalled the folk-pictures or character sketches given later by Miss Jewett, Miss Phelps, Miss Woolson, Eggleston, Bret Harte, "Charles Egbert Craddock," or Cable.

A certain special significance, among all the novels of this period, has often been claimed for a story that is certainly curious and individual: "Margaret; a Tale of the Real and the Ideal, Blight and Bloom," by Sylvester Judd. Lowell, in "A Fable for Critics," declared it

> "The first Yankee book
> With the *soul* of Down East in't, and things farther East,
> As far as the threshold of morning, at least,
> Where awaits the fair dawn of the simple and true,
> Of the day that comes slowly to make all things new."

He even went so far in praise of its author as to tell his countrymen:

> "His name
> You'll be glad enough, some day or other, to claim,
> And will all crowd about him and swear that you knew him,
> If some English hack-critic should chance to review him."

Judd's recognition, however, never came in any general way, though a fit few have always bestowed upon his book that sort of admiration which is supposed specially to distinguish the thing praised, and also to reflect peculiar brilliancy upon those who praise. "Margaret" very narrowly escapes being unreadable, as an entirety; the accumulated purpose of years was required to make successful my own second attempt to reach its close; for it is crude,

Sylvester Judd, 1813-1853.

"Margaret."

careless, irrelevant, improbable, and at times weari-
somely sermonic. The author's ultimate plan was
to make of this novel a sublimated Unitarian and
American "Pilgrim's Progress," portraying true
Christianity and the large means of its propaga-
tion among a free and enlightened people. That
which another brilliant and efficient Unitarian
believer—Hale—attempted a generation later in
the most realistic and practical of stories, Judd
sought to achieve by combining pure faith and
pure moonshine in an idyllic and sensational
novel of New England village life at the close of
the last century. There can be no question, however, that this eccentric story is marked by crude
power and irregular beauty. The social and
religious "progressive" notions of the time, the
homeland love of a patriotic New Englander, and
the thoughts of a prose-poet were curiously jum-
bled together, so that "Margaret" is dream, picture, and riddle in one. The merit of loneliness,
or isolation from other books of the sort, it clearly
possesses, and its religio-poetic feeling is at times
almost impressive. Judd was an idealist through
and through, loving nature with all his heart, yet
burning with a still stronger love for humanity.
His novel is a sketch-book of snow-storms and
summers, drunkenness and murder, bird-songs and
sunbursts, vulgar poverty and flawless virtue
blessed with all gifts that mortals can long for,
and marching onward toward a beatific and regenerated future of humanity. The faults in "Margaret" are so numerous and conspicuous as to

remove it utterly from the list of great books, but
its scattered beauties of thought and word are
such as to make the reader regret that the author
so lacked all shaping power of art.

Description of nature and of out-door experiences had now become a settled element in many
American novels ; and naturally, in a country still
new, the fields and personages con-
nected with pioneer adventure attracted
the pens of writers in nearly all the several sections of the United States. " Nick of the
Woods ; or, The Jibbenainosay "—how could such
a title fail to interest eager young readers everywhere, and turn their minds once more toward the
unfelled forests of the far west ? Its author, Dr.
Bird, had been an experimenter, deemed successful in his day, in the writing of divers melodramatic plays, and had produced two historical
romances of old Mexican life. It was his good
fortune to give that robust actor Edwin Forrest
one of his more conspicuous successes, in the
tragedy of " The Gladiator," with its muscular
hero Spartacus. Something exciting or imposing
was then demanded by the majority of people
who turned to the play or novel for their amusement ; " The Gladiator " was thought to merit
both adjectives, and " Nick of the Woods " at
least the first. It was dramatized, and long held
the boards without impinging very seriously upon
the domain of the standard literature of the play.
Such stories, after all, are better read than heard,

Robert Mont-
gomery Bird,
1803–1854.

notwithstanding the obvious temptation they offer
to playwrights.

The most marked characteristic of the tales of
adventure produced in the period under review
rests in their general uniformity of style and
merit. Parts of "Nick of the Woods," selected
at random, might easily be supposed to be ex-
tracted from one of Cooper's land-stories, while
Cooper's sea-tales are not essentially different
from some of the opening pages of Dr. Mayo's
"Kaloolah." Even "The Dutchman's Fireside"
of Paulding, notwithstanding the would-be humor
and the playful touch which connect it with the
work of the "Knickerbocker school," falls into
general line with the other novels of exciting episode. Poe, who was certainly very clever in some
of his criticisms upon contemporary work, said
justly in a review of a previous novel by Bird—
"The Hawks of Hawk Hollow : a Tradition of
Pennsylvania"—that "upon the whole the style
of the novel—if that may be called its style,
which style is not—is at least *equal* to that of
any American writer whatsoever." Elsewhere he
declared it to be, "in many respects, a bad imitation of Sir Walter Scott," "composed with great
inequality of manner—at times forcibly and manly
—at times sinking into the merest childishness
and imbecility." Fifty years do not add much to
this criticism, which was applicable to dozens of
books written in that fertile period. The pre-
scription was simple. A manly adventurer on
land or sea, an "interesting female," a tomahawk-

ing Indian after scalps, a British frigate with too
few guns and too clumsy sails, together with
various affluent squires, imposing commanders,
cowardly villains, rustic wits, and housewifely
matron, were all that was needed; the plots and
escapes, the inland or marine scenery, the earth-
quaking thunder and the swollen torrents, and
the final matrimonial adjustments could be in-
serted at will. Scott was the distant but powerfully regnant monarch, and Cooper the master of
ceremonies; those who, like the latter, created
original characters of manly force, survived the
" mutability of literature," while those in whom
" the merest childishness and imbecility " were too
generously manifest lost very promptly their
quickly-won fame.

The Indian, as delineated in "Nick of the
Woods," is a darker and more repulsive creature
than Cooper's red man. Dr. Bird's view of the
aboriginal character approximated more nearly
to Custer's than to Crook's.* Accordingly he did
not hesitate to introduce descriptions merely
brutal and gory, illustrating and appealing to that
sentiment in human nature which got boundless
delight from a gladiatorial combat in Rome, and
which still falls into paroxysms of joy when a
half-starved bull, in Spain or Cuba, is at last
tortured to death by a dozen men. It must be
said that Dr. Bird had plenty of intelligent sup-
porters in his estimate of Indian ferocity and
bloodiness; but its literary effect, in his own case

See vol. I, p. 4.

at least, did not prove advantageous. Twenty or thirty years after the appearance of " Nick of the Woods," similar stories were produced in abundance by obscure or anonymous writers, bound in salmon-colored paper covers, and known everywhere in America as " dime novels," the literary diet of the lower classes.

Turning southward, as we follow the scenes depicted by the novelists of the period, there is found in the books of John P. Kennedy a gentler temper and a more delicate and finished touch. The very title of his best work, "Swallow Barn," forms a euphonious introduction to its leisurely and pleasant descriptions of rural scenes and character in the Old Dominion. It is a sort of Virginian " Bracebridge Hall." Kennedy, like Paulding, filled the office of Secretary of the Navy, and well illustrated that union of wholesome manliness with bookish tastes which was beginning to be a characteristic of our literature. The turmoil of American politics has over and over again left place, in diplomatic service or public station at home, for historians, essayists, novelists, or poets who also have been, like Kennedy, efficient and honored servants of their country and leaders of their party. The " scholar in politics" is an old, old figure in the United States ; the problem to-day is to keep him in, not to get him in.

John Pendleton Kennedy, 1795-1870.

Kennedy was a Marylander, and his " Rob of the Bowl," " Swallow Barn," and " Horse-Shoe Robinson " were all of the South, being devoted respectively to scenes and times of his native state (in the Roman Catholic Proprietary days), Virginia, and South Carolina (in the revolution). The first and last differed from "Swallow Barn" in that they turned definitely to the field of historical fiction rather than to the portrayal of country life in a placid story. Had Kennedy's graceful pen been driven by a genius more forcefully creative the result of his life-long devotion to literature would have been more considerable.

The representative Southern man of letters, after Poe and before Cable, Hayne, and Lanier, was William Gilmore Simms. His brain and pen were never idle, and he essayed nearly every sort of writing. Though far removed, in his South Carolina home, from the greater publishing centres, libraries, colleges, and author-coteries, Simms was poet, dramatist, Shakespearean editor, essayist, aphoristic philosopher, historian, biographer, lecturer, commemorative orator, legislator, pro-slavery apologist, journalist, magazinist, critic, and, above all, novelist. Authors have been hacks, helpers, or wage-earners since the art of writing was invented; but Simms' industry and fertility are remarkable in view of his environment, which was not favorable to such facile and miscellaneous productiveness. The novels, naturally, have survived the other writings, so that the "works" of Simms have come to mean, in publishers' parlance, merely the best of his romantic or historical fictions. The most attractive part of the novels, to

William Gilmore Simms, 1806–1870.

tell the truth, is their titles. One rolls from the tongue, with a certain pleasure, the names of Simms' best books: "The Partisan, a Romance of the Revolution"; "The Yemassee, a Romance of Carolina"; "Beauchampe, or, The Kentucky Tragedy"; "Southward Ho! a Spell of Sunshine." When Southerners took up "The Wigwam and the Cabin" or "Mellichampe, a Legend of the Santee," the very names made them feel that a literature had sprung from the sod. The whole list of his writings is here and there suggestive of historic men and events in the Carolina belt, or of the romance of adventure and discovery elsewhere in America and abroad; as well as of miscellaneous domestic or cheaply sensational themes. Purely exciting methods—the bowie-knife, the struggle, the revenge, the rescue—were often employed by Simms, whose hurried and careless pen would turn from "Eutaw" to "Richard Hurdis, or, The Avenger of Blood"; from "The Damsel of Darien" to "The Kinsmen, or, The Black Riders of the Congaree"; or, again, from far-away "Pelayo, a Story of the Goth" to "The Golden Christmas, a Chronicle of St. John's, Berkeley." Simms was a sort of American G. P. R. James, without James' regularity in quality of literary product. His tales highly interested a local audience because of their patriotic and sectional pictures and temper, and they were valued elsewhere as contributions toward the delineation of an important American region in an indigenous fiction. The romantic novelists of

the time turned most eagerly toward themes of
Indian adventure, pioneer settlement or Revolutionary struggle, and therein they began, at least,
to do wisely, according to the limitations of their
day. The portrayal of living folk-life was to
come later, for in Simms' time a "historic background" was commonly deemed essential. Indeed, the unpolished style, and the constant
striving for immediate and striking effects, which
characterized his fiction, were unfavorable to the
production of novels of society, in the full sense,
or of stories recording the characteristic vitality of
actual existence in the region best known to the
author. This fault was partly incident to the
time, which influenced the man unfavorably; for
Simms sometimes excelled in spontaneous picturesque description, while his familiar letters or
comments on men are couched in excellent and
telling phrase. There is no inconsistency in saying that Simms won considerable note because he
was so sectional, and has lost it because he was
not sectional enough. His stories are Southern
and characteristic, but to paint actualities and
things present—as do Cable, Miss Murfree, and
the interesting group of young Southern writers
—was not his chief purpose. The tinge of the
past and the imaginary is thrown over most of the
plots and descriptions, yet without that full and
deliberate idealization which is needed. Hawthorne, in "The Scarlet Letter" or "The Marble
Faun", so describes things far in time or space
that the men and women seem of our own spirit-

ual world, and yet are helped or tempted by moral and mental forces from out the infinite. Cooper, with all his faults, is a novelist of large humanity, and hence a novelist of many lands and of more than one time. We do not ask Simms to be a Hawthorne; but in Cooper's field, at least, he should have been either a romancer of the past or a picturer of the present, if he could not be both. Between the two fields of fiction, as we now insist upon separating them, he has no place. It may be that future fashions in literature will restore to him some part of a lost fame; but such is not likely to be the case. Save for the masters, the world turns its face not backward in the search for stories.

The best novel written in the Southern States before the civil war is "The Virginia Comedians" of John Esten Cooke. Its author, like Simms, was an inveterate book-maker, and belonged distinctly to the romantic-sentimental school, not the realistic. He aimed to produce novels and novelettes of incident or passion, rather than sketches of local scenes and characters. The John Esten Cooke, past of Virginia was more vivid, in 1830–1886. his mind, than her present. But his stories are not sensational, in the sanguinary sense; and they describe certain conditions of an ancient and half courtly society. Instead of wigwam and cabin, Cooke presents the chariots and brocades, the "palace" and capital, the statesmen and beauties of picturesque old Williamsburg, once the Southern Boston. To its streets and mansions, its

26

Raleigh Tavern and early theatre, he returns more than once, and in and near them occurs the action of "The Virginia Comedians." John Esten Cooke was himself an honorable representative of the best blood of the *ancien régime*—gentle, courtly, affectionate, unselfish, and brave ; and his masterpiece is a series of historic pictures, warmed by bygone sunshine and given true spirit by the sympathetic promptings of the maker's heart. If "background" is needed in our fiction, it assuredly is here—that background in front of which stood, in his college days, the first statesman, after Washington, of the early republic. If we seek color and action in a varied society, Thackeray himself asked no better, though he understood the scene and time less perfectly. Cooke, a fierce fighter in the war, was as sensible and kindly as Lee at its close, nor in his books did he display Simms' silly contempt for his Northerners, nor Cooper's or Poe's angry hatred of New England. His aim, says an anonymous eulogist, "was to do for Virginia what Simms had done for South Carolina, Cooper for the Indian and frontier life, Irving for the quaint old Knickerbocker times and Hawthorne for the weird Puritan life of New England." The modesty of the author himself would have made no such claim, for none more clearly perceived or frankly stated his general failure. He was, like Cable, wisely philosophic as to the futility of special pleas in literature. "If," said he, "there is anything endurable in Southern literature, I feel sure that it will take care of itself." But this "Virginian of the Virginians", as he has been termed, this cousin and fellow-worker of John P. Kennedy's, left his state no unworthy literary legacy. When "The Virginia Comedians" fell out of print, it was for years one of the most sought of American novels; re-issued, it was welcomed; nor does it cease to interest those who turn, from time to time, to the study of a phase of life not less attractive because its antique grandeur now seems as faded and thin as the garreted satins in which it once was resplendent.

At this period English and American literature (of course including poetry and prose fiction) were beginning to feel the scientific and economic influence of the age,—an age which on its superficial side was searching for facts rather than dreams or fancies. Periodical literature, too, was multiplying a miscellaneous but in its way somewhat definite sort of information, and was thereby responding to a public curiosity, and creating it as well. Reflective or imaginative sentimentalism was presently to yield, in part, to the wide-spread wish for some new thing. The clever pseudo-scientific tales of Poe made answer to this wish, yet without sacrifice of integrity of literary merit; and were followed by a long line of American, English, and French imitations. Another response was made by Herman Melville in his brisk and stirring tales of the sea or sketches of travel, in which fact and fancy were mingled by the nervously impatient author, in

Herman Melville, b. 1819.

the proportion desired by his immediate public. Melville's own adventures had been those of a modern Captain John Smith in the Pacific islands and waters; so that the *pars magna fui* of his lively books gave them the needed fillip of personality, and duly magnified their elements of wonder. That brilliant power of delineation which, in Melville's conversation, so charmed his warm friends the Hawthornes, is apparently not heightened in his books, but would seem to be rather diminished by the exigencies of writing. But the personal narrative or fiction of " Typee," " Omoo," and " Moby Dick," with their adventurous rapidity of description of Pacific seas, ships, savages and whales, represented the restless facility which has always been an American trait, and which occasionally develops into some enduring literary success.

Dr. W. S. Mayo, like Melville, had endured many vicissitudes of travel and adventure, and in his African romance " Kaloolah, or Journeyings to the Djébel Kumri, an Autobiography of Jonathan Romer," he drew upon his experiences abroad and at home, reverting to his school-days in northern New York, and to his father's marine exploits. That " Kaloolah " has barely outlived Melville's sprightly but now forgotten improvisations in literature is due to the combination, in its pictures of a far-away world, of the improbably romantic and the obviously satirical. Melville made some essays in the same direction, but failed completely

William Starbuck Mayo, b. 1812.

for lack of a firm thought and a steady hand. In Mayo's book the marvellously adventurous Jonathan Romer, at last the husband of an African princess, turns a reflective eye back upon the triumphs and foibles of the Anglo-Saxon political and social system which he has left behind. Often, since the coarse and strong "Travels of Mr. Lemuel Gulliver," have adventure and satire been mingled, and not infrequently with some such moderate success as Mayo here won; for no device is simpler than to change one's outlook in place and time, and survey mankind with the amusement found in a new perspective.

In the same search for novelty of theme, scene, and time, American fiction turned far backward toward the picturesque history of the classic past of Rome. Ware's "Zenobia," "Aurelian," and "Julian," with their occasionally stately—and sometimes stiff—descriptions of venerable bygones, really indicated, as truly as "Moby Dick" or "Kaloolah," that American writers were trying to broaden their field at the demand of a broadening public. Ware failed to equal such later books—in themselves not comparable with "Hypatia" or "Uarda"—as Wallace's "Ben-Hur" or Crawford's "Zoroaster"; indeed, the whole world never produced ten great historical novels, aside from those of Scott. Historical fiction is as tempting and seemingly easy as blank verse, but few men are so masterly as to win success in either. But Ware, in his "Letters from Palmyra" ("Zenobia") showed himself not

William Ware, 1797–1852.

destitute of that poetic imagination which is able to reproduce some part of the pageantry and the persecutions, the might and the weakness, of Rome in her splendid decline.

It should not be supposed that the fiction of the period was wholly given up to tales of pioneer adventure, romantic travel, or glorious antiquity; to the Virginian historic pictures of Cooke; or to Judd's utopian dreams of regenerated man. Stiff moral sentiment, dressed in a garb that now seems somewhat artificial and extravagant, but which exactly suited the fashion of the day, was the lay-figure that stood beside the desk of many a novelist. Catharine Sedgwick, who connected the earlier and the later days, could write a story of adventure which some were once ready to assign to Cooper's pen.

Catharine Maria Sedgwick. 1789-1867.

But her axiomatic novels chiefly aim to show that honest poverty is better than hollow wealth; that mistresses should know something about housework and treat their servants humanely; that self-improvement should be a constant study; that deportment portrays the inner man; that single life is an honorable estate for woman; and that the New England homestead is a pleasant place.

Miss Sedgwick, in addition to her novels, wrote several stories for children. It is not customary, in literary history, to include juvenile books in the list of works worthy of serious mention, nor to discuss them as related to the intellectual tendencies of the time. The classics of childhood were not, it is true, primarily written for children; the

" Arabian Nights " are folk-products; the " Pilgrim's Progress " is the most serious of allegories;
" Robinson Crusoe " is a tale of a typical Englishman, thrown utterly on his own resources; while
" Gulliver's Travels " aimed to be a vitriolic satire
upon humanity itself. But in the nineteenth
century, when the Grimms in Germany, Hugo in
France, Scott in England, and Hawthorne in
America address a child-public and meanwhile
attract child-hearted readers of every age, it is
manifestly too late to ignore the " juvenile " as an
honorable contribution to literature in the department of fiction, and not measure it by general
canons. In America many writers, from Lydia
Maria Child to Miss Alcott, have developed the
juvenile; but the representative name of all, a
name well entitled to consideration here, is that
of Jacob Abbott.

In the course of a literary life of unremitting
activity, Abbott wrote one hundred Jacob Abbott,
and eighty volumes with his own pen, 1803-1879.
and in addition wrote in part, or edited, thirty-
one. Most of these were not of great size, but
not a few of them called for patient and sometimes extended research in historic or scientific
fields. I know not what American author has
produced a larger library, or one more wholesome
and helpful throughout. These books fall naturally into six divisions: religion, education, science, travel, history, and juvenile fiction; the
representative types of which are " The Young
Christian," the " Little Learner Series," the " Sci-

ence for the Young" series, "A Summer in Scotland," "Abbott's Illustrated Histories" (written in part by John S. C. Abbott, the author's brother), and the "Rollo Books" and "Franconia Stories." Abbott created and systematically continued and popularized a characteristic style, in which didacticism and interest were pleasingly joined. To tell an instructive story in an attractive way, and thereby to impress his mark upon his time, was his life-work in letters. The clear style, the manner of the dialogue, the introduction of anecdote and explanation, the choice and arrangement of pictorial illustrations, and even the typographical appearance, were the author's own, and have never been exactly reproduced by any of his many imitators. Abbott was as closely related to his day as the authors of "Evenings at Home" were to theirs. If, as his son and biographer says, "The Young Christian" is his most representative work, the long list of historical biographies, and the "Franconia Stories," are his best products. To the former Abraham Lincoln professed his indebtedness for about all the historical knowledge he had; to the latter belongs the name of New England's classics for children. The United States is a nation of readers, and in an altogether exceptional degree a nation of young readers; Abbott found the inclination, and at once addressed it and developed it by his work. To claim that his stories and biographies have a high literary rank would be unwise; to deny their place in the development of American letters would be false. In themselves, and yet more in their indications, they stand for a nineteenth-century habit of authorship which, notwithstanding the production by some hands of a wearisome amount of worthlessness, is likely to increase in importance with the passing years.

Turning again from the juvenile story to the general field of fiction, one notes, with not unkindly interest, that a "phenomenal success," in days of eager reading and impressionable "sensibility," was won in particular by three stories, all written by women, and all attaining a circulation to be reckoned by hundreds of thousands. Of the three "The Wide, Wide World" of Miss Susan Warner was the worst in itself and the best-loved by the public. All literature cannot show so lachrymose a book; the heroine burst into tears, silent or paroxysmal, in accordance with a numerical average amounting to every-other page of the two-volume novel. The piety of the work is unquestionable, and it is still deemed a strong story by those who read it in impressionable girlhood and have not since refreshed their memory by recurring to its briny springs. "The Lamplighter," by Miss Cummins, though somewhat exclamatory and didactic, was more natural in its honestly human tone; had it been compressed by an artist within the limits of Dickens' "Cricket on the Hearth" it would have been a worthier addition to the literature that lives more than a decade.

Susan Warner, 1818–1885.

Maria S. Cummins, 1827–1866.

Midway between the appearance of "The Wide,
Wide World" and "The Lamplighter," two years
after the one and two years before the other, was
published, in 1852, that novel which exerted a
moral force in politics unequalled in
the history of English fiction. Harriet Beecher Stowe, had she never
written "Uncle Tom's Cabin," would have held
at least a respectable place among American
authors. New England home-life on the coasts
of Maine and Rhode Island is aptly described in
"The Pearl of Orr's Island" and "The Minister's
Wooing"; while "Oldtown Folks" and "Oldtown
Fireside Stories" are excellent additions to our
rich library of folk-sketches. In Sam Lawson
Mrs. Stowe created a character as true to the life,
in his way, as Lowell's Hosea Biglow. All this
other work, however, is not indispensable, and
pales before the intense fire that has long glowed
in the pages of "Uncle Tom's Cabin." In the far
cold North, where her husband was at the time a
professor in Bowdoin College, Mrs. Stowe looked
toward the sunlit South, and beheld beneath fair
skies all the horror of the wide-spread and blight-
ing evil of human slavery, with its curses of lust
and lash, broken homes and bleeding hearts; hate
and cruelty and greed on the one hand, and the
dogged endurance of hopeless woe on the other.
The horrible system of slavery was not unmitigated by occasional kindness; many a freedman
has sincerely said that sorrow and suffering never
came until abolition severed him from the old

[margin note:] Harriet Elizabeth
(Beecher) Stowe,
b. 1812.

master and mistress, and threw him all unfit upon the world, with a ballot in his hand but no wisdom in his brain. Yet no question of past political expediency, no consideration, even, of exaggeration in the book, as regards the average condition of the negroes in the Southern States, can blind our eyes to the essential and enduring success of the novel. It is far from faultless in development of plot, delineation of character, or literary style ; but it strongly seizes a significant theme, treats it with immediate originality and inevitable effect, and meanwhile adds several individual characters to the gallery of fiction. It was everywhere an anti-slavery argument because its pictures of episodes in the history of slavery were so manifest and so thrilling. Read in every state of the North and in parts of the South, and translated into twenty languages of Europe, it aroused the indifferent and quickened the philanthropic. Its power was felt, perhaps unconsciously, before a quarter of its pages had been read.

The author of " Uncle Tom's Cabin " had the wisdom—not possessed by the pessimistic or self-blinded delineators of later woes in Russia—to brighten her pages by touches of humor and kindly humanity, and to obey the canons of the novelist's art as well as those of the moralist's conscience. Thereby her force was quadrupled, for literature both popularizes and perpetuates morality, while morality without art is fatal to literature. The book remains a vivid panorama of people and scene in a bygone time, now remanded by final war to a past that must ever be historic and can never be repeated. The " abolition of tribal relations in Christ" was the broad theme of a Christian woman ; and in treating it she produced an art-result of such inherent merit that the hand helped the soul as much as the soul the hand.

CHAPTER XII.

As the closing years of the nineteenth century have worn away, fiction has monopolized more and more of the attention of writers and readers in England and America. As a means of popular amusement it has completely overshadowed the drama; and it has demanded for itself three-fourths of the circulation of many public libraries. The masters—Thackeray, Dickens, George Eliot, Hugo, Tourguéneff, Cooper, Hawthorne, Poe—have departed, leaving no successors for the time being; but the hope of easily winning money or notoriety, mayhap even fame, has crowded the literary ranks with story-tellers of every temper, theme and residence and of every ability save the highest. Watching the motley procession of fiction-makers, the critic is tempted to say with Omar Khayyám:

> "A moment's halt—a momentary taste
> Of Being from the well amid the waste—
> And lo!—the phantom caravan has reach'd
> The Nothing it set out from—oh, make haste!"

But the later and younger story-tellers, novelists, and romancers of America have brought to their work a zealous if irregular ambition, a com-

prehensive eye, and a skilful pen.   Their best
short stories are unsurpassed in the literature of
the time ; and while few indeed of their books or
names will live,—half a generation sometimes
envelops a novelist's " fame" in permanent shade,
—the average excellence of their work proves
clearly enough the general resources of the American mind in this division of literature, and the
certainty with which " the long result of time"
promises to produce, once more, works of genius
and imagination in the full sense.   American
story-tellers since the civil war have shown powers
distinctly in advance of those of the lesser novelists in the years immediately preceding that conflict; and their keener vision and simpler methods
have summoned before us many American types
and scenes previously unnoted or unfamiliar.
This manifest improvement in the quality of
minor fiction since 1861 has been chiefly due to
an honest attempt to describe American life as it
is, in its breadth, height, and depth.

These later writers of fiction, however, though
they fill a large place in the immediate literary
landscape, have not completed their work nor
given sure indication of their ultimate place in the
intellectual history of their country.   Many of
them are still in youth or middle life, with their
larger hopes unfulfilled and their more ambitious
plans unmatured.   The only valuable method of
studying their works is obviously to pay small
heed to single volumes or individual writers,
though intrinsically more praiseworthy than some

of their predecessors chronicled in these pages; and simply to take note of the principal tendencies of the American fiction of the time. This may readily and profitably be done, for the lines of subject and method are drawn with sufficient clearness to serve both as a record and as a prophecy.

The first and most significant tendency, as I have said, is toward the production of novels of the soil, and the presentation of American types and scenes. The earlier writers had indeed followed to some extent this obvious and common method, but their successors have discovered new fields and characters, even more typical and interesting because less enveloped in the haze of the authors' own intellectual fancy. They have given large play to humanity, with its hopes, fears, loves, hates, and ordinary experiences; and a true realism has portrayed men and women as they are,—creatures with souls as well as bodies and minds. The portrayal has been more successful in sketch than in finished picture, in short story than in rounded novel; but it has been well worth making, and has been well made. The dash, and fresh wholesomeness, and full-blooded life of the hastily-written and posthumously-published tales of Theodore Winthrop, issued in the midst of the civil war, fitly ushered in a fashion of plain truth-telling in fiction, which never- Theodore Winthrop, theless remembered that life has 1828–1861. its color and romance as well as its dun tameness, and that from its wood and ashes the fire of aspi-

ration flames up toward the ideal. The war itself
produced, North and South, no novel of commanding importance—wars seldom effect general
literature with immediate force, though their ultimate stimulus is greater; but this circumstance is
of small significance in view of the fact that upon
the pages of our fiction are fully drawn the character and lives of the men—and women—who fought
that war and who make the nation what it is.

New England itself, already old, sometimes
conventional, and not previously destitute of authors of ability, has been newly painted by several
of these later writers.   Sarah O. Jewett portrays
Sarah Orne Jewett,   the ancient, decadent, respectable,
b. 1849.   gentle,   and   winsome   seaboard
town, and tells of the life therein.   The courtly
old lady in black lace cap and mitts, living in a
great square house with a hall running from door
to door, and rich in mahogany and cool quiet;
the New England girl of the better class, well
educated, of good descent, and sufficiently aware
of the proprieties of life, yet fresh, happy, and
fond of a "good time"—these two figures are
alone worth more, as contributions to fiction,
than any artificial portrayals of the "sparkling,"
sensational, or satirical talking-machines which
are sometimes supposed to represent American
life.   In the New England which Miss Jewett so
pleasantly and faithfully portrays, are self-respecting people, aristocratic in the only true sense;
bringing up their daughters in freedom, and yet
in homes, modestly but not conventually; speak-

ing the good English which their ancestors
brought from old England two centuries ago ; and
making, as well as finding, "life worth living."

Naturalism, by which term Miss Jewett's
general method may be fitly described, also characterizes the literary work of other New England
women. Thus, for instance, let him who would
know the real Yankee—Doctor Jekyll and Mr.
Hyde—read such grimly humorous stories as
"Freedom Wheeler's Controversy with Providence," "Miss Lucinda," or "The Deacon's
Week," by Rose Terry Cooke. The Rose (Terry)
longer and shorter stories of Miss Cooke, b. 1827.
Elizabeth Stuart Phelps are more intense than
those of Miss Jewett ; but they Elizabeth Stuart
are also local in scene and color, Phelps, b. 1844.
and, like Mrs. Cooke's, are pervaded with
a moral idea. Miss Phelps deals with stormier
moods and with profounder aspirations, but
the New England books of the three writers
differ in selected type and intensity of tone rather
than in kind. If it be said that Miss Phelps'
glimpses of the unseen in "The Gates Ajar" and
"Beyond the Gates" open a heaven that is little
more than a reconstructed New England, and fail
to portray adequately the tender human hopes
and deep and true beliefs which lay in the author's
mind, let it not be forgotten that hope and faith
and sympathy, on the human side, find a fit expression in such stories of hers as "The Tenth of
January," in which the tragedy of life and the

tragedy of art combine, before the background of a New England factory town.

A simpler, less intense and nervous, and more genial and humorous naturalism is the distinguishing note of the stories of Louisa M. Alcott. Their fresh and staid spirit—for childhood is demure as well as frolicsome—make them acceptable to adults and children alike. Any juvenile story, aiming to be swift and cheery rather than artistic, and accompanied by numerous predecessors and successors from the same pen, is likely to be lost in the multiplicity of the lesser books of literature; but Miss Alcott's wholesome young New England girls and boys represent types, at least, which will remain, in fact and in fiction, long after her essentially ephemeral books are forgotten. Miss Alcott, like Miss Phelps, was not oblivious to the deeper romance and shadow of American life, which brightened or darkened the strong pages of " Moods," her first considerable novel.

Louisa May Alcott, 1833–1888.

Another, deeper, and more artistically significant and serene delineation of New England life is made in Higginson's " Malbone, an Oldport Romance." Here are environment and background fit for the most thoughtful artist in prose fiction: the ancient sea ; a town already venerable and courtly, by American standards ; a moist climate that marks the English complexion and restful temper upon the faces of the young American residents ; and a modern, sensational, fashionable life surging

Thomas Wentworth Higginson, b. 1823.

around the slowly-moved landmarks of the chief of our watering-places. Here Higginson viewed life and put some part of its vital blood into a book of quiet literary strength, of romantic action, of lambent humor, and (in its capitally-drawn character of Aunt Jane) of fidelity to that shrewd and indigenous New Englandism described elsewhere by Mrs. Stowe or Miss Phelps. "Malbone" is an Emersonian novel in its view of inanimate nature as mirror and monitor of human nature,—the eternal theme of romancer and poet.

I have been considering some novelists and story-tellers of New England. In the two books of Mr. Philander Deming, one of the least sensational but one of the most praiseworthy of recent writers, the scenes are laid in the Adirondack region of Northern New York, or in the neighboring cities of Albany and Burlington. In Mr. Deming's work the form is something like that of Mr. James' stories, but the Philander Deming, b. 1829. spirit is the author's own. In "Lida Ann," or "Tompkins," for instance, Mr. Deming shows that he possesses the double power of describing details minutely, and of delineating the life behind the details. By little touches we are made to see character and scenery; and we are also shown, in deeper tints, the kind of existence led by the personages of the tales. Their works and ways are humble, like the grim and mean but pathetically human love-making in Mary E. Wilkins' somewhat similar Vermont story called "A Humble Romance." But the essential spirit of

the better fiction is never lost. In "Lida Ann" a
commonplace little Adirondack girl marries a
coarse, "emotional," and pretentious revivalist;
then she runs away with a "Spiritualist" humbug;
but at last come the real regeneration of the
revivalist by the gospel of hard work and
modest self-sacrifice, and the return of the foolish
wanderer to a respectable life. In "Tompkins"
is merely the life-story of a Vermont girl who
silently supports an unsuspecting loved one in his
college course, and who goes to her grave before
he learns the secret. Yet these "simple stories,"
in very truth, are told with such art, with such
fidelity to petty detail and to high purpose, that
they cannot be omitted in any estimate of our
later fiction. They portray in clear lines and firm
tints the plain or rude American country life from
which come the very bone and sinew of the nation.
Rectitude and hope lie behind the simplest American society; a rectitude based on an essentially
noble self-reliance, and a hope that may lack
refinement or intelligence but not spiritual
strength. Even in the Adirondack wilderness
is a view of life that forms a striking contrast
to the pale pessimistic woe of the Russian countrymen of similar social grade, as shown by such
local masters as Tourguéneff or Tolstoi.

The most successful pictures of American characters and characteristic scenes, whether chosen
from the east or the west, from city or from country, have unquestionably been presented in such
short stories as those of Miss Jewett, Mrs. Cooke,

Miss Phelps, or Mr. Deming, rather than in long novels. Bret Harte is distinctly at his best in his brief stories and sketches, and at his worst in his larger books; Mr. Cable's "The Grandissimes" and "Doctor Sevier" are, at best, no more than equal to the separated studies of "Old Creole Days"; while Miss Murfree ("Charles Egbert Craddock"), an apparent exception, writes novelettes, or long-short stories, rather than novels. Others of the newer and younger Southern writers are sketchers, not romancers ; and as we look at the whole field of the new American fiction we note excellence in the small, rather than any largeness of creative ability. But a short story, like a short poem, is as legitimate as a long one ; and if our large and fine new creations in fiction are few indeed, at least we escape thereby the weariness of prolixity. The explanation is not far to seek : our broad and varied national life, from the Maine ship-builders to the Louisiana Creoles, from Miss Woolson's lake country to Miss Murfree's Tennessee mountains or Bret Harte's mines and gulches, affords as yet so abundant material for description that the literary painters naturally multiply portraits, and little groups of figures, and *genre* pictures, rather than inclusive or ideal scenes. One such sketch as "Peter the Parson," in Miss Woolson's "Castle Nowhere : Lake Country Sketches," is so true and therefore

Constance Fenimore Woolson, b. 1845.

so valuable that I care not if the author's ambitious books, "Anne" and "East Angels," despite

manifest touches of a strong hand, seem altogether unimportant in comparison. In "Peter
the Parson" we have the cold, raw, scantling-and-
boards life of a hateful little Philistine settlement
in Michigan; but we have also high if mistaken
religious devotion, the half-hopes and crushed
possibilities of a real love, and a supreme self-
sacrifice like that which lies at the very heart of
Christianity—and that is enough.

A little farther westward lie the scenes of
Edward Eggles-
ton, b. 1837. Edward Eggleston's tales of pioneer
life in the "new west" of 1840. The
author was able to put into his books sights and
experiences of which his own life had taught him.
As an itinerant preacher among the Methodists,
and later as a Sunday-school worker, he well
learned of the shifting borderland between civilization and barbarism; and his novels tell us
truly of the life lived at the outposts, in log cab-
ins built on virgin soil. The very titles of his
works—"The Hoosier Schoolmaster," "The Cir-
cuit Rider," "The Mystery of Metropolisville,"
"Roxy"—illuminate the scenes and characters
described. The scenes are rough and the characters "tough," in the better sense and sometimes
in the worse; but the fidelity with which youth
and age in the backwoods are painted makes the
books, like so many other American works, at
least valuable essays toward that full delineation
of the whole country which our novelists seem
surely, though irregularly, to be making. America includes many a "Metropolisville," as well

as Boston or New York. Eggleston's western stories present passing phases of a life-character that is in itself permanent. Thin and poor as that life may be in externals, it is even opulent in courage, cheer, and manly helpfulness. The men and women of these Hoosier tales may live in bark-covered log houses, but their hearts are full of true blood and their sinews are of steel. It is fortunate that they found a chronicler who understands the true relation of fiction to the study of life.

With a humor less spontaneous but neater and more deliberate than Eggleston's, Bret Harte has made the early Californians, good and bad, known throughout the world of readers. An evident disciple of Dickens, he joins wit and pathos in that union which has ever marked their near kinship in English fiction. Some of his tales almost seem the apotheosis of mere grit and friendship, at the expense of all other moral qualities; they are full of sentiment, but so far removed from sentimentality that they appear to revel in coarseness and general badness, only caring that they laud devotion and self-sacrifice, courage and rude tenderness, and scarify treachery and hypocrisy. Mr. Harte can give the best of reasons for this nature of his stories: it was and is the real nature of the characters described. If his realism brings very near us such things as gamblers, prostitutes, robbers, "speculators," pistols, knives, cards and dice, it does not forget the community of human nature, and

Francis Bret Harte, b. 1839.

the higher moods and tenderer impulses of hearts covered by rough flannel or tawdry finery. Bret Harte's best stories—usually the shorter ones, such as "The Luck of Roaring Camp," "The Outcasts of Poker Flat," "How Santa Claus came to Simpson's Bar," "An Apostle of the Tules," or "A Ship of '49," set forth with large truth and with accuracy of detail certain passing episodes in America. The life they portray with kindly and swift humor, with grim impartiality, and sometimes with a coarseness not essential, is genuine; it is a life which is apparently brazenly selfish in the struggle for existence or gain, but is, after all, deeply stirred by generous instincts and helpful humanity. Bret Harte's sharpers or miners of the far West, his owners of ranches, rough pioneer farmers, and rude, uncultured women, are for the most part united in favor of sincerity and "bed-rock" honesty, traits which are by no means least common in the slums of New York or the gulches of California. The life of his stories, miserably limited as it may be in breadth and wealth of opportunity, is yet a full and rich life in those things which most make existence desirable and progress possible. Its Americanism is genuine; that of the national or quaintly local earth and sky, but also of universal man shown in new scenes and phases. Harte's wit has greatly helped his rise in public favor,— the wit which tells us how suddenly the rascally gambler, outwitted by the "heathen Chinee," discovered that "we are ruined by Chinese cheap labor." But the wit of "Plain Language from Truthful James," or the pathos of others of Harte's poems, finds a better expression in his prose idyls of the land of rough ore, and is chiefly to be valued not for its own sake, but as an aid to the presentation of interesting and actual types of unfamiliar character. The presentation is irregular, often hurried or weak, and not more than once or twice marked by the highest art; but, in the author's own words, it is "quite content to have collected merely the materials for the Iliad that is yet to be sung."

After the end of the civil war and the violent death of slavery, there appeared in several of the Southern States a self-reliant literary spirit,—shown especially by many young story-tellers and poets whose fame is still unknown,—and a habit of faithful portrayal of men and things close at hand that promise much for the future of American fiction. Southern provincialism before the war, though intensely local in its pride, was self-complacent, and not sufficiently keen-eyed to see that provincial types and scenes, accurately and impartially presented, may be made contributions to national or even universal literature. Instead of mere pride in the soil has come a living interest in the characteristics and products of the soil; in place of a somewhat artificial and perfunctory praise of Southern writers, we now have a spontaneous and hearty recognition of the inherent merit of their writings. The old temper might have expressed itself in the words: "It must be good because it is Southern " ; the new says : " It is good, and it is also Southern." * Like Bret Harte, Miss Murfree and Mr. Cable rely for success upon the fidelity with which localism is given a universal interest. To sight they add insight ; and their painstakingly minute touches are directed by a knowledge of humanity beneath eccentricity. In presenting " The Prophet of the Great Smoky Mountains " of Tennessee, and the rude folk to whom he preached, Miss Murfree adds to description that ideal or imaginative

Mary Noailles Murfree (" Charles Egbert Craddock"), b. 18—

power which, while sacrificing no jot of truth, sees the soul through flesh and bones, and discerns the meaning of life, however sordid or coarse it apparently is. The mighty mountains, and deep gorges, and overshadowing trees in her books, as in Bret Harte's California stories, at first seem to dwarf the vulgar men and women who crawl about them ; but Miss Murfree's Prophet, and Harte's Apostle of the Tules, and Miss Woolson's Peter the Parson are yet able to rise to a Sidney Carton height of self-sacrifice for others. The externally hateful and wicked and mean, in our worst American life, is yet instinct with the higher optimism ; for

---

* An able, unquestionable, and admirably concise and strong expression of the true Southern attitude toward American literature is made by a very competent authority, in a personal letter to me from which I am permitted to quote. Colonel J. Lewis Peyton, of Steephill-by-Staunton, Virginia, is peculiarly qualified to speak on this subject,—by descent, by remarkably extended family connections with the great men of the South, by important services to the Confederate States when their representative in England, and by his own relation to literary work. He writes : " In the South (as

"It is not only in the rose,
It is not only in the bird,
Not only where the rainbow glows,
Nor in the song of woman heard,
But in the darkest, meanest things,
There alway, alway, something sings."

The tone and color may be strange, and certainly
are presented with grim accuracy; if the moral
appears, it is not because these writers preach,
but because human life preaches, however unwelcome to finical critics its sermon may be.

The new Southern writers have much to do and
much to learn. They have not, as yet, begun to
exhaust a rich store. Before the war was the
ancien régime, picturesque and peculiar; then
came the storm and stress of a conflict that
burned the South—far more than the North—
with searing flame; now rises the new South, a
patriotic part of the common country. The field
for fiction, whether romantic or realistic, broad
novel or narrow sketch, is wide, and seems reason-
ably sure of cultivation. If the large mind and
large manner are not apparent as yet, the same is
true in the case of the writers of the West. By
and by the masters will come, here one and there
another, it may be at long intervals; for not

with you) nobody now thinks of the birthplace of an American writer; we
only wish to know what he has turned a sheet of white paper into, with pen
and ink. And I hardly think any but a man of diseased mind and imagination, like Poe, would ever have uttered such sentiments as he did as to
Edward Coate Pinkney. The enlightened men of this region, as of yours,
know no North or South in literature—only one grand Republic of Letters,
in which every man standeth according to the soundness of his heart and
the strength of his understanding."

often, at the North or anywhere, appears an author deserving to be called great. The localism of a narrow field does not in itself, of course, prevent a book or an author from attaining greatness or showing the large manner. The single name of Hawthorne is enough to prove that high genius may cultivate the narrowest field with noble literary results, and that the ablest mind finds and almost makes its *locale* in New England or Old, beneath the shades of Puritanism or of Romanism.*

Mrs. Frances Hodgson Burnett, a writer of English birth but of Southern residence, has shown how mental character and literary preference choose their field, and how the author's thought may profitably revert to old scenes or distant types. Her bright and fresh little love stories are as unimportant as they are numerous, and her portrayals of certain Southern characters and life-phases are entertaining but not significant, with the exception of occasional portraitures of self-re-

Frances Eliza (Hodgson) Burnett, b. 1849.

---

* "Literature as a profession has until quite recently found but few followers in the South. . . . . The institutions and traditions of Southern life were unfavorable, if not openly antagonistic, to the establishment of the literary profession. The leisurely and cultivated, among whom literary productiveness would most naturally have its rise, preferred, as their fathers had preferred, the career of the statesman, and its honors were their ambition, to the attainment of which the legal profession was the natural stepping-stone. The art of expressing thought on paper they regarded as an elegant accomplishment, to be cultivated as a gentleman's recreation, not the serious business of his life, for which he was to receive remuneration. That they were a race of polished letter-writers family archives conclusively prove; and able essays on political subjects not infrequently came from their pens. Thus there were men who did literary work, and good work

liant girls like Esmeralda or Louisiana. Such blatant and let us hope passing types as the American young woman whom Mrs. Burnett calls "A
Fair Barbarian" may entertain an hour; but
better than a hundred such studies is her picture
of "That Lass o' Lowrie's," and life in the Lan-
cashire mines of England; or the unmitigated
pathos which we are made to share in "Surly
Tim's Troubles," a sketch of transatlantic grief
that appeals to the worldwide heart.

The renaissance of literature in the South has
produced no more interesting result than George
W. Cable's tales of picturesque Louisianian life.
A keen observer and a fearless painter—for fearlessness is needed if one would faithfully depict
the life of a sensitive folk—Cable is also a fine
artist in his touch and at the same time a wholesome moralist. New Orleans and Louisiana, far
and unfamiliar, half French and therefore half foreign, a later addition to   George
the territory of the United States, both   Washington
Cable, b. 1844.
rich and poor, chastened but not humbled or
crushed by the civil war—what better scene could

too, to whom the writing of books was neither the prime aim in life nor yet
purely a pastime. . . . . Simms made the prophecy that there would never
be a Southern literature worthy of the name under a slave-holding aristocracy. Social conditions were against it. When the result of the war
brought about a new state of affairs, and the people of the South, at first
stunned by the mightiness of the blow, went bravely to work to meet the
demands of the situation, the pen, heretofore a political weapon or the attri-
bute of cultured leisure, was soon made to take its place beside the plough.
In Southern life was presently perceived abundant material, rich and varied,
possessing high literary value and interest. Letters as a career found a
larger following."—Charles Washington Coleman, Jr. (of Williamsburg,
Va.) in *Harper's Magazine*, May, 1887.

a novelist find? It was Cable's by birth and residence, and he made it his anew by the larger purpose and the lesser art of his books. Here are
the romantic and the picturesque in theme, and
the dainty and welcome in treatment. "Old
Creole Days" and "Madame Delphine" happily
illustrate that union of local and limited study with
unconsciously large and free presentation which is
a mark of true literature; and these best of his
books, as well as the longer romantic novels called
"The Grandissimes" and "Doctor Sevier," view
the ideal sky through the lower atmosphere of
the real. *Post nubila lux:* here humor and pathos
and tender humanity do not long leave tragedy in
unmitigated gloom, nor is the riddle of existence
without some suggested answer. Whether these
delicate books will live I do not know; but it is
certain that few recent American novelists have
shown so uniform an average of attainment in
thought and art, or have thrown upon the quaintly
real such new tints of ideal light.

What is to be understood by the term "realistic," as applied to the method of some later
American writers of fiction? Defoe was an early
realist; he so clothed fiction in the garb of truth,
in his "Robinson Crusoe," "Strange Apparition
of Mrs. Veal," and other writings, as to deceive
the very elect, and to interest the reading public
as few writers have ever done. Fielding, too, was
a realist, in that he described low life as he saw it,
and turned his back upon the academic traditions
of his time. Goldsmith, in prose and verse,

painted certain classes of English and Irish society in real colors. Even Scott, with all his sentiment and romanticism and old-fashioned Toryism,
cannot be called untrue to the soul of humanity,
or unable to see and describe life in a real world.
Dickens walked and talked with the London
poor, familiarized himself with suburban and rural
English life in many grades, and at least thought
he described Americans as he had seen them.
Thackeray mirrored certain parts of British society, and portrayed its shams and foibles, as well
as the hearts of some true women and men, without essential exaggeration. Charlotte and Emily
Brontë in Yorkshire, Blackmore in Devon and
Somerset, George Eliot in rural England, may in
justice be called realists, whatever their differences
of method and style. Yet none of them would
come under the application of the term as nowadays employed. It was their aim to be true ; but
they differed from the present transient school of
" realists"—led at a distance by the finished and
woe-begone Tourguéneff and the strong and
individual Tolstoi—because they gave a greater
place to sentiment, even though most of them
shunned sentimentality.

What, then, is modern American realism ? To
attempt to define it may be easier than to define
poetry or beauty, but it is not easy. For the purpose of the present study it may be sufficient to
say that it stands without, not within ; gives no
evidence of personal sympathy ; seldom indulges
in reflections upon the narrative it offers ; leaves

the reader to draw his own conclusions concerning
right, wrong, progress, and remedy ; describes by
implication or by a minute rather than large
characterization ; is fond of detail ; devotes itself
chiefly to a limited and uninteresting set of tolerably intelligent people ; makes much of transcon-
tinental travel or international episodes and social
exchanges ; insists constantly upon the duty of
portraying life as it is ; and yet omits many of the
most important factors in life's problem. It has
been the most conspicuous, though not the most
important, the most discussed, though by no means
the most read, division or development of later
Henry James, American fiction ; and its leader has
b. 1843. been Mr. Henry James. This quiet
innovator, without self-assertion or the use of
adventitious aids to success, has at least entitled
himself to a place in the limited list of those who
have been influences in American literature. I
remember reading, from the pen of some anonymous English critic, the statement that " American novelists almost give us (the English) lessons
in careful elaboration of style, in reticence, and
well-calculated effects." If this be true, the compliment—or rather its first two parts—belongs in
some measure to a writer sometimes distinguished
for careful elaboration of style and always for reticence, whatever his verbosity ;—" the refraining
to speak of that which is suggested."

Mr. James did not adopt at first the constructive method by which he is best known. The
New York magazine called *The Galaxy*, now

dead, used to be his common vehicle of communication. Its earlier volumes contained many stories from his pen, which differed from the usual magazine work not so much in plot and in larger elaboration as in a certain neatness of finish and lack of intrusion on the writer's part. Some of his earlier work, printed in this or other magazines, has been abandoned by the author, but several stories are preserved in book form. In these, though the external style is sufficiently calm and cold, is an element which forbids them to be classified with Mr. James' later productions. There is more than a touch of romance in "A Passionate Pilgrim"; "The Last of the Valerii" is an essay toward the Hawthorne manner—with the usual result; "The Madonna of the Future" is an essentially humanitarian tale; and "The Romance of Certain Old Clothes" is distinctly sensational. The prevalent note of the stories in Mr. James' first collection was not that of the realism now connected with his name. His earlier criticisms and descriptions of travel showed more of his later method than did his short stories. The influences of travel, of cosmopolitan culture, and of his instinctive calmness of mind, served to develop his final man-without-a-country manner. He needed no *ars est celare artem* motto, he simply followed his bent; and the soberer years of manhood naturally turned him from his essays toward the sensational and the romantic, though he never quite lost his humanitarian element, to which he occasionally yields.

28

It is not necessary to pass through the tolerably
well-known list of Mr. James' books, reviewing
each in minute detail. They are rather weari-
somely numerous, and some of them, written
after the first, show a lack of that literary finish
which is supposed to be connected with his name.
Of all his books "The Bostonians" is the best
illustrative type : long, dull, and inconsequential,
but mildly pleasing the reader, or at times quite
delighting him, by a deliberate style which is
enjoyable for its own sake, by a calm portraiture
which represents the characters with silhouette-
clearness, and by some very faithful and delicately humorous pictures of the life and scenery
of Eastern Massachusetts. Its method is somewhat dreary and narrow, but is in its way sufficiently admirable.

Mr. James has three "manners" : " The Passionate Pilgrim " book represents one ; " Daisy
Miller " the second ; and "The Bostonians " the
third. In "Daisy Miller " Mr. James depicts a
characteristic American girl, from his own point
of view. The picture is unattractive to those
who, recognizing Daisy as a "type," refuse to
regard her as a more prominent or representative
type than Mr. Howells' "Lady of the Aroostook," Miss Jewett's " Country Doctor," or Mrs.
Burnett's " Louisiana," to select three young
women of equal self-reliance but greater sense.
The novelette aroused, perhaps, a needless attention, since the author's method evidently was
impartial, in his own view, and since he gave his

little heroine some attractive qualities, which may
well enough be recommended for European imitation. The defect which the reader feels in
this booklet, as in so much of Mr. James' work,
does not relate to what is said, but rather to the
author's apparent lack of heart or human interest in the matter. We may call Mr. James a
faultless photographer, in the "Daisy Miller"
class of his stories, but not an artist. He is, at
best, a French painter in fiction, not a master in
the older and larger and better manner. He has
deliberately chosen his plan, and must pay the
penalty while he receives the reward.

In his longer "international"—or, as they have
been cleverly called, *émigré*—novels we recognize
more clearly the artistic touch. "Roderick Hudson" and "The Portrait of a Lady" are the best
of his longer stories, and "Confidence" is the
poorest, but all are constructed on the same
scheme,—the scheme first fully elaborated in his
novelette of "Watch and Ward," published in
1872. Behind all his books stands the author,
never more visible than the live man in Maelzel's
automaton chess-player. There passes before
him a procession of people ; he notes and chronicles their characteristics, and he tells some of the
things they say and do, with fewer of the things
they think. These personages, men and women,
are not knights, Pathfinders, dark mysterious villains, dazzling beauties, or damsels forlorn, subjected to plot and intrigue ; nor are they melodramatic creatures of the Nancy Sykes order.

Mr. James describes commonplace people of the better kind; and though they feel, and act, and are acted upon, their environment is irreproachable. Seldom does he seem to be working toward a definite result in his books, though most of them have what may in a sense be called a moral. A part of the *outside* of the complex life of the last quarter of the nineteenth century is his theme; he delineates it, and he analyzes and sub-analyzes; but that is all. If it be true that he is preëminently the American novelist who represents "life" and reality, without artificial idealism in adornment, then life nowadays is a sadly shrunken and shrivelled thing, cold, thin and incomplete.

Later American prose has been distinctly broadened and enriched by the work of William Dean Howells. Of Ohio birth, and thoroughly American in his fresh, self-reliant, alert, observant, and optimistic tone of mind, Howells has strengthened his natural powers by a wise assimilation of the results of study, travel, and European residence. In his broad field of work he has shown his ready acceptance of the national necessity—or temptation— to do many things: he has been editor, critic, traveller, comedian, novelist, poet, and even (like Hawthorne) a writer of the "campaign biographies" called forth by the demands of American quadrennial politics. But his novels, in number and importance, have overshadowed his readable biographies of Presidents Lincoln and Hayes; his incisive, witty, or too swiftly laudatory reviews of

William Dean Howells, b. 1837.

fiction and poetry in America, England, Italy, and Russia; his graceful but relatively unimportant verse, dominated and saddened by the influence of Heine; and his serene sketches of life in Italian Venice or American Cambridge, the scenes and characters of which he has illumined by the lambent light of a humor which not seldom recalls the pleasure the masters give.

Howells' stories and novels are American in scene, in portraiture, and in spirit. In "Their Wedding Journey," "A Chance Acquaintance," and "A Foregone Conclusion" he fairly entitled himself, by his freshness, faithfulness, and wholesome humor of description, to be called the most successful literary painter of contemporary American life in the better classes. His field was somewhat limited; he did not essay to treat of noble tragedy or utter pathos; of inexorable necessity or glowing romance; but within that field his success was manifest and his method was his own. After the publication of "The Lady of the Aroostook" (1879) and "The Undiscovered Country" (1880), the one a fine portrait of a true and womanly girl and the other an interesting study of some phases of New England "Spiritualism," Howells distinctly changed his manner and manifestly fell under the influence of Henry James, his junior in years and certainly not his superior in ability, reputation, or mastery of style. This change was clearly for the worse. Henceforth Howells, though never becoming indifferent to the deeper truths of life, was to be ranked with

the new-realists. The stories, he said, had all
been told; therefore he presented passionless and
elaborately minute studies of certain types—characteristic in their way, but non-significant—of
New England men and women. With keenness
and clearness of vision, and with the humor which
is a part of his nature, he simply told his readers
what he had seen and heard. The telling would
have been faultless had the subjects been representative. By perpetually portraying a part of
life, and that not the most significant, this painstaking realist has produced an unreal effect.

Of the books in Howells' later manner "A
Modern Instance" is the strongest; it is Howells'
representative novel, as "The Bostonians" is
James' masterpiece. The men and women, boys
and girls, and winter life and landscape of a typical New England village are delineated with a
fidelity that would be perfect were it not that the
heart and soul of New England are almost out
of sight. "A Modern Instance," placed beside
"The Biglow Papers," "Snow-Bound," or "The
House of the Seven Gables"—all three of them
minutely realistic—almost seems an artistic falsehood. Its separate elements are true, but its
whole is misleading. Howells returns again and
again to the porch or the heap of builders' débris,
but shuts his eyes to the skyward cathedral.

> "What parts, what gems, what colors shine,—
> Ah, but I miss the grand design."

The influence of the two chief American real-

ists, and of their European prototypes, has of
course affected some of the younger novelists in
the United States. Occasionally one of them has
devoted himself to realism pure and simple; others, with a more or less romantic motive, have
followed the general method of cold and unimpas-
sioned delineation; and still others have only
employed the realists' international plan. On the
whole, however, the smaller American fiction, as
well as the larger, seeks to portray the ideal in
the real, not the real without the ideal. A finer
and truer art is demanded in this attempt. It
would be a sorry day for fiction if it turned its
back on life and truth, in a chase after mere
romance or invention. Life was field enough for
Shakespeare, and ought to be for nineteenth century novelists. But Shakespeare did not forget
the romantic, the ideal, and even the supernatural
in his treatment of human life, which was far
indeed from that of Tolstoi or Tourguéneff.
What is the life that the novelist is to describe?
Is it action, movement, story? or is it existence,
attitude, pictorial representation? Again, which
is the more important, the thing told or the way
of telling it? The former; because all art is
grounded on the necessity that the subject should
have some reason for existence and delineation.
Last of all, what is life itself? The career of
upward-moving souls, answers the chorus of the
world's greatest authors, in fiction as in every
other department of literature. Man always has
been and always will be a creature of ambition,

hope, love, enthusiasm, and the idea of duty; thus only, by rectitude and hope, can he explain the mystery of life, and look forward with confidence to "the long day of eternity."

Midway between the realists and the romanticists of later days stands Arthur Sherburne Hardy, whose "But Yet a Woman" (1883), like the realistic novels, presents an effective contrast to the representative books of preceding American fashions in fiction, with their dark and sombre scenes, their stirring melodramatic adventures, their commonplace sentimentalism, their gentle aspirations, or their bursts of bitter tears. "But Yet a Woman" is a characteristic novel that could not have been written save in the later, maturer, and quieter days of fiction in the United States. Its characters, as usual in the novels of the day, are few, and its tone is almost quietistic. Yet the lives and hearts it brings before us are far from being those superficially and hence imperfectly presented in the pages of the ordinary realistic and impassive novel. The author's sympathy is shown, and the reader's sympathy is tacitly asked, for things significantly vital and deeply human. The novel endeavors to be, in some sort, a "criticism of life"; indeed, its chief merit is to be found in the aphorisms and pithy sayings with which it abounds. It would be the thoughtful reader's companion, and not merely his stimulant or amusement.

A further reaction from realism, in England

and America, has produced in recent years a large
number of stories, long and short, which have
ranged from highly-colored oriental or even African romance to sensational novels of intricate
crime, clever detection, and ultimate punishment.
Of these stories it may be said, in Tennyson's
phrase, that "some are pretty enough, and some
are poor indeed." At one extreme, in England,
stands "The Strange Case of Doctor Jekyll and
Mr. Hyde," a valuable addition to the select
division of English fiction ; at the other, certain
improbable, loosely-constructed, and even ungram-
matical romances not worth mention. But in
speaking of this reaction, let us not forget that
"realism" has never affected more than a somewhat limited minority of novel-readers, in England or America. In the former the sway of
Dickens, the prose poet and master-mind, is still
undiminished ; in the latter, where Dickens is no
less potent, the many have been stirred to flame
by "Uncle Tom's Cabin," or have eagerly bought,
for political reasons, tens of thousands of the
novels portraying scenes in the "reconstruction
period" of the Southern States. Their highest
favorite is a writer who, beginning with a story
of the great Chicago fire of 1871, gave them
a long series of tales in which the humanitarian,
the domestic, and the sensational elements were
combined in what proved to be the desired
proportion. Meanwhile two hundred thousand
copies of "Ben-Hur, a Tale of the Christ"
have been distributed among pleased readers,

to whom its religious suggestions and its occasionally vivid pictures have been most welcome, though the construction and—to me at least—dull literary style are of the amateur rather than the true historical novelist. "Uncle Tom's Cabin" will always be a historical landmark in American literature; the literary future of the other books just mentioned is of very insecure promise; nor can mere popular favor, so thoughtless and so ephemeral, be elevated into a critical judgment. But it is plain that, in America at least, literary agnosticism will be received with no more favor than religious; and that American literature will not chiefly be influenced by books in which

"The heart somehow seems all squeezed out by the mind."

English literature has long made a clear distinction between the story or short tale, whether romantic or natural; the novel or long story, dealing with passions and experiences not essentially improbable; and the romance, in which the action or the study of character is more ideal, imaginary, unusual, improbable, picturesque, or tinged with the supernatural. Other languages make a similar distinction, in varying methods of nomenclature. In American fiction, as elsewhere, the boundaries of the three divisions are not clearly defined. Brown's "novels" are essentially romances; there is a romantic element in Cooper; and Poe's "tales" are little romances. But it is plain enough, in the general view, that

Irving wrote stories, Cooper novels, and Poe and
Hawthorne tales or romances. The conscious
humor in Irving's stories minimizes the romantic
element. In later fiction there is of course an obvious difference between Deming or Miss Murfree
and Crawford or Julian Hawthorne. Through the
works of Brown, Judd, Cooke, Winthrop, Cable,
there runs a glittering thread of romance, visible
even, as we have seen, in some of the earlier work
of Henry James. Fitz-James O'Brien, a brilliant
young Irish son of fortune, killed in the first year
of the civil war, showed in his remarkable
story called "The Diamond Lens" how a
minute realism, the most rigid art, and
a seemingly unfettered imagination could combine
to produce a valuable and original result within
no more than thirty pages. A more thrifty man-
of-letters would have elaborated the idea in a long
romance. But the prodigality of American literature has in it something regal as well as something wasteful; and nowhere has its wealth been
more manifest than in the tales of three of our
greater, and some few of our lesser, writers of
fiction. Occasionally an author of no higher rank
than Harriet Prescott Spofford, by the very carelessness of opulence, apparently throws away
renown. Her earliest volumes, "Sir Rohan's
Ghost," "The Amber Gods and Other Stories,"
"Azarian," displayed to American readers a
romantic element of unwonted luxuriance and
ostentatious wealth. The stories in the "Amber
Gods" volume in particular, were fairly resplen-

Fitz-James
O'Brien,
1829–1862.

dent in color, rich in tone, and oriental in per-
fume—"and all Arabia breathes

Harriet Elizabeth
(Prescott) Spofford,
b. 1835.

from yonder box." "The Amber
Gods" and "Midsummer and May"
are something more than curiosities in American
literature. The author's later work has not fulfilled her early promise nor added to her fame;
the ready magazine-market for common love-stories has tempted her pen to easier toils and less
exhilarating or exhausting mental states; it may
be that the books of her youth now seem to their
writer—as indeed they sometimes are—altogether
careless and extravagant. But the irregular
dramatic fire of these individual tales has not
burned itself away in a quarter of a century; and
there is still a place—however far below the
highest place—in our literature for "the complete
incarnation of light, full, bounteous, overflowing";
"attars and extracts that snatch your soul off
your lips"; or the "little Spanish masque, to
which kings and queens have once listened in
courtly state, and which now unrolls its resplendent pageant before the eyes of Mrs. Laudersdale,
translating her, as it were, into another planet,
where familiar faces in pompous entablature look
out upon her from a whirl of light and color, and
familiar voices utter stately sentences in some
honeyed unknown tongue." Not often appears a
writer capable of describing the effect of tone-
color in eight words like these: "*the instrument
seemed to diffuse a purple cloud;*" but in fiction
and in life there is in very truth

"A tone
Of some world far from ours,
Where music and moonlight and feeling
Are one."

The romantic tone occasionally marks some single book among the many boasting of no more than ordinary success. From the hurried international experiments of Francis Marion Crawford, ranging from an unfamiliar "Mr. Isaacs" in languid modern India to an im- Francis Marion possible "American Politician" at Crawford, b. 1854. home, there emerges the noble figure of "Zoroaster," surrounded by a Persian environment of dramatic scenes. Here are somewhat of the swift carelessness of mere romance and somewhat of the effective force of restrained art. Another writer, turning from pretty little unimportant village love-stories of New England, Blanche Willis portrays in "Guenn" a nobly pa- Howard, b. 1847. thetic picture of the hopeless love of a Breton peasant maiden for a painter innocently oblivious of the life-ruin he is making. To the smaller novelists as well as the greater there sometimes comes that ideal vision, that clearer insight, which peers to depths and heights of life unseen before. If the thought and the power be those of romance, the resulting life-picture need not be less true because less commonplace or familiar.

Such life-pictures are not hard to find in the tales, novels, and romances of the younger Hawthorne. Over his broad field hang both European and American skies, but they are not seldom illumined by "the light that never was on sea or land." Internationalism, in his method, is but a convenience in the portrayal of minor character; it is not a mere matter of external amusement. "Analysis" he reserves for such essays as those printed in "Saxon Studies"; soul he deems a thing somewhat deeper than may be shown by mere study of attitude or lesser act. His studies in stories are of life, not of society; and he prefers to create rather than to record. The soul and its struggles, deep sin and grim inexorable penalty, inner loveliness and spiritual triumph, are his higher themes; and though he occasionally writes some compact tale of mere crime and discovery, he usually turns to subjects far more intricate and psychological. His lighter tales are long-removed from the intense romance called "Sinfire" or the original creation of "Archibald Malmaison"; yet even in the former there sometimes appears the romancer's profound impression of the depth and half-guessed meaning of the mystery of life, and his constant search for some utterance of that impression.

Julian Hawthorne, b. 1846.

The careless opulence of which I have just spoken, as a sign of the strength and the weakness of later American fiction, finds no better illustration than in Julian Hawthorne's books. They crowd upon each other in their rapid appearance; their construction and language are too often so faulty that they almost seem wayward; and now and then the figures are blurred upon the mental retina. "Archibald Malmaison" seems to me the most original and the strongest of the author's books, a remarkable example of the romance pure and simple; yet even here, where the elaboration of the peculiar plot demands the utmost nicety, are occasional signs of haste. Julian Hawthorne has not yet applied to fiction the constructive art and the gravely decorative detail which make his "Nathaniel Hawthorne and his Wife" the best biography written in America. In "Sebastian Strome," which is not unable to endure mention beside "Adam Bede," of which it is a sort of unintentional counterpart, the author shows his most sustained strength. I prefer, however, to find in the general, rather than the particular, those qualities which led a living critic*—a critic thoroughly familiar with the work of Nathaniel Hawthorne and Edgar Allan Poe—to declare that Julian Hawthorne "is clearly and easily the first of living romancers."

None knows better than Mr. Hawthorne himself the perilousness of so confident a statement as this. But it is certain that his published books display the originality and power of genius. Their general purpose and literary trend, their unswerving idea, whatever their irregularity of theme and merit, may fairly be summed up in these words from a critical essay by Mr. Hawthorne, written of course without the slightest autobiographic intent :

* Richard Henry Stoddard.

The heterogeneous mass of material phenomena is destitute of order, proportion and purpose, and in their unregenerate state these phenomena are and must remain unavailable for a work of art. Only after the mind of the artist has impressed its form upon them, moulding them to its image, choosing the good and rejecting the bad, vindicating them and vitalizing them with its overruling purpose, can the facts and circumstances of the physical world become fit to assume their station in the immortal temple of art. . . . . You cannot bind a human mind with iron fetters, and the laws which control fixed matter cannot be applied to the regulation of free spirit. . . . . To what end is this royal gift of imagination bestowed upon the race? Is it to chronicle small-beer, which speaks sufficiently for itself? or shall it be applied to the creation of an "Iliad," a "Divine Comedy," a "Hamlet," a "Paradise Lost?" Is it better to show the seamstress and the dry-goods clerk an elaborate imitation of their own petty existence and contracted ambition? or to thrill a nation with a grand romance and elevate a generation with a sublime poem? If we have any Horace Walpoles, any Chesterfields, any Boswells among us, let them appeal to us as students of manners and biography and they shall receive their due welcome and recognition; but why should they assume the tones and the titles which have been made reverend by Shakespeare, Fielding and Balzac? A work of art should partake of realism only as to its substance; in its design it should be not realistic, but ideal. . . . . The idealists should draw their materials from the accumulations of science, and the realists should forbear the attempt to carry physical law into metaphysical regions. The value of fiction lies in the fact that it can give us what actual existence cannot; that it can resume in a chapter the conclusions of a lifetime; that it can omit the trivial, the vague, the redundant, and select the significant, the forcible and the characteristic; that it can satisfy expectation, expose error and vindicate human nature. Life, as we experience it, is too vast, its relations are too complicated, its orbit too comprehensive, ever to give us the impression of individual completeness and justice; but the intuition of these things, though denied to sense, is granted to faith, and we are authorized to embody that interior conviction in romance. Everything is free to the imagination, provided only—as a great imaginative writer has said—it do not "swerve aside from the truth of the human heart." And stories of imagination are truer than transcripts of fact, because they include or postulate these, and give a picture not only of the earth beneath our feet, but of the sky above us, of the hope and freshness of the morning, of the mystery and magic of the night. They draw the complete circle, instead of mistrustfully confining themselves to the lower arc.

Moral struggle and spiritual aspiration, as portrayed by the majority of later American novelists, have for the most part been shown in limited fields, in separated or imperfect types. Not often does a romancer or story-maker essay the largest manner or the highest reach of thought. But in their seeming narrowness these lesser novelists but follow life, wherein the petty struggle and the common home are environed by all the broadening spheres of the universe. The highest thought may be born of what seems the meanest brain. The writer, too, may find a universal lesson in the narrow fact. Not yet, aside from the works of Nathaniel Hawthorne, have the prob- Edward Everett lems of life been broadly spread upon Hale, b. 1822. the pages of our fiction. But a writer so studiously and narrowly realistic as Edward Everett Hale finds no clod too mean on which to stand while his eager eyes turn with the upward look. His sketch of "A Man without a Country" is a word-token of all that humanity has ever connected with the idea of patriotism; and his simple and almost rollicking novelette " Ten Times One

29

is Ten" outlines no smaller scheme than the regeneration of a world by means wholly practical.
It is no wonder that the lessons of Hale's "Ten
Times One is Ten" and "In His Name," with
their optimism and cheery helpfulness, have been
caught up here and there by many a "Harry
Wadsworth Club," "Look-up Legion," or "King's
Daughters" society. This is proper Americanism
in the closing years of the century—the father's
gift and the son's duty:

> "To look up and not down,
> To look forward and not back,
> To look out and not in,—and
> To lend a hand."

When such thoughts are embodied in books the
thoughts, at least, cannot die. The life of books
and authors is of minor importance.

Some of the writers whom I have named may
do better work than they have hitherto done, and
others may do worse; the field of fiction will be
occupied by new figures; literary fashions will
change; art will ever be followed, and will be
brought to higher developments; but in novels
as in life the coming world of readers will ask not
only *whence* but *whither*, not only *how* but *why*.
Whether or not the "great American novel"
will ever be written is an unimportant question.
But if it be, it will spring from the character which
has made the nation in the past, and which must
be its future reliance.

INDEX TO VOL. II.

A

Abbey, Henry, 245
Abbott, Jacob, 407–9
Abbott, J. S. C., 366, 400
Adams, Sarah Flower, 235
Agassiz, Louis, 198
Alcott, Louisa M., 407, 418
Aldrich, T. B., 265–8, 269; an American Herrick, 266–7; rememberable poems, 267–8
Allen, Mrs. E. A., 223
Allen, Paul, 325
Allston, Washington, 28, 241
America, art starvation in, 283–4
American fiction, see Fiction, American
American literature, see Literature, American
American novelists, lesser, see Novelists, lesser American
American poetry, see Poetry, American
American soil, poetry of the, 227
American song, the future, 281
American verse, see Verse, American

B

Bacon, Delia, 373
Bancroft, George, 173, 305
Barlow, Joel, 12, 13, 23, 35
Bartol, C. A., 165, note
"Bay Psalm-Book," The, 3–4, 6, 172
Beers, H. A., 221
Bird, Robert Montgomery, 17, 394–7
Boker, George Henry, 17, 249–50
Bowring, Sir John, 235
Bradstreet, Anne, 4–5, 7, 8, 9, 35
Brainard, J. G. C., 31–3
Bridge, Horatio, 369, note
Briggs, Charles F., 250
Brooks, Maria, 34
Brown, Charles Brockden, 286–9, 291, 442, 443

Brownell, H. H., 224
Bryant, William Cullen, 137, 138, 144, 148, 149, 167, 173, 177, 194, 200, 210, 220, 235, 240, 245, 250, 253, 323–9; writings of, 35–49; "Thanatopsis," 37–8; poetic product, 38–41; solemnity, 41–2; uniformity of work, 42–3; prose, 43–4; a poet independent of time-conditions, 46–7; translation of Homer, 47–8; career, 48–9, 57
Bucke, R. M., 278, note
Burnett, Frances Hodgson, 428–9, 434

C

Cable, G. W., 398, 400, 402, 421, 426, 429–30, 443
Carter, Robert, 216, note
Cary, Alice, 238
Cary, Phœbe, 238
Channing, William Ellery, 173
Channing, William Ellery, Jr., 233, 236–7
Chamberlain, Mellen, 6, note
Child, Lydia Maria, 407
Cilley, Jonathan, 366, 373
Coleman, C. W., Jr., 428, note
"Columbiad," The, Barlow's, 12, 33
"Columbian Muse," The, 23
"Confederate Flag," The, 224
"Conquest of Canäan," The, Dwight's, 9, 17, 33
Cooke, John Esten, 401–3, 406, 443; "The Virginia Comedians," 391, 401–3
Cooke, Rose Terry, 417, 420
Cooper, James Fenimore, 24, 80, 110, 173, 283, 287, 292, 294, 295, 296, 339, 358, 359, 361, 395, 396, 401, 402, 406, 413, 442, 443; writings of, 297–329; "The American Scott," 298–9; prodigality in fiction, 299; his irregu-

larity of work, 299–301 ; minor writings, 301–2 ; as controversalist, 302–4 ; naval history and biography, 304–5 ; lesser novels, 305–8 ; series of novels, 308–9 ; as dogmatist, 309 ; great merits, 310–12 ; " Leather-Stocking Tales," 312–14. 320, note ; his domain, 314 ; sea-tales, 315 ; our novelist of action, on land or sea, 315–16 ; " The Spy," 317 ; " The Pilot," 318 ; " Lionel Lincoln," 318, 320, note ; " The Red Rover," 319 ; " The Bravo," 319 ; his special achievements, 320 ; conditions of his time, 320–2 ; Cooper, Irving, Bryant, and Webster, 322–4 ; Cooper in the early days of American literature, 324–7 ; a national novelist of international fame, 327–8

"Craddock, Charles Egbert," see Murfree, Mary N.

Cranch, C. P., 233, 236, 241

Crawford. Francis Marion, 405, 413, 445

Cummins, Maria S., 409

Curtis, G. W., 198, 293

Cutler, E. J., 224

D

Dana, Richard Henry, 28–9, 324

Dawn of imagination, the, 23–49

" Day of Doom," The, Wigglesworth's, 5–8

Deming, Philander, 419–20, 421, 443

Dial, The, 233

Dowden, Edward, 333. note

Drake, Joseph Rodman, 24–7, 35, 283

Drama, The, in America, 16–22

Dunlap, William, 18–19, 23

Duyckinck, E. A., 221

Duyckinck, G. L., 221

Dwight, J. S., 233, 234–5

Dwight, Timothy, 9–11, 23

E

Eastburn, J. W., 324

Edwards, Jonathan, 6, 391

Eggleston, Edward, 422–3

Emerson, Ralph Waldo, 8, 40, 41, 42, 46, 50, 51, 54, 59, 60, 63, 70, 89, 94, 102, 103, 110, 136, 173, 194, 200, 202, 204, 208, 210, 219, 220, 233, 235, 236, 237, 239, 240, 245, 247, 275, 277, 278, 279, 282, 341, 345, 346, 375, 377–8 ; as poet, 137–71 ; poetry and prose, 137–9 ; poetic theme, 139–40 ; method and limitations, 140–2 ; spontaneity, 142 ; " The Rhodora," 142–4 ; a poet of nature, 144–5 ; thought and expression, 145–9 ; the test of popularity, 149–50 ; Emerson and the greater poets, 150–2 ; evenness of his work, 152–6 ; conciseness, 156–7 ; " The Snow-Storm," 157–8 ; " Hamatreya," 158–60 ; " Brahma," 161–5 ; general estimate of his poetry, 165–71 ; its future, 167–8 ; success as far as success was sought, 168–9 ; the poetry of an optimist, 169–71

English, Thomas Dunn, 223

European impact upon American literature, 240

F

Fessenden, Thomas Green, 373

Fiction, American, later movements in, 413–50

Fiction, the belated beginning of, 282–96 ; fiction the highest prose, 282–3 ; fiction and poetry, unity of, 283

Fields, J. T., 165, note ; 217

Finch, F. M., 223

Foster, S. C., 225–7 ; " My Old Kentucky Home," 226

Franklin, Benjamin, 36, 371

Freneau, Philip, 13–16 ; " The House of Night," 15–16, 23, 286

Fuller, Sarah Margaret, 238

G

Gilder, R. W., 243–4

Godfrey, Thomas, 17

Goethe, J. W. von, " Wilhelm Meister," 55

Greene, Albert G., 223

" Greenfield Hill," Dwight's, 11

Griswold, R. W., 222

H

Hale, Edward Everett, 393, 449–50

Halleck, Fitz-Greene, 24, 26–28, 35, 211, note ; 324

Hardy, A. S., 440

Harte, Francis Bret, 421, 423–5, 426

Hawthorne, Julian, 341, 347, note; 368, 443, 445–9

Hawthorne, Nathaniel, 54, 93, 101, 102, 110, 121–3, 125, 136, 173, 194, 282, 283, 287, 292, 296, 297, 300, 306, 310, 311, 390, 400–1, 402, 407, 413, 428, 436, 443, 447, 449; writings of, 330–89; literary artists of the beautiful, 330–1; Dante and Hawthorne, 331–2; "Hand and Soul," 332–3; literature as art, 333–4; Hawthorne as artist, 334–5; the romancer of the human heart, 335–6; art and ethics, 336–7; moral law in English fiction, 337–9; an inevitable race-principle, 339–40; his foundation, 340; was he morbid? 340–2; the extremes in his universe, 342–4; attitude in the sentimental era, 344–5; his outlook, 345–6; philosophy of life, 346–7; a realist and an idealist, 347–9; "Ethan Brand," 346–52; the universe of morals, 351; the stony heart, 351; "The Threefold Destiny," 352–4; "Lady Eleanore's Mantle," 354–5, 357–8; his background, 355–6; creator, not follower, 356–7; his romances, 358–60, 375–84; his humanity, 360–1; his youth in Salem, 361–3; at Bowdoin College, 363–6; as recluse, 366–9; "Fanshawe," 360, 369–70; "Twice-Told Tales," 359, 370–1; juvenile stories, 371–2; quiet charm, 372–3; "The Snow-Image, and Other Twice-Told Tales," 373–5; "Mosses from an Old Manse," 359, 373–5; "The Scarlet Letter," 359, 375–7; "The House of the Seven Gables," 359, 375, 376–7; "The Blithedale Romance," 359, 375, 377; "The Marble Faun," 358, 377–83, 387; "Life of Pierce," 379, note; art and environment, 380–1; "The Dolliver Romance," etc., 360, 383–4; note-books, 384–5; "Our Old Home," 360, 384; his faults, 385–6; place in literature, 386–9

Hawthorne, Sophia, 347, 348, 382

Hayne, Paul H., 229–231, 232, 398

Hedge, F. H., 165, note

Henry, Patrick, 173

"H. H.," see Jackson, Helen

Higginson, T. W., 368, note; 418–19

Holland, J. G., 227–8

Holmes, Abiel, 17

Holmes, Oliver Wendell, 71, 138, 165, 172, 235, 240, 246; poems of, 204–18; wholesome American conservatism, 207; his essays and novels, 208–9; personality of his poems, 209–10; as lyrist, 210–12; occasional verse, 212; "Rhymes of an Hour," 212–13; his masterpieces, 213–17; "The Last Leaf," 210, 213, 214–15; his career, 217–18

Hooper, Ellen Sturgis, 233, 235

Hopkinson, Joseph, 26

Howard, Blanche Willis, 445

Howe, Julia Ward, 223

Howells, W. D., 434, 436–8

I

Irving, Washington, 23, 36, 250, 283, 302, 305, 311, 314, 323, 324, 339, 356, 358, 361, 402, 443; stories of, 289–92; the true beginner of American fiction, 289–90; as novelist, 290–1; his fields and triumph, 291–2

Irving, William, 292

J

Jackson, Helen ("H. H."), 238–9

James, Henry, 419, 432–6, 437, 440

Jefferson, Thomas, 402

Jewett, Sarah O., 416–17, 420, 434

Judd, Sylvester, 392–4, 406, 443; "Margaret," 391, 392–4

K

Kennedy, J. P., 306, 397–8, 403

Key, F. S., 26

Kinney, Coates, 223

L

Landor, Walter Savage, 155, 167–8

Lanier, Sidney, 231–2, 242, 398

Larcom, Lucy, 238
Lathrop, G. P., 379, note
Lazarus, Emma, 240
Lincoln, Abraham, 173, 200-1, 408
Livingston, Edward, 324
Livingston, William, 12, 23
Literature, American, idea of freedom in, 172-3
Longfellow, Henry Wadsworth, 8, 17, 40, 41, 42, 45, 101, 125, 128, 137, 138, 140-1, 148, 149, 158, 167, 175, 176, 183, 187, 188, 194, 198, 200, 206, 210, 219, 220, 223, 230, 235, 240, 245, 248, 249, 266, 275, 283, 331, 342 ; writings of, 50-96 ; the questioned leader of American song, 52 ; transient work, 52-3 ; "Kavanagh, a Tale," 53-4 ; "Hyperion, a Romance," 54-6 ; early poems, 57-8 ; causes of popularity, 58-61 ; as lyrist, 61-2 ; the poet's soul and the poet's hand, 62-3 ; poetry and the religious sentiment, 63-5 ; successive volumes of minor poems, 65-7 ; sonnets, 67-9 ; "My Books," 68 ; "Victor and Vanquished," 68 ; "The Spanish Student," 69-70 ; "Evangeline," 69, 70-8, 89 ; hexameters, 73-8 ; "The Courtship of Miles Standish," 74, 78-9 ; "Hiawatha," 69, 79-87, 89 ; trochaics, 81-7 ; spontaneous beauty, 85 ; repetitions and parallelisms, 85-6 ; "Christus" (comprising "The Divine Tragedy," "The Golden Legend," and "The New England Tragedies"), 70, 79, 87-9 ; "Tales of a Wayside Inn," 89, 90-1 ; translation of Dante, 91-2 ; "Michael Angelo," 92 ; the man and the poet, 93-5 ; limitations, 94 ; "Morituri Salutamus," 95-6
Lounsbury, T. R., 304
Lowell, James Russell, 50, 89, 138, 158, 172, 205, 206, 207, 210, 213, 242, 250, 261, 283, 302, note, 410 ; poems of, 186-204 ; early poems, 187-9 ; "A Fable for Critics," 189, 195, 196 ; manly sincerity, 189-90 ; humanity, 190-2 ; lavishness, 192-3 ; philosophic thought, 193 ; verbosity, 194 ; poems of freedom, nature, and human nature, 195 ; varied demands of American life, 195-6 ; "The Vision of Sir Launfal," 193, 195, 196 ; "The Biglow Papers," 184, 195, 196-7, 198-200 ; delineation of Yankee character, 197 ; his best lyrics, 197-8 ; man and artist, 198-9 ; secret of his successes and failures, 199-200 ; a poet of the time, 200 ; the American song, 201-3 ; "The Cathedral," 198, 203

M

Marvell, Andrew, 2
Mather, Cotton, 6
Mayo, W. S., 395, 404-5
McClurg, James, 13
"McFingal," Trumbull's, 11-12, 13
Melville, Herman, 403-4
Miller, Cincinnatus Hiner ("Joaquin"), 232-3
Milton, John, 1
Morris, G. P., 223
Motley, John Lothrop, 173, 203, 381
Murdock, Frank, 17
Murfree, Mary N. ("Charles Egbert Craddock"), 400, 421, 426, 443

N

Novelists, lesser American, 390-412
Novels of "feeling," 284-5

O

O'Brien, Fitz-James, 443
Osgood, Mrs. F. S., 220
Otis, James, 173

P

Packard, Alpheus S., 364
Page, William, 250
Paine, R. T., Jr., 26
Parkman, Francis, 80, 173
Parsons, T. W., 242-3
Paulding, James Kirke, 292-5, 395, 397
Payne, John Howard, 17, 19-22, 250
Percival, James Gates, 29-31, 302, 324

Peyton, J. Lewis, 426, note
Phelps, Elizabeth Stuart, 417-18, 419, 421
Piatt, Mrs. S. M. B., 240
Pierce, Franklin, 379, and note
Pinkney, Edward Coate, 427, note
Poe, Edgar Allan, 8, 33, 40, 50, 51, 52, 69, 70, 138, 148, 149, 150, 190, 200, 210, 211, 215-6, 221, 222, 230, 240, 245, 246, 250, 260, 269, 275, 283, 287, 292, 311, 341, 342, 356, 358, 361, 395, 398, 402, 403, 413, 427, note, 442, 443, 447: writings of, 97-136; personality, 98-100; literary field, 100-2; measure of success, 102-3; a poet of beauty, 103-7; "To Helen," 103-4, 105, 107; "To One in Paradise," 104-5, 107; "Annabel Lee," 105-7, 191; the eternity of the individual soul, 107; a poet of weird woe, 108; the singer and his hearers, 108-10; originality, 110; failures, 110-12; "The Bells," 109, 112-15; "The Raven," 108, 109, 113-14, 126; "Politian," 104-16; prose, 116-136; "Ligeia," 107, 117-18; definiteness of tales, 118-19; "The Fall of the House of Usher," 107, 119-20; divisions of tales, 120-1; "Arthur Gordon Pym," 121; "Eureka," 101, 121, 128; Poe and Hawthorne, 121-3; could he create characters? 123-5; mind and heart, 125-6; analytic power, 126-7; clearness of speech, 127-8; his product the best he could offer, 128-9; prose poems: "Silence, a Fable," 130-4; time and Poe, 135-6
Poetry, American, to-day, 244
Poetry, American, tones and tendencies of, 219-81
Poetry and fiction, unity of, 283
Poetry of the American soil, 227
Poetry of thought and culture, 233
Poets of freedom and culture: Whittier, Lowell, and Holmes, 172-218
Preston, Margaret J., 238

Q

Quincy, Edmund, 199

R

Read, T. B., 223, 241
Rhys, Ernest, 278, note
Richardson, Samuel, "Sir Charles Grandison," 58
Richter, J. P. F., 56
Roe, E. P., 441
Rowson, Susanna, 283, 285-6, 391

S

Sanborn, F. B., 165, note
Sands, Robert C., 43, 324
Saxe, J. G., 228
Sears, E. H., 235
Sedgwick, Catharine M., 324, 406
Sentimentality in American verse, 219-20
Sigourney, Mrs. L. H., 220, 222, 223
Sill, Edward Rowland, 237-8
Simms, William Gilmore, 398-401, 402
"Simple Tale," A, 295-6
Spofford, Harriet Prescott, 443-4
Stedman, E. C., 206, 247, 250, 269; poems of, 256-65; a lyrist and idyllist, 258-9; life and the poet, 260; the old thought in new times, 260-5
Stoddard, R. H., 264, 269, 447, note; poems of, 250-6; "Hymn to the Beautiful," 253-6
Stone, John Augustus, 17
Story, W. W., 241-2
Stowe, Harriet Beecher, 283, 410-12, 419; "Uncle Tom's Cabin," 391, 409, 410-12, 441, 442

T

"Talisman," The, 43-44, 296
Taylor, Bayard, 210, 228, 246-8, 250, 269
Tenney, Tabitha, 283, 285-6, 391
Thaxter, Celia, 238
Thomas, Edith M., 240
Thoreau, Henry David, 233, 235, 237, 345
Timrod, Henry, 229, 231, 232
Tones and tendencies of American verse, 219-81
Transcendentalism, 233, 235, 236, 237
Trowbridge, J. T., 228

Trumbull, John, 11–12, 13, 23
Tyler, Royall, 18, 19

U

Unitarianism, 235
*United States Literary Gazette,
The,* 57, 58

V

Verplanck, Gulian C., 43, 44
Verse, American, tones and ten-
dencies of, 219–81
Verse-making, early, in America,
1–22
Very, Jones, 233–4

W

Wallace, Lewis, 405 ; " Ben-Hur,"
441–2
Ward, William Hayes, 246, note
Ware, William, 405–6
Warner, Susan, 409
Warren, Caroline Matilda, 286
Washington, George, 10, 41, 402
Webster, Daniel, 127, 173, 178, 323
Wheatley, Phillis, 8–9
Whitman, Walt, 63, 89, 110, 194,
200, 240 242 ; writings of, 268–

81 ; prose, 269–71 ; " Leaves of
Grass," 271–80 ; its limitations,
275–6 ; its verse-form, 276–7 ;
what it is not, 277–9 ; what it is,
279–80 ; the future American
song, 281
Whittier, John Greenleaf, 40, 42,
51, 89, 137, 138, 158, 172, 188,
194, 196, 198, 200, 203, 204, 223,
228, 240, 275, 365 ; prose works,
177, note ; poetical works, 173–
87 ; character of the man, 176–7 ;
his country-heart, 177–8 ; transient and permanent writings,
178–9 ; lyrical power, 179–81 ;
nature and exercise of his powers,
181–2 ; " Snow-Bound," 175, 177,
183–6
Wigglesworth, Michael, 5–8
Wilde, Richard Henry, 33–4, 35
Wilkins, Mary E., 419
Willard, Samuel, 391
Willis, N. P. 200, 220–1, 223
Willson, Forceythe, 224–5
Winthrop, Theodore, 415–16, 443
Woman in American literature, 240
Woodworth, Samuel, 223
Woolson, Constance Fenimore,
421–2, 426
Wordsworth, William, 35–6